BERLIN

BUTTERFLY

RELEASE

Book Three

BY LEAH MOYES

ISBN 9781705397381

Edited by Irene Hunt

Cover Design by Allie Hext

Published by:

SpuCruiser Media

Leahmoyesauthor@gmail.com

Facebook @BerlinButterfly

Twitter @authormoyes

To Marla

May you always know how much I love you!

ACKNOWLEDGEMENTS

When writing a book series, an author takes on a world of challenges, many of which are unforeseen in the first book. For example, the writer must map out the story start to finish, yet be willing to take a curve ball if one presents itself. (Take Mari, for instance. When I brought her in at the beginning of book two, I had no idea how integral her role would be in this series.) The characterization requires growth but consistency, questions must be answered and ideas finished at the end, and above all, nothing can be written that will infuriate your fan base. That's a lot of pressure on an author!

Berlin Butterfly began as a dream I had in 2014. I dreamt of a restricted boundary, a man in uniform, and the woman he loves getting shot. I hope that if you're reading this, you know which scene I'm referring to in *Deception,* however, I'm not a spoiler, so I won't say much more. After seeing that scene, I immediately started writing down the details. Several days later, its location came to me—the Berlin Wall—but look how long it took me to get to that scene . . . one and a half books. My point is simple. Series can be quite challenging, and I have been blessed a thousand times over to be surrounded by people who have fallen in love with this story as much as I have. Most likely they have not been told enough how much their input and contributions mean. Even here, my acknowledgement is quite small in comparison.

To my editor, Irene Hunt, for the days and nights and everything in between, I appreciate your ability to hash out the mistakes I make—repeatedly, even after you tell me how to do it right. Whether it's my overused commas (unless it's the ever-elusive Oxford comma), passive language, filter words, or telling, I am forever indebted to you and your talent as an editor. Thank you for being honest with me and challenging me as a writer and for your invaluable friendship. Above all, thank you for sacrificing three years of your life to Berlin Butterfly.

A warm hug to the extra pair of eyes: Greg Moyes, Taylor Moyes, and Ashlyn Owens. Thank you for your support and love of this story and your willingness to read, listen, and critique.

Allie Hext, my cover designer, your talent and gift as an artist always amazes me. I can tell you what I'm thinking in my head, and through your skills, it always materializes on paper. I am lucky to have your artwork represent my story.

Much gratitude to my advance critique team for your willingness to read the raw version of "Release" and share your thoughts and insights as experts of Ella's mind. Many of your comments and suggestions made a difference in the final draft and the direction her story went. You will always have a special place in my heart Dawne Anderson, Maria Carrasco, Wendy Hargrave, Melisa Harker, Stacy Johnson, Susan Provost, Katalina Taunima, Lani Taunima, and Jody Turpin.

Danke, mein Freunde Jan Mengeling and Maria Carrasco for bringing me one step closer to Ella's life in Germany through conversation, experiences (Carnival!), and adventures like Cochem. I love you both!

To Christa Moak who listened to me express my thoughts on this crazy story back in 2015, thank you for your suggestion on how the ending should go, considering the first book hadn't even been finished.

Last, but never least, my family. Your continued support in my writing addiction encourages me to share the stories in my head. Thank you Greg, for always listening to my ideas, encouraging me, and being my confidence when I have none. Thank you, Taylor and Coty, Ryan, Harlie, Faith and Serenity, Jace and Samantha, Alex, Chad, and our "blind side" boy Bubba. Your love and inspiration mean everything to me.

Contents

Prologue

In the Deutsche Democratic Republic, the decade of the 1970s brought increased fear and control surrounding the fortifications of the Berlin Wall. The double-strengthened concrete barrier was armored with wires, traps, motion sensors, and mines, and a new order to shoot on sight was instituted. Residents continued to exhibit little trust and hope in a city where simple resources—including food and adequate living conditions—remained scarce, thus, driving more people to attempt escape. Victims from both East and West Berlin, as well as foreign travelers at the checkpoints, raised the number of deaths into the hundreds.

The ranking political organization—the Socialist Unity Party (SED)—and their methods of government power and domination had been portrayed to the world as cruel and inhumane punishment against the people of East Germany. In an effort to change their image and improve international Relations, the SED's state security—the Stasi—was tasked with reducing their overt persecution, including torture and imprisonment, and turning to more obscure measures in their procedures. The espionage and psychological terror established for this purpose was known as *Zersetzung*. It included tactics such as breaking into homes and moving objects, damaging personal property, manipulating medical results, and sending falsified compromising photos or documents to family members as a means to torment with subtlety.

Many times, the psychological anguish was so effective, the victims believed they were going crazy, and mental breakdowns ensued, many times ending in suicide. Due to the proficiency and elusiveness of how *Zersetzung* was conducted, the acts were often easily denied and the perpetrators never brought to justice.

The 1980s in West Berlin, with its freedom of speech and assembly, began to stir the hearts of the youth in the East through music and voice. Though their lyrics and publications were restricted in the DDR, artists such as Wolf Biermann and author Robert Havemann, continued to rouse resistance underground. Opposition groups IFM, KvU, Women for Peace, and the Justice Working Group began to organize after a Priest, protesting against the atheist beliefs of the State, lit himself on fire, forcing the Protestant church back into the fight. With the Protestant Churches protection of the dissenters, Punk music gained popularity, and its members' change and rebellion set events in motion with no intention of stopping until the Berlin Wall came crashing down.

One

WAKING UP

20 September 1983

The fine layer of dust appeared like a fragile first snow across the floor. The cold, hard wood pressed against my cheek bringing my eyes parallel to its caked presence. Flattening my palm against it, I allowed the dirt to coat my skin. I examined it carefully before rubbing it between my thumb and forefinger. My thoughts flickered with strange fascination between it and the sudden vibration that thumped against my face. Emil, my landlord, had become quite bold in the last few months, his entry and criticizing scold expected any moment. I held still, but he never came.

Rolling onto my back, my eyes surveyed the long crack in the ceiling. The melodramatic exhale that followed, resembled more of a whimper than a whine. *Did I fall asleep on the floor again?* Goose bumps rippled across my arms before an aggressive shake drove me to pull a blanket off Mama's chair. The clank of glass startled me as the linen knocked a *wodka* bottle to the floor. I stared at the container as it tumbled to a stop on its side next to three other bottles. An impetuous craving surfaced . . . *Is there any left?* Tightly clutched in my other hand, a single piece of paper drew my attention away from the liquor.

I released my grip and let the letter fall. A trail of dark-red blood stains splattered across the parchment, my fingers, and the floor. With hastened breath, my chest heaved. *Whose blood? Mine or . . .* Scanning all directions, I patted my cheeks and neck then ran my hands through my matted and tangled hair. A few black strands fused to the sticky fluid as I pulled away. Painful throbs shot through my fingers as if they'd been thrust into a bed of nails. Fresh blood seeped freely from open cuts at each tip.

What happened? Was I alone last night? Why is there blood? I knew my arrival at Wilhelm's pub came late, close to ten, but the harder my mind tried to recall the events afterward, the heavier my head became. Instantly my stomach lurched. An all too familiar sensation rose. Scrambling on all four limbs, I crawled towards the nearest wastebasket as the contents in my stomach erupted. Missing the wide opening at the top of the basket, it drizzled down the side, joining last week's retch. Weakened, my body continued to hurl in waves. The clear bile revealed an obvious lack of solids. I failed to recall the last time I'd eaten anything.

Dropping flat to my back once again, a single hand remained clenched to the rim. The other covered my mouth as if this could prevent another round of vomit. Useless . . . I rolled to my side, apathetic to the mess produced on my clothes and anything within launching distance. The repetitive heaving nearly drowned out the incessant pounding on my front door.

"Ella! Ella! *Öffne diese Tür!*" Emil's angry demands to open the door thundered through. My throat seared like coals on fire. Alcohol definitely tasted better going the other direction.

"*Ich kann dich hören, ich weiß, dass du da drin bist!*" His pitch elevated with each connection his fist made against the wood. Though I never answered, Emil's surety of my presence followed up with a threat. *"Ich bin fertig mit der Gewährung von Zulagen, Sie haben eine Woche Zeit,"*

His eviction warning merely words I'd heard before.

Sitting up, I brushed the back of my hand across my mouth while my bangs tangled irritatingly with my eyelashes. Wet to the touch, I grabbed the strands and twisted them tightly into a bun. Though their length was shorter, it resembled the kind I wore when employed at the Franke's.

The Franke's—ages ago—twenty-two years since I walked into their home for the first time, to be exact. Young and naïve, almost sixteen. Having entered an agreement to work and pay off the debt on my father's burial, little did I know then my association with them—one specifically—would change my life forever. Now, at thirty-eight, the past left its mark, scars both inside and out. My fingers, still bloodied and bruised, skimmed my shoulder briskly until the raised scar of a bullet wound materialized. My jaw set tightly behind clenched teeth . . . anything to halt my cry.

Stefan's image appeared before I could forbid it. *Why do I allow myself to think of him? Shame on you, Ella!* His defined physique, eyes that fluctuated alternating shades of blue, sexy cropped hair, and the playful manner in which his smile only lifted halfway on one side. The intrusion reproduced a toxic thirst. My top teeth depressed firmly into my bottom lip, partly to stop another round of barfing but mostly to invoke pain, pain necessary to draw the agony away from my chest. Stefan was only a memory now, a memory that—even twelve years after I'd seen him last—proved difficult to erase.

Leaning my heavy head to the ground once again, I spied a bottle under the chair. The watery discoloration inside pointed to a triumphant find. Clambering to my knees, my fingers stretched for it as if my life depended on it. The moment the liquid touched my lips and melted down my throat, the unquenchable desire to empty the bottle quickened. The sting of hard alcohol and the twinge of guilt no longer bothered me like in the early years of drinking. I recalled that first time in the back room of the pub where I *celebrated* Stefan's release from the military with my first taste of wodka and a black-market tattoo. The ink engraving of a blue butterfly never faded over the years, and its association with the bullet hole transpired into a constant reminder of Stefan and what would never be. A tormenting memory. My only relief, the back of my shoulder remained out of sight.

"*Ella, Ich komme rein!*"

Once again, my stomach rejected the alcohol vehemently. The subsequent lurch knotted my stomach muscles and drove sharp spasms through my chest. Without the strength or will to move back to the can, I wretched on myself and the floor beneath me. Emil's forewarning of entry went from earsplitting knocks to the quiet tap of a pencil as blackness swallowed the limited light my drawn curtains allotted. Darkness absorbed the last of my blurred sight as a pair of cold hands gripped my arms tightly.

"Ella! Ella, wake up."

Pungent smells alerted my senses, yet my eyelids remained shut. The touch seemed softer now. . . so did the floor.

"Ella, do you know where you are?" Foreign reassurance came in the form of a female voice.

I swung my head towards the sound and attempted to open my eyes. The bright lights of the room forced them closed again. Soft blankets surrounded my body, both beneath me and on top. It had been a long time since I felt this warm.

"Do you know where you are?" A stern voice repeated the woman's question.

I squinted against the harsh lights. A man in a white lab coat stood at the foot of my bed. His rigid stance matched a pitiless glare. My eyes, suddenly wide, darted frantically about. White walls, a small window, and noisy machine next to my bed . . . the room whirled, strange and unfamiliar. Gasping for air, I reached for the tubes connected to my arm but stopped when I caught sight of my bandaged fingers. Holding them up, I examined the wrapped gauze.

"Wh—" Choking and spurting, nothing logical came out of my mouth.

"Calm down, Ella." The woman in a nurse's uniform used her hands to block mine as they went for the tubes once more; her hold firm and unyielding. "It's okay. You're safe now."

My stare jolted back towards the man. Despite the twist of disgust on his face, elements of familiarity tugged at my mind. *Where have I seen you before? Maybe the same Doctor who treated Mari all those years ago? Mari! She probably doesn't even remember me.* The last time we spoke, she had just turned fifteen. She'd be twenty-three now and should rightfully hate me for deserting her.

My hands shielded my eyes from more than just the intense lighting. Somehow, I wished they could guard me from the pain I'd inflicted in the last few years, when a drink became all that mattered to me.

"You need to answer me," the man intoned, clearly obstinate. "Do you know where you are?"

My hands quivered, though they remained flat against each temple, allowing only a simple head bob in reply. When I attempted to speak, only air escaped my dry lips. I licked them with an equally parched tongue. The nurse lifted a glass to my mouth, and I took a large gulp before she pulled it away.

"In . . . a—" Something coarse lodged in my throat. "—Hosp . . ." It took every ounce of effort to spit out half a word. *What's wrong with me?*

"Good." The man seemed unaffected by my inability to articulate. "Do you know what day it is?"

My eyebrows curved inward. *Monday? Maybe Thursday?* This time my head shook side to side, still unable to speak clearly.

"What about the year, Ella? Do you know the year?"

1983 How can I forget? Despite my attempt to ignore time, it suffocated me.

I held up eight fingers, staring at the white tips and then let one hand drop to leave three digits upright.

5

The man turned to the nurse. "She's making progress and should make a full recovery." His pause fixed my direction. "Another few days, and we can release her."

Few days?

"Wh . . . wh" Stuttering, I reached for the nurse. The man left the room.

"Don't push yourself, Ella. You've been through quite an ordeal."

My brows lifted for clarification. I hoped she could read the need to elaborate. My grip on her wrist tightened.

"It's okay." Her hand covered mine with a gentle pat. Her compassion exceeded that of the man who left; I assumed him to be a doctor. "You were brought here just in time." She smiled and lifted the water glass to my lips once again, only longer this time. The cool liquid soothed my irritated throat. I tapped on my neck.

"We put a tube down your throat to pump the alcohol out." Then she whispered, "You almost died, but Dr. Weib worked fast to save you."

I gazed at my bare feet sticking barely out the bottom of the sheets. *Dr Weib? Why does his name sound familiar? Could we possibly be acquainted?*

"Just rest. I'm Dorothy, your nurse. I've been taking care of you."

Over the next several days, the strain on my throat and stomach calmed, and the more Dorothy assisted me, the better I felt.

"How long have I been here?" Words began to flow much easier.

"Let me see . . ." She tapped her finger against her forehead. "Today makes one week exactly." Heat drained from my face. *One week?* I could only remember the last two days. *What happened to me?*

"Who brought me here?"

"I'm not sure. A man; he didn't stay long. He gave us your name and condition when he found you."

"Must've been Emil," I mumbled, "afraid he wouldn't get rent if he didn't."

"I never saw him."

"Do you know why my fingers were stitched?"

6

Dorothy paused, "I believe you sliced your fingers on glass, somehow. All but one pinkie needed to be sewn. I found small shards in most of them."

"Oh." I tried to recall anything about the night leading to my arrival.

"How are you doing today, Ella?" The doctor interrupted our conversation, walking over and pressing the back of his hand roughly against my forehead." I cringed at his abrasive touch.

"What's her temperature, Dorothy?"

"Normal. Thirty-seven range for a day now."

"Good." He grabbed my wrist and squeezed tightly.

"Ouch!" I cried, his grip unmovable.

"Shhh," he demanded, his lips moving subtly as if talking to himself.

Irritated, I huffed openly.

He let go quickly and without asking, propped one of my eyes open with his fingers. A blinding light assaulted me. I swatted his hand away. His hand recoiled in trepidation, but it didn't stop a second attempt. I smacked his hand once more.

"Stop it!" he ordered. "I need to check your pupils."

"No. Dorothy can. I don't want you to touch me."

"She's not the doctor."

"Well, you're being cruel. Don't touch me."

His eyes switched intently between me and the nurse. He waved his hand as if he didn't care and wrote something down on his clipboard.

"Please make sure she's drinking plenty of liquids, Dorothy." He paused and then added—as he zeroed in on me, "Water only!"

I gritted my teeth with regret for not smacking him harder. His stance remained stationary, although no words came forth. Again, his countenance reflected disdain. *What is it that nags me?* My eyes narrowed.

"How do I know you?" I whispered.

He turned away. His hands nervously shuffled papers as he spoke. "Dorothy, will you see to Frau Stevens in the next room?"

"Yes, sir." Dorothy hustled out quickly.

The doctor circled back to face me, his steps placing him within a metre of the side of my bed. I adjusted to a sitting position and peered closer.

Immediately, my mouth fell open. "Is it really you? Edmund?"

He rubbed his chin briefly before he nodded affirmatively.

"Oh my . . ." I gasped. *It's Katharina's husband!* My gaze dropped to hands now resting in my lap. The weakness in my voice conveyed shame. "H-How is she? How is Katharina?" The few friends I claimed were quite neglected, but she was more like a sister. Nobody should treat a sister the way I'd treated her. His reaction now seemed justified.

"She is—" He stopped and shifted the weight from one foot to the other. He appeared to be holding back. "—She's well. She gave birth to our second."

"Second child?" I spit it out, shocked, finally meeting his eyes again. "When did this happen?"

He continued without hiding his frustration. "A year ago, but you would know this if you actually stayed in touch!"

The room fell silent for a long period of time.

"She went to your flat a dozen times, Ella. When you didn't answer, she left you notes. Even Lena tried to reach you."

I remembered the knocks; I never read the notes. My grief over Stefan seeped into my relationship with everyone. Closing off seemed the easiest way to endure, though my choice of survival was hardly logical.

"I've been busy," I whispered.

"Killing yourself," he hissed, "I know. Remember, I saved you."

My cheeks heated up, resulting in a resentful stare.

"This would be the second time, Ella, in case you don't recall the first."

A fierce burning rumbled deep in my chest, determined to rupture. "I never asked you to." Edmund's lips parted, but nothing came out. After an insurmountable silence, I whispered, "When Stefan shot me, I wanted to die."

"There's a reason you were meant to live. Why are you throwing that away?"

"You don't know anything about me. You know nothing."

"I know you never used to drink, yet here you are recovering from alcohol poisoning. I know you're a talented artist that probably hasn't painted in years." He inched closer with each item on his list. "I know you've experienced great loss and survived. I also know you're loved! *Scheisse*, Ella, loved by Katharina and Lena at the very least." He turned a deeper shade of red. "Why, I'm not really sure. Over the years, Katharina has cried for you—she actually misses this." He pointed to my form from head to toes.

Chewing on my lower lip, I resisted the desire to snap back. A tear tried to break free. It had been a long time since I'd cried. With no intention of doing it here in front of *him,* I held fast.

His voice lowered, "Why, Ella? Why this?"

"You don't know what I've been through," I mumbled.

"I know more than you think I do. Katharina told me everything. She's worried sick over you and since the death of her mother, has been beside herself trying to piece her loved ones together."

"Her . . . her mother died?" Somehow everything slowed: my thoughts, words, even breath. My emotions, driven to anger seconds ago, melted away. This woman who callously schemed to distance me for years was *dead*. I struggled to wrap my head around this, believing her to be practically immortal, incapable of death.

"How?"

"Frau Franke succumbed to a fever. We tried to save her, but she never recovered."

Although no tears would ever be shed for her, my curiosity prevailed. "When did this happen?"

"Two years ago. Katharina is now managing the mortuary on her own. My work here offers little time to assist, and with Stefan gone, she only has her father, who is practically inept.

"Stefan never returned home?" I muttered, afraid of the answer either way.

"No." I'm sure both our minds went to the night at the mortuary after Frau Franke dragged me out, and Stefan appeared only long enough to tell us he would be leaving forever. The sharp pains of heartache never ceased, the memory of him in those final moments imprinted into an endless torture.

"I've always been led to believe you were one of Katharina's closest and dearest friends." His insults returned. "Some friend!"

"Stop it! Just stop! You don't know me," I countered through gritted teeth. Any closer, I would have slapped him, doctor or not.

"I know you better than you think I do. For years I've heard the stories. Ella, the strong, brave friend, separated from her family in the West."

The sting in my nose amplified. The onslaught of tears I fought fiercely to restrain reached the surface. Angry, I pulled the blanket up over my head, but Edmund persisted.

"I understand you miss them and wish to be together. The sorrow you experience is not unlike many others here on this side. Why should your pain be any different?" His tone softened, but the damage was done. "And I believe . . . even though you and Stefan are not together, there is always hope."

"Don't!" I shrieked, pulling the blanket down in heated response. He had no right to say such personal things.

"You're alive. You're breathing. There's a reason for that, and you're trying to kill yourself!"

"Alive?" My voice trembled insignificantly compared to the violent shaking of my body. "You call this living?" Wet lines traversed freely along my cheeks and saturated the linen now pulled down to my chin.

"You chose to live this way."

10

Every nerve in my body flared as if electrified. "Just stop!" I screamed.

The shrill of an alarm sounded only briefly before Dorothy ran through the door. Shock blanketed her face as she glanced between us.

"Doctor, what is going on? Why are you just standing there?" She ran to the monitor and pressed buttons and then gently grabbed my arms and forced me to lie back. Her brows pulled tight, but the calm in her voice demonstrated patience. "Doctor, I think you're needed elsewhere."

Edmund's stiff stance and bobbing mouth exhibited panic, his skin pasty-white.

"Now!" she insisted sternly.

He shook his head. "Um . . . I'm sorry," he mumbled as he walked out. "I'm so sorry."

Dorothy reached for a linen and wiped my forehead. "Please, Ella, you aren't strong enough yet; please calm down." She said nothing about what just occurred. "Please take a deep breath and exhale slowly. Whatever it is that's upsetting you, you can deal with it when you're recovered. Not now." She stayed with me another hour until my vital signs reached normal and my breaths became regular. Pretending to fall asleep, I hoped she would leave. I needed to be alone.

Through the night, my eyes closed more for relief than rest. My thoughts drifted to the last time I'd seen Katharina, nearly nine years ago. Two months from giving birth to her first child, she was heavy and tired but continued to check in on me after my shoulder wound. Yet once again, selfishness prevailed, and jealousy over her unending good fortune destroyed my reason to remain close.

From there, my thoughts betrayed me. Stefan's words imprinted permanently in my head like a broken record, a devastating song that played over and over again . . . *"This is goodbye . . . forever."* Many times I wished his gun aimed at my heart and not my shoulder, and then I wouldn't have been forced to live through this never-ending nightmare—from the twinge in my arm every time I lifted, it to the chasm in my chest. The anguish could hardly be forgotten.

*****

"Alright, Ella. You will be released today. Your blood work is good, and the poison has cleared your system." It had been nearly two days since the argument ensued and I'd seen Edmund last. Quite surprised he stood here now, I braced for another attack, but nothing came. My eyes studied his hands—the way they fidgeted mildly at his sides—and how he repetitively paced the room. Finally, he slowed and then stopped. Dorothy laid out a skirt and a blouse on the end of my bed, her focus clearly on the clothes while the doctor spoke.

"Please stay away from alcohol, Ella," Edmund said and then lowered to a whisper, "You really have more to live for than you think." His hand grazed mine with a tenderness quite foreign before. "And please find a way to reach out to Katharina; she needs you as much as you need her." With a final nod, he stepped out of the room.

"He's right, you know," Dorothy commented without peering up. "There are many reasons for death here. Don't let drink be one of them. Here—" she patted the clothes. "—I brought these from home. The clothes you arrived in were not salvageable, and I figured you wouldn't want to wear a hospital shift when you leave." She laughed at herself then walked over and handed me a personal mirror and a compact. "You're still a bit on the pale side. This will bring color to your cheeks." And she left the room.

It had been quite some time since my reflection appeared before me. Even at the flat, it was avoided quite carefully. Only now, curiosity prevailed. Raising the mirror, I steadied my fingers in a tight clasp around the handle. Dorothy was right. For someone with my darker skin color, it now hovered between tan and gray. A lighter tone wouldn't have been disappointing if it didn't come across so unearthly ashen. I studied the image. The wrinkle Mama G playfully teased me over, the one between my brows above my nose, deepened—as well as the lines extending from the corners of my eyes. The youthfulness in my countenance faded, accelerated by sorrow and alcohol, I was sure. Popping the compact open, I found the blush and pad untouched. Dorothy purchased this new. Even here, amongst strangers, traces of compassion and kindness emerged, though I refused to allot that same charity on myself. I felt far from deserving.

With prolonged effort, I dressed, knowing full well the reality I must confront once I left the security of the hospital. After only a few steps, my slumped shoulders and defeated spirit acknowledged the truth of utter soberness. *What do I really have to live for?* Happiness remained as elusive as before I entered the hospital. Glancing up at the blackened street, my future paralleled the setting sun. Everything that meant anything to me dimmed with it.

Two

ANTON'S HEARTACHE

30 September 1983

As I stepped into my flat, an overpowering smell of waste and vomit filled my senses. Teeth, tightly clenched, I fought to keep the rancid scent from weakening what little strength I owned. Fumbling for the nearest lamp, rubbish and glass clattered deafeningly at my feet. With a flick of the knob, my eyes enlarged to the disturbing sight before me. I glanced around the room with increasing clarity. *What happened?* Without question, evidence of a mental and physical collapse proved much longer than a ten-day hospital stay . . . years of abandonment lay before me: A failed attempt to drown out the past and forget Anton, Josef, and especially Stefan. But the more I drank, the deeper hole I dug.

Rustling through a kitchen cabinet, I located some unused rags. With a clean handkerchief tied around my mouth and nose to reduce the smell, I filled a bowl with warm, soapy water and went to work on the long-neglected filthy flat. In all, the empty bottles piled in the rubbish bin totaled a couple dozen. With no recollection of my drinking binge, I was unaware if they had been consumed in one sitting or over time. Quite possibly, due to the medical consequence, it was the former.

On the floor next to one shattered bottle, the trail of dried blood led to a letter and a scattered pile of unopened envelopes. Glancing at the sender's names, they all varied in origin: Josef, Anton, Lena, and Katharina. I reached for the only open letter and glanced to the bottom. Anton's signature.

Studying the paper, blood stains concealed some of his words. Why or when I chose to open this specific correspondence evaded my memory, especially when all the others went unanswered. Faint, I slid to the floor and leaned against the counter. Gripped in my fist, I began to read.

Dearest El   *3 Mar 1983*

   I don't   you will get this letter. I don't know if

you have mov   or if you are aliv   that matter.

It's as if you've disappeared complete   Wherever

you are or whatever you're doin   re happy. It

has always been my greatest hope   long as I have

known   we talked about saving our sentiments

until we faced one another, but because this will be my

last correspondence, I must confess my whole life

became centered around the hope you and I would one

day actually be face to face. In the East, my only dream

was to marry yo   my life was over the night I

left you and until I met my wife, Elizabeth,   lieve I could love anyone but you.

I can't begin to describe the fear of that night when I watched the soldiers begin to roll out the wire. I knew that your   deathly sick, but I hoped with all of my heart I   you to come with me. Yet deep down, I knew you would never leave him. Saying goodbye and seeing you at the window, I thought I would never forgive myself. Even though Josef became the family I never had, it was Elizabeth who made my life worth living again. She didn't replace you but filled a hole I never believed could be filled.

But Ella, I don't know if I can get this out. The most painful and agonizing thing has happened. My beautiful bride has passed away while giving birth. I now have a four-year-old son and a six-month-old daughter I can barely look at, barely hold without seeing the face of my beloved and now I'm raising them entirely on my own. If it weren't for Heidi, Josef's wife, my infant daughter possibly would not have lived this long. I'm weighed down with disabling grief. After   the only person I could think to share my misery   is you have you forsaken my friendship. No word, no sign, not even a note of life . . . and when I reach out to you, you're nowhere to be found. It's as if I have the weight of a double loss strung around my neck, and I'm inches from jumping. Why would you ignore me in my greatest time of need? With this blasted wall between us and so much pain and heartache   years, I cannot continue waiting for a letter or a phone   or worry if an escape was possible or successful. A foolish dream I had but your silence has confirmed I must let you go. I cannot hold on to nothing. Josef believes you are dead. If you're alive, you must've chosen to keep us away. Please know, I will always carry you in my heart, but in order for me to survive the torment, I must force it away. I love you more than you will ever know, but for my sanity, I must say goodbye.

Love Anton

Pressure built in my chest with each passing word, trapping my movements, sounds, even air until an agonizing moan tunneled through my throat when I reached the end. The sting thrust through every part of me. I clutched the letter, holding it to my chest as cries of agony burst forth, rivaling those at the time of my papa's death. No doubt the news led to my drunken state, drove me to break bottles and sear my fingers, then consequently consume until the bristly spines of guilt fostered numbness. I betrayed Anton's friendship. Everything we shared and experienced became invalidated by my own self-pity.

I read the letter two additional times, willing tirelessly for the words to change. My heart agonized over his pain, his suffering, his undeniable greatest loss. I knew some of what he felt. My own torment plagued my dreams, and occasionally, during the day, Stefan's apparition baited me with authenticity until I blinked and the hallucination was gone . . . alcohol had been a cruel companion.

I didn't blame Anton for giving up on me; he spoke the truth. We knew for years we may never see each other again, but to see it in writing, knowing it was initiated solely because of me, was like taking a knife to my wrist and slicing very slowly.

The doorknob rattled, and Emil walked in much calmer than the previous months, although he kept one sleeve over his nose as his eyes darted about the room.

"I'm sorry, Emil." My voice carried deep sincerity as I waved my hand about the room. "I'm sorry for everything."

He nodded, his unblinking eyes scrutinizing me from head to foot. I shifted awkwardly under his stare and searched for what to say next.

"I promise to have the rent by next week. I'll get back to work."

"Your rent is covered," he said, "but get this place cleaned up . . . and Ella, get your life together. You're a mess."

I sprang to my feet with a strange eagerness and reached out to shake his hand. "Thanks, Emil. I appreciate it and also . . ."—my eyes fell to my feet humiliated—"also for taking me to the hospital."

"I didn't," he said with little sympathy before turning towards the door, my hand left hanging midair. "I also didn't cover your rent."

My nose wrinkled in confusion, and because I could no longer see Emil's expression, I rushed to his side. "What do you mean?"

"Some mate showed up when I tried to open your door. He took you himself then came back and paid your past dues through next month."

"Who?"

"I don't know, and I don't really care." He slammed the door behind him.

Stumbling towards the bed, I could feel my knees giving out. *Who would have done that for me?* Did Katharina or Lena send someone? Impossible. Edmund would have told me. Hans maybe? I hadn't had contact with him for years, but I saw him once in a bar with a woman.

18

We never spoke. I'm not even sure he recognized me. Could he have possibly seen my suffering and acted on it? Anton and Josef! Of course, when I stopped responding to their letters, they could have sent someone to look for me. Maybe Heidi's brother, Herr Volney.

The last letters I wrote my friends and family were sent December 1974, shortly after my move to Leipziger. Everything about my former flat brought tender memories forward that needed to be purged. It took over three years to finally realize Stefan fully intended on keeping his promise to stay away. Over time, my drinking increased. Believing a balance would come if I got every reminder of Stefan out of my sight, I buried his memory deep into my new closet. This included the phonograph, records, the picture of Cochem, but especially his love letters. Yet even with those efforts, his image— both before the shooting and after—continued to haunt me. Alcohol became my constant companion.

Glancing back at Anton's letter on the floor where I left it, I shuffled to my feet, grabbed my sweater, and burst out my door. Long overdue, the walk to *Do Nothing*, now from the other direction, brought me face to face with a stranger behind the bar, a young man with feathered bangs and a button-down pin stripe. I didn't recognize any of the patrons seated before him. Maybe it had been too long and Jörg no longer owned or managed the place. As I approached, my eyes shifted behind the barman to the rows of bottles. The deep-blue label of the *Gorbatschow* called to me. I blinked. Next to it, the *Zaranoff* waited for an invite. I shuffled closer, the stool only an arm's length away. I scanned the room. Nobody here recognized me, nobody would know if I took one little sip. A tiny glass would not kill me; I tried to convince myself I could stop after only one. I slipped onto the seat, and the young man nodded in acknowledgement before finishing another patron's order. As he approached, he wiped his hands repeatedly on the apron at his waist.

"What would you like?"

Each syllable caught in my throat. "Uh." Perspiration built on my upper lip. "Um . . ."

He let go of his apron and waited, eyeing me curiously.

"Ella!" The cry from behind caused me to jump. I swung around and met the familiar, mature visage of an old friend.

"Jörg." I smiled.

He came towards me for a quick hug. "I haven't seen you in ages. How are you?"

My eyes shifted nervously as I stuffed my trembling hands beneath my knees. "Fine," my voice cracked. The barman left to serve someone else. Both relieved and disappointed, I focused on Jörg.

He sidled up next to me and pulled one of my hands out to hold. It shook in his grip. He studied me carefully. The weight of his eyelids over time did not dim his sight in the least bit.

"When did you stop?"

"Stop what?" I challenged nervously.

"Stop drinking."

"I—um, I don't drink, remember?"

He patted my hand and placed it back in my lap. "Patrick, *wasser* please." Then he turned to me, "Still?"

"Yes, please."

"Still, Patrick."

"You forget, dear, I own a bar. I'm quite familiar with the effect alcohol has on one's body and soul."

My eyes dropped to my lap. Each time I visited in the last decade since we met, I never ordered alcohol. I knew Jörg would be disappointed. He became the *opa* I never had.

"I guess the better question is, when did it start?"

I mumbled, "July 1973."

He nodded processing this. "You're an alcoholic, Ella."

"I know." My lips quivered. Jörg handed me the water then waited for me to finish drinking before he spoke. "I may receive my earnings from how much people drink in my bar, which may seem hypocritical to some, but I'm not naïve to its destruction."

I nodded.

"Seems we have a lot to catch up on, darling. Patrick, bring me a plate of currywurst and papas please, in the corner." Jörg held out his hand again and led me to an isolated booth. I eagerly complied. If anyone had advice for me, it would be him.

Three hours later, I stepped away from Jörg's warm embrace and outside to where a drizzle of rain began. With my sweater pulled up over my head, I hopped childishly across the puddles both on the sidewalks and streets, pondering everything we discussed.

In true honesty, I exposed my entire life. Jörg's keen mind and warm friendship somehow found my reset button and led me back on a moral path. Moving forward, I knew finding a way to live beyond the wall, beyond Stefan, and beyond the drink would be my saving grace. As tough as penance is meant to be, Jörg had faith in me, and right now, his faith needed to be enough for the both of us.

*****

It took nearly a week to clean the flat. Twice, I found small bottles of alcohol stuffed in various places. The temptation boiled extreme. Both times I placed it to my lips and let the liquid rest against them. I wanted to part my mouth and allow the contents to enter. It took Jörg's face and the bandages on my fingers to stop me. Even then, I knew in my heart this wouldn't be the first or the last craving I encountered.

Pulling the drapes aside, I opened the windows for the first time in several years. The crisp autumn air seeped through and helped clear out the stale smell. I washed my linens in the sink and hung them to air dry on the roof. Some of my clothes and much of my kitchenware didn't survive the relentless mistreatment. Holes, stains, and rust infiltrated nearly every corner of the room.

The late October rains continued as I worked vigorously to bring sensibility back into my life. With a mug of black tea between my palms, I sat on the bench near the window. For the first time in weeks, I allowed myself to relax. Glancing around the room, a calm washed over me. The room no longer appeared like a scrapyard or smelled like a water closet. The warmth of the drink radiated to my skin easily as I rested my head against the pane. My eyelids grew heavy with the synchronized weight of the drops as they pattered gently against the glass. Larger drops pooled on the leaves of the linden tree next to the building, smaller than the oak on Max-Beer, its spring bloom no doubt prettier. It had been years since my body and mind slowed down enough to enjoy a serene moment with mother nature. The balmy liquid slid soothingly down my throat while I watched the drizzle graduate to a downpour.

Movement on the sidewalk drew my eyes from the tree. The outline of a figure, most assuredly drenched from the deluge, shifted between pacing and leaning against the nearby lamppost. The vision blurred. *A person or ghost?* I unlatched the lock and opened the window in an attempt to see better, but the increasing barrage narrowed my visibility. Repeatedly wiping the wetness from my eyes, I fought for recognition, yet trickery reigned. A green military jacket pulled tight to a chin., eyes shrouded by long bangs below a snug gray cap. When the delusion stared my direction, thundering erupted from my chest.

My mug fell to the sill, tea splashing wildly against the window pane as I sped through the flat, ignoring my own jacket on the way out. Fleeing down the stairs from the third floor, I missed a step or two. By the time I reached the road, the apparition disappeared. The rain, appreciated only moments earlier, now pelted me annoyingly and doused me.

"Why?" I cried aloud. Water cascaded down my forehead and nose to my open mouth, but my shrieks continued "Why is this happening to me?"

A man with a perfectly poised umbrella stopped next to me. "Are you alright, Frau?"

"No!" I screamed, "No, I'm not!"

He jumped from my reply then hustled rapidly the opposite direction. Grabbing each side of my head, my fingers raked through the soggy, tangled hair. Rage consumed me. Tired and worn from these stupid fantasies, I cursed my gullibility. The illusions grew more and more frequent. In the last year, Stefan's image had been conjured at Friedrichstrasse, Alexanderplatz near St Mary's, Mont Klamott in Volkspark, and now here. Yet each time I rushed to where the figure emerged, nothing resulted. With no logical explanation for the hallucinations, I'd blamed the alcohol . . . maybe its use altered my brain. Totally sober today, that excuse no longer held weight, unless the alcohol poisoning caused irreparable damage.

I sat on the step leading to my building door and let the water continue to soak through my clothes. My emotions bounced feverishly from doubt to anger. *How long can I endure this vicious persecution—imagining Stefan still in my world although he is clearly not? How long must I suffer?*

Three

Josef

4 November 1983

Settling into Mama's chair with the stack of unopened letters, I cringed. Despite their small size, the unknown contents intimidated me. After Anton's letter, I truly feared what else might surface after years of neglect and no contact. Placed in order according to the post date, the envelopes rested warily on my knees. Within seconds, a physical yearning, accompanied by sweats and a tremor, crept through my soul like an infectious disease. An easy out, the fog I functioned in became my means of forgetting, dealing, and ignoring life. It replaced sense and logic and became the only relief to numb my pain. With tightened fists, I drove my fingernails into my palms, anything to lure the impulse from my lips. With small strides I was making progress; this one only lasted several minutes.

I tore open the first envelope.

Dear Ella,   21 September 1974

Thank you for sending your new address, but why don't you call more often? Correspondence every few months is not enough. I miss you. Last month I graduated from the university in law and have taken employment with a notary who specializes in emigration. There is so much to tell you that cannot be said on paper. Please call. I need to hear your voice again. Or meet at the platform. It has been too long since I saw your face. Just tell me when. I'll be there.

I wish I didn't have to say this in a letter, but I cannot wait any longer to share my news . . . Heidi and I are getting married! 13 August next year. The date of course because of its significance for both of us, with you and Cade on the other side of the wall. Have you met him? We gave him your name but have not heard if you two have become acquainted yet.

If by some miracle the wall will be torn down by then, it would be our greatest hope that we celebrate this occasion as a family. Please, dear sister, let me know of your welfare.
Josef

I glanced at the calendar on the wall, 1983 in bold type at the top. This letter is nine years old. Not only did Josef marry but could have a family by now. Resisting the urge to scold, I promised myself respite from the abuse and continued reading.

Sweet Ella,   12 December 1974

I'm glad you've found a place close to your work. Edmund and I are hosting the Christmas Eve party this

25

December 24th. We would love for you to join us. You may bring a friend or friends if you choose. Lena is bringing Freddy. It will be like old times, all of us together. I can't wait for you to be acquainted with our son, Jonas. He recently turned six months and is the joy of our lives. Please let me know. I will send the automobile for you. I miss you, my lovely friend.
Katharina

Dear Ella,   17 February 1975

Elizabeth and I are going to be parents. I'm terrified. I know nothing of child rearing and with little learned from my own parents I'm afraid I'll fail. Why have you not called? When Josef and Heidi came for dinner last night, they too mentioned they have not heard from you . . . not even a letter.

We are desperate to know of your health and happiness. I know we've had stretches of time where we haven't heard from you before, but this seems to be the longest by far and with a telephone within reach you can contact us anytime. Josef and Heidi live in the flat below us and will be getting their own telephone shortly but until then he can use ours. Only you must be the first to reach out, I believe you still use the public ones.

26

Josef has much to say. He has learned a great deal about travel between the East and the West, he believes he has the means to get you home. Please, Ella, please just reach out to us. We are concerned.
Love Anton and Elizabeth

Anton a father? I knew this to be true from his last letter, but to see his anticipation here so fresh, unaware of what was to come. The patter in my chest was subtle but overwhelming. Setting the pile aside, I went to the window and opened it. Inhaling the clean crisp air, I wiped my brow with my sleeve before I scanned the posts on the chair. I needed to continue but labored to get my feet to move that direction. I placed the kettle on the stove and reached for the next letter to read in the kitchen.

Dearest Ella,   *18 July 1975*

We missed you at the Christmas Party then the new year dinner as well. Why have you disappeared from my life? Did I do something to offend you so? Freddy and I went to Zur for dinner and the manager refused to speak of your whereabouts. He would not even let me know if you were still employed there. The waitress said she only knew of your name, nothing else was shared. Please, please come to our Carnival celebration. I'm including our address and would be beside myself to see you again. I'm with child. I haven't told my mother yet, at only a couple months along, I fear for the child's safe carriage. Please, please come, I have much to share with you.

Love, Lena

Everyone's lives moved forward, and mine regressed in a sinkhole. The whistle blew, and I fixed a soothing cup of lemon tea before I took my place in the chair again.

Ella,   15 November 1975

    Nearly every month we are informed of news involving a shooting at the wall, and it frightens me even more as I do not know of your current welfare. The reports of the recent shooting a week ago of a young man only 21 years of age by the name of Lothar Henning state it was apparently a case of mistaken identity, however, he died of his wounds. The story in the press included a disparaging comment by the border police who transported the injured man to the hospital. The officer said "It is the dead man's own fault. It really angers me personally since I now have to clean up the very filthy car".

    Such disregard for life and morality is what you're living in every day, and for this very reason I continue to make pleas on your behalf in the West. I beg you, dear sister, respond to a letter, any letter. Pick up the phone, go to the platform . . . your distance tears me up inside, especially knowing what kind of wolves prey upon you. Please write soon. Josef

The strain in my jaw from the clench of my teeth prolonged as I continued.

Ella,   *26 August 1976*

I went to your flat twice in the last month, and there was no answer. Are you well? I also went to Zur and was told you don't work often. A woman by the name of Angelika was kind enough to tell me your next scheduled day, so I returned when your shift started, but you were nowhere to be found. I don't want to assume the worst since your friend assured me you're alive, although, she was less forthcoming on your well-being. Nothing has changed at the mortuary. I work quite regularly while Edmund assists at the local clinic. I know your first question to me would be if I'd heard from Stefan, and I take no offense, yet also have no news to share. He has not been seen since that dreadful night in 1971. Please come and visit us. My son turned two this week and has not met you, my dearest friend, Ella. Please, even without Stefan you are family to me.

All of my love, Katharina

Ella,   28 December 1976

I send you our condolences as it has been made aware in the West of Erich Honecker's succession in office following Stoph. I guess we all expected him, the man who was responsible for the wall in the first place, to again have some sort of power over the people in the East. They have already built a death strip. What more can they do to break you? I realize I'm bolder in my correspondence over the years, but since studying the law, my awareness to how much the SED has broken it, has increased. They're evil.

The real news of my letter and much more enjoyable is this . . . we have a son, sweet sister, You're a *tante*! He is strong and healthy, and we named him after Papa . . . Heinrich Albert Kühn. He has wisps of my auburn hair and strong hands, but his face belongs entirely to his mother's and thank goodness for that. She's quite beautiful.

I fear for your existence, your safety and anything else. We have never been out of touch this long. Please do not continue to make us suffer.

Cade said he has tried to locate you but to no avail, I'm including Cade's information. Find him so we may know of your existence. If for some reason you're angry with me or Anton, at least we won't fear the unknown.

Here is a picture of your nephew.

Love, Josef and Heidi

The photograph felt foreign in my fingers, with only two in my possession over the years: the one of my mother, and the one Stefan and I posed for during his leave, which I sent to him. *Does he still have it? Could it have been taken from him as a prisoner in Vietnam? If it wasn't, would he have kept the photograph all this time?* Without control, my mind sprinted down a dark path. *Has he married and moved on like everyone else around me . . . weddings, children . . . futures . . . without Ella?*

Dear Ella,   13 July 1977

Elizabeth has offered to go to the East in search of you. As you know, Josef and I could never do so with our past in the East. Our papers would be confiscated, and we would be detained. However, Elizabeth has two friends who have traveled there twice and were successful in locating their family. Please just contact us. Call and we can discuss the details. Elizabeth knows how much you mean to us and feels the need to help where she can.

Love Anton and Elizabeth

Ella,   4 March 1978

   Heidi is pregnant with our second child, due late September. Heinrich, the eldest, is now fifteen months old and is full of energy and very much a boy.

   It has now been four years since we've heard from you. Maybe you moved again or maybe you've chosen not to communicate with us. No matter what, I will never stop writing, Ella. You're my sister and will always be in my thoughts. If you need help, please find a way to let us know. We would do anything for you.

Love, Josef and Heidi

Dearest Ella   17 September 1978

   I'm not sure if you received the invitation to our daughter's christening. I know you're not religious, neither am I, but Freddy was raised in a church and I agreed to have our child christened. It's just that every correspondence I've sent has not been responded to nor returned. Do you not want to maintain a friendship? I believed with all we experienced since the day we met back in 1961, we were better friends than this. If I'm wrong, please tell me and I'll leave you alone. I only want to know of your health and safety.

Love, Lena

Ella,   18 November 1979

What do you want me to do? Should I stop writing you and no longer bother you with our letters? It seems quite apparent that you no longer wish to communicate with us or have any relationship of any sort. This by far is the most difficult thing we have faced since our separation. Five years, Ella, and no word!

I thought if I continued to write and pursue our friendship that whatever you might be going through might pass and you would know I was here for you. That will never change. I live in the same place I always have. If you ever find your way back, you're welcome in my home. We have faced difficult times. Nothing to bore you with but I'm not sure where to go from here. Elizabeth went to the East twice without waiting for your consent. She went to the café, the restaurant, and your address. Nobody knows your whereabouts. Despite some knowing who you are, they have not seen nor heard from you. Have you disappeared entirely from our lives . . . from everyone's lives?

Anton and Elizabeth

The rawness of reality stung.

Dear Ella,   30 January 1980

   I'm unsure if you're receiving my letters, but in case you are, I just needed you to know how much I miss you. Clara is almost two and the highlight of my life. Freddy is the lead barman at the first neon bar due to open in Berlin the end of March. There is a special occasion night for the employees, spouses and select friends. Would you please join us March 25. It is called Café M in Berlin-Schöneberg. Let the doorman know you're a guest of Freddy Wagner; your name will be on the list. I have much to tell you. It has been too long, my sweet friend.

Love, Lena

Dearest Ella,   12 July 1980

   I stopped by your flat this week and although I was positive someone was home, nobody answered the door. I left a note. Maybe you have a roommate or a friend that could somehow get word to us of your welfare.

   Jonas is a strapping young man of six. He is sure to turn the heads of many young girls as he gets older, for he looks like a miniature Edmund, so handsome. Speaking of Edmund, he has now accepted a full position at the hospital while I continue to run the mortuary. I hired a student to *assist in the afternoons, since father is unavailable and rarely leaves the house.*

I've not received word from Stefan. I often walk past the wall and wonder if he is still there or if he found peace outside of Berlin. Although it is strange, there are times I've imagined him near . . . at a bus stop, in line at the bakery or reading a newspaper. I know this is my mind wishing for him to be happy, leading a normal life, but more often than not it is a torturous game. With the absence of my dear brother and now my closest friend, it is hard not to feel abandoned. Please, in your greatest mercy, would you please find a way to let me know you're alive and whether you want to associate with me or not. I just need to know you exist.

All my love, Katharina.

Dear Ella,   22 September 1981

I'm trying not to be angry with you. I can't believe my own sister would choose to ignore me, your own brother for all these years. I can only assume the worst has happened. Our life here has not changed much. Heinrich and Savannah are both healthy and strong and happy. Although they hear the stories of their *tante* Ella, they have not heard from her. If you are alive, please find it in your heart to send word. We think about you every day.

Love Josef and Heidi

Dear Ella,   12 April 1982

It has been announced the American President Ronald Reagan, the one who was a Hollywood star before he became involved in politics, will be visiting Berlin, of course from the West. Even he, I'm sure, would not be allowed to view the East from the inside. I have not forgotten how the DDR likes to portray its image differently than how life really is. I haven't been there for twenty years, but I could probably describe the condition of the buildings from the foundations to the rooftops, and it would not be a positive report. Here in the West it's almost like we are living on an island, not that I would know what that feels like except we are a city isolated in the middle of East Germany, and growth is limited. Being in construction there was a lot of work to accomplish from repairing the war-torn buildings but now as we move forward into the 1980's, open space is not as available as it is outside of West Berlin. It is challenging and has forced me to experiment in new areas. Thus far, business has been successful.

Elizabeth is pregnant with our second child due in September. I can't believe I will now be the father of two children. I need my friend, Ella.

I do not know what is going on, but I cannot give up on you. I cannot stop writing and cannot believe you've chosen to stay away on purpose. Please know I'll always care for you and hope this silence ends soon.

Anton and Elizabeth

My eyes fell to my empty lap. This being the last letter Anton wrote before Elizabeth's death, severe remorse rekindled. Elizabeth came looking for me. She did this for Anton and Josef—on her own—to get answers, and now . . . now I couldn't even thank her for trying. She is gone and Anton's torn to pieces. I didn't deserve such people in my life.

I picked up the pile of letters and set them on the shelf, plagued by what to do next. With too many years between us, where did I fit in? Would I be refused? Could I have been forgotten or buried like what I attempted to do with Stefan?

With no idea on what to expect, I wandered towards the public telephone three streets down. I stood outside the empty box, staring at the device. Before my "disappearance", I phoned Anton and Josef nearly once a week for almost two years, the number imprinted in my head, never forgotten, but what if it changed or they moved? Nine years was like an eternity in Berlin. The cold air whipped wildly around me, and I stuffed my hands into my pant pockets. I stepped inside the booth, inviting and warm. Sweating nervously, I gripped the receiver, lifted it, and placed it to my ear while my other hand reached to dial. Both quivered excessively, requiring multiple attempts. When the ring came through, I nearly hung up.

"*Hallo?*" A woman's voice materialized.

"Uh, um."

"Hallo?" she pressed.

"Uh, yes, I'm looking for Josef."

"Josef?"

"Josef Kühn." My tongue snagged on the dryness of my lips.

"He does not live here." My pulse raced.

"Is, is this Anton's home?"

"Yes. Yes, it is. May I ask who's calling?"

"Uh . . ." My mouth struggled to form the words. "Uh, it's Ella."

"Ella?" The voice lifted unexpectedly. The woman nearly screeched into the phone. "Ella? Ella from the East? Hold please."

The line went silent. The tremble in my hands now shook my knees.

"Ella? Ella, is it you?" The desperation in Anton's voice suffocated me. "Ella? Are you there?"

"Anton?"

His voice resonated even deeper than before. "Yes. Yes, it's me. What happened? Are you alright? Ana . . ." His voice became muffled as if he held the phone away. "Ana, get Josef!" His voice came back strong, "What happened to you?"

"I got sick."

"Are you okay now? We've been worried. I can't tell you how concerned I've been. Why didn't you write? Why didn't you tell us? Why did—"

"Stop. Anton, please stop."

"I'm sorry. I'm just . . . I'm surprised is all."

"I know."

"Can you tell me what happened?"

"I have no logical answer. I never really do . . . I wasn't well. Please—" My nose stung. I sniffled. "—Please forgive me."

"Ella, did you—" Anton's voice wavered. "—did you get my last letter?"

I choked back a sob. How could I possibly begin to tell Anton how sorry I was for his loss. "Yes. I—I'm sorry."

Static interrupted. I tapped the receiver against the window then checked the connection. "Anton, are you still there?"

"I'm here."

"You have no reason to forgive me. I've been selfish and cruel."

"Yes, my world collapsed, and all I wanted was to talk to you, to hear your voice tell me everything would be okay like you did all those years when we were children."

"I'm sorry I wasn't there for you."

"You deserted me when I needed you most."

"Anton, I promise I'll never do that again."

"Where did you go? Are you . . . are you married? Children?"

"No. No none of that. I, uh . . . I didn't recover well with Stefan's disappearance. I—I became an alcoholic." I waited to hear the disappointment which never came.

"I'm sorry, El."

"Anton, it wasn't you or Josef. I forced everyone out of my life. The only thing that mattered for a very long time was a drink. It was the only way I knew how to numb the pain."

"There's so much you've had to face alone. We don't fault you for any of it. We just miss you. Are you better?"

"I'm recovering." My lips parted long enough to allow a deep breath to fill my lungs. I hesitated before my next words. "I'm truly sorry about Elizabeth."

"I wasn't sure how I would go on. It has been hell."

"I only read that letter a month ago, and I'm sorry to say, all the other letters just today. I missed a great deal. You have children, Anton!"

"Yes. Two."

"A boy and a girl?"

"Thomas, he's eight and . . ." His tone wavered, "my daughter is 16 months old now."

"What's her name?"

"It was Elizabeth's idea. We talked about this during the pregnancy." He coughed. "But I wanted it as much as she did. Her name is Ella."

A dagger went straight for my heart. With all I'd done to Anton, Elizabeth, Josef, and others . . . they still believed in me . . . all this time . . . they believed in me!

"Anton," I wept. My head fell heavy in defeat, tears freely moistening my palms. "I'm truly sorry. Will you ever be able to forgive me?"

I wanted to hang up the phone, to take cover, run, scream, hide, and—above all—I wanted to drink.

"Ella?" Anton whispered, "Please, please don't leave us again."

His pleading strangled my heart.

"I don't know what you've been through. I barely know your life since we separated, but I know you. You've always been my closest friend, my family. Please don't leave us."

My voice raised with an unknown confidence. "I won't." It was the very thing I needed to hear aloud. "Never again, Anton." Tired of feeling sorry for myself, tired of being weak, I made the one promise I intended to keep. Time for the old Ella to return. "How can I reach Josef?"

"He's here. My help, Ana, the one who answered the phone, retrieved him while we were talking. He's here, Ella."

Josef's anxious voice blasted through the earpiece, "Ella! Ella, why? What happened? Why didn't you reach out? What were you thinking?"

"Josef." My voice faltered; I could hear Anton whispering in the background.

"I'm sorry, Ella. I don't mean to yell. I just can't believe it's you. I've waited too long to hear your voice. Are you okay? Just tell me if you're okay."

"Yes, Josef, I believe I will be now."

After speaking to him for over an hour, I wrote down his own phone number. He and Heidi lived in the same building as Anton, only a floor beneath him. One thing was certain in the course of our conversation, though the boys saw to the needs and nurturing of their own families, they themselves remained inseparable after all these

39

years. This small realization brought forth a great deal of comfort at the close of this long-overdue telephone call.

"Take care of yourself, Ella. Call us anytime."

"I will, I promise."

"I love you, dear sister."

"I love you too, goodnight."

Darkness hovered by the time I left the booth. Outside, nobody waited their turn, and even if they did, I wouldn't have ended my conversation out of politeness . . . not today anyway. As I walked back towards my flat, I realized my amends only reached half of those offended. There were others I owed enormous apologies to, but through the daunting guilt, a feeling of unfettered freedom emerged. The terrible burden of remorse began to gradually lift, lighten, and release!

Four

WHO ELSE WOULD IT BE?

15 November 1983

The tapping on the door grew annoying.

"Hold on, Emil!" I cried. He was the only one who stopped by anymore. I hesitated. *He doesn't wait this long before walking in. Maybe its Katharina or Lena? Am I ready to see either one?* I had resolved to make things right but wasn't sure how or when. The knocks continued.

I cracked the door with a caution that quickly dissolved. A pretty, young woman stood before me gripping a single suitcase in her hand. Her short brown curls bordered a light, flawless complexion and big brown eyes.

"I knew it! You're alive," she cried and entered without an invitation.

My eyes blinked rapidly. *Can it be?* "Mari?" I whispered.

"Of course, Ella. Who else would it be? I doubt you have friends these days." The truthfulness in her words stung. "You obviously forgot about me."

Driven by the bottle, an unforgivable separation lengthened from my justification that she would be disappointed in me.

"What are you doing here?" The door still ajar, I studied her, stunned. "H—how did you find me?"

"I'm moving in," she announced decisively.

"Wait. How did you find me?" I repeated, staring at how beautiful she'd become in the years since I deserted her. At least seven, my mind struggled to remember her appearance the last year of my visit.

"I'm twenty-two." Suddenly the confidence Mari exhibited upon arrival, swayed. She set her suitcase down. Her voice quivered. "Nurse Margret is gone now, and the *Waisenhaus* can no longer house me. You're my only family. Please don't turn me away."

I lunged for her. My arms wrapped around her torso so snug she squeaked from the pressure. "Too tight," she cried and rested her head on my shoulder when I loosened my grip.

"Why here?" I whispered. "Why me?"

"You're the only reason I'm standing here." Mari's words vibrated in my ear, although only part of her statement spoke truth. Stefan initiated her entire recovery when he offered his gold watch to the doctor for payment.

"I don't deserve your forgiveness."

"That's not what Margaret said," she muttered, and I leaned back to face her again. She left a dampness on my cheek.

"Nurse Margaret?"

Her smile filled both cheeks and gradually shrunk to a straight line. "Ella, I've been in the orphanage for sixteen years. I don't know how to live outside of it. Nurse Margaret always assured me you'd be there for me when I needed you the most."

"Yes, Mari, of course." Entirely at fault for the absence of her radiant spirit in my life, I guided her farther inside and closed the door. "Nurse Margaret passed?" Sorrow stirred in my voice. Much like a mother, Margaret's influence was deeply rooted.

"Sadly, yes. She's the only reason I stayed past eighteen. She said not to worry, you would come for me." Her voice trailed off.

Fighting a desire to cower in a corner, I reached for a handkerchief on my dresser and handed it to her. "I'm sorry." I wanted to give her an excuse, but I had none. Sitting on the edge of my bed, my head hung low.

She came to my side and brushed my hair off my forehead. "Let's not dwell on the past." Her encouragement, meant for the moment, struck close to my recent thoughts.

I wiped my nose and grinned back at this astonishing young woman next to me. "My flat is small, but we'll make it work. Of course you can live here."

As I cleared a drawer for her clothing, I inquired again, "Mari, really, how did you find me?"

She paused. Her long eyelashes fluttered several times. "Just know, I understand you were in need of me too."

Even though her answer left more questions, her perseverance to keep another's confidence touched me. Surely Edmund recognized his criticizing behavior in the hospital and told Katharina of my condition. Having been made aware of Mari years ago, it would've been easy to find her and bring her to be my companion at this crucial time in my life. A twinge of guilt arose. Even after all this time and no contact, Katharina sought to help me. That evening, we made *Beamtenstippe*, giggled like girlfriends sharing secrets, and divulged news from the past seven years. Her presence generated an energy long forgotten within these walls. For me, it was as if I relived life in the Waisenhaus, only in a different body. She spoke of nearly everything I knew or experienced at the orphanage.

"Mari, did you ever play in the closet?" my question feigned innocence.

"The closet? The hallway closet?" Her nose wrinkled with curiosity.

"Yes, I did."

"Anything unusual happen?"

"Maybe . . ." She hesitated, but her eyes glistened. "Why?"

"Just wondering."

"Wondering if I found the secret room underneath?"

"Yes!" My cry made her jump. "You found it?"

"Oh, yes. My friend Ginny and I went down there. The space is dreadful."

My mind floated back to the musty smell, dirt, rat feces, and shell casings, but comfort filled my heart at the joy of my find. The linen, the game Anton and I played—despite its outcome, the memory brought forth a wide smile.

"Except this . . ." Mari jumped up and went to her drawer. When she returned, a pink handkerchief wound through her fingers. She handed the linen to me. Although the color differed, the same initials emerged, perfectly stitched into one corner . . . שכ.

I brushed across them. My memory continued: Anton retrieving the kerchief for me, knowing full well it represented something he despised.

"I have one too," I whispered.

"You do?"

"It's not here. It's with Anton."

"Anton, your friend in the West? The one who's with Josef?"

I nodded.

"Why?"

I glanced at the clock; its small hand drifted next to the number eleven. Darkness seeped through the open curtains. "It's a long story." Although one I truly yearned to share.

"Well, I'm not going anywhere." Mari chuckled and wrapped the quilt around her shoulders, wiggling comfortably as if she waited for me to begin.

Five

ZUR LETZEN INSTANZ

"Okay!" Mari bounced into Mama G's chair and crossed her legs, holding a paper and pencil. Being the chair's only occupant since Mama passed, it was surprising that I neither protested nor experienced the usual twinge of ownership. When both Stefan and Hans stopped by the old flat, I carefully guarded their proximity to the chair.

Mari continued, unaware of the memories and emotions playing out in my head. "How do I find employment?" She peered at me with a freshness I hadn't known for years. Her enthusiasm spread contagiously and somehow passed vitality into my aging bones. I sat on the floor near her feet.

"You, my dear, will not have any trouble finding work if you keep smiling like that. Everyone will love you!"

She giggled. "Where do I start, and what do I say?"

I considered the few jobs in my past, the first being the Franke's, of course—intended to be a repayment of debt, not a life-altering

45

event—and then a few small delivering jobs until Hilde hired me. Hilde, another person cut out of my life. And now Zur Letzen Instanz. I hadn't had any contact with Zur since before my hospital stay nearly two months ago, but even before then, my reliability was loose at best. I might not have a position there anymore. Although employed longer than any other waitress, now twelve years, I may have exhausted my last privilege.

"First, you need to write down duties you'd like to do, and make a list of skills you might have."

For the first time since she arrived two days ago, she frowned. "I can't do anything."

"Of course you can. See what you did here, turning this apartment into a place that looks like people actually live here?" It was true. With minimal resources, she transformed my psychiatric ward into a home. She took small scraps of fabric and tied the curtains back. To my paints, nearly dry from neglect, she added water and painted my shelf, vase, and headboard all bright colors. Afterward, she hung from the ceiling small paper birds she'd learned to fold.

"I don't think there are jobs decorating homes."

"No, I suppose not—not here anyway."

I reached for her paper and started writing what I believed her qualities were on one side and on the other, typical jobs with possible openings. "I don't know who might be hiring, especially since jobs have become more complicated with the government involved, but I really think you would do well at the shop around the corner. The crabby old woman who assists customers scares half of them away before their purchase is over. I think she's the grandmother of the owner, but once they meet you and see how delightful you are, they might hire you."

Her countenance lifted. "Yes, I could help people."

"Then I think you should check this neighborhood first. I wouldn't go too far and spend your money on transportation when you can walk, at least for now."

46

"Okay, I'll start checking this afternoon. What about you, Ella? You mentioned you might not be at the restaurant any longer. Why not?"

I'd resigned to being honest with Mari, but confessing the choices I'd made in the last decade proved quite challenging. "I was in the hospital and missed a lot of work. They may have replaced me by now."

She reached out, laid her hand on my shoulder, and kissed my cheek. "I'm sure *you* are irreplaceable." Then she rose quickly to dress and start her search.

After she left, I washed the dishes, swept the floor, and made the bed. I knew the inevitable needed to be addressed but delayed. Grabbing a cloth, I walked to the shelf, recently painted a deep yellow. Mari had carefully placed everything back exactly as before. The box of unused stationary caught my eye first. Other than her brief handling of it, the paper remained untouched. A fine layer of dust was its only companion. My book collection, doubled in size since Mama G's, now occupied half the space. On the far end, next to Papa's medal and Josef's marbles, Anton's tinnie pin leaned against the wall.

Carefully brushing the contents, I held them with reverence, each representing a significant time, purpose, or event. When I reached the pin, it reminded me once again of Anton's last letter. Forefront on my mind, I couldn't help comparing our loss; it was if our basic emotions subsisted in a parallel universe without intertwining. The strain in his voice when we spoke, the pain in his words, his despair and profound agony. The anguish I endured over Stefan penetrated my ability to think, sleep, and function.

The inability to have Stefan—to physically feel his body and spirit—taunted me at every possible moment. Every time I envisioned him near, he wore the same green military jacket and black boots. His blond hair extended from the edges of a close-fitting gray cap, and he appeared as still as a mannequin until I blinked . . . and then he vanished. A cruel joke my irrational mind manipulated for years. If my own brain devised this extreme reaction concerning someone possibly still alive, I couldn't imagine Anton's devastation over Elizabeth's death.

Lifting the tinnie pin, I rubbed the ridges. This precious piece tangled with a lifetime of heartache: the night Anton left it to me, Frau Franke's clutches, the Stasi remand room, the underground tunnel, and now my shelf. A faint smile emerged from the memory of how it had been faithfully worn inside my dress until the time I fell in love with Stefan. Pressing it against my lips, and placing it back on the shelf, I conceded my love for Anton never stopped; it only changed. He would always be a part of my heart.

An hour later, I approached the entrance of Zur Letzen Instanz. Despite the fact that nothing changed structurally in the centuries it served, Zur's familiarity vanished. When I stepped inside the open door, Conrad swiftly left the bar.

"Ella." His strict stance blocked my progress. "Let's step outside."

Nodding, I feared what my gut told me. Though a chill nipped the air, he guided me away from the warm entrance and towards the outer bench.

"I'm sorry, Conrad," I squeaked. "I should've tried to get word to you. I'd been hospitalized."

"I know. Angelika went to your building, and the superintendent told her."

"Emil?"

"Yes, I believe that was his name." His eyes darted around the neighborhood, an unusual behavior for him. "I hope you've recovered."

"I'm doing much better."

He sighed heavily and glanced at his hands, unable to look me in the eye. "I'm afraid you can no longer be employed here."

Heat flushed my cheeks. I slid my trembling fingers underneath my legs, ignoring the rough scratch from the wooden bench. "Conrad, please," I whimpered, "I need this job. I've been here a long time."

"Yes." He finally met my eyes. "Yes, you were always one of my best waitresses."

"Were?"

He shifted uncomfortably. "You—you changed, Ella." His brows curved inward. "You were barely here, and when you were . . ." The sympathy evident in his countenance silenced his lecture. He never had trouble telling me the truth before.

"I was ill."

"Yes, but I'm referring to much earlier, the weeks with no contact."

I remembered little of this. He most likely gave me multiple concessions because of my seniority. "I see," my whimper choked back a cry.

"You don't recall the last time you were here, do you?" he continued.

My mind frantically reeled for the memory. *What did I do?*

Conrad answered the question, though it never reached my lips.

"You came to work drunk . . . again." Conrad shook his head. Apparently there was more to the story, but he stalled. "It should probably be forgotten. Please wait here. I need to retrieve your final pay." He stood, and although he'd always been a rigorous employer, empathy lingered behind him.

So many memories here. This small corner of Berlin never aged. My eyes shifted from the cobblestone road to the black iron gate a stone's throw away. Even the tall tombstones and thick shade trees in the cemetery dated centuries. These sights had become part of me. I gazed back at the windows of Zur, the brown trim stacked in mismatched proportions yet identical to the door frame. Many times I entered and exited over the years from the spiral stairs and niches to the brick wall and biergarten. Tears flowed without a fight this time.

"I'm sorry, Ella." I whirled around as Angelika appeared next to me. She pulled her sweater tight across her chest and reached for my hands as I stood to hug her.

"That bad?" I questioned. I knew she would tell me the truth. "Was what I did really terrible?"

She nodded. "An *SED* lunch." She referred to the Socialist Unity Party, the one Herr Franke had been a member of for many years. "You're actually lucky Conrad intervened. You should've been arrested."

I bit my lip. At one time, Angelika teased me about my choice to never drink alcohol.

She laughed coolly, "Actually, when I go, I think I'll follow suit. After your clearly hateful speech—which ended with an accusation of them being killers—you flipped your finger on your way out. They probably deserved it."

My lower lip dropped slightly. Not only did I not remember the act, I didn't recall ever being vulgar to anyone, although it could've been suppressed after decades of falling victim to their control. *I must've lost it.*

"You gettin' help?" She peered at me strangely.

Having witnessed her blackout on a dance floor, grope a stranger in the street, and dump her glass of rum on a barman because he didn't make her *Echte Kroatzbeere* correctly, I must've practically fallen off the earth to have her ask me this. "Yes, I am."

Angelika's eyes darted upward as Conrad cleared his throat. She kissed me on the cheek. "Come visit," she whispered and turned away.

"Here's your final due. It's not much." Conrad held out an envelope.

"I truly apologize, Conrad, for everything."

He nodded. "I know."

I smiled. "Thank you."

He walked back inside the restaurant.

I sat on the bench for only a few more minutes. *If I'm going to sulk, it needs to be far from here.* As I stumbled along the street, my body pined for the closest *kneipe*, and in typical German fashion, there were many to choose from.

I stopped outside the entrance of a bar frequented often in the beginning, to slip a few drinks in before work. Poorly lit, my entry went unnoticed. The steps to the bar lugged as though cement filled my boots. Finally reaching a stool, I slid on but couldn't lift my eyes. My hands gripped the edge of the bar while every vein protruded from my fingers to my wrists. *What am I doing here?*

"What'll it be?"

My hands fell to my lap. "W-wodka."

"Startin' early huh, lass?" The barman's foreign accent did not hold back his sarcasm. My glare answered for me. "Rachmaninoff okay?"

I nodded. As he poured, the liquid flowed smoothly, and when it settled, it appeared like solid glass, no fizzes or foam. I scanned the surface, laden and tempting, imagining the relief provided as it passed my lips and slithered down my anxious throat. I stared.

I thought of Mari, how she needed me now—how we actually needed each other. *What will she say?*

It's only one drink. I can handle one drink . . . can't I?

Will she be disappointed in me if she knows?

She may already be when she finds out I lost my position at Zur.

"Is there a problem?" The barman stood in front of me.

I shook my head.

"Do you want a different one?"

"No," I snapped. He quickly retreated.

As I ran my tongue across my parched lips, the desire to bring the drink to my mouth brought a familiar yearning to my bosom. My hands cupped the glass. *No one will know.*

I rubbed it with my thumbs. *I will know.*

My teeth clenched tightly behind sweltering cheeks. *How am I going to fight this? How am I going to overcome this?*

My hands jerked toward my lap; they were no longer trembling but graduated to a full shake. I shoved them in my pockets. The barman watched me warily from the other side of the bar, but he didn't approach me again.

I pulled my lips in and braced for impact. Every muscle in my body tightened. My eyes watered incessantly. The moment might have only lasted seconds but seemed like eternity before a wave of relief washed over me as if I had climbed a peak and reached the other side. Weak and fatigued, I slipped a mark from my pocket and placed it on the bar next to the full glass and walked out. Taking my first real breath, I inhaled the scent of the city. Despite its flaws, it brought oxygen to my soul. I clutched a nearby lamppost to steady myself. My watch revealed two hours had passed when it only felt like minutes.

The walk home offered little satisfaction. Leaving the bar without a drink should have held a more victorious state, but it hurt. The physical rawness that tore through me seared more painfully than anticipated and with strange accompaniment. A gaping hole emerged, one that needed to be calmed and quieted, yet I lacked the knowledge of anything to possibly do the job.

Six

I'M AN ALCOHOLIC

4 December 1983

"I may have found work, Ella." Mari smiled with gentle hope the moment I entered the flat. "I went everywhere these last two weeks, to all the Geschäfts in a couple kilometre radius, and nothing came of it. I went to banks and transportation, but they offered nothing. I finally went to the *Fleishcherei* you spoke of and met the butcher, Herr Volney. He's in need of a stockperson but looking for a man to fill the position because of the meat." She stole a quick breath before she continued, her brown curls bouncing spiritedly atop her shoulders. It would be hard to picture her petite frame working in a butchery. "But I told him my job at the orphanage was to unload the carts and stock the pantry, even the heavy bags of wheat or flour, and I could do it. He said *no*, but I remembered I'd been advised to seek him by you." She paused. My head bowed low as she continued. "Taken aback, he asked me to come back tomorrow." She placed a warm cup of tea in my hands. Her tone turned sympathetic, "Ella, your skin . . . it's pale."

It's not often anyone noticed, being that *my pale* is another's healthy glow. Her hand cupped my cheek. "You're cold. Come. Come sit." She led me to the chair and grabbed a quilt to wrap around my shoulders. "Are you well?"

My lips curved upward in a false motion and quickly turned down. *This is Mari. I need to be real with her.* "I'm happy for you. I really am."

Mari swiftly stepped to the stove, turned the knob for the soup she was making, and returned kneeling by my side.

"Herr Volney asked about you." She searched my face for a reaction. "He said his sister is married to your brother. Is that true?"

I nodded, embarrassed I left specific information out when I told her to check for employment with him.

"Why didn't you tell me, and why don't you know him? He's family, Ella."

I tugged the blanket tighter around my body and sighed. "I kind of kept to myself for a while."

"Yes, that's what I assumed. How did things go with your restaurant?" She returned to the kitchen and poured the soup into two bowls.

I debated telling her. It would be quite disappointing after her good news. She approach me, the bounce in her step matching the spring in her curls. She deserved to know the truth. *Always the truth.* "I lost my job, Mari." I accepted the food but placed it on the small night table nearby and covered my head with the quilt, unable to watch her reaction. I mumbled, "I'm an alcoholic."

Within seconds, her fingers gently drew the blanket away. "I know."

"You do?" I sat forward in surprise.

"I know you have a drinking problem. It's part of the reason I'm here." She lifted my hand and kissed it, smiling at me through growing tears. "You saved my life, Ella. Please let me save yours."

"How—"

54

Mari cut me off. "It doesn't matter. Just know I'm here for you, and we'll figure it all out together."

I reached around my precious Mari, no longer small and frail, and pulled her to me. Strong and beautiful and exactly what I imagined her to be as a grown woman.

"Thank you," I whispered.

*****

Six weeks after Zur released me, the January cold made the job hunt miserable and discouraging. Every day I passed a bar, a pub, or café. Alcohol called to me from every direction, and every minute I fought the desire to give in. The cravings relentlessly wracked my body to the point of physical exhaustion only hours in. Despite the discouragement in my pursuit of finding employment, I promised Mari I wouldn't drink again, and it took every ounce of strength to fulfill my vow.

"Why did you leave your previous employ?" The typical question hovered, but more comments followed.

"No experience? We need experience."

"We don't have any positions open."

"Nothing here."

"You shake like an addict. We don't employ *alkoholikers*."

I even made my way back to Checkpoint Charlie, reaching a humbling low when I turned to Hilde for help, having not spoken to her since she and the soldiers revealed the news about Stefan back in 1971. Memories of that time—his assumed demise, the tunnel, the drunk man dead at the wall, Stefan's duty—led to him shooting and deserting me. Cringing with trepidation, I entered the café.

A quick assessment revealed potted plants replaced by colored vases, my butterfly paintings by photographs of Berlin, and the wooden tables now metal stands with stools. Even the counter donned a bold red color.

"Are you eating in?" The woman who met me near the front wiped her hands on her apron and grabbed a menu. I squinted to find familiarity.

"Is Hilde here?"

"Hilde?"

"Or Gus?" I added, craning my neck towards the kitchen, no longer exposed.

"I . . . I don't know who . . . Wait. The former owners?"

"Yes." I nodded excitedly. "Former? This is Gustav's, right?"

"Oh yes, it is. We kept the name, but they no longer own the restaurant."

"They sold Gustav's?" I repeated her answer but mostly for myself. I believed they'd be here to the very end.

She nodded her head.

"Do you know where they are?"

"No. They mentioned Saxony, but I have no contact information. I'm sorry."

My once-over was brief. Many memories packed this room, especially the one that lingered the longest . . . the reunion with Stefan. I quickly thanked the woman and fled outside. Even though the inside of the café varied from what I remembered, the exterior remained exactly the same. I stood below the white box sign that advertised *Gustav's*, but my eyes couldn't resist floating towards the nearby brick wall where the reunion continued. Stefan's arms wound tightly around me; his lips sweetly immersed with my own.

Angered by the interference Stefan's memories caused, I shielded my eyes and hustled away. On the bus ride home, I rebuked myself for allowing Hilde to disappear from my life but also for the grief my daydreaming caused. I needed to stop allowing those past fantasies to surface. They brought nothing but heartache.

Glancing around the bus, hopeless expressions joined mine. Each day, life in the East grew darker and graver. Russia's threats to withhold assistance and Germany's prideful refusal to accept foreign aid made access to healthy food and adequate medical care limited.

Finding work had never been a problem for me before, and my determination to avoid going to the government for help drove me to continue my personal search, despite discouragement. Though the state offered employment opportunities, I wanted nothing to do with the SED and their corrupt politics.

In the last decade, fortifying the wall with motion sensors and trigger mines drove people to seek alternate routes to freedom. Successful escapes included a hot air balloon, an air mattress across the water, and a man who used meat hooks to scale the wall. Interwoven between those were many more disastrous outcomes. Of the twenty-four documented deaths since 1973, Lothar Fritz Freie from West Berlin became the only recognized fatality last year. Yet I knew better. Numberless victims without a name and a voice lived and died among us . . . but something began to change.

People started to speak out, meet, and organize. One such society known as "Working Group 13th of August" arose, founded by a man in West Berlin. Their purpose was to publish annual updates on the victims, their names, their murder dates, and as much of the circumstances they knew. Several smuggled copies made their way to the East, and although I'd had never seen it personally, many testified of its existence. Thankfully, once again, people demonstrated they remembered us.

After a disheartening bus ride home, I spent another two hours moving from the window, to the bed, to the kitchen. Nothing settled my anxious mind. I finally resolved to making dinner shortly before Mari came home.

"How was your search today?" Wrapped up like an onion, Mari drifted towards the radiator at the same speed it took to remove her various layers. She wasted no time jumping straight to the point.

I set the lid back on the pan. The *maultasche* needed a few more minutes to simmer. "Oh, Mari. It's discouraging. Nobody will hire me. I've never faced such rejection."

"Don't fret. Something will come up." Her smile lit the room. "Herr Volney offered me more hours."

I watched her expression carefully. "Your hard work must please him."

"Oh, Ella. He's kind and answers all my silly questions. I'm learning a great deal about the leg of a chicken and the behind of a pig." Her laugh filled the small space. "He's quite anxious to meet you, though." She stepped to the stove and lifted the lid for a whiff. "Ohhh, my favorite," she cooed.

"It doesn't have the spinach. I couldn't find it this time, but the meat is fresh." I finished smashing some crackers to sprinkle on top of the pasta. "Wait . . . me? Why does he want to meet me?"

"Don't be ridiculous. He said Heidi sent him your name over eight years ago. He even stopped by once. So . . ." —she reached for two plates— "he's coming to dinner a week from this Sunday."

"What?" Pressure in my chest stifled me. My hand froze an inch above the pan. "I don't . . . think that would be a good idea."

"It's a very good idea. He's your brother's family, which makes him yours too."

"Oh, Mari. I—" I finished dropping the crumbs and then leaned against the counter, my palm pressed against my cheek. "—I'd be an awkward host."

"Well, thank goodness I'll be the hostess, then." She clapped her hands together. "It's settled."

I lifted my chin and a slight grin emerged. Her radiance was infectious. How did I survive all this time without her?

At dinner I carefully avoided conversation regarding Cade and relayed my job-hunting adventure to Mari's more than gracious ear, including the sad update of Hilde and Gus.

"What about Katharina?"

"Katharina?

"You told me in the Waisenhaus. Don't you remember? You shared the stories of the Frankes, her *and* Stefan."

The breaded dough clumped thick in my throat. *Stefan?* Meticulous about not mentioning him since she arrived, the twist in

58

conversation stunned me. Of course I remembered the times I shared news of Stefan with her . . . his letters, our plans, and our wishes.

"Why Katharina?" I managed to swallow the morsel with difficulty, although it left my throat tingling. I reached for the water glass and took a long sip.

"Maybe she'll offer you a position."

Mari's naivety regarding my past became evident. I hadn't told her everything, and even with Frau Franke no longer there, if Herr Franke didn't kill me, the memories of Stefan would.

"No. I'll keep searching. I have some ideas."

"Okay." Mari paused, deep in thought. "Ella, on my way home today, I saw a curious display outside a building. Since I'm quite unfamiliar with the city, I don't know exactly what it was, but people wore signs around their necks by string, held hands in a circle, and chanted."

"What were they chanting?"

"For human and civil rights and democratization of state."

"Ah, yes." I nodded my head. "More and more people are organizing into opposition groups."

"What are they?"

"People who are tired of being controlled by socialism and communism. A few factions started in the West and have filtered over here, but in the last year, more and more residents of the East are uprising."

"Can they stop the government?"

My head leaned forward as I contemplated her question. Having seen *what* the government can do first hand, I was skeptical. "I'm not sure. It would take a lot of people, pretty much everyone in East Berlin—possibly East Germany—to take a stand against them. We would need a great deal of courage."

The next day after Mari left for work, I warmed some water for tea and paced the room with agitation. Confined with guilt, I told Mari I had employment options when truthfully, nothing transpired. Facing the shelf, I rummaged through the stack of letters read after my recovery. I held Papa's pipe firmly between my teeth and pulled an incredibly dusty Immensee off the shelf. Settling into Mama's chair, I waited until the kettle whistled. I knew I was stalling, but each day seemed gloomier than the one before. My true fear was disappointment—mine and hers. If not carefully restrained, my discouragement could potentially lead to another bar, another stool, and ultimately, another drink.

I let Papa's pipe rest on the armchair while I sipped my tea and watched a light flutter of snow brush the windowpane. Guilt reared its ugly head. *I'm reading a book, sipping tea, while sweet Mari is walking to and from a butchery job in the freezing cold. How can I let her continue and not keep trying?* I set the mug on the window sill, slammed the book closed and proceeded to replace the book on the shelf. A card protruded from the back of the book and caught my attention. *I must've used this to hold a page.* I pulled it out and instantly the memory of an over-confident teenager who openly criticized authority and plotted escape . . . *Karl-Heinz* . . . came to mind. My grin swelled at the flattering memory. His energy, wit, laughter, and absurd flirtations the night we met played in my head. My lips pulled into a frown, recalling his final words wishing us farewell, his intent to leave the East only hours later. I never searched the missing lists for his name but believed I probably would've found it.

The dust on the card tickled my nose. I held my sneeze to read the one sole name. *Darek Mayer.*

I knew several underground resistance groups actively promoted anti-fascism through different scenes. Unsure who Herr Mayer was acquainted with, my interest piqued. With the shift in my longings from escape to survival, I wondered if I could be helpful . . . or useful, maybe get paid. Karl-Heinz, himself, mentioned the cause needed someone like me. Of course, back then confidence and conviction surged through me. Now, cowardice reigned.

Seven

ARE YOU FOOLISH?

14 February 1984

"I'm seeking Darek Mayer."

"Nobody here by that name." The barman glanced up at me with deep black eyes that matched the liner heavily coated above his lids. My own eyes stirred in response. A black strip of hair centered the man's bald head and settled on his neck like the mane of a horse. I labored to speak, but nothing came forth. The chains dangling against his leather waist clinked as he turned away.

"I know he's here." The tone in which I spoke exhibited forced assurance, but my legs quivered at the knees.

"Who's asking?"

"Ella," I spit out. "Ella Kühn."

He circled back towards me, his upper lip curled at the corner.

"What do you want, Ella Kühn?"

"I received his name from a friend."

61

"I told you" —he placed both his hands on the bar— "no one here by that name."

"I know he's associated with this place. An acquaintance of his sent me here."

"You need to leave!"

"Look—" I bit the inside of my cheek. "—Truth is, I hoped Darek might have work. I . . . I need a job."

"We're not hiring," he snapped curtly before he waved me off.

"Wait!" My hands raised in defiance. It had taken me an entire week to track Darek to this place in Prenzlauer, and I wouldn't give up easily. Mari's job at the butchery brought in a small income, but without my contribution we were headed for dismal times. I'd reached my absolute last straw. *We need this.* "I was referred by a friend. I want to help."

His fingers turned white gripping the edge of the wood. A slow throaty murmur discharged. "The bar is *not* hiring!"

"I'm not talking about the bar," I shot back.

His countenance appeared confident, although the slight flutter of his eyelashes told me this was not expected. He scrutinized me from head to foot—my hair worn in a bun, a thick conservative turtleneck topping a plaid, knee-length skirt—and I knew exactly how I appeared. An ordinary middle-aged woman. He browsed the empty room, one patron sitting in the corner.

"Who referred you?" he whispered.

"Karl-Heinz."

His mouth rolled into a scowl. The escaping hiss was unmistakable. "Liar."

I jutted my chin out. No kid half my age was going to call me a liar. "I'm not lying!"

He wiped his brow with the cloth he just used to dry a glass. "Get out. Get out now! You don't belong here!" he shouted.

A man quickly appeared in front of a curtain behind the bar. The barman steamed. "I'm handling this fine."

"Thank you, Nikolaus. I can take it from here." Dressed moderately conservative in comparison to his mate, the man wore jeans and a sport jacket. Nikolaus threw his rag on the bar in protest and turned his back on us both. The man motioned for me to follow him to the back room. Flanked by boxes and supplies, it bordered a narrow hallway where voices drifted from another room, yet we remained in the tight space. His trust seemed to have limitations.

"Are you Darek?"

He ignored my inquiry and proceeded with his own. "When did you see Karl-Heinz last?" Kind but skeptical, his tone remained even, his gaze fixed.

"I guess it would be about fourteen years now." Trying to recall the exact date, I remembered the bitter cold night Lena and I went to the pub. "December 1970, I believe."

"Describe him."

"He had brown hair, brown eyes."

One of the man's eyebrows rose. "Really?" A typical description of half the men in Berlin.

I continued, unruffled, "He wore a jacket with torn pockets and a hole in his shoe. His big toe slipped out when he danced, and when he smiled, the dimple in his chin deepened." I grinned at the memory. "And he loved the Beatles."

Folding his arms across his chest, he held firmly in place. His eyes gazed briefly upward before they reached mine again "Karl's dead." His words were only confirmation. I knew in my heart when Karl-Heinz left the bar that night, his life was over.

"I'm sorry." My smile disappeared, solemnness taking its place. "I should've tried harder to stop him."

The stranger continued to watch me carefully. "He was a foolish kid."

"He wanted a better life."

"He could've had one . . . had he waited."

"Waiting is difficult." The sorrow in my voice rose, absolute.

He ignored my grief. "Are you foolish, Ella?"

Clearly my answer was yes as I reflected on my checkered past, but desperation outweighed the truth. "I'm loyal."

"How did you locate me?" His eyes narrowed. I found Darek.

I contemplated how to answer. Espionage, a learned skill in the East, meant nobody could be trusted, not family, friends, or strangers. If I told him he'd been relentlessly tracked through associations, he might question my motives. "It was difficult."

Nikolaus walked in from the front and handed a stack of papers to Darek. He leaned in. "We need to get these leaflets out tonight."

"I can help," I insisted, surprising them both. Nikolaus shot me another irritated squint I quickly ignored. "I can do anything you need me to. I need work."

Darek scanned the length of my torso. "I can't see you having trouble getting a decent wage with respectable work, Miss Kühn." Again, it had to be my moderate appearance. "Why come to us?"

"I—" *Oh*, I groaned in my head, *how much should I tell him? Truth. Tell the truth.*

I waited until Nikolaus turned down the hall before answering softly, "I'm a recovering alcoholic."

"No way," Nikolaus snickered. I hoped he hadn't heard, but his aggravating laugh reverberated in my ears as I continued.

"I served tables at Zur Letzen Instanz for the past twelve years. I lost my job because of my addiction."

"Well, we won't have any addict here," Darek insisted. "Our work requires people to be alert at all times. There are too many people looking to take us down."

"I'm recovering. Five months sober. Please, Herr Mayer, give me a chance."

Following Darek's stare down the hall to Nikolaus, who stacked boxes near the entrance of the other room, I waited nervously for his response. The man I'd come to loathe in such a short time didn't shy from his dissent. Nikolaus's mohawk whipped sternly side to side. "Darek . . . *sie ist Neger.*"

64

Shocked, my lower lip fell. It's been years since my darker skin rendered caution.

"That's not my concern, Nikolaus. The cause is bigger than color. You know this."

They spoke as if I weren't present.

"She's not the right fit," Nikolaus mumbled.

"I'm a hard worker. I can do it." My defensive plea began Nikolaus's direction but ended by locking eyes with Darek.

"Not a good idea," Nikolaus huffed.

"Don't mind Nikolaus, Ella. He's bitter . . . barely six when Karl died. He was his cousin."

"Oh." A brief moment of apologetic remorse emerged. "That's awful."

Nikolaus continued shuffling boxes around and refused to acknowledge me.

"What can you do, Miss Kühn?" Darek continued.

"I . . ." Instantly, I made a mental list of my capabilities. They all included taking or filling meal orders. "I can distribute those leaflets for starters, deliver messages or packages, anything you need."

Darek hesitated. Nikolaus continued to utter disapproval.

"Okay," Darek agreed. "I'll give you a trial."

I wanted to leap for joy, but my relief was short lived. A seriousness entered the room as Darek grabbed the top leaflet and started to scribble notes on the back. "You first need to know several things. I'm not sure exactly how you found me, but you must understand our work here is potentially life or death." He continued to write on the paper. "It might be exciting to be part of the beginning stages of change, but this is not a game. People disappear and die over information. When you come into the pub, make sure you're not followed. You never say our names in public, and if caught, no matter what they do, you never expose the organization."

My thoughts went to my previous torture, years ago. After considerable time in the darkness—the sound of my dripping sweat and tormenting verses—I willingly talked. Did I have the strength now to resist if I got caught?

"How have you been able to stay... well, you know..." I inferred the word *secret*.

He seemed to know exactly what I meant.

"By who we involve," Nikolaus snapped. "You've told her too much already." His discord grated on me.

Darek ignored him. "Loyalty." He used my own word against me and then handed me the stack of leaflets Nikolaus had organized.

"A concert... at a church?" I read the paper for the first time, obvious skepticism in my tone.

"Yes, a concert. Change can be stirred through freedom of choice, music, lyrics; and many times a social event is the best place to set a trap."

"A trap?"

"That's all, for now." Darek pointed to the curtain, urging me to leave.

I studied him briefly. There was much I didn't understand, but my need for a paycheck meant I must also trust him.

"Make sure you get these leaflets everywhere. Lampposts, sign boards, shop windows, and parks, Annika."

"It's Ella."

"Not to us."

I mulled over this sudden change. "So Darek's not your real name?"

He smiled and pointed to the door.

Before I left, I twisted back his direction. "After I do this, then what?"

"Come to the concert. A smart woman would see for herself what she's getting into."

I left the bar feeling strange. I'd never been a fan of the SED or their domineering thumbprint, but my introduction now to the underground movement didn't sit comfortably either. With little knowledge of this growing faction, including the culture known as *punk rock,* I wavered. My only resource had been the papers, printed by their enemies. In the words of the *Berliner Zeitung,* the bold, brazen haircuts, brash clothing style, and abrasive music initiated rebellion. Nikolaus's appearance placed him well into that category. *A smart woman would see for herself . . .* Darek's words repeatedly infiltrated my thoughts. I considered myself that type of woman most of the time, but today, as I entered the foreign world of the underground, doubt reared its ugly head.

After dropping the leaflets in public places all over several neighborhoods, I ventured towards Alexanderplatz and the Centralmark. With only a small stack remaining, I meandered close to the world clock. A boy played the violin underneath, his case opened against the concrete, hoping to earn some change from those passing by. Unfamiliar with the tune, I became engaged with his long stirring notes. Glancing upward, my eyes rested on each bold number that represented a different time in the world . . . 19, 20, 21 . . . the gleaming gold shone brightly against the setting sun.

A memory awakened and brought me back to the day I stood here with Stefan. Only an introductory poster appeared at the time. It wasn't the clock, however, that triggered the tears but a recollection of his body pressed securely against me, holding me, comforting me. My eyelids descended with the gentle sway of the boy's tune. The exaggerated notes from the instrument dragged me deeper into my mind. When my eyes opened, the green military jacket and gray cap appeared against a distant column underneath the rail station. I gasped. With blurred sight increasing by the second, I sprinted the direction of the apparition. Slapping my cheeks with vigor and brushing the wetness away, I fought for clarity, only to reach emptiness when I arrived.

Slamming my fist against the post, I wilted to the ground beside it. Bursts of anger, mixed with pain, blazed through me. *Why is this happening? I haven't had any alcohol for months*—my fists balled against my eyes—*why are the hallucinations still coming? I must be crazy . . .* I reached

67

the only explanation for the constant delusion and torture. Could the effects of the alcohol have damaged my brain? *Will this ever get easier?*

"Are you alright?" A woman with a child stood before me. She held out a handkerchief, her toddler cowering behind her leg. A simple question with no answer. I reached for the handkerchief and wiped my eyes.

"Do you need help?" she continued.

I shook my head and handed it back. "Thank you, but no." I forced a fake grin that allowed her to leave. Despite my rejection for help, gratitude surfaced, knowing people still cared for one another in these uncertain times. The fear and darkness that infiltrated our lives for decades hadn't stripped us entirely of compassion or sympathy.

After several more minutes, strength occupied my limbs once more. On my feet, I pulled the remaining leaflets out of my jacket pocket and glanced around the plaza until my restless eyes settled on a small store. Anxious to be done, the record store next to the bank would be the perfect place to leave the rest of the pamphlets.

Once inside the shop, sight of the growing selections brought forth an honest smile. Multiple rows of at least a hundred back-to-back vinyls materialized before me. I recalled previous years and my desperate search in record stores to find one album—*La Vie en Rose* by Edith Piaf—only to have discovered it, of all places, at the Franke's. I leafed through the titles and found only European-approved bands. No Beatles, no American, and definitely no punk.

I hesitated to do it but asked the attendant, "Do you have any punk rock?"

Examining my dress from my shoulders to my toes, his expression spoke for him, just as it had everyone else today.

"Punk?" he whispered, although we were alone.

I nodded.

He shifted awkwardly for several seconds before stepping into his back room. When he returned, his hand clutched a single record jacket. The title *London Calling* bordered the edge of the cover in colorful type. The band *The Clash*, appeared along the top. I pretended to know who they were. "How much?"

"Well, . . ." His eyes flashed towards the door. We were still alone. "You know it's banned, right?"

I dipped my chin and repeated my question. "How much?"

"I could be arrested if it's traced back to me." His stalling grew annoying.

Convinced he attempted to make a better deal, I fanned it off. "Forget it." I turned away.

The man's voice croaked hastily, "Wait."

Hesitating at the door, I hid my growing smirk before I met him again.

"Ten mark."

"Five," I rebutted.

"You can't get this anywhere else."

"Oh really?" I handed him the leaflet I posted. "Maybe I can." Though the flyer promoted a different band, the punk association carried some weight.

He glanced at it and my direction again. "Okay, five."

My last marks . . . ridiculously spent on a record I wouldn't normally care about. Music over food. What had things come to?

I paid, offered him the last of the leaflets for interested customers and quickly rushed home.

In the flat, alone, I struggled to open the closet door. Behind it, all my carefully hidden memories lay buried next to the phonograph. Every letter Stefan wrote me, the dried flowers, the note he put on my bed, the Cochem painting, *La Vie en Rose*, and of course, the ring stuffed in a small box. I hadn't laid eyes on that most precious jewel for ten years, nor could I part with it.

Tugging on the light cord, I held my breath. My intent was to remove the phonograph quickly and seal the space once more.

"What are you doing?" Mari's inquiry caused me to jump. I hadn't heard her enter.

69

"I am . . ." My mind couldn't construct a reason fast enough. She appeared at my side.

"You have a phonograph?" Her squeal chilled my ears. With a swift lunge, she retrieved it and placed it on the kitchen counter. "Ohhh, I saw one in a store window once. I can't believe I'm looking at one now." Her fingers explored each knob, openly mesmerized.

"Is this the record you want to play?" She held the cover of the vinyl I'd purchased.

I quickly grabbed Camille Felgren's album from the closet floor and switched records with her. I wasn't ready to confess my new responsibility nor introduce her innocence to the dark side of punk rock. "Here, this album has Mama G's favorite songs. I think you'll like it."

As she toyed with the machine, I carefully hid *The Clash* under the bed and helped her set the record. Mari was in love. She swayed faintly at first, but as the music picked up, she fell into a full twirl about the room. What a joy to see something that had brought such happiness into my life now shaping hers.

The next day, finding myself alone again, I retrieved the newly-purchased vinyl and carefully listened to the two songs. *London Calling*, on side A, was a politically-charged rant regarding everything from war to police brutality, including a strike against the Beatles. Side B, titled *Working and Waiting*, described a clampdown of oppressive governments, urging youth to fight the status quo. No wonder the record store attendant expressed concern. This is precisely the type of music people get arrested over.

After listening to both sides repeatedly, I had difficulty finding the appeal in the bristly beats. Although lively and stimulating, it was actually the lyrics that generated familiar emotions for me—poetry portraying a people tired of being controlled.

While the music played, I retrieved the instructions Darek handed to me. On it he also listed several western media papers and a couple of books he recommended I read. It seemed as though he valued knowledge as much as I did, and that impressed me. After reaching

70

the end of the list, I carefully folded it and slid it in the front cover of my Jules Verne poetry book, one title Mari hadn't shown an interest in reading yet. With a resolve of careful concealment, I acknowledged the less Mari knew about my latest exploits, the better off we'd all be.

Eight

CADE

The simple knock was as far from threatening as humanly possible, but it still caused my anxious form to shudder.

"Don't worry." Mari lit up as she hopped down from the kitchen counter. "I'll get it."

I paused my preparation to hear his voice.

"Hello, Mari." Younger than I expected. I stretched my neck enough to peek and nearly fell over in my awkward stance. More handsome too. "Oh . . ."

He caught me.

"You must be Ella."

I fumbled to get my feet solidly beneath me and stood forward, embarrassed. Cade held a bouquet of flowers I'm sure were meant for Mari, but he pointed them my direction.

"Thank you for inviting me to dinner."

I wanted to say it wasn't my idea. Yet, unable to put two logical words together, I only nodded and reached for the flowers. After taking his coat, Mari sidled up next to me and rubbed me gently with her elbow. "She's delighted you accepted." Then gave me a hard stare.

"Yes—yes I'm glad you came." I turned back to the kitchen and scrambled to find a glass to put the flowers in. We rarely had such luxurious gifts, therefore no vase.

We had borrowed a card table and three folding chairs from our neighbors the Mengeling family. With five children in their small two bedroom flat, they depended on the compact furniture for space. Mari reached for the glass of flowers and placed them on the center of the table, previously set with simple tableware: three plates, three forks, and three knives. Between the two of us, we managed to find mushrooms for the breaded *schnitzel*, and Mari traded a scarf for fresh eggs to make the *Spätzle* as a side dish.

While Mari showed Cade to his chair, I slipped back over to the kitchen to check on the food. More than ready, I deliberately delayed. When I brought the meat from the oven and set it on top of the stove, I caught sight of Mari's face as they visited without me. She practically glowed. Instantly, I became defensive, like a mother hen protecting her chick. *Herr Volney must be thirty. What are his intentions with someone this young?* My jaw clenched tighter the more I dwelt on the idea. A hand appeared on my arm.

"Can I help you?" Mari had noticed my sudden stupor. Ashamed at my more-than-obvious selfishness, I conceded.

"Yes, of course. Here, put the meat on this plate, and I'll put the Spätzle in a bowl. "Sorry, I'm dawdling."

"Not to worry. There's no rush," she whispered in my ear a moment before her lips blessed me with a tender kiss on the cheek. That one small act calmed my heart. Smart, responsible, and capable, Mari didn't need me to protect her.

I brought the food to the table and after taking a seat, extended my right hand to Cade, my smile genuine. "It's finally nice to meet you. It shouldn't have taken this long."

"I'm grateful to make the acquaintance of the famous Ella. Josef speaks of nearly nothing else." When he laughed, a dimple in his chin deepened, and his hazel eyes brightened like stars. It even pressed me to laugh back.

"Do you speak to Josef often?"

"Mostly Heidi, but several times a month to Josef as well." Instantly, a jealous gene stirred, although, the only one responsible for our lengthy silence was me. Herr Volney's fork stopped mid-air. "I understand you spoke to them recently."

"Yes." My heart warmed. "Yes, I did."

"According to Heidi, it was the best thing to happen in years."

Although not said aloud, I agreed. "And how is your sister?"

"She's well, along with the children. Here, I have a photograph." He reached into his trousers pocket and retrieved a small black-and-white photograph of Josef's family. Filled with adoration, I rubbed the surface with a deep longing. My younger brother, standing quite father-like behind his wife and, at the time, two children. His face aged tenfold since I saw him at the platform.

"Would you like to keep it?"

My eyes betrayed me. They danced with the possibility of his offer. "Yes. Please. I don't have any pictures of Josef."

"Then it's yours."

"Herr Volney?"

"Cade. Call me Cade."

We spoke as if we were long lost friends reacquainted. It had been ages since I spent time with a man this charming and likeable. Any fears or concerns I harbored had vanished, and if anything, I sanctified the possibility of a union even though nothing led me to its surety, except the way they look at each other—a mixture of pure happiness and admiration.

"How old were you when the wall went up and Heidi became separated from you?" I asked

"Eight. Heidi's the oldest of three. I also have an older brother who—" His pause lengthened. I waited to see if he would finish his sentence.

Mari glanced to me and spoke for him, "He disappeared in 1976, twenty-five years old." The fact that Mari knew this revealed much about their growing friendship.

"Disappeared?"

She nodded, but no other information came forth.

"Where are your parents?"

"They've both passed on. I run the butchery myself."

I studied Cade with a newfound respect. He too faced enormous loss and sorrow and somehow survived.

"How *is* the butchery?" A question meant for either one, Cade motioned for Mari to speak first. *He's quite the gentleman.*

"I never knew how much work goes into a slab of meat before we purchase it." She laughed and waited for Cade to respond.

"I wasn't sure this petite, lovely woman could handle such difficult work." He smiled widely, and her cheeks flushed under his gaze. "She has proven otherwise. You should see her in action. No man could do a better job."

"That doesn't surprise me," I chuckled.

After dinner, he taught us a game using playing cards called *Skat.* I had never seen it before. We took turns being the *declarer* and the *defenders.* Every round seemed to get louder than the last. It wasn't until a shout from downstairs reminded us we were not alone in the building and brought us back to respectable levels. I couldn't recall a time in recent years I'd laughed this much. When the hour came for Cade to leave, I found myself eagerly inviting him back.

"Please join us anytime for dinner and games." I went to shake his hand, but he hugged me.

"We're family, Ella. I'm glad we didn't wait another eight years to meet."

Embarrassed, I glanced briefly down to my shoes. "Me too."

Mari appeared with his coat. When she held it up, a patch exposed from the inside pocket. My hand reached for the round badge before I stopped myself. The image of a man with a sword and plough emerged.

"Oh? This is interesting." I pulled it into Cade's view. Bold and forward, my inquiry seemed to catch him off guard. I had never seen anything like it before. "Why do you wear this hidden on the inside?"

"It's important to me." He quickly replaced his jacket, which buried it against his chest. My interest piqued but shifted to understanding from all the years I kept Anton's tinnie pin concealed against my breast.

"Thank you for coming, Cade." I winked as subtly as possible Mari's direction and then stepped into the bathroom, the only place in our flat with a door. I had no need to be there, other than offering them privacy, and pressed my ear on the door's backside in curiosity.

Minutes later, the doorknob jiggled. "You can come out now," Mari chuckled.

Met with the sweetest face, I beamed as she clutched my hands, swung me around, and then let go only long enough to put a record on.

"Do you like him, El?"

"Like him?" Surprised she didn't already know what I thought, I elaborated, "He's fantastic. He is more than I ever imagined and then some." She giggled again and twirled around me. "Are you two . . . ?" I paused, not sure how to ask if they were together.

"What?" Her expression suggested naivety but failed when she burst into another tittering spell. "Oh, I can only hope."

"I think you have nothing to worry about. He seems quite taken by you."

"I haven't been around many men, but he's the kindest person I've ever met. He's respectful and honorable. I think . . ."

My eyebrows arched as I waited for her to say what I knew in my heart.

"I think I might really like him."

"You know what I think?"

"What?"

"I think you already do."

Mari fell to the bed and clasped her hands over her chest. "It's such a wonderful feeling. Is this how you felt with Stefan?" Mari's question conveyed innocence but sailed through me like a grueling spear.

My countenance fell flat. I remembered the patter of butterflies in my chest, the inability to frown, and the exhilaration that filled my soul when Stefan gazed upon me. *Yes, it's exactly how I felt.*

Mari's hand patted my cheek. "I'm sorry. Did I say the wrong thing?" Her other hand squeezed mine. "Forgive me."

"No. Oh no, love." I forced a grin. "I just miss the feeling, is all. Don't let me ruin it for you. It's the greatest of all emotions. Enjoy it." I kissed her cheek. "Enjoy every minute of it."

Nine

NO SELF-RESPECTING PUNK

3 March 1984

Scanning my closet, I pushed the clothes aside a dozen more times trying to find anything that would not scream *middle aged woman completely out of place!* My enthusiasm to attend the concert teetered far to the left, where a big fat zero would have appeared on my imaginary scale. I moved to the floor, my knees cracking the entire way down. "I'm too old for these games," I groaned and contemplated my situation. Darek didn't require me to go, this wasn't part of my job description, but between his comment and a nagging feeling in my gut, I felt the choice was made for me. Too many times I entered a situation completely naïve and, in the end, paid the price. It wouldn't hurt for me to go, observe, and try to understand more about this growing opposition. I knew it wasn't going to be as easy as walking into a record store. To do this right, I needed to be invisible and feared its impossibility.

"Ella, what's the matter? Why are you sitting down there?" Mari walked in from work.

"I've been invited to go with friends, but I'm not sure I want to now."

"Oh," she squealed, "you must! Here let me help you find an outfit to wear." She practically flew to the closet. Her intentions were sweet, but I knew there wouldn't be anything in there that would help me tonight. She pulled out my olive dress and brushed the dust off the sleeves. "This is beautiful. Wear this one."

I smiled and let her hand it to me. I wrestled the memory that came with it and then stood and hugged her. "Thank you, Mari," I whispered.

"I'm sorry I can't help with the other details." She giggled, "I have a date."

"With Cade?"

"No." She frowned. "A man who comes to the butchery for meat every week asked me to dinner. I don't think Cade is interested in me that way."

"Impossible. I saw the way he gazed at you the other night. Give him time. He's probably nervous. Maybe going with this other gentleman will make him a little jealous and give him the shove he needs."

Mari wrapped her arms around me. "I hope so." She quickly changed, and before applying her makeup, twisted her hair on top of her head with a barrette.

Ideas came too fast; I could hardly contain myself. *If I change my appearance, this might work.* The years employed at the Frankes, I learned a few things while serving their guests. The more alcohol both informants and soldiers consumed, the looser their lips got, and many times secrets were revealed: tips on how to follow and watch without others knowing, where to stand, or even what to do. The more I thought about it, the more I remembered.

"May I borrow some of your makeup?" I changed into the dress as she finished.

"Of course." She gaped at my reflection in the mirror since lipstick was the most I wore at any given time. "You're welcome to anything of mine."

"Thank you." I zipped up the dress. "Don't wait for me tonight. I might be late."

She turned and beamed. "Oh, wonderful! I'm happy you're getting out."

I obliged a grin. Her excitement triggered enormous guilt, but I kept it hidden. She grabbed her purse, gave me a quick peck on the cheek, and disappeared.

Once the door closed, I went to the mirror in the bathroom and glanced over her shelf of makeup she worked hard to purchase. *I can't do this!* My mind chastised my plan. Yet the fact that she's the only one bringing in a paycheck made me feel worse.

Back to the bed, I reached for a stack of old newspapers and flipped through until I came to a page with a series of photographs. Several young adults leaned against a wall making obscene gestures to the photographer. I didn't care about the article just the detail in their appearance. I walked to the closet, stripped the dress, and reached for a rarely-worn pair of jeans. With a careful glance over the photos, I retrieved a kitchen knife and made several stabs and then sliced them open horizontally at both thighs. Lastly, I cut one knee completely out. Instantly stricken with remorse, I realized there was no return. Those jeans cost me a month's worth of wages two years ago when I bought them. No matter what, I had to proceed now.

I put them on and found a blue tee-shirt I occasionally wore to bed. Removing the ribbed neckline, I opened it enough to slide off my shoulder, exposing my butterfly tattoo from the back. In the bathroom, I cringed at the sight, having never worn anything this revealing or ridiculous. I tugged at the shirt and pulled it back to my neck, but it lay awkwardly. Sliding it off my shoulder again, I reached for several of Mari's barrettes.

Taking a fistful of hair on both sides, my hands swept it upward similar to Nikolaus's mohawk without the bald sides. With it all pulled to the center, it appeared as outrageous as it felt, which meant I was on the right track.

With her dark eyeliner, I followed my upper eyelids then looped it outward in a dramatic curl at the ends. Next, I traced my lips with the same black stick and filled them in entirely. Like death itself, my countenance exhibited a hideousness I had never seen.

Lastly, I knew the punk style always had something shiny or noisy dangling from various body parts. I searched, but neither Mari nor myself owned any trinkets. Glancing about, I noticed the pull chain hanging above the toilet, a small ring dangled at the end. Dismantling it, I went back to the bed and the pictures. Returning to the mirror, my frown confirmed I knew exactly where it needed to go. I pried it apart enough to create a separation and then secured it to the center of my nostrils where the silver ring hung lightly above my black lips. Examining my appearance once more, I wilted, horrified. No trace of Ella remained. The guise was necessary, but I hated every bit of it.

Grabbing my scarf in one hand and my long coat with the other, I headed for the door. Bundling as if a heavy snowstorm were about to hit, I slipped out of my flat and to the street. With one leaflet in my hand, I maneuvered to a bus stop. Everywhere I went people stared. A joke on both sides of the fashion aisle. No self-respecting woman would dress this way, and I imagined no self-respecting punk would cover up.

After an uncomfortable twenty-minute ride, I reached the right stop and stepped off the bus. Peering around, nothing in this neighborhood seemed familiar. Regardless, I had no trouble pinpointing the location of the concert. Noise emanated from every open crack of the church on the corner. Frozen in place, I tried to muster the courage to continue. Embarrassment reeked; I may have dressed the part, but could I act it too? Again, I thought of Mari and knew I needed to continue. I whipped off my coat, the chill in the air shooting through the exposed areas. I shivered uncontrollably while rolling my only sources of warmth and tucking them carefully under a nearby hedge. *I'll get them on the return.*

Bolstering weak confidence, I pushed my shoulders back and stiffly walked towards the church. Down the path, two people talking with each other peeked my direction and laughed aloud. I wanted to cry, sensing this was all wrong. Instantly, the only punk rocker I'd ever interacted with came to mind. Nikolaus. *Okay, Ella. Relax. Be rude. Sneer. You'll be fine.* Releasing my shoulders, I sauntered casually the rest of the way. Each person I passed got a wrinkle of the nose or roll of my eyes.

Upon entering, I should've felt relief from both the dim lighting and the tight crowd, yet I cringed at the manner in which this "House of God" was being treated. I personally had no allegiance to a God who I felt abandoned me years ago, but desecration of others' beliefs went beyond my understanding. My first few steps past the door and through a wall of smelly, drunk adolescents confirmed my challenges had only just begun.

Met with a deafening sound, I cupped my hands over my ears. The band's music seemed to bounce off each wall and reverberate around me. When I realized no one else cowered from the noise, I quickly removed them. The devotees seemed to actually relish the higher decibels.

Clenching my teeth, I meandered around, constantly reminding myself not to gawk. Each person emerged more shocking than the last. Although my own appearance felt mortifying, it was relatively conservative in comparison. With the growing crowd, less and less space became available. Bodies merged with no clear boundary of where the dancing started or ended. Twice, within minutes of my arrival, a body flew violently into me . . . no apology offered. My sneer in response was the only honest action I rendered. Rubbing my sore arms, I searched for open spaces between the arched doorways and took cover. Unaware of what I scanned for, I watched everyone.

Not intending to stay in one place too long, I wandered carefully from room to room. Expecting only young people, I discovered a few my age dancing, socializing, and involved. This surprised me. I wanted to say *grow up*, but reminded myself *I* was standing here with black paint and a ring in my nose.

Spotting Nikolaus nearby, I deliberately aimed for him. Walking briskly, my elbow extended as far as possible—and as intended—we collided. The pain irrelevant, my agony was a fair exchange for his suffering. In my mind he deserved more than a clip of his wing for the way he treated me.

"Schiesse!" he cried and shook his arm. I narrowed my eyes his direction and lifted one side of my black upper lips. "Schiesse back, *arse.*" I hid my smile and turned away, satisfied he didn't recognize me. He really was an ass. If anything, that could end up being the only highlight of my night.

After three complete turns of the room, I slithered towards the makeshift bar. My progress slow and hesitant, my eyes shifting around seeking assurance no one was here to judge. Two tables pushed together created a separation between the patrons and a large stack of barrels behind. *This will be much easier with alcohol in me.* Justifying my reasons, I waited in line. *It will help with the realism,* I told myself, but once I reached the front, my body froze, unable to speak.

"*Willst du ein Bier?*" the barman yelled over the music. My eyes blinked excessively to his question about beer, but my lips didn't part in response. "*Wenn sie nicht bestellen warden, greaten Sie aus der Reihe.*" Even after he told me to leave, I remained motionless until the girl behind pushed me aside with a string of cuss words. "*Bewege es Schlampe.*"

I only caught sight of her tattooed neck and pierced lips before I slithered away. Fighting the tears, I shoved my way through the crowd to a wall. *I should have gotten a drink.* Thankfully, the darkness concealed my emotions fairly well as I leaned against the partition for strength. *What am I doing here?* I questioned over and over. *This isn't my job.*

I stepped towards the exit when someone bumped into me again for the hundredth time. "*Verdammt!*" I cried, tired of the whole scene.

"*Es tut mir leid.*" The mumble came out quickly but enough to force me still. This man apologized? I stared for another second when a whiff of his zesty cologne filled my nostrils. He continued on his way, seemingly unaware of my confusion that he didn't smell like everyone else's bad body odor. Intrigued, I followed him casually. Each time his form began the motion of turning back, I slipped out of sight. When he stopped for longer than a minute, I deliberately advanced a bit closer, unseen, and took watch from a nearby niche.

Studying him, something felt off. His hand shook when he lit his cigarette, and his eyes bolted around nervously. I scanned his attire. The high collared shirt and pressed denims stuck out here, no rips, holes or stains. His hair—although spiked in the front—was combed too neatly in the back. He had a fat, gold ring on one finger and glanced at his watch three times in less than a minute.

This is what Darek is talking about . . . people trying to infiltrate. My heart fluttered with anxious excitement, but I kept my cool and leaned casually. With the number of bodies present, the heat was stifling, but the man didn't appear to have been here long enough to sweat. I continued to watch. Several minutes later, a different man knocked into him. Dressed head to toe in leather, his silver chains draped his skinny waist heavily while one hand constantly rubbed his short, blue hair.

Initially, the impact appeared to be accidental. Fully expecting a fight to ensue, I stared with fascination as neither one spoke. With full sight on the first man's lips, I never saw them move. Yet he apologized when he bumped into me. The apology could've been offered because I was a woman, though I doubted it really mattered here. The punk should've been set off from their encounter, yet their interaction almost appeared intended. Once separated, the cologne man slipped his hand into his pocket and walked the opposite direction.

My mouth opened in awe. *Did I witness something?* Unsure, I glanced around, wondering if anyone else saw what I did, but everyone played in their own world—drinking, dancing, kissing—nobody cared. I thought of Darek and wondered if I should find him, but realized, in all my wanderings, I never saw him. *Is he even here?* I doubted he would've missed the concert, but maybe he had others watch for him. Questions began to tumble through my mind at rapid speeds. Should I mention it when I see him next? Would he think I invented it? What if he asked questions I couldn't answer?

I roamed the church for another thirty minutes to see if I saw the man, the punk, or Darek but didn't. Satisfied I had seen enough of the culture and the spectacle, I departed. Thankfully my coat and scarf remained untouched under the brush, and the rain that fell in my absence left them only slightly damp. Covering up for the ride home, I felt less concerned about how I appeared to others, my thoughts continuing to flip-flop between the men, their strange behavior, and the concert.

At the top of my building stairs, I caught sight of my reflection in the door's window and remembered the horror story I had become. Quickly, I scrambled for the tissues in my coat pockets and wet them on the edge of the sill where rainwater still pooled. I removed the ring and wiped the tissue against my lips and eyes furiously. My watch showed half past twelve, and I hoped with all my might that Mari had already fallen asleep. Examining the tissue, now covered in streaks of black makeup, I envisioned unsightly smears across my cheeks. I rubbed harder and then gave up, stuffing the shredded material into my pocket. With my coat wrapped tightly around me, I entered the flat as quietly as possible, believing the motionless lump in the bed was Mari. I rushed to the bathroom and turned the water to full strength. The hot water not only melted the horrendous paint and grime off my skin but seemed to eliminate the foul feeling that accompanied it. Dimming the bathroom light, I waited for my eyes to adjust to the darkness, and then tiptoed towards the bed. At the edge, I listened for Mari's steady breath to confirm she slept soundly before I stuffed the smelly, ripped clothes into a spare pillowcase. Anxious to distance myself from them, I shoved the case deep under the bed next to *The Clash* record and crawled under the covers.

Lying awake, I struggled to process the night. Defending my decision to attend the concert, I believed it was important for me to see what I was getting involved in, though I still faced serious misgivings about the secrecy, rebellious attitudes, and a possible uprising in the works. *Am I too old for this?* Years ago I would have jumped at an opportunity like this. I thought of Darek who seemed like the only normal one around—well educated, level-headed, and cautious—everything the punk movement was not.

By the time light filtered into the room, my eyelids fell heavy. Regardless of the questions, for now the only answer was to continue with the tasks Darek asked me to do. Above all, the job and the paycheck remained my top priority.

Ten

HERR COLOGNE

The next day I went to the pub hoping Darek would have another task for me. Comfortably back in my simple clothes, I showed more gratitude for my pleated pants and sweater than ever before.

My appearance didn't matter, however. Nikolaus's typical contempt surfaced in his snub. Three times I asked for Darek, and all three times Nikolaus ignored me. Tempted to point out his ignorance last night when we crossed paths, I bit my tongue—more from my inability to admit what I'd turned myself into than to see him squirm from stupidity.

"Fine, whatever," I mumbled and walked over to a table. "I'll wait here until I see him." As the hour dragged on, boredom reigned. Determined to stay, my stubbornness stretched, both for payment and to show Nikolaus I'm not fragile. Reaching into my purse, I retrieved a pencil and grabbed a nearby napkin. Several years had passed since my fingers sketched the familiar strokes of a butterfly, but somehow it flowed naturally. Despite its lack of color, stunning qualities emerged. Taking little satisfaction in this small accomplishment, I glanced impatiently at the curtain . . . .still no movement. Turning the napkin over, I randomly started to list the details of the men from the concert.

Herr Cologne:

- *Appealing smell*
- *Out of place clothing*
- *Trimmed hair*
- *Peculiar actions*

Herr Blue:

- *Signature-colored, spiky hair*
- *Possible turncoat?*
- *Ripped leather*
- *Chains*
- *Body piercings*
- *Spiderweb tattoo the length of one arm*

This stupid and simple diversion, certain to be a mystery invented in my own mind and from my own ignorance, forced me to laugh aloud.

"Annika?"

Jumping at the voice next to the table, I peered up to see Darek standing there. I placed one hand over the napkin as subtly as possible, but his eyes darted its direction. "What are you doing here?"

"I came to see if you need anything more . . . you know . . . if you have work."

"Why didn't you ask for me?" His eyebrows met in the middle.

88

"I did . . . several times."

Both our eyes flashed towards the bar. Nikolaus's mouth snaked upward before he turned his back on us.

"I'm sorry." Darek seemed truly apologetic for Nikolaus's behavior. "I could actually use your help with a delivery today if you're up for it."

"Yes!" I practically leapt from the bench, leaving the napkin exposed. Grabbing it quickly, I scrunched it tightly in my fist.

"What's that?" he asked.

"Nothing, just some scribbles."

He nodded his head. "I have a small package to go to the Bäckerei off of Kastanallee."

"Okay, I can do it." Walking behind Darek, I stuffed the napkin into my pocket.

As he neared the bar, he whipped around and studied me carefully. His stare had a way of generating insecurity. "Is there a problem?" I asked, afraid he'd say yes.

"No, there isn't. You surprise me is all."

"Surprise you?" My inquiry encouraged elaboration, but he shared nothing more.

"Wait here."

While at the curtain, I watched Nikolaus continue to *pretend* to work. Nobody sat at the bar, but he moved around as if every stool was occupied. When he turned my direction, he snickered. I wanted to slap him for wasting my afternoon, but a part of me took silent satisfaction in the fact that I fooled him at the concert. If Nikolaus knew of my presence last night, he never let on, and since he's supposed to be aware of these things, his incompetence felt even more gratifying.

"Here's the address this package is to be delivered to and your pay." Darek appeared with an envelope and a small brown paper bag folded twice, flat enough to fit into my purse. "If Tomas isn't there to receive it, you'll need to bring it back."

"Thank you." I smiled and shifted towards the door when he grabbed my wrist. "And leave the napkin."

"What napkin?" A stupid response. Surely he'd seen me grab the napkin off the table. "It's nothing . . . really."

"Then it won't be a problem to leave it behind." The muscles in his jaw tightened. I hardly had the choice to argue.

Cringing, I retrieved the wadded paper, left it in Darek's hand, and swiftly exited the pub. *You are such an idiot sometimes, Ella!* I chastised myself the entire walk to the bakery. He's going to think I'm a silly woman. The only one to offer me a smidgeon of employment, he'd see these reckless actions as a hassle and let me go. Thank goodness he never saw me as a drunk. Even after that first drink in the kneipe the day of the tattoo, my drinking had limits for a few years. Then the hallucinations started, the dreams, visions . . . my reality became distorted and the more I tried to bury my past, the more it pestered me. *No matter what, I can never return to that world!*

En route, the paper bag remained tightly concealed in my purse. With no inkling of what it contained or what role Tomas played in the organization, I kept my curiosity in check. The irresponsible amusement I engaged in back at Darek's bar—scribbling nonsense onto a napkin—could have cost me my wage and I was in no position to screw this up or chance any additional suspicion.

With gratitude and relief, Tomas received the bag at the bakery. He didn't scrutinize me as heavily as the others, but I was, of course, just the delivery girl and nothing more. I relished in relief that no return to the pub was required. I couldn't face Darek so soon. The napkin, a foolish amusement to pass the time, may have created more questions about me and possibly planted more doubt.

That afternoon I made my way towards the telephone box. I yearned to hear a familiar voice and, above all, a voice of reason. Everything in my life seemed to spiral out of control, and the one person I could always count on was only a few digits away.

"Ella?"

"Anton, hi."

"Oh, El, I'm glad you called. I hoped your first phone call wasn't by chance and you were serious about staying in touch."

"Yes, I am. Sorry for causing so much worry. I'm trying harder. Please believe me when I say I won't do that to you or Josef again."

"I'm glad. We miss you immensely." His voice held evident relief.

"I miss you too." I'd always known this, but somehow, in this moment, those words cut deeper than normal.

"How's Mari?"

"She's wonderful—Wait . . . Why are you asking about Mari?" I was taken aback since she moved in after we spoke last.

"Josef told me she lives with you and works for Heidi's brother, Cade. I'm glad you have someone there to call family."

Relieved, I sighed. "Me too. I haven't met a more perfect person on earth." I laughed and he joined me.

"Heidi of course is trying to manipulate a romance, but Cade doesn't say much. I can't wait to meet her."

"Cade came to dinner a couple weeks ago, and there's definitely an attraction between them. Tell Heidi it might help if she encouraged him to ask Mari out. If he waits too long, she'll be snatched up by someone else."

"Yes, he shouldn't wait." Anton's tone revealed pain. "He may regret it one day."

A brief period of silence emphasized our own personal remorse. "Yes, you're right." I quickly changed the subject. "So, I called you specifically because I didn't want to get Josef too excited. You know how he can get sometimes."

Anton's heartwarming laugh on the other end brought tears to my eyes. Oh, how I missed our walks and talks and the times we ate pfannkuchen by the Spree. That image opened the door to another— our kiss. How strange that after all this time it would enter my mind. I shook my head aggressively.

"Yes, I know how he gets. That's probably why he's successful as a notary. What's on your mind?"

"Well, in the letters I read, the ones written over the years . . ."

91

"The ones you only recently opened?"

"Yes, those. Well, I . . ." Standing at the public telephone booth, my hands started to sweat under a tight grip of the handle. I knew things needed to be worded carefully or prying ears would misunderstand and flag our conversation or release the call.

"You are asking about your options, aren't you?"

"Options?"

"Yes." Anton's words came across clear and slow. "Options for you to *visit* us, right? Like Josef mentioned in the letters."

"Yes, to come *visit* you." Our emphasis on the word *visit* was expressed only for the purpose of the operator. We both knew that if I ever got permission to get across to the West, I wouldn't return. "Josef mentioned he knew some people who might be able to help me get a tourist visa, but I wanted to talk to you first. If I said something to him now, he might get a bit overzealous, and well, I figured you could keep things under control."

"Oh, Ella, it would be the greatest gift we could ever ask for. Is this something you really want?"

"Yes, I'm ready."

"What about your friends over there? Mari? And what about Stefan?"

"Stefan?" I choked his name. "Anton, I told you he's . . . he's no longer in my life." My mouth dried up. I licked my lips vigorously.

"I know you told me that, but—"

My teeth clenched together, and I spit the words like venom. "But what?"

"I thought—"

"What?" Blood rushed feverishly to my head and pounded behind my eyes.

"Never mind. Please calm down. It's nothing."

My knees wobbled, and one hand braced myself against the door. How in the hell did so many conversations follow that path? My cheeks flamed hot.

"I'll speak with Josef tomorrow, Ella. We should have some answers in a week, possibly two. Can you meet us at the platform at Bernauer in two weeks?"

I opened my mouth for more air, desperate to release the anger anywhere but at Anton. "Okay, let's plan on Tuesday, 20 March at 6pm. We can talk then."

"Okay, Ella. We love you."

"Love you too, Anton."

Eleven

IT MATCHES YOUR TATTOO

"Annika."

With no sign of Nikolaus, Darek stood alone behind the bar. Only one other man occupied a nearby stool. I blew a light sigh of relief, equally thankful I didn't have to wait two hours to see him nor put up with Nikolaus's childish harassment.

"I got your message that you wanted to meet with me. I hoped you might have more work."

"I expected to see you sooner. It's been nearly a week since the delivery to Tomas."

"Yes, I—I was busy." Truthfully, I feared what would come of the napkin and still did, only the twenty marks I received disappeared too quickly. I needed to return.

"Do you have a minute?" he asked as he poured himself a drink. He peered at the other man wordlessly, and the gentleman quickly departed. Unease prickled my skin as a quick scan of the room confirmed our complete seclusion.

"Yes." The answer came out more as a whisper.

"Can I get you something to drink?"

"No, thank you."

"On the house."

"I'm fine, thanks."

"Let's go back here and talk."

I cringed when he pointed to the curtain. I'd only been invited in once before, my first day. Why did he need to conceal this conversation with no patrons present? I shoved my trembling fingers into my pockets and obeyed. Nothing Darek had done or said caused me fear. In fact, his open defense of me to Nikolaus brought quite the opposite reaction—immense respect. Still, why did we need to talk in another room?

Safely behind the curtain, he produced my crinkled napkin. My heart sunk and eyes fluttered rapidly in motion. *I knew this would happen.* I only hoped somehow it vanished with my absence.

"Explain this."

I glanced as he unfolded it, the list side facing upward. I considered talking about the butterfly, but Darek was sharp. I couldn't play dumb with him.

"It's a stupid list."

"Indulge me," he insisted.

I wiped the growing perspiration off my upper lip and wiped it on my pants, but Darek's eyes didn't stray from mine. "I saw something strange happen between two men, so I wrote down some details of their appearance and interaction." I tried to be vague, but again, he was no fool.

"Where?"

"Where what?"

"Where did you see them?"

I hesitated. I didn't want to tell him I attended the concert, one of the most humiliating moments of my life.

"Where?" he repeated.

My lips pulled into a thin line. I needed to get this over with and move on.

"The concert."

His expression shared nothing, not even surprise. "The concert, huh? Explain."

"I . . . I saw these two men bump into each other, and it appeared as though the punk handed the cologne guy something," I stammered, "th . . . the way it happened . . . it didn't seem right, but it's probably nothing, only my mind playing tricks on me."

"Had you seen either man before that night?"

"No, never."

"This list is quite detailed. How did you remember all this?"

My heart finally stopped beating in double time. "I have a good memory. I see things, and somehow the specifics stick."

Darek reached for my arm and led me towards the curtain. His fingers barely parted it. He pointed outward and whispered, "Is that the man you saw?"

My brows arched. We came from the empty bar minutes before. Darek jerked his chin towards the curtain again. "Tell me, Annika. Is this him?"

I peeked through, and there on a stool against the bar sat "Herr Blue". He sported the same scowl Nikolaus perfected and wore the same clothes from the concert, but his hands were clinched over the bar, tightly wringing. The man who'd been on the stool when I arrived sat next to him as if he never left. I flinched and stepped back. "Yes, that's him. How did you . . . ?" Then I glanced to my list, still gripped in Darek's fingers. Every feature recognized now sat only metres away.

Darek's expression appeared difficult to read. His brow bent while his head tilted downward. A moment later, he parted the curtain once more and nodded the other man's direction. When he circled back to me, he smiled. "So, what did you think?"

"Of what?" My thoughts spun once more over any aspect I may have withheld about the punk in the bar. Nothing came to mind.

"The concert."

"Oh . . ." I paused, "the concert." Apparently, our conversation over the two men was over. I studied Darek, still grinning in a strange boyish way, odd for an adult man in his thirties. Hesitating for only a moment, I let my true feelings over the experience roll out. "It stunk like a sewer, the music played so loud I could barely hear myself think, and I'm still bruised from people slamming into me every thirty seconds." I bit my lip to keep myself from adding to the miserable list when Darek's head rolled back and lips opened into a long, full laugh. "Oh, Annika."

I smiled at the way his laugh helped shave some of the tension off the moment. A peculiar man, but the more time I spent around Darek, the more I liked him.

He patted my shoulder. "You're a gem." He chortled and grabbed a stack of leaflets off the box next to him. As he placed them in my hands, his voice steadied. "This is for a peace protest next week. It's very important that you place them everywhere, just like last time."

With the pamphlets in my arms I made for the curtain, but Darek wasn't finished. From the corner of my eye, I watched him flip the napkin over. "Did you draw this?"

I nodded slowly, believing full well this wasn't the first time he'd seen it. Based on the course of the earlier conversation, I was convinced he thoroughly surveyed every centimetre of that napkin. Still, I wondered what his interest could be in my sketch.

"It's quite good."

"It's only a hobby."

The way he viewed me felt more like an examination. "It matches your tattoo."

"Ye—wait. How do you know about my tattoo?" Instantly self-conscious, my tone grew anxious.

Darek pointed to the curtain. "Have these distributed by tomorrow, and come by next week for payment. Good day, Annika."

I knew better than to argue or demand an answer, but when I left the pub, frustration consumed me. How much did Darek know about me? *Am I being watched?* Then as quickly as my defenses materialized, it suddenly became clear how foolish I'd been. *The concert.* That must've been where he saw my tattoo. My shirt hung off the edge of my shoulder for a couple hours. Somehow, in all my rounds, he remained unseen.

Walking down the street, my conclusions reached transparency. I may have deceived Nikolaus, but one thing's for sure, Darek is way too intelligent to outsmart. Despite his often-times ambiguity, my conclusions were evident—we were lucky to have someone like him leading this most-important cause. If we were going to get one step closer to freedom, we'd need men like Darek.

Twelve

DO NOTHING

20 March 1984

"Ella!" Josef's eagerness sailed above all else in this noisy district. Although cars couldn't drive along Bernauer anymore, the sounds of the city on both sides of the wall were no-less silenced.

I waved anxiously. The distance of the sperrzone spanned twice as long as it used to, and talking evolved to yelling, which meant our conversation could be heard by the soldiers guarding the wall. Even though our interaction never entertained the idea of escape, anything about leaving the East and going West would be targeted.

"Josef! Anton!" Both men stood stately side by side. Young adults who'd transformed into full-fledged men with careers, wives, and children. The wrinkles around Anton's eyes and above his nose had deepened, no doubt hastened by grief. Josef appeared a bit rounder in the belly, an indication of his contentment and sure to be the result of Heidi's good cooking. I peered past them, scanning for little bodies.

With both hands on my hips, I exclaimed, "Where are my nieces and nephews? They need to meet their Tante!"

Both men laughed simultaneously, their mannerisms so identical they could pass for brothers. I smiled at their youthful natures.

"Oh, they will meet their Tante Ella soon, no doubt," Josef cried. His eyes swept back and forth from the tower to the guards patrolling, evidence that this conversation needed to remain on the surface today. "My friend is looking into papers."

My sight, too, took in the patrols. We can't talk on the phone, our letters are read, and now here—where we used to be able to speak more freely—proved to be quite difficult. How were they going to tell me what to do without it being flagged?

"Brother," I cried, "can you tell me your friend's name? The one you want me to meet. You know . . ." I stuttered a bit, making it up as I went along, "for a . . . date."

Anton's eyebrows curved, his confusion obvious, and then he smiled, whispering to Josef. Josef's grin filled his face.

"Yes, my friend, the one who you'll go on a date with is Paul Wagner. He's a colleague of mine and comes to Mitte every other month. His office is in the emigration building. He's quite anxious to meet you, Ella."

"Do you know what day he has in mind?"

"Yes, May 13th. Would that work for you?"

"Yes!" I pulled the pencil from my purse and quickly jotted down the information before I forgot and peered back to *my* men. My heart ached physically for them, my hands yearning to touch them. I gazed in quiet observance for nearly a minute.

"You look good, Ella," Anton cried. The olive dress Mari gave me the night of the concert still fit like a glove. More and more women in the last decade shifted to wearing pants, especially jeans, but I still preferred skirts. This particular dress, until now, spent an immeasurable amount of time in the back of the closet.

"You too, Anton . . . and Josef," I quickly added. They were both in shirts and ties. We all appeared as though we were going to church or out to dinner, but that's how one would be expected to dress for an occasion as special as this.

We spoke about the children, Heidi, and their jobs for another thirty minutes until we said our goodbyes. I blew them a kiss before the tears came. They were so close yet so far, unreachable and untouchable. Stepping down from the boards, piercing pain shot through my chest. No doubt the recognizable distress of a breaking heart. Each time it occurred, the agony felt like the first time, equally raw and tormenting.

I walked to *Do Nothing*, where Jörg stood behind the bar. His eyes lit up until he saw my distress. He hurried to my side and immediately led me to a booth for privacy. The one thing I loved about him, no matter what he was doing when I arrived, he dropped everything for me. More than a friend, he became family.

"Oh, Jörg. I miss my family so much. It's like I go through a slow, painful death every time I see them, which is probably why it took me this long to meet again. It hurts so much."

"Sweet Ella," He reached for my hands. The layers of wrinkles covering his hand multiplied, although mine were now beginning to show more wear, as well. "I know you'll see them again; I know you'll love them and embrace them. It's going to happen. I know it."

"It just seems that every year the wall gets stronger, the control harsher, and nothing changes."

"Oh, change is coming. These old bones feel it."

"What kind of change do you think? Good or bad?"

"Good. It's in the air, it's on the streets. The voices of the oppressed are getting louder."

My eyes narrowed with wonder. *Should I tell him? Should I tell Jörg that I'm delivering papers and packages for an opposition group?*

"What do you know of the voices?" Out of curiosity I decided to bait him. Without a doubt, I could tell him anything, but my thoughts went to Lena and Christoph. My involvement in secrecy back then destroyed their future. Jörg had experienced much in his many years, but I could never live through the guilt of another friend paying the price for my choices.

"Why don't you tell me what you really want to say, dear?"

I chuckled. He knew me practically better than I knew myself. Leaning in, my voice whispered, "I'm helping with the cause. Nothing big or extraordinary, just small ways."

"Which group?"

I paused. All this time, although it crossed my mind, I never asked Darek. My intent in knowing more by going to the concert seemed irrelevant now that I lacked knowledge of the biggest question of all.

"Actually, I don't know." Shielding my eyes, I attempted to hide my shame.

"Ella," Jörg's palm went to my cheek and gently removed my hand. "You're too hard on yourself."

"I should be smarter, Jörg. I'm older now. I'm not a dumb teenager."

"Maybe its best you don't know. You're only doing small tasks, right?"

"Yes."

"Well, if you were ever caught, I suppose the less you know the better."

I balanced his logic. It made sense, but not knowing exactly who you work for shows naivety too.

"I say keep your head low, and don't stress about it. This could all be over soon."

"You really think so?"

"Yeah, I really do."

I wrapped my arms around him with my warmest embrace and kissed his cheek. How did I get lucky enough to find him?

"Now, don't wait too long to come back, Ella. I miss you."

"I promise not to."

I decided to stop by the pub and pick up my pay for the peace pamphlets on my way home. Remembering Darek's instructions, I wound through varying alleys before arriving carefully at his front door. When I entered, Darek sat in a booth with two other men I'd never seen before. Both dressed much like him and not the alternative punk way. The manner in which they whispered led me to believe it involved business, so I hung back on a stool until he finished. Nikolaus remained behind the bar, though neither of us acknowledged each other, which I preferred.

"Annika, the very person I hoped to see." Darek said goodbye to the two men who promptly left, leaving the three of us alone.

I pointed to my chest and scrunched my nose in surprise. "Why me?"

"Well, we've made some changes recently, and I believe you can help."

"How?" My conversation with Jörg lay fresh on my tongue.

"Have you ever sketched a person?"

"A person, like a man or woman?"

"Yes, that's what a person is," he laughed.

"No, most of my work has been—well you saw it, the butterfly."

"Yes, I've seen the butterfly—" he paused in the usual Darek way "—several places actually."

The heat in my cheeks rose, unpreventable. Unsure if it was embarrassment or anger, I waited for him to continue.

"You're the one, aren't you?"

"One what?" Nikolaus chimed in uninvited. Though he slid near us, my eyes stayed only on Darek.

"She's the one who drew the butterfly murals all over town."

"No way!" Nikolaus huffed.

"Right, Annika?"

Darek's unparalleled ability to force the truth out of you proved he could make a powerful Stasi officer. His calm voice, leading questions, and facial expressions all played with your head.

"Yes."

He smiled. Nikolaus scoffed as if still in disbelief.

"I'm going to pay you twenty marks for delivering the pamphlets and another twenty marks to sketch Nikolaus right now."

"WHAT?" we both cried simultaneously.

He ignored us and retrieved a piece of paper. "Do you have a pencil?"

"Yes—but I—" The money tempted me and Darek seemed to know that. "Fine. I'll do it."

"Oh, hell no." Nikolaus refused.

"You'll be fine." Darek turned to Nikolaus. "Continue working as if she weren't here."

I didn't see the exchange of looks, but I imagined it wasn't friendly. Nikolaus lost. Retrieving a pencil from my bag, I sat in a booth.

Unlike sketching a person, a butterfly allowed for more creative freedom, however, much of the technique and skill was the same. Nikolaus actually wasn't hard to draw, even while he deliberately rotated his back on me several times. Once again, my ability to retain specific details when he faced me were mentally noted for when he turned away.

"Alright, I'm done."

Both Darek and Nikolaus's faces shot my direction, as if they didn't believe me. Darek walked over immediately. "Fifteen minutes, Annika? You did this in fifteen minutes?"

"Yeah." I took advantage of the moment. "It wasn't hard." Nikolaus grunted and disappeared through the curtain.

Darek continued to scan the image. His countenance shared more in this brief minute than most of our acquaintance. "I'm truly impressed."

He pulled the marks from his pocket but didn't let go when I reached for them. "I have a proposition for you."

Again, my mind flashed back to Jörg and his advice to keep things simple. "What?"

I need someone to sketch at a concert."

"A concert? Uh, no . . . I'm not the right person."

Darek's brow arched. "You don't have to dress up this time. You'll sketch without being seen."

104

Although masked by my skin color, warmth singed my cheeks. *He did see me and my ridiculous attempt to blend in at the last concert.* I remained silent for several seconds before I asked. "What will I be drawing?"

"People. Like the men you saw before."

He never told me if my observation proved anything until now. I smiled. Maybe I did have more talent in noticing these things than I believed.

"Seventy-five marks for the night."

"Seventy-five?" I spit the words in haste. *Where is all his money coming from?*

"Yes, Annika. What's your answer?"

I didn't want to come across as desperate, but the amount of money enticed me. Still, he must've seen a talent, or he would've never offered me the opportunity.

"Alright. I'll do it. Just tell me where and when."

Thirteen

BULL'S EYE

5 May 1984

The night of the second concert, I reached the church precisely thirty minutes before, exactly as instructed. This time I wore a pair of denim jeans (*not* the ones I shredded), a casual top, sneakers, and I let my hair fall freely to my shoulders. I even wore makeup, though nothing black or remotely close to the last concert. As I passed the line of devotees, satisfaction that there was no resemblance to me in the least came swiftly.

Nikolaus's characteristically arched brow met me at the door with as close to a compliment as he would probably ever get. "That's an improvement." His eyes scanned my apparel loosely as if he expected redundancy.

"Can't say the same about you."

He ignored my juvenile banter and didn't say a word until we reached a second-floor balcony that overlooked the center floor. "You'll sketch from here."

"Who am I sketching?"

"Anyone out of place."

"Like me."

Nikolaus's lip actually lifted in what almost appeared as a smile.

"Exactly." He pointed to the front. "The doors open in fifteen minutes. We have enemies to our cause trying hard to infiltrate the scene. See if you can find and sketch them, so we can put a name to a face. If you need anything, I'll be . . . unavailable."

"Wait" —I reached out—"Why here? Why are the concerts always in a church?"

"Why not?" He snickered and walked off.

That didn't really answer my question, although I wasn't remotely surprised. I placed my bag on the floor and leaned over the railing for a better view. Aside from the sconces on the walls and a few bright lights at the front where the punk band *The Company* set up their equipment, the room appeared darker than the last time. As my eyes adjusted, the emergence of a typical chapel formed . . . arched doorways, circular windows, pews, columns, and an enormous cross on the wall. Although this church differed from the last one, the same question lingered, *why here?*

Thick columns limited my viewpoint, so I positioned myself in a way that allowed me to see the entire space below through the wooden railings. Using what illumination existed, I opened my book and steadied myself for the doors to open.

The opportunity to make more money was the strongest motivator for accepting the job, but ultimately, I wanted to prove to myself I could do it. The sketch of Nikolaus seemed easy because I'd seen him so many times. Here I'd be drawing strangers in brief appearances.

Stricken with panic, my body turned to the incoming crowd, once again hardly respectful of the fact that we were in a church. They entered with one purpose ... to be entertained. My eyes flashed rapidly about, too many people and all dressed provocatively outrageous. Pointed mohawks, ripped skirts, fish nets, spikes, leather, plenty of black eyeliner, and every shade of lipstick possible. Exactly what I'd seen before, only from this angle it seemed as though they reproduced and doubled in numbers. Instantly flustered, I wiped the growing sweat from my forehead and tucked my hair behind my ears. *This will be harder than I thought.* It only got worse. Once the music started, they became one blurry blob, smashed together collectively, their radical movements too hard to follow.

I cowered in failure. Why would they keep me on as an artist if I couldn't complete the first job adequately? My head felt heavy; my composure defeated. Again, I thought of Mari. My deliveries barely made a dent, while she worked longer hours for a couple months now to bring a small contribution to our debts. I pulled my thoughts together.

Okay, I can do this. I inhaled deeply and scanned the room by sections. If I wasn't supposed to be here, how would I dress? Would I be all decked out, tattooed, and pierced? Probably not. Considering my own recent attempt to infiltrate a concert, the whole disguise process does not come as naturally as one might think.

Next, how would I act? Confident or nervous? Recalling the cologne man and how shifty and suspicious he appeared, I searched for these characteristics. Then I remembered that some agents are smooth and convincing, like Captain Scharf. Scanning patiently by sections, this time I focused on deliberate, measured actions.

Bull's eye.

My sights fell on a man and woman moderately dressed for the concert, no shaved heads or piercings. Their black leather jackets were shiny and lacked rips or tears, something that definitely stood out in comparison. What little I knew about the punk style confirmed the vast majority were poor, homeless, and teenagers to mid-twenties. Some appeared older like me, but still maintained the squatter look. The woman's boots were quite fashionable, and the man wore sunglasses. Inside. They moved together slowly, whispering, and looking about without socializing or dancing. I began to sketch furiously. Obviously, the glasses didn't help, but my precision with their body type, hair color, and facial structure—her high cheek bones and full lips, his long nose and square chin—prevailed. At one point, when they stood nearly beneath me, I noticed her gold bracelet and matching locket around her neck. Within the hour, they met another man in passing. So brief it wouldn't have raised an eyebrow, the woman slipped him something, just like the blue-hair punk before. I turned my sketch to him and his long mustache and cynical eyes. I studied them for another hour in their various directions and behavior before they departed, but by then the profile on all three filled my pages.

Two hours and a heavy headache later, I emerged from my perch. Aside from the band who were now packing their gear, only Darek, Nikolaus, and one other man remained in the vast room. I stepped over a pile of rubbish and couldn't keep my nose from wrinkling. How could the Priest or Preacher of this House of God tolerate this kind of treatment? Even when I approached, the men were all smoking.

"Annika,"

—I need to get used to hearing that—

"this is Klaus." Darek pointed to the man I didn't know.

Klaus, hearing the name again produced shattering images of a man I had come to know only through our escape attempts. Our final moments—the tunnel, the shooting, the bodies—I fought to keep the dreadful memory buried and focus only on the stranger before me.

"*Gute nacht.*" Reaching to shake his hand, I wished him a good night, but both his hands held onto a similar sketchpad as mine. I peered around at each of them.

"You didn't trust me?" My expression betrayed me. *Was I set up?* Apparently, I wasn't the only artist. Where did he sketch from?

"You didn't think you were the only one, did you?" Nikolaus jeered. "Seriously, put this entire night into the hands of an amateur?" Aggravating me more than usual, I frowned back.

"Don't get offended, Annika. Leave your sketches with Klaus," Darek prompted. "Meet us tomorrow at the pub, 3 pm."

When I exited the church, my discouragement reached every muscle, exhaustion and defeat weighing heavily on my long walk home. I tried hard to enter the flat unnoticed, but the lamp glowed, and Mari instantly met me at the door.

"Oh, Ella. Thank goodness you're here. You didn't leave a note of your whereabouts," she cried as she embraced me—but instantly drew back, the repulsion evident in her creased brow.

"Oh dear, you smell—" she covered her nose with her sleeve "—you smell like tobacco and . . ."

"And what?" I couldn't personally identify any of it. It could have been anything.

"Sweat." Her lip curled.

"Yes. I worked tonight."

"In a pub?"

"Kind of."

"Is that a good place to be?" Her concern over my weakness emerged, justified.

I stripped to my underclothes and fell to the bed. "I'll clean up in the morning. I'm quite tired."

Mari retrieved the reeking garments off the floor, tossing them in a corner, and walked over to tuck me in. "We can talk tomorrow. I'm just glad you're safe."

I grinned as my head hit the pillow, as if Mama G had been reincarnated into Mari. *Sent here to look out for me.*

The next day I checked for employment at every establishment along the way to Darek's pub. The same answer everywhere. No work. Sure that I botched my first sketching assignment and was only arriving to receive the bad news in person, I dragged my feet. How could I have been reasonably observant and not seen the other artist? Klaus must have been hidden quite well.

By the time I reached the bar I was a silent wreck. When the door closed behind me, Nikolaus glanced up.

"Is Darek here?"

"Sit over there and wait." He pointed to a back booth.

Wait, he said . . . wait for bad news, of course.

When Darek and Klaus sat across from me, my eyes barely reached them.

"How did you come to sketch those two?" Darek asked first. He laid my pictures flat in front of us.

"Nikolaus told me to find someone who didn't quite fit in."

They exchanged obvious glances.

I continued, "Their leather jackets appeared expensive, as well as her jewelry and shoes. He wore sunglasses inside and checked his watch nearly every two minutes until they met with the third man who appeared older and grumpier than everyone else and never danced. After less than a minute together, they spent the next fifty minutes wandering around separately and didn't meet again until they departed."

"She has talent." Klaus pointed out specifics on the sketches and spoke once again as if I weren't present.

Darek nodded and responded with frustration, "She picked up on Gregory . . . who you missed."

Klaus stuttered, "My . . . sight . . . was skewed. She had the advantage."

"Excuse me," I interrupted, "*she* is still here."

Darek smiled. The first genuine smile shown my way since this whole sketch thing started.

"Yes. Yes, you are. Well done, Annika. Check in with me in two days, and I'll have more work for you." He handed me an envelope, and the two left the table.

I peeked at Nikolaus as I stood to leave. He shook his head annoyed, but at least he didn't speak. The envelope remained sealed

111

until I got home. Alone, I opened it. A patch slid to my palm. Chills raced up and down my back. *What does this mean?* My fingers rubbed the raised exterior that bore the words *"schwerter zu pflugscharen"*. Exactly like the patch found on Cade's jacket liner, a man turned a sword into a plow. *Could he possibly be part of an opposition group? Did they all have the same button and motto, or could he be associated with Darek?* Questions flowed but were ignored once my attention went from the patch to the money inside the envelope. Seventy-five Marks totaled more than I'd received in quite some time. *I can finally buy some decent food!* I grabbed my coat, slipped the patch into my pocket, and practically ran to the store. We won't starve tonight or several nights to come.

Fourteen

A HAUNTING PAST

13 May 1984

"Ella!" The man reached out for my hands as if we were long lost friends. His chin wiggled under his round face and large black spectacles. "Josef told me you would be by today."

"Yes, Herr Wagner, thank you for meeting me."

"Oh, I would do anything for Josef. He's a favorite colleague."

"How is it you're colleagues if he's there and you're here?"

"When the wall went up, many professionals had already made the exodus to the West. Fortunately for me, the DDR pays well for me to bring my services here one week every other month."

"So you travel freely back and forth?" My astonishment was hardly masked. "Doesn't it worry you that they could decide to keep you, and you wouldn't have a choice?"

"Yes, that's definitely a concern both my wife and I have, but I've been doing it now for fifteen years, which brings us to the state of your predicament." His smile puffed his cheeks even further. "I understand you would like to be with your brother."

"Oh yes. He left the night they rolled out the wire, only eleven years old, me . . . fifteen." Glancing around his office, the friendly ambiance calmed my concerns about being forthcoming. "I've seen him a few times at the platform, and we've spoken over the phone, but we're practically strangers, having lived away from each other for so long."

"How heartbreaking."

"He's my only family, Herr Wagner. Although I have friends I consider family, I miss Josef immensely."

He grinned and with the warmest hands, led me to a chair. "Well, the emigration process is complicated, and to be honest, there's no rhyme nor reason to it, which means that could be good or bad."

"I understand."

"Have you applied for an exit request?"

"Yes, several times in the beginning, back in 1961 and 1962. It returned, denied."

"Everyone was. They lost so many people prior to the wall that the emigration department became a front. Nobody was actually awarded papers to leave."

"I didn't know that, but it makes sense."

"Well, now things are improving, but its progress is found mostly through government connections. There are some loopholes, but Ella, I have to be honest. Overall, the process could take years."

"Years?" I cried, slapping my hands on my knees.

Herr Wagner peered at me skeptically. "Do you have someplace to be otherwise?"

"No," I whimpered. "I've waited so long, I hoped it would be sooner, that's all."

He patted my shoulder. "I understand. Josef feels the same way. Would you like some tea?"

"Yes, sir, thank you."

He brought me a mug of black tea and sat across from me, behind his desk. Several stacks of papers appeared dauntingly high before him. I suppose if he only came here one week every other month, his work must accumulate easily.

"Once we get the process started, there might be ways to move it along quickly."

"Thank you for doing this."

"Like I said, anything for Josef or his family."

Herr Wagner spent the next few minutes going over personal information and making notes. He seemed quite engaged in his details, which added a layer of comfort for me. The whole idea of leaving the East was thrilling, except, of course, for Mari. When Anton mentioned Stefan, my initial reaction to his inference bordered anger, but Mari . . . she was a whole different story. She might truly be devastated with my absence. My only solace would be to bring her, as well, unless she married.

"Herr Wagner? What's the possibility of another person getting a tourist visa as well?"

"Another?" He looked up, peering through the bottom portion of the glasses perched on his chubby nose. His eyebrows crunched with concern.

"I have a friend, an orphan, who lives with me. She's an adult now, but she doesn't have anyone here either, and I'm curious to know if it would be hard for her to come as well."

"An orphan . . ." He sighed. "It might be complicated if we can't show a reason—no family to visit. They might suspect she's escaping."

I hesitated. My mind tossed possibilities around—*if the process takes years, she surely would be married by then, but if she's not, could I really leave her?*

"Should we proceed?" I hadn't realized he'd been waiting for me.

Drawing a deep breath, I nodded. "Yes, let's do it."

After another twenty minutes of questions, he placed his pencil down and stretched his fingers. "This is a good start, Ella. From what I see, you should be a good candidate." He placed the papers in a file folder and wrote my name at the top. "Oh, one last question, a formality of course. You haven't been in trouble with the law have you?"

I paused. A heaviness built in my chest. *Could there be a record of my detainment with Colonel Anker and Captain Scharf?*

My silence brought Herr Wagner to my side. "I need to know the truth."

My head hung low while my teeth gnawed at the inside of my cheek.

"Ella?"

"I . . . I don't know."

"What do you mean, you don't know?"

"Well, It's complicated. Something happened back in 1963 . . . an accident. I didn't harm the man intentionally."

"What man, and what did you do?"

My lower lip began to tremble spontaneously. Having spoken of the incident to very few people other than Stefan and Mama G, I delayed. The trauma buried for quite some time now.

"I can't help you if you don't tell me everything."

My hands fidgeted in my lap. *Verdammit, Ella! What is your freedom worth to you?* I cried in my mind.

"Frau?"

"Please promise me you won't tell Josef." My eyes matched my pleading voice as I peered up to him. "It's very important."

"Tell him what?"

I spent the next thirty minutes sharing the details of the horrible torture and attack. Twenty years later, its remembrance stirred the same emotional upheaval, nonetheless.

Herr Wagner, a father of two, reached for a tissue. Then handed me the box as he continued to listen to my painful confession. Upon conclusion, I conceded, "I don't know if this was recorded as a crime, if I have a file somewhere, or if it all disappeared. I just don't know."

"Hmmm." His full cheeks drooped solemnly while he patted my hands. "I'm sorry this happened to you."

Though his tone reflected sympathy, I couldn't ignore the lack of color in his once-rosy appearance. "This is bad isn't it?"

He sighed loudly. "It's definitely a concern. I'll see what I can find out."

"What if . . . what if something does come up? Does that mean I might never get papers to visit the West?"

He didn't answer right away, removing his glasses and wiping the moisture from his eyes. "Yes, Ella, that's a possibility."

I couldn't prevent the tears from falling. With one tissue box depleted, he scrambled to find more. "It's not my fault."

"Truly, I believe you. Your situation sounds dreadful." With one hand on his full chin, he paced the room. "There are many here who find themselves at the wrong place at the wrong time." He paused and glanced over to me. "Are the shooting victims at the wall at fault? No, nobody is guilty except the ones pulling the trigger. I have no doubt of the corruption here, but it doesn't change the fact that it affects good and innocent people."

"Please—" I launched to my feet and placed my hand on his arm. "—Please promise me you won't tell Josef."

"If you ask me not to, I will heed your request, but may I offer some advice?"

I nodded.

"He's your brother, and although you haven't lived together for decades, from what I know about Josef, he will love you no matter what."

I smiled through a series of sniffles. "I know. I only hoped that part of my life had been buried and gone. It will only cause him undue pain."

"I will heed your request until you say otherwise." Herr Wagner stepped to his desk and scribbled something on a notepad. "Here's my telephone number. This might take a while, but give me a call in a few months, and I will update you on my findings."

"Thank you. Thank you so much."

"Anything for Josef's family."

"I would ask you to give my brother a hug for me, but that might be awkward." I chuckled and he joined me. "Please tell him how much I miss and love him."

"Now, that I can do." He showed me to the door and shook my hand firmly. Although he tried to appear positive, I sensed his worry and doubt. Instead of the optimistic thoughts I imagined having after today's meeting, my journey home swelled with additional angst. Especially since my "history" might affect my chances to apply for papers and ultimately, freedom.

I passed the Babylon. Suddenly drawn to its alluring vibrancy, I stood for several minutes scanning the curves of the theater's unique architecture until I glanced at the open, inviting patio café across the street. I couldn't afford to attend a motion picture now, but consuming a cup of coffee and enjoying a visit with good memories might be enough to force the damaging ones, generated earlier, away.

My thoughts swayed to the night Hans accompanied me to the cinema. The stroll up to the balcony, the privacy of the booths, the way he kissed me as if we were the only two people in the building. Despite my deceptive reasons for the association, Hans cared for me, and for this brief moment I missed him. My mind, however, tried to untangle additional thoughts flinging rapidly inside my vulnerable brain. Maybe I simply missed the idea of being wanted and loved.

The sign board lights flickered on. The bulbs' brightness drew anyone within a three-block radius their direction. With the setting sun, a series of glowing streetlamps heralded my departure. A glance at my wristwatch confirmed my leisure time at the café spanned over two hours. *Mari will be worried again.* I hustled to the nearest bus stop and home to where my guardian angel waited for me, confirming my earlier thoughts in Herr Wagner's office and the possibility I might not be able to leave the East without her.

Fifteen

CHURCH OF RECONCILIATION

22 January 1985

"Josef!"

"Ella, what's wrong? What happened?"

The burning in my lungs and throat magnified from my run to the nearest public telephone. "J—Josef . . . it's gone. It's gone!"

"What's gone?"

"Th-the chu-church." I squeaked out.

"What church, Ella?"

"Reconciliation. They tore it down."

"Tore it down?" his voice resonated. "Who's they? What are you talking about? I saw it last week. How come I didn't hear about this?"

"It just happened this morning. The tower fell."

"Why now?" Josef's growl seeped through. A thump reverberated through the receiver, and I imagined his fist connected with something hard. "Why would they let it sit empty all those years and demolish it now?"

"I . . . I don't know." I hadn't realized I was weeping. With no real attachment to religion, and only once inside as a child, it should've been painless, but the building—its symbolism, the perseverance—made it different. As the last remaining structure from the Bernauer corner, its significance meant everything. They destroyed our home years ago, and although the church remained empty and vacant since 1961, its silhouette always provided a sense of hope positioned exactly in the sperrzone between East and West Berlin.

"Meet me there, Ella. Can you get to the platform?"

"I don't know if I can. The plume of smoke can be seen from here."

"Try. I'll be there."

I hung up quickly and ran back to my flat for my jacket. Having left in such a hurry; I didn't initially recognize the frostiness outside. Mari met me at the door.

"That rumble, Ella. What happened?"

I broke into tears again. "The church, the Church of Reconciliation at Bernauer."

"The one by your old house?"

"Yes." I grabbed the jacket

"Where are you going?" she cried, worried

"To Bernauer."

"I'll come with you." I should've expected this. Above all, Mari's first and foremost concern always befell anyone but herself.

By the time we reached Invaliden, Anklamer swelled with a growing mass of people who came for the same reason as I, and many clearly as emotional. I searched for the steeple that no longer reached for the sky. Thick, brown dust lingered in the air, and the absence of the old red-brick spire brought many to their knees. A large number of soldiers blocked the way near the wall. Their commands hollered fear for our welfare, but ironically, we didn't know what or who was concerned about our safety anymore.

120

Angry shouts filled the air as I stepped closer to Sophien Cemetery. I spied the podium next to the cemetery wall, thankful it remained untouched. Away from the church, and what I thought to be out of the chaos, I easily ascended to the top. Once my sights rested on the West, however, I realized *their* platform disappeared, obstructed and restricted. The West Berlin police held an equally angry mob back.

My eyes flashed across the scene. With double the number of soldiers, the Eastern spectators grew by the minute. Under specific instructions, the squaddies linked up in rows. A half dozen men in crisp, perfect uniforms stood behind them and smirked over their accomplishment. They must be the officers who oversaw the destruction.

"*Warum?*" A sole woman's shrill voice rose above the rest.

Her question why expressed what we all wondered, but she seemed to be the only one brave or naïve enough to ask it aloud.

I held my breath. The men ignored her initially, but her desperation and anger surged through.

"Warum, Schweine? Warum?" She continued calling them pigs and pushing forward until they no longer ignored her. With one nod of his head, an officer sent a message. Instantly, two soldiers grabbed her by the arms and dragged her, kicking and screaming, into the sperrzone, past the wall, and out of sight. Within seconds her piercing cries no longer resonated, and silence crept through the crowd.

The remaining soldiers waved the spectators off, commanding people to return to their homes. "*Nach hause gehen!*". Mari reached for my hand.

"Ella!" resonated above the confusion.

My eyes scanned until I saw Josef's head barely above the western side of the wall, shaking his hands high into the air. Jumping back up to the stand, I pulled Mari with me.

"Ella, hang in there!" he cried standing on top of the roof of an automobile. "There will be an end one day."

I beamed through tears. Like a child again, he hopped, eager to be seen.

Suddenly remembering that she stood next to me, I shouted, "Josef, this is Mari."

"Mari, nice to meet you!" he cried.

A soldier came to our side. "*Nach hause gehen.*"

"I'm not near the rubble," I snapped, still trying to keep one eye on my brother.

"*Gehen Jetzt. Dieser Bereich ist geschlossen.*" He tapped the end of his gun on the boards and demanded for us to leave the area immediately.

Irritated, I shouted to Josef, "We're being forced to leave."

The soldier grumbled and pulled Mari to the sidewalk by her arm.

"Bye, brother," I hollered and jumped to Mari's side. "Let go of her." I smacked his hand off her forearm. His face shot up in surprise and irritation materialized. I didn't move.

"We are leaving. Thank you, sir." Mari flashed her sweetest smile. This distracted him momentarily as she grasped my hand and hustled away with me in tow.

Still walking, her grip on my hand remained firm. "Are you trying to get yourself killed?"

Her response seemed overdramatic to me. I chuckled at what little she knew of my past. A brief recollection of my encounter with a similar soldier only days after the wire was rolled out flashed before me. Though separated by decades, familiar defiant emotions roused, unrestrained.

"Do you think this is funny? You saw what they did to that woman."

My chortle grew louder.

A safe distance away, Mari stuck her heels in the ground, and we came to a sudden stop. "This is not a game," she scolded. I'd never seen her countenance twisted in anger this way.

Her cheeks pale, my lips pulled tight. "I'm sorry, Mari. I wasn't thinking. I didn't intend to be condescending."

"Please don't be so reckless. You're my only family."

Her form mildly shook as I embraced her. "I really am sorry. I just get tired of the whole thing."

"I know," Mari whispered.

Holding her hand, we walked leisurely back to the flat. The rest of the night we spent in solemn reflection. While Mari fell asleep easily, I struggled to get the image of the church in rubble out of my head. *What's next?* If they could justify the destruction of the Church of Reconciliation, there wasn't much they feared, and a fearless enemy is the most dangerous of all.

After Mari left early the next morning, I made my way back to the telephone booth. This time I called Herr Wagner. Driven by the anger I felt over the church and soldier, I hoped for good news.

"Hallo?"

"Herr Wagner, it's Ella. Ella Kuhn."

"Ah yes, dear. How are you?"

"Not good today. Did you hear about the Church of Reconciliation?"

"Yes. Yes, I did. My wife attended that church as a child; she was devastated."

"Though I didn't attend, it belonged to my neighborhood. Herr Wagner, the sight is now one ugly heap of brick." I seized a deep breath before I continued. "I'm tired and lonely."

When he didn't answer, I continued. "I'm calling to see if anything has changed since we spoke last. Actually, I really hope you have good news for me."

"I'm sorry, Ella." His voice dipped to a whisper. "I don't have an update for you. The records request has been delayed, again."

"But it's been almost a year since you started. Why is it so difficult?"

"It's the East. Everything is difficult."

"Do you think it's because of what happened?" I tried hard to keep the conversation simple, knowing, of course, it was being listened to.

"I don't know yet. There's difficulty getting answers when it involves the Stasi."

"I see." Frustration tunneled through my veins while I wrestled to keep it from reaching the handset or my mouth. Resting my head against the glass door, my eyes closed tightly as tears attempted to squeeze out the corners.

"Ella?"

"I'm here." Defeat infiltrated my whisper.

"It's not over. I will keep trying."

"Okay," —I lifted my head— "when should I ring you again?"

"Try me again this summer. If anything changes before then, I'll deliver a message to your flat with a time we can meet."

Forcing a goodbye, my hand reached for my throat upon disconnect. Rubbing my skin brought minimal comfort to the scorching strain that developed inside. My efforts to curb emotion failed, tears welled regardless. It wasn't Herr Wagner's fault for the delays. He'd always been truthful with me. From the beginning he said it would be complicated, and with all I knew of the Stasi organization, this should not have come as a surprise.

Shuffling back to my flat, disappointment settled in my heart and on my shoulders. Not necessarily for a past I could never change but for allowing hope to materialize unrealistically again.

Sixteen

EINE SCHLANGE IM GRAS

March 1985

"Annika!" Darek greeted me happily as I entered the pub. His exclamation generated the most emotion I'd seen from him in months. His arms wide open as he approached, I hesitated with caution.

"You did wonderful work on the last assignment. Exceptionally detailed, remarkably talented!" His touch surprised me. Although I did not complete the hug, he seemed unaffected. "Nikolaus, hasn't she accomplished impressive work this past year?"

Nikolaus shrugged. "It's decent. It did the job."

"Yes it did!" Darek ignored his mate's sarcasm and chuckled. "I'm glad we didn't keep you confined to concerts. Your skills have expanded with the various environments."

Picking up the latest publication, my two recent sketches appeared on the front page. The drawing depicted a Stasi agent named Günter

Holt shaking hands with another man. A woman lingered nearby, a child gripping her hand tightly. A carousel spun behind them. Below the sketch, an article titled in bold letters appeared: "*EINE SCHLANGE IM GRAS.*"

"A snake in the grass?" my question, not necessarily directed to Darek, was voiced out loud. He patted me on the back.

"There are many, and we're finding them one by one."

I rarely knew what my drawings led to, but this one appeared on the front page of the underground news. A sense of pride flourished, knowing I played a small role in the disarmament of dishonest people. As I read, the more stunned I became. The man Herr Holt met with held the position of a priest, someone who listened to confessions and apparently turned over his parishioner's secrets to the Stasi. He went unsuspected until dozens of people started missing. *I thought priests don't marry* . . . I didn't really know much about his faith or his possible connection to the woman and child.

In the next section of the article, a list appeared of the people who trusted this man and ended up missing or dead. I thought about their families and the grief they suffered because of him and how his life might change now that his dirty deeds were exposed. Maybe he'd no longer have a congregation, leading to unemployment and searching for food like the poor he betrayed. *How could anyone do this? Listen to a confession or a confidence and turn it over to the very people who destroy? Especially a person who knew first-hand the sufferings of the oppressed.* It disgusted me to read further, so I put it down. Darek's proud countenance remained stationary in front of me.

"Don't you think a photograph would be more efficient?" I questioned, though I didn't want to put myself out of work.

"We use them occasionally, but a camera isn't as discreet. They can be identified quickly and confiscated. An artist on the other hand . . . somebody as talented and inconspicuous as you, well . . . that's a hidden treasure."

I shrugged. I didn't believe my skills exceeded those of the other two artists he employed, but I allowed him to think that.

126

"What's the next assignment?" I asked, anxious to keep busy and shorten my time in the pub.

"What's your hurry? Why don't you join us for a drink?"

"A drink?" I glanced over to Nikolaus, who stacked the glasses under the bar. He met my stare and peered at Darek who waited. Everyone present knew of my former addiction.

Each day I came to receive my assignments, I fought my urges, and each day I left without drinking became a personal success. Eighteen months of sobriety was no easy task.

"No, thank you, Darek. I'll be on my way."

His expression was smooth and unfettered, except for his eyes, which drilled through me. Was this another test . . . or his way of dispensing comradery?

"My assignment?"

"The information is in with your pay." He handed me an envelope.

"Thank you. I'll see you in a couple days."

*****

Zur, located less than a kilometre from Darek's bar, stirred a sentimental reaction as I passed by. Maybe if I convinced Conrad I no longer drank, he might take me back. Some might think it's crazy to miss the bustle of filling orders, demanding customers, or aching feet, but the immersion of succulent aromas, steady work, and modest appreciation outweighed the negative, and I missed it. I truly missed the restaurant life. Glancing between the biergarten and the active assignment in my hand, I stayed the course. Zigzagging down the brick path behind a handful of buildings, I sauntered towards the river.

Always lovely in the spring, the Spree outdid itself today with its glassy surface and fluctuating shades. The wooden bench next to the bridge, historically one of my favorite places to sit, drew me over. Fortunately for me, my target would be dining at the café on the corner, which bordered my serene location. According to my information, he preferred to sit outside on the patio. If this were true, I could remain in place while he dined and I drew. I sketched the water. It's gentle rolls amid a soft breeze hypnotized my sight and teased my relaxing eyelids. From there my drawing shifted to the lampposts on the west side. The sharp, clean angles and stylish design exaggerated the differences between each side, separated only by a body of water. Peeking towards the restaurant, nothing changed; the target remained unseen. *Maybe he chose this day to eat inside?* After adding the nearest apartment building and shops, I conceded. My target evaded me. I decided to pack up when something caught my eye. Why I hadn't seen this before confounded me, but my focus primarily swung between the café and the landscape. Not far from my bench, a man leaned coolly against the river railing. Nothing about a simple bystander's presence should alarm me, except the small details my mind had come to detect. His back stayed to me, and although the weather seemed more than comfortable without a coat, he sported a thick, lengthy one. Bending to one knee, he appeared to tie a shoe. I remembered the concert and Nikolaus's advice, *Look for anyone out of place.* When the man stood and turned around, our eyes met. I quickly began sketching again, but my fingers glided freehand while my thoughts scrutinized the situation. I reached for a different color of chalk as a means to steal another glance, and his focus remained solely on me. The hair on my arms raised. He lit a cigarette.

My chalk scratched as I drew. Sschhhk, sschhhk, sschhhk . . . *Don't look up.* Sschhhk, sschhhk . . . *He'll know.* Sschhhk . . . My skin flushed as his intense eyes shortened the distance between us. My attention drifted along with my fingers. *Oh scheisse!* A smudge blurred the window. I grabbed a tissue and peeked again. He moved closer. My heartbeat echoed in my ears. The recollection of the night the NVA officers came for Simon at the café surfaced. I remembered how my knees rattled until Klaus clamped his hands on them. Nobody sat here to stop the quiver this time. My lips parted enough to let a mouthful of air enter as subtly as possible, the man now a mere two metres away.

I peered up the moment he passed. His eyes deliberately scanned my artwork. He never paused nor did he speak. Afraid to follow his steps, I pulled my eyes back to my sketch and waited another thirty seconds before I released the captive breath. Wiping my face with the tissue I retrieved, I instantly recognized the magnitude of my risk. *I need to be more careful. What if I'd been drawing the target when this man came by?* The result could've been quite different. The tall man with the long coat and jet-black hair couldn't be a casual bystander, too interested in me and my work for this to be happenstance.

With one last glimpse of the empty patio, I closed my sketchbook and placed it in my bag. Either Darek's information proved to be incorrect, which rarely happened, or the target could've been warned. Either way, today marked the first time I truly realized the dangers of my job and the jeopardy I placed myself in for money. When I started with the organization, I never stopped long enough to ask the hard questions. *Is it possible the Stasi is baiting the group I work for? If so, how long am I willing to risk my safety for this?*

Walking home as the sun began to dip and the streetlamps flickered on, the sounds around me switched from day clamors to night hums. I reflected on the strange man, his expression when he passed, and the way he stared at my work. *Who is he? Could his interest be random or was he sent by someone? Has he followed me before?* By the time I reached my flat, my contemplations snowballed into a long list of doubts. Yet, once again, when met by Mari, those inhibitions were carefully tucked away. Even after all this time, the true responsibilities of my job remained undisclosed to anyone.

Seventeen

DEATH BY FIRE

16 June 1985

"*Tod durch Feuer! Tod durch Feuer!*" the young boy carrying a handful of newspapers on the corner cried as we approached Bäckerei Balzer.

"Death by fire?" Mari sighed. "What a terrible way to die."

I nodded. It must've been the black smoke seen yesterday in a neighborhood near Mitte. Although not close, the smoke could be seen for miles.

We settled at a table on the patio. The afternoon not only brought the warmth of the sunshine, but with my steady work for Darek, summer also generated steady financial means. With many lean years behind me, I enjoyed the pleasure of dining out.

In the last three months, my assignments proceeded without a hitch. The mysterious man and failed target were only memories now. Darek brushed it off as missed timing, but it didn't feel that way. I chose not to mention the stranger. He actually didn't do or say anything that made him a threat. It may have been a worry conjured only in my mind. Nevertheless, I contemplated the subtle changes needed to make sure my work remained discreet. Specifically, arranging two sketchbooks before me, one with a scene of the area and the other the target, easily interchangeable in a moment's notice. Above all, I needed to be aware of my surroundings and safe places to reach in a hurry if necessary. None of this had been a concern before.

"May I take your order?" The waitress interrupted my internal contemplations.

"*Germnoedel,* please" —Mari handed her the menu— "and a cup of black tea."

The poppyseed pastry sounded good. "The same, please. Only mint tea."

After the waitress departed, I turned to Mari. "I used to come here often with a friend. We would eat Pfannkuchen and giggle like schoolgirls. "Once," —I pointed to a nearby table.— "we sat right over there after a military parade. I'd never seen these streets filled with so many people before." My genuine smile reflected the ability to reminisce without tears.

Mari grinned. "Who's your friend?"

"Lena . . . she . . . she was very special."

"Was?" Mari's brows nearly met in the middle. "How come everyone and everything is a *was* in your life?"

I shrugged and accepted my tea from the waitress.

"You can change that, you know." Mari too reached for her cup.

"I'm worried it's been too long. Lena's married and has a child, maybe two. I might not fit into her world anymore."

"Ella, I don't know why or how, but it seems to me you were blessed with very good friends in your past and chose to separate for some reason." Tenderness emanated in her touch when she placed one hand over mine. "Friendships don't have expirations."

Her last sentence resonated as more names appeared on my mental list. My capacity to shut people out, not once or twice but many times, should've kept them at bay, yet they continued trying. I wove my fingers through hers and squeezed. "I promise you I'll try harder."

The patio now overflowed with happy patrons enjoying their summer, as well. Mari giggled and took a big bite of her dumpling, cream seeping from the corner of her mouth. My laugh could not be suppressed.

"So how is Herr Volney doing?"

Mari grinned. My suspicions that there might be something blossoming seemed apparent. "He's a wonderful manager," she exclaimed safely.

My chin dipped with a wary glance. "Just a manager?" I inquired with a hint of tease. Her cheeks blushed a brighter pink to confirm my guess.

"Yes!" Her grin matched the light in her eyes. "Well . . ."

"Mari, you must share!" I squealed

A voice bellowed quite loudly from the table next to us, "He was a man of the cloth. It seems appropriate he should die in his parish." I twisted my head slightly to see him reading from the newspaper to his small company, and then I peered back at Mari, waiting for the man to continue. Something about the story struck a chord. "It says here, three charred bodies were found in the ashes. Two adults and one child."

My hand flew to my mouth. *Three bodies were found . . . a priest . . . a child.*

"Ella, what's wrong?" Mari asked, quick to react to my expression. She reached to comfort me, but I held her back with one hand and spun around to face the stranger.

"Sir, may I please see your paper?"

His party appeared surprised at my sudden request, but he easily conceded. There, on the front page, a photograph of the priest emerged. The same cleric I sketched. My eyes sped across the words that confirmed his death, but not only his. Two others perished in the fire with him . . . a woman and a child. *Could it be? Could it possibly be the woman and child I sketched as well?* I muffled a quick thanks and jumped to my feet, hoping I could reach the toilet in time. I vomited the entire contents of my stomach by the time Mari appeared at my side.

"What's wrong, Ella? What's going on?" she cried, reaching for a handkerchief in her purse. Moistening it, she pressed it against my cheeks and forehead.

"I recognize the man—the one who died in the fire."

"How?"

"Someone I met a while ago." A lie of course, I could never tell her the truth.

Heat radiated from my forehead and cheeks while my eyes clenched shut to keep my body from falling dizzily to the ground.

"You're burning up," she cried, placing the freshly cooled handkerchief against my skin once more.

I'm the one who sentenced them to death. I'm the one who brought this malicious act upon them. I heaved into the toilet a second time. No matter what evil deeds he did, nobody deserved to die in this violent manner.

"Let's get you home, Ella."

As Mari and I walked home from Bäckerei, my spinning mind refused to settle. Unruly fears and judgements ricocheted sharply within. The gentle hum of Felgren's tune coming from Mari's lips should have calmed me but didn't. It'd only been a couple months since my sketches of these very same people were printed in Darek's magazine. Was it a coincidence his demise came suddenly? Maybe a vengeful family member of the victims? Or someone with more authority? A ripple trailed down my back. *The Stasi, no doubt, are capable of such carnage.* Their cruelty evidenced in the scar on my mind and the wound on my hip. Although faint now, each time I caught sight of the damage in the mirror or in dressing, the colonel's countenance and evil intentions surfaced. The remand room, the sound of sweat dripping below my elbows, and the way they psychologically tortured me. They must've seen the printed pictures and suspected the priest would expose their connection.

Why is this upsetting me? This man comforted his church goers with one hand and knifed them with the other. He turned a dozen innocent people over to the slaughterhouse. He earned his punishment . . . didn't he?

Once home, I showered and got ready for bed. Mari fell asleep immediately, but I could not get the images of smoke and ash out of my head. I remained at the windowsill. The lamplight glowed against the tree's leafy branches, casting gloomy shadows across the sidewalk, building, and me. I held the envelope for that deadly assignment in my hands and trembled as I reopened it. Skimming the directions, the description of two men were clearly detailed. One the agent, the other the priest. Though no description of the woman and child appeared, their fate intertwined. *I'm the one who added the woman and child to the sketch. Because of me, their identities became known. Were they aware of the man's deceit? Did they suffer?* My head fell to my hands, my chest heaved with sorrow. Unable to stop the tears, I cried for their fate and my hand in it.

In an instant, my own future unraveled. If the Stasi gained access to the magazine, did they know who sketched the artwork? Have they sent less conspicuous people to watch me? Spy on me? Though I hadn't *seen* the black-coat man recently, he could still be in the shadows watching my every move, reporting to Stasi where I go and what I do. What might happen to me if my involvement is confirmed? Could they already be devising my fate . . . my death?

Eighteen

SEEKING FORGIVENESS

20 June 1985

The next few days, I stumbled around the apartment in a daze. Unable to think clearly, much less work, I sent a note by messenger to Darek. My excuse would only bide him for a short time. I needed to use this time to figure my next step and lay my thoughts out logically. Pacing the flat, I pondered my position. *How much danger am I in?* The man Lena loved when I met her, Christoph, didn't do anything wrong, and he disappeared, presumably at the hands of the Stasi. His fate never became revealed.

Have they targeted Darek and his group? I still didn't know the name of the opposition faction I worked for, though my ignorance was intentional. Jörg's suggestion that the fewer details I knew the less chance I myself became a target justified my ignorance. I agreed until the strange man appeared and the gruesome deaths were discovered. Now my ignorance resembled stupidity.

Despite the Stasi's violent thumbprint, my mind considered various suspects linked to the murders. Once the priest's identity surfaced, it wasn't improbable to believe the victims' families took matters into their own hands.

What about Darek? He never showed any signs of violence in the year and a half I worked for him. Always kind and professional, especially when others weren't, he listened to any concerns in respect to my assignments. He even defended my skin color multiple times. No, there was no logical reason to suspect him. Now his followers . . . I wasn't so sure.

In the beginning, when Darek advised me to read and research I did. The pamphlets and protests from the West ignited a desire to rebel, not only from the students and young adults, but eventually from people of all ages. Enraged at the abuse of power, dwindling resources, and lack of choice, their courage increased along the border. True, they were disrespectful and rude, but their brashness showed no proof of violence and quickly squashed my suspicions.

All in all, the answer still circled back to one. The Stasi. They must've seen the paper and realized their source had been compromised and proceeded to take action themselves. With no conscience and no trouble erasing people, it was the only thing that made sense and the only explanation that helped me sleep at night.

That evening, Cade came home with Mari.

"Hi, Ella." Mari met me with a squeeze. "How're you feeling today?"

"Much better, thanks." My gaze went past her to Cade. A grin filled his face.

"Oh, sorry." She winked without him seeing her. "Cade invited me to dinner."

I returned his smile. "Wonderful."

He held his hat in his hands. "And if there's time, we'll go to the Babylon as well."

"The Babylon?" My heart twitched at the realization that it was nearly a year since I sat on the terrace across the street watching people enter the theater. My thoughts flickered on my own cinema experience with Hans. "It's a beautiful theater."

"You've been there?" Cade sounded intrigued.

"Only once."

"What picture did you see?"

"A . . ." I caught myself before the answer. The movie, recommended by Hans' border guard friends, might cause unnecessary misgivings. Cade wouldn't understand why I willingly watched "KLK an PTX" and that was not a history I could divulge. "I can't remember." I went to the shelf and picked up *Icarus*. "What picture is showing at the Babylon right now?"

"*Das Boot.*"

"Oh yes. I've heard of it, the World War II movie."

"It's shown around this time of year. It's one of my favorites." Cade leaned against the counter comfortably. "Have you spoken to Josef recently?"

"Not since last month. When I called a week ago, only Heidi could talk. Your sister is a saint," I chuckled.

"Not in her youth," Cade snickered. "I believed her wild ways would be forever demonstrating against something . . . now it's the wall. Nothing makes her angrier than that."

"Yes, I understand. We're the same in a way . . . being the only one separated from our family." I thought about this. Heidi was in the West, where we all wanted to be, but alone until she met my brother. "Well, she's a good wife to Josef and sweet to help Anton with his two when she can, but between them, five children is quite a handful."

"I can't imagine one, let alone five." He grinned, but his smile targeted an unsuspecting Mari who entered the room after changing into a red skirt. It flattered her figure well and didn't go unnoticed.

"You look . . . beautiful," Cade stuttered, paled by his forwardness.

Mari blushed and grabbed her purse. "You don't have to wait up for me, dear sister." Her grin swelled as she naturally slipped her arm through Cade's.

I closed the door behind them, recalling the nights I'd dressed up for Stefan. The excitement built with anticipation of his arrival, and although we dreaded the end of the night, our farewell kiss rivaled the date itself.

Stop it, Ella!

To sit here and sulk only aggravated me. I needed to get some air. Changing into my jeans and sweater, I left with no clear destination in mind. No matter how low my spirits were, I needed to avoid the bars. With nearly two years of sobriety, my determination to stay clean took precedence. It didn't go without its challenges. The urges and temptation brutally persisted, but my strength gradually returned as well.

Meandering down the sidewalk, my smiles were genuine, even at all the happy couples I passed. Beyond the cafes, the parks, and stores—dark after a hard day's work and service—I continued to stroll. It wasn't until I paid attention to my surroundings that I realized my steps led me towards my old flat, the one on Anklamer near Bernauer. The street remained empty. The recently washed cobblestones glistened under the lamplights as I shuffled to the middle of the road, Sophien cemetery on my left and remnants of the homes in the Bernauer district on my right.

Once I reached the corner, where the platform stood vacant, I cast my eyes past the wall and followed the outline of the westside skyline in the moonlight. The bright lights of the sperrzone flickered in familiar ways, though the newly constructed guard towers flaunted a larger intimidation. Now twenty metres high, their width matched that of a narrow building, easily accommodating more than four guards and, of course, more guns. *What's next? What more can they do to reinforce the border? Any more fortification and all of East Berlin will become a labor camp.*

A rumor circulated recently that Stasi buried explosive mines inside the death strip and brought additional tanks into areas where more attempted escapes occurred. After twenty-five years, the words from Herr Mielke rang true, "We'll make sure nobody leaves the East alive."

My watch revealed that the time fell well past 10 pm by the time I reached the flat again. Darkness filled the rooms with Mari's absence. I beamed; young love was nearly the best thing to ever happen in my life. I could only wish its reality for her as well.

Alone in the apartment and alone in my head, I knew one part of my past had been avoided far too long. Snuggled in Mama's chair, I retrieved my unused stationary and constructed two letters. After multiple attempts, and a handful of discards, a final draft emerged.

Dearest Katharina,   20 June 1985

I'm sorry for all the pain I have caused. You were always kind to me and never deserved to be treated badly. My decisions in the past few years have progressively gotten worse and although I haven't found a way to overcome foolishness, I'm trying to move forward with more clarity and responsibility. In time I will beg for your forgiveness in person, until then please be patient. Each day I make progress, but I want you to see a better me. Thank you for your compassion and love. It has helped me more than you could ever imagine.

Love, Ella

And the second one:

Dear Lena,   20 June 1985

It is cowardly for me to ask for forgiveness through a letter and not in person. I fear my behavior has cost me one of the best friends I ever had. I know you've tried to reach out to me, and in my selfishness I abused our relationship.

139

I hope that as I work to rectify my wrongs you might be able to forgive me. My choices over the last ten years have brought consequences I must overcome, but in time I hope I can see you again.
Love, Ella

The messages were brief but composed with intent to repair the friendships. They deserved much more than a note, but before I issued mental punishment, I forced the negativity away. Jörg insisted the last time we met that I needed to be kinder to myself. He emphasized that every step I took forward should be celebrated.

"Ella." Mari nudged me awake.

Curled up in Mama's chair, I yawned and glanced at my watch. "Did you just get home?" Well after midnight, I eyed her familiar dress and grinned. "You must've had a nice evening."

She smirked and gripped my hands to help me up. When my feet hit the floor, so did the forgotten envelopes sitting in my lap. Mari swiftly retrieved them and although their identity remained sealed, she placed them back in my hands and whispered, "Don't worry, Ella. They will forgive you."

Nineteen

ACCIDENT OR MURDER?

July 1985

When I arrived at Darek's the following week, a tolerable
Nikolaus surprised me.

"You better?"

"Yes," I stuttered, "th-thanks."

Still in shock, I stepped behind the bar and through the curtain.
When Darek didn't appear, I walked towards the back room. I tiptoed
lightly, being the first time I ventured this far. A printing press, coils
of paper, and stacks of freshly inked newspapers sat on both the floor
and a nearby desk.

"Welcome back." I didn't hear him come from behind and
jumped at the sound of his voice. "Did I frighten you?"

"Uh, no, I just . . . uh . . . never mind. I'm fine."

141

"We missed you last week. I'm glad you're healthy again. Things are starting to heat up with the protests. We have another concert at the end of the month. Can you sketch it?" He handed me a leaflet.

"The Church of the Redeemer?"

"Yes, in Lichtenberg and in the cellar this time." He winked. He seemed aware of how uncomfortable I'd been previously.

"Sure, I can be there. Anything now?"

"One, tomorrow. Are you up for it?"

I nodded. Darek stepped away, and I picked up one of the newspapers while I waited. A drawing of the famous kiss between Erich Honecker and Soviet Leader Brezhnev appeared on the front page, "**THE KISS OF DEATH**" in bold block letters centered above. The photograph, shot back in 1979, only now gained speed.

"It's good, huh?"

"Yes. Well, the kiss is disgusting, but yes, it's good you're exposing these men for who they are."

"I'm glad you think that." He patted my shoulder and handed me an envelope. My heart stirred in remembrance of the last envelope I held. I quickly brushed it away. *Darek is not responsible*, I reminded myself sternly. Exposing them didn't make him guilty—the Stasi were the real culprits.

"Thank you. I'll be in touch."

The next afternoon, I rode the bus to Alexanderplatz. My target, a married security guard named George, manned the entrance of a shoe factory west of the plaza. Darek listed the possibility of the man's after-hours activity with a mistress. Apparently, the unnamed mistress sells the secrets he reveals about the factory workers. Other than her being an attractive blond, my note disclosed no additional identification of George or his lover.

Fortunately for me, the Haus des Lehrers stood nearby and made a wonderful cover to sketch. Small twinges in my chest reminded me of the time Stefan and I came to view the building's artwork and instead found a small child. My eyes shifted around until I found the walk where Mari's little makeshift home existed. Not much had

142

changed in the landscape. Rubbish, wood, and broken concrete still littered the area, but obvious relief escaped my lips when I found no *obdachlos* children living here.

I settled on a bench near a bus stop. The constant coming and going of commuters would be a great addition—busy was always better—and with two sketchpads as planned, I began to draw my cover piece before George's shift ended at six.

I didn't have the talent to replicate the abstract images that wrapped the exterior, but after the initial outline, drawing people living life in Berlin proved to be more natural than expected. Shortly after finishing the mother holding her child in front of a fruit tree, a man dressed in uniform stepped away from the entrance of the factory in question. He meandered slowly towards a building on the opposite corner—the suspected hotel. Thankfully, he stopped long enough to purchase a pretzel and enjoy it in one solitary spot. Easy to sketch, the man of average height sported a strange assortment of hair on his head: a receding hair line, long sideburns, and a scruffy moustache to top off the oddities. His uniform shirt, tucked tightly in the front, hung out of his belt on one side. Even after he consumed the bread, he loitered.

He must be waiting for her.

If they disappeared into the hotel too quickly, a well-timed glance might be essential. Afraid to blink, I continued to watch and wait.

Within minutes, a tall, shapely woman stepped off the trolley and strutted confidently down the walk towards George. She wore a ruffled gold skirt significantly above the knees, a loose blouse with a wide neckline partially slid off one shoulder, and a strip of black lace tied her blonde hair back. Despite the limited description of the mistress, my instinct signaled her as the target. I sketched swiftly during her short walk.

Observing any potential interchange, I narrowed my sights. She sailed coolly past George, and if I hadn't suspected her, I would've missed the flick of her hair his direction before she sauntered into the hotel alone. Curious to see how long it took before he joined her, I counted numbers silently in my head—less than thirty seconds. The poor man nearly salivated. I laughed aloud and collected my tools. Once stuffed into my bag, I froze.

The man—long coat, black hair—stood across the street staring my direction. Petrified, I threw the strap over my head and jumped to my feet, no question his stare zeroed in on me. I turned and hustled towards Alexanderplatz. One peek back confirmed his stride reached halfway across Otto-Braun Strasse now.

My first few steps were cautious before I flew into a dead run and sped towards the closest tram. The doors opened, and a rush of people exited. I pressed my way inside to the dissention of those trying to depart. I didn't care about them or which direction the train went, only that it needed to move soon. Very soon. From the inside, my body huddled tightly between passengers, peering carefully the man's direction. Though he remained unseen from my position, my imagination envisioned his approach. The exhale I allowed filled the small space as the train squeaked into motion.

Three stops later I exited with caution and clambered to find a bus to ride home, glancing behind me practically every step of the way. There's no way in a city this big that our encounter could be a coincidence. *He watched me! His eyes seemed to be upon me only!*

Before Mari got home, I sketched him as much as I could remember in my panicked state. Covered by a brown leather cap, his black hair fell evenly to the sides and barely below his ears, which led me to believe it must be parted down the middle. A coat of solid black hung heavy and low to his knees. He may have worn boots, but I hardly glanced at his feet. His eyes were small and set close together with no facial hair on his chin. Scanning the sketch, unexpected goose bumps rippled my skin. Everything about this image screamed fear.

Should I say something to Darek? Would he think I'd become careless? Would he label me a risk and release me? If this man found me and followed me to more than one job, it's very possible he could follow me to the bar, or already had. The hair on the back of my neck prickled with unease. Wandering around the flat, my anxiousness magnified with indecision.

Finding peace at the windowsill, I began to think more clearly. This man's bold appearances struck panic into me much the way an enemy emotionally provoked a victim, however, trained spies were traditionally less conspicuous. The more I contemplated his identity, the more convoluted it became. Regardless, I needed to be more vigilant in my surroundings, with a plan to leave at a moment's notice.

Despite the alarm he conjured, I decided to wait until after the concert to speak to Darek. Maybe by some crazy luck this man would appear and his role would be identified as either part of the resistance or an informer.

The next day I turned my sketches of George and his mistress into Darek.

"Well done, Annika. These should make the next edition."

My thoughts immediately diverted back to the priest, the woman and child, and the dreadful result of *that* particular sketch being printed. What if our information proved inaccurate? What if the person reporting to Darek issued false intelligence and these people were innocent? With no proof the artwork triggered their tragic demise, I wrestled the suspicion in spite of the coincidences.

"Annika?"

I blinked.

"I've called your name several times. Are you alright?"

Far from alright, my head bobbed sluggishly. It occurred to me, in this very moment, I always accept the information in my envelope as fact. I never question it or where it came from. A small bead of sweat rolled down my temple and tickled my cheek. I swiped it away as Darek handed me a glass of water.

"Are you sure you're well? You seem—" He paused, and my eyes followed every curve of his profile. "—Did something happen?"

I picked the water up and drank it faster than I should have. The man in the black coat appeared in my mind. The liquid tumbled down my throat like a mouthful of rocks. I sputtered and choked. Any liquid left on my tongue spilled to the floor.

"Sit down," Darek insisted. One hand gripped my arm and forced me to a nearby stool. "What's going on?"

My hands covered my eyes. I wanted to tell him about the strange man, but nothing felt right.

"Annika!" Darek's tone increased.

"I'm fine!" The answer came out stronger than anticipated, confused as to where the strength drew from. "It's nothing. I want this wall to come down, that's all. I'm tired of it all." I let my hands fall to the bar and stared back.

Relief immediately swept across his visage. One of his hands patted my back. "We all are." He moved towards the curtain and turned back around. "We don't have any work for you right now. I'll see you at the concert."

I didn't see the final publication of my sketch, although Darek implied its printing. Instead, I picked up the Berliner Morgenpost every day for the next three weeks out of curiosity. I didn't really know what to look for exactly. The incident with the priest could have been accidental, but the gnawing in my gut told me otherwise, and on the twentieth day I found something. Hidden between military news and photographs of the *Pfingsten* festival, a small article centered the third page. A shooting death of a man and woman in the Hotel Berolina. The same hotel George and the mistress entered the day I sketched them. The bodies were discovered by a maid the next morning. No known assailants were apprehended, and despite the vague identities of the deceased, I was sure they matched my sketches. One was presumed to be a security guard based on the uniform found and the other a sex worker.

Placing the paper down, I felt the blood drain from my cheeks. Another *accident?* The vengeful response of his wife? A family member affected by their treason? Or much bigger—a plot for death? A disturbing notion formed and suddenly, not enough air reached my lungs. Nothing about Darek, Nikolaus, even Klaus—anyone I met involved in the movement—frightened me until now. My hatred for the Stasi—their threats, the fear and control—was real, but could my suspicions about the underground and their powerful influence also be correct? If so, they could be equally as dangerous. If they were the ones behind these murders, how do they justify their actions? Evil against evil?

The room spun slowly. *What am I going to do? Quit, run, and hide?* A thin layer of sweat built on my skin. *Do I have a choice? Is leaving even an option? Is it possible that once involved you're always involved?* I didn't have a shred of evidence Darek could be dangerous or that my life would be at risk from him or his group, but I also couldn't shake my reservations. Too many unknowns. By far, the greatest concern weighed heavily in my mind—how will I live or survive without this job? With the generous income I received in the last year, we became comfortable. We'd saved a little, enough money to live on for possibly another year, if we were careful. But then what? What if I still couldn't be hired anywhere?

The thought of trying Zur materialized again. I missed serving and helping. Maybe Conrad would give me another chance with my sobriety closing in on two years now. But what if he didn't? No matter what scenario I whipped up, the answer seemed the same; for now, I needed to do my job and not think past the paycheck. The aftermath of my sketches or their trail must be forced entirely out of my head.

Twenty

CORPSE CELLAR

August 1985

Like before, Nikolaus met me at the door and led me down the brick staircase thirty minutes before they opened for the concert patrons.

"Welcome to the corpse cellar."

"Corpse cellar?" Hearing the name sent goosebumps rippling. Southeast of Prenzlauer Berg and near the border of Kreuzberg, the area remained foreign to me.

"Unless you prefer the name piss pot." Nikolaus snorted when we entered the dark stairway. I held my sleeve up to my nose almost immediately. My belief that all churches were similar immediately extinguished once we arrived in a basement devoid of an ecclesiastical footprint. The windowless room resembled a prison more than anything else: damp, cold, and dark except for a string of lights looped along the ceiling corners. On one end, several bulbs flickered on and off, magnifying the disturbing scene. Geometric designs shadowed anarchy rants and littered the walls in blasphemous bright graffiti.

"What is this?" I struggled to hide my uncertainty. A distillery moaned in one room where bottles of what I assumed to be beer were being filled and placed in barrels.

"A morgue," Nikolaus grunted with his usual condescension before leading me to the largest room at the end of another dark hallway.

My body stiffened at the word. Even after all this time I didn't know Nikolaus well enough to recognize if he were joking. Maybe this banter seemed comical to him, but there was nothing funny about it. I switched my focus to the band. Several musicians unpacked their equipment, including a Lute guitar, an instrument I recognized from Freddy's bar.

"Who's playing tonight?"

"*Der Bruch* and *Kein Talent.*"

I nodded as if the names stirred familiarity, but they didn't. "Where am I supposed to sketch from?" My eyes narrowed in search of a balcony.

"Over there." Nikolaus pointed to what looked like an old wardrobe sorely in need of repair.

"What is it?"

"You never did confession?"

"Confession, like with a priest?"

"Protestants don't, but somehow this piece of junk ended up here."

"It looks like it's about to fall apart."

He ignored my concern and opened the door. Once I stepped inside, he closed the door behind me.

"This window makes you invisible to anyone on the outside."

I brushed my fingers across tightly crisscrossed wood slats, but my fear rested less in being seen and more about what *I* could see— more specifically, draw. I cracked the door as Nikolaus walked away.

"I can't see the entire room like before."

He ignored me.

"Nikolaus, what if someone stands in front of it? I won't be able to see."

He stopped and slowly turned around; his shrewd sneer lacked sympathy. "You're the artist, figure it out." Then he left me alone.

"Scheisse!" My cry rang loud enough for anyone within range. Set up for failure, I wouldn't be able to do the same job as last time. I flung the door open wider. Its resentful moans reminded me that if it came unhinged, I would have worse things to worry about. Carefully, I sealed it shut behind me. The tight space brought a layer of claustrophobia with it. I located a small bench at my knees. Not knowing how long I'd be hidden, this fortunate find offered simple relief as the night wore on.

Once the noise began to swell from the crowd moving closer, I readied my sketch book. The room filled quickly. Black hair, black clothes, black makeup added to the indiscernibility. Placing the book down, I scanned the patrons. One by one they passed my hideaway, or more appropriately, my asylum. Strong smells of hair spray and body odor mixed with the earlier scent of urine nauseated me. I flipped the collar of my jacket upward toward the corners of my nose while I continued to study the devotees carefully. The loud music and limited lighting helped to keep my identity secret. Nobody seemed to care about the cracked wood closet in the corner.

The greater struggle came when trying to distinguish individuals. My job was to find people out of place, but I could barely identify *anyone*. I continued to scan as the music got louder, the dancing more erratic. Then I saw him.

The man—long black coat, black hair. I stared hard, looking for anything more I could add to my earlier sketch from home. A pointed chin, small gold chain, a scar on his upper lip. He stopped. Nikolaus assured me no one could see in, yet the mysterious man's eyes never diverted from my side of the room. My skin moistened under the weight of his presence. Both eyes dropped to my hands as a minor tremor evolved to a full-fledged shake. When I glanced up again, the man disappeared. I searched for his destination, but too much blackness kept him camouflaged.

"I hate my job." Only loud enough for me to hear, my whisper confirmed everything I felt at that moment. Grabbing my pad, I penciled what I'd seen. Possibly in his late thirties, unemotional, and when he stood close, his height towered. Could he be affiliated with Darek and the cause, possibly sent to keep an eye on me? A logical explanation of how he appeared at the Spree, the Haus de Lehrers, and now here. Maybe he knows everything? The gloom which emanated from him didn't stand out, but maybe he's Stasi and figured out how to blend in. Darek would need to know.

"You need to leave." The whisper came clear and quick, my sight suddenly blocked. A body, possibly a piece of clothing, or a drape—something obstructed me. His demand came again. "You need to get out."

"Who is this?" I whispered back, more angry than scared. "Nikolaus?"

"Now!" The voice strained with urgency.

What if the black coat guy had been sent to warn me. Nothing made sense, but it didn't matter. The voice sounded serious. I turned to throw my sketchbook into my bag, and by the time I faced the door again, the obstacle vanished. I flipped the latch open and slid out, hesitating briefly as I struggled to recognize anyone, but couldn't. *Should I stay or leave?* With no identifiable threats, I lingered outside the cabinet for over a minute deliberating my next move.

I decided to go.

With the patrons clustered heavy like before, I found it easy to slip through the rooms and up the stairs unnoticed. I passed a dozen attendees spread around the grounds outside, some smoking, others drinking. They never acknowledged me, and I never made eye contact. I gripped my bag tightly and pulled my hat low over my eyes. My arms pulled my jacket snug and tugged my collar farther up my chin. A light rain fell the moment I hit the railroad tracks. Besides the noise from the cellar, the neighborhood sounds passed quietly.

Nothing indicated danger, as warned. What if the black-coat guy aimed to stop me from working—to prevent me from sketching a meet?

Walking to the nearest bus stop, I berated myself for fleeing so easily. If the ploy meant to get rid of me, it worked. Between my hindered sight and the loud music, the mystery person could have been anyone. *How will I explain my departure to Darek?* Only recently, doubts and questions began to surface. On the bus, my pounding head made an honest explanation for my flight, and by the time I reached my flat, my heart pumped laboriously. At the front door, I couldn't get my hands to settle long enough to insert the key. I knocked hastily until Mari opened up.

"What happened?" Her arms enveloped my quivering form, and unable to answer, I wept on her shoulder. "Ella, what's going on?" She led me inside and to the bed. Her mouth drew into a frown as she tucked me in, fully clothed. "I'm going to make you some chamomile." She left long enough to warm the tea, but I struggled to keep my eyes open for her return, my body and mind exhausted from the night. Another night in a long string of nights I wanted to forget.

Twenty-one

FOLLOWED

September 1985

"Darek, do you have someone following me?" The words seeped through exasperated breaths the moment I stepped through the curtain to the back room.

"What do you mean?" Sorting more leaflets into piles, he didn't glance up.

"I've noticed the same man at three different assignments. The most recent being the concert. Are you having me watched?"

"Speaking of the concert, where did you go?"

Stunned he changed the subject, I stuttered in response. "I . . . I . . . um . . . didn't feel well. I needed to leave."

"You should've told me."

"I left in a hurry."

"You missed the encore."

"Encore? I didn't really listen to the music—"

"No. The Polizei."

"Polizei?"

"Ja." He eyed me carefully. "You didn't see them when you left?"

My mind whirled anxiously. I didn't see any soldiers. Nothing in the area or on the street seemed amiss. My thoughts instantly went to the warning. *Who warned me?* Nobody who apparently worked for Darek. He seemed to have been taken by surprise, which rarely happened. My hesitation to answer compelled him to face me fully. I sputtered, "My head hurt. I left and saw nothing."

"Fortunate timing, wouldn't you say?"

"What are you suggesting?" The fire in my tone rose unmistakably.

"Nothing in particular . . . simply curious." His warning had been launched.

"I had nothing to do with any raid, Darek. After all this time, haven't I proved to you I can be trusted?" My steps inadvertently closed the gap.

"Trust can be cyclical."

"Not from me. Why would I jeopardize my income when you are the only one who'll employ me?" My voice rose with obvious agitation, nevertheless, the question caused him reason to pause. Our shared expressions remained unreadable until mine softened into a genuine inquiry. "What happened?"

His jaw relaxed, and for the first time it appeared unshaven. He glanced at the curtain before he spoke and whispered, "The Volkspolizei know the church is a place of refuge, especially for our kind, and their authority is limited inside. They waited until the concert ended and arrested people trying to leave."

"How many?"

"Over fifty."

"I'm sorry. I didn't know."

His eyes searched mine for the truth. I hoped after two years Darek believed me, but he was right, trust ran a fine line in the East, and doubt consistently rotated. I met his stare with nothing to hide,

154

yet I held my breath. The warning received through the lattice held no origin. Telling him would only cause more wariness.

"Tell me about this man you see."

Desperate to take a short breath, I exhaled briefly and continued, "Tall, late thirties, early forties maybe, hair past his ears, wears a coat and hat. Although he never makes contact, he looks right at me. I'm positive it's not a coincidence."

"He's not one of mine."

"Do you think someone could be onto me?"

Darek turned back to his leaflets. "Possibly." Rubbing his hands against his stubbly cheek, he paused. "It has happened before."

My lip started to tremble before my hands did. Danger followed me. "What should I do?"

"Did you draw him?" Darek understood me well and most likely knew my answer before I gave it.

"Yes."

"Good. Let me think on it. Come to this address on Friday for your next assignment," —he scribbled some numbers onto the back of a leaflet— "and bring the sketch."

"Why here?"

"We need to switch things up a bit. Adjust your route."

"Okay. Thanks." I didn't show it openly, but I was relieved for the break.

"Don't forget, Annika," Darek placed his hand on my arm. "We're good at what we do, and protecting our loyal assets is part of the plan"

His intentional use of the word "loyal" made me wonder if that too implied another caution.

I nodded and rotated to leave but took a long peek back at Darek who didn't meet my gaze. For the type of work he did, his demeanor appeared abnormally calm. Maybe he hadn't been in a Stasi building or under interrogation before and had no idea what they're capable of, yet something about his methods made me believe he was quite well aware.

The next Friday, I deliberately pulled my bangs back with a barrette, wore pink lipstick, wrapped a scarf around my hair, and donned a pair of shades. With a borrowed jacket from Mari whose style varied from mine, I endeavored to be different. Although my skin color remained the biggest distinction between me and many others, it was one feature I could never change.

"Hi, Darek."

"Annika?" Arriving easily at the different location, I took note of its similarities to the last pub. Few customers, another door behind the lengthy bar, and Darek comfortably at the bar pouring himself a glass of liquor when I walked in. He didn't invite me to drink with him this time, and I appreciated that. "New look?"

"Something different."

"I'm sending a person to observe you." His long sip emptied his glass. Although his words should have brought me comfort, his hesitation troubled me.

"Will I be safe?"

"Your safety is always my priority." He filled his glass once more. "We have some new recruits. For your next few jobs, they'll monitor from afar. You won't know them. Do what you always do, and we'll see if this man is truly watching you or not."

"Okay." The idea of having support in the vicinity—mindful and protecting—instilled an element of confidence. If for some reason this man is there for the wrong reasons, it felt better to know reinforcements stood by.

"If you happen to see him again, don't let on that you're aware of him. Carry on like always."

"What if he approaches me?"

"It'll never get that far."

Not sure what his comment meant, I thanked him. "I appreciate your help."

He nodded.

"Anything else?"

"Here's your next assignment."

"Thank you, Darek." He slipped into the back room, and I went to the water closet to open the envelope in private.

Neptune Fountain 3pm, white female early forties 5'7 with short blonde hair, blue eyes. White male fifties 5'10, black hair, brown eyes, carries an umbrella and can be found reading a newspaper on a bench. Sketch their contact.

Even with a fresh assignment in hand, I couldn't help but allow my mind to drift to the stranger and his purpose. Though I'd trained myself to focus on my targets quite well, the reality part of me remained detached wondering who lurked nearby. *Is he here? Studying me, watching me?*

It brought enormous comfort to know someone from *my side* also watched. An ally looking out for me *and* for the man who might stalk me. With my detailed sketches of the targets complete, I lingered near the fountain, drawing the simple spray of happy water. How nice it would be to have one solitary purpose, like a bead of water. You dance in the fountain, and at some point you're drawn in and shot out to dance once more. How effortless and trouble-free my job would be. Chuckling as I packed up my sketches, I realized in my daydreaming that my one true wish and desire had been reduced to live the life of a droplet of water. What had I become?

Twenty-two

THE TELEVISION TOWER

March 1986

"Ella, did you hear about the bombing?" Josef's cry amplified through the phone. We hadn't spoken in over two weeks.

"A little," I whispered. "The explosion rocked some plaster off the walls at the Sophien Mausoleum, and one condemned structure collapsed." I glanced through the glass telephone booth at a sea of people on the sidewalk. Everywhere I went now, I scanned for anything suspicious. "The Morgenpost hasn't published a reason. What happened?"

"A bomb. It exploded at a popular discotheque here, *La Belle*. Three people died but hundreds were injured. Many were soldiers,— American, French—they all frequented the place."

"What terrible news, Josef. Anyone you knew?"

"Not personally, but two of Heidi's Uni friends were injured. She couldn't get near the hospital to check on them. It's surrounded by soldiers."

"Who's responsible?"

"Terrorists, most likely. Possibly Libyans."

"How awful. Does this happen a lot over there?" Uncertainty laced my question. I had envisioned West Berlin as a perfect place, free of danger, threats, and fear.

"Only recently. Most attacks happen at military bases. This was the first I'd heard it occurring in public."

"Will you be safe?"

"I know it doesn't sound like it, but life is much better here." The initial excitement in his voice relaxed. "The Americans are good people. It's only a matter of time before Communism is defeated, El. Secretary Honecker can only lie for so long—"

The line went dead. I tapped the receiver a couple times before placing it back on the hook. When I lifted it up again, the operator responded tersely, "*Diese Zeile ist nicht mehr verfügbar!*"

"I don't understand," I demanded. "It was working fine."

She disconnected.

Peering around the area again, this sudden reaction brought an added element of vulnerability. It's no secret our conversations were monitored. That's why the government installed public telephones to begin with. But I hardly believed they would be offended over a conversation about a bombing in West Berlin. If anything, they might celebrate it.

Stepping outside of the stall, my body shuddered, not only from the increasing wind but an uneasy likelihood I wasn't alone. No longer content with the comfort of anonymity in my own neighborhood, I wandered as though trepidation hung profoundly from my neck. Maybe the disconnect came from whoever is following me or monitoring my whereabouts. *What if they're closing in?*

Running to a different telephone booth several streets away, my head swung in all directions for fear of being followed. Safely inside the stand, I picked up the handset again, only this time I dialed Paul Wagner's office.

"Herr Wagner? It's Ella." Allowing my first breath since arriving, it all came out harried.

"Oh yes. How are you?"

"Not great." "The operator disconnected me from Josef. He told me about the bombing."

"Yes, such an unfortunate situation."

"Is your family safe and well?"

"All is well. Thankfully, we were nowhere near it."

"Herr Wagner, . . . I'm calling to check in again." A flash of déjà vu crossed my mind, these exact words expressed only six months earlier. "It's been quite a while, and I hoped to hear of some progress." Heavy breathing seeped through the receiver, which confirmed a connection, but no words came forth. "Is everything okay?"

"Well," his mumble was further muted by an obstruction, possibly his hand. It sounded like he was speaking to someone else. I waited. "Sorry, Ella. I'm quite busy today. Let me see when I will be back in the East. Can you hold please?"

"Yes, of course." As people passed the booth, I wondered if any were there for me. My fingers found their way to my lips, and I began to gnaw on my nails.

"Not until June."

"Three months?" My cry came louder than expected.

He continued with a regretful sigh, "I apologize, but there has been an increase in work here with the British. Can you come by my office, say 12th of June in the morning?"

"Yes," I hid my frustration. "I will be there. Thank you." Placing the handset down, my lips curved into a frown over the two discouraging phone calls in a row: Josef's call forced to a close, and Herr Wagner's conversation brimming with skepticism.

Less than an hour later, I devised a different route to work. Maneuvering with vigilance around five different blocks, I entered a cafe, ordered a tea, and exited out the back to an unfamiliar alley. A long line of women caught me off guard. Mothers, grandmothers, even young daughters waited with pails or bags in hand. Curious, I edged closer. The bright-orange skin of a plump Cuban orange exchanged hands at the back window of a shop. My lips licked twice with a fond childhood craving, a coveted Christmas gift received once in the Waisenhaus. I could practically feel the juice drip down my chin as I glanced at my watch, debating my next step. Ultimately, the choice was made. Darek expected me, and this line could last for hours. My eyes beheld the glorious shade of sunrise until I could no longer keep it in view and departed.

Since working for Darek, Mari and I hadn't lacked for much. The steady income provided well for us, and if a product could be found in a Geschäft, we could afford it, but fresh fruit was always a rare find. Superficial maybe, but turning my back on the chance to smell and eat a lovely orange saddened me.

Despite our comforts, the prosperity came with a tradeoff. My time with the underground brought more risk to me and my family than my attempts at escape ever did. I was always looking over my shoulder, wondering if I'd been followed home, or worrying my home life would be exposed. What if something happened to Mari? My friends? Cade or Katharina? Even knowing this, I continued.

Crossing the street, I walked through an apotheke and out their back door before I entered the rear door of Darek's pub to receive my next assignment.

Fernsehturm. Lift operator (older man, mid-fifties, gray hair, glasses) exchanges information he receives in the lift with a woman said to be attractive with dark hair, brown eyes, vibrant smile, usually wears a skirt. Sketch anyone you see who might fit this description conversing with him more than an average visitor. You may have to take the lift to the sphere.

The Television Tower. Having passed it dozens of times walking through Alexanderplatz, another memory effectively shoved into a quiet compartment in my brain, sealed for a very long time. Anyone in Berlin can see this iconic structure that rises 365 metres into the sky, but not all could say they were there back in 1966 during its beginning stages—but Stefan and I were.

Settling on a bench south of the tower, I studied the view. As the sun reflected off the steel panels of the ball, the appendages of a cross emerged. How ironic that this dome oversees all of Berlin, watching and spying, and now with the arrival of a Holy symbol, it appears as if God had some hand in it. My eyes trailed the cylindrical shaft that widened the closer it got to the ground. Several triangle canopies extending from the base provided shade but prevented me from seeing the lift from outside.

Darek sent me on assignments with specific timing in mind. His ability to predict the window when a target arrived had only been wrong twice. His intel was generally spot on. Only here, besides the minimal information to go on, my ability to sketch inside the lift seemed impossible. Without question, the need to recall every detail without paper in hand became real.

I wrapped my strap over my head, walked to admissions and bought a ticket. There were two operating lifts for visitors. From a distant corner, I observed the suspected man. He appeared older than described, an *opa* for sure. Stepping into his line, I waited. Once inside, the reason why he may have been targeted materialized almost immediately—he talked nonstop.

"Welcome to my spaceship little one." He shook the hand of a young child. "Is this your first time at the television tower?" The child nodded then cowered at his mother's leg. "What about you?"

I glanced at the child's parents who met my expression curiously. Realizing he addressed his question to me and not them, I murmured, "My first time going up."

"But have you been here before?" The doors closed with only eight of us aboard.

I nodded. "When it reached one hundred metres."

"Back in '67?"

"Yes."

"You are a true Berliner then."

"Yes, my—" I stopped abruptly. My eyes shifted to the other patrons and then to the outside windows. Nervous, I skimmed the area for anyone observing us. It occurred to me, if *I* was watching, I would've sketched *me!* I loosely fit the description—having a conversation with the target as a woman with dark hair, brown eyes, wearing a skirt, and attractive—at least I'd been told similarly in the past. I backed up, pretending something fascinating had caught my eye elsewhere and shuffled behind one of the mothers. *What if this is another test? What if I'm being set up?*

My stomach lurched with the rapid ascent. The lift rose so fast it was hardly conceivable that information could be exchanged in such a short amount of time. Only seconds passed before we reached the sphere. When the doors opened, I sprang to exit first.

"See you on the way down." He grinned wide, tipped his hat, and turned his attention to the guests who were ready to enter his lift for the return.

Blocked by panoramic windows, my need for air grew. I pressed my palm against the closest one. *Closed, of course.* Stumbling to a bench, I leaned over until my head rested between my knees. *How do I always find myself in these situations?*

"Are you well?"

The voice floated melodically towards me, but I didn't budge.

"I'm fine," I mumbled. "Maybe a bit queasy."

"Let me get you some water."

I lifted my hand and waved an *okay*, afraid if I actually moved I would leave the contents of this morning's breakfast on the floor beneath me. Minutes later, a hand brushed my arm. "Here, drink this. It will help. Happens to me all the time."

When I glanced up; my bottom lip fell open. A woman in a blue, pleated skirt, perfectly coiffed brown curls, brown eyes that lit up the room, and a smile that melted glaciers appeared next to me.

"Uh . . . um, thank you."

"You're welcome."

"D-do you work here?"

She tipped her head back gracefully and laughed. "I suppose I do in a way. I'm a tour guide."

"Tour guide?" I stopped drinking. "Who do you tour?" The question reeked with stupidity. I knew people from all over the world came to the East to take advantage of the currency exchange, although I suspected many wanted to say they visited the eastern side of the wall.

She laughed again. "We do have some very nice places to see here. You happen to be in one of them."

I nodded and finished the water. My head pounded, but I no longer felt the rippling unease in my stomach. A pang in my chest replaced it. I *knew* she was my target.

"Thank you." I passed the empty cup back to her. "Thanks for helping me."

"My pleasure. What's your name?"

"Uh," The panic this harmless question created filled my mouth with confusion and tasted like cotton. *Which name do I give?* "Um, it's Annika. And yours?"

"Maren. Pleased to meet you, Annika." She reached out to shake my hand. I met it with apprehension, but she didn't give the impression she noticed. "It gets easier each time. I'm here quite often. Every day, it seems." She flashed her brilliant smile once more, every tooth perfectly aligned and as white as I'd ever seen.

"Nice to meet you too." The words came out more of an afterthought, this being the first time I'd ever made physical contact with a target. There was something surreal about the idea I would be sketching the very hand that touched me.

I remained on the bench, watching and waiting. Maren's energy lit up the room. Not many people in the East demonstrated enthusiasm about life anymore. Made from a rare mold, she dazzled everyone she engaged.

Despite the longer line, she chose to take her small group down the old man's lift. When he saw her, he met her smile comfortably in return. Their interaction appeared normal, friendly, and almost innocent. Yet innocence in the East was debatable.

I waited another few minutes before the old man's lift returned. Once inside, I pressed deliberately against the farthest wall and kept to myself. The man continued to chat. Despite the short rides, he multi-tasked quite efficiently. Yes, without a doubt he was privy to information, but in a little over thirty seconds, how does he induce people's secrets?

Outside, I returned to the small bench where my day began and retrieved the sketchbook from my bag. It wouldn't be hard to reconstruct the distinct details of her image, even the twinkle in her eye. Only it was more than that now. We spoke. She helped me. She was kind. The significance of interacting with my target for the first time flooded my mind. Though completely unintentional, it couldn't be ignored. It *did* happen, and now obstacles I've never faced before, emerged.

The coincidences between my drawings and negative consequences were too real. After the priest and the security guard, I deliberately stopped checking the newspapers, afraid of what I might find. Could I sentence Maren to an indisputable destructive outcome? *Maren! I know her name now. We have been acquainted!* Digging through my past years, I tried to recall any time the intel was misleading. Only two possibilities surfaced, and even then, it might have come down to missed timing. When my thoughts shifted back to this woman, affable and kind, I struggled to picture her as either a spy or an informant. Each role lacked empathy and compassion, and in my observations, she had mastered both qualities.

I needed time, time to come back, possibly tomorrow or the next or the next. Reassurance—one way or another—suddenly became a crucial quest for me. I couldn't live with the results if I didn't.

"Mari, would you go to the television tower with me today?" Washing the last of the breakfast dishes the next morning, I proposed the idea. "I know it's your day off and you might have plans, but I haven't seen you in a long time, and we could catch up."

"Absolutely." She stepped out of the bathroom as she brushed her hair. "I've never been past the platform; I'd love to see it from the top."

"Oh, good. I didn't want to go alone."

"Let me get my sweater."

The crisp spring air sweetened the walk to Alexanderplatz as Mari and I maneuvered through the neighborhoods under the fresh blossoms of the Linden trees. She'd been quiet most of the time, listening to me jabber on about different music groups I recently found interesting. After several minutes, she spoke. "Ella?"

"Yes?"

"I have a question about something."

My lips pulled tight; it could be any number of things she questioned. I hoped it had nothing to do with my work.

"Anything." Which wasn't entirely true.

"Cade and I have been spending a lot of time together . . ."

My lips curved with a small sigh of relief. "I've noticed." I laughed. "I've barely seen you."

"It might be getting serious."

My insides burst with happiness for her. "Has he kissed you?"

"Yes." She grinned sheepishly.

I reached for her hand and squeezed. "Then yes, it's serious."

She became quiet again. I stopped and turned her toward me. "What's wrong?"

Her sigh brought subtle unease on my end as she continued, "Well, what I wanted to ask you has more to do with his friends."

"What's wrong with his friends?"

166

"Nothing is wrong with them, actually. I'm not sure if they are really friends or just associates . . . like a group."

"A group? What do you mean a group?" My heart skipped several beats. We remained in place.

"Have you heard of *Kirche von Unten?*"

My jaw grew rigid. *KvU*, an opposition group—*the church from below*—formed out of rebellion with the recent church restrictions on grassroots groups. Their anger was fueled by the cancellation of the peace workshop intended for next year. Darek told me the workshop, still in the planning stages, had been anticipated by all resistance groups, though somehow the 1987 event, scheduled to be the biggest protest rally to date, provoked KvU the most.

Only months ago, *Der Tages Spiegel* wrote an article on KvU and their strong demands for "Glasnost in the state and church". Their outspoken behavior had enraged authoritarian structures, and as expected, the government placed a target on their back.

"Yes, I've heard of it." With no intention to alarm her, my tone remained flat, but my breath quickened a second faster. This information explained the patch Cade wears on the inside breast of his coat.

"How did you and Cade get involved?"

"Some customers of Cade's invited him to a meeting. He went alone at first, and then he brought me several months later."

"What did you think?"

"Well, I'm conflicted. They all seem to be good people. They want rights and freedom, but as you know, I'm not as familiar with their concerns. I'm not separated from anyone. I grew up protected in an orphanage. I don't really relate to their discussions. In fact, I feel out of place."

"Have you told this to Cade?"

"No. He's kind to me. I don't want him to think I'm ungrateful."

"Telling someone the truth about how you feel, especially someone you care about, shouldn't be taken the wrong way." A hypocritical thought entered my mind before I could stop it. *How can I convince her to stay away from this without exposing my own precarious involvement?* Knowing what I knew about this dark corner of the world, I shuddered to imagine her a part of it. Her inexperience and innocence must be protected. Cade needs to know this! "He's a good man, Mari. He'll understand."

"Do you think so?"

"Yes, I do, and I also think—"

My eyes caught sight of the pretty tour guide. She led a handful of visitors from the clock towards the tower.

"Think what?" Mari followed my gaze. "What's wrong?"

"Uh . . . nothing. Nothing's wrong." I turned back to her. "I think you should trust your instincts. If you feel uncomfortable about going to the meetings or being involved, you know yourself better than anyone. Maybe intuition's telling you it's not right." I tried not to sound too eager in encouraging her to avoid the KvU, but my protectiveness shifted to high alert. Any underground defiance could be targeted by the Stasi, and I feared my sweet Mari experiencing torture similar to what I endured.

"Okay, I'll tell him. I enjoyed it more when we were going to cafes and the cinema anyway." She giggled.

"Two tickets to the sphere, please." After I paid, I pretended a need to go to the water closet and waited to time our arrival to coincide with the tour guide's. If I managed to get into the elevator the same time as her, maybe I'd see something or nothing at all. Either way, it would make me feel better to know.

"Okay, Mari, let's get in this line for the lift."

As we waited our turn, I told her about the construction, how I came once a week to see its progress for the three years after Stefan and I were here.

"Oh. Well, hello." The beaming smile hit me before anything else did. "I see you have the courage to try again."

"Try again?" Mari's forehead wrinkled.

"Yes, I tried coming here yesterday. I really wanted to enjoy it but got sick going up." I frowned a bit dramatically. "I thought if you came with me today, I might be too distracted to be ill."

Mari laughed, "We'll see."

We stepped into the elevator. The old man from yesterday was gone. A younger, yet just as friendly operator, greeted us. My expression did not hide my discontent.

"It's okay." Mari slid up next to me and gripped my hand at the side. "I'm here." She had mistaken my disappointment as fear. I forced a grin her direction and closed my eyes. Mari started to hum, loud enough for me to try and guess the tune. It took only a short time before I recognized the song "Goodbye Yellow Brick Road" by the British artist Elton John. It came from the album Cade bought her a month ago. How he found and purchased it confounded us both, but his connections seemed endless.

When the doors opened and we stepped out, I realized I hadn't felt an ounce of wheeziness. It worked; her distraction really worked. As the tour guide slid past me, she patted me on the shoulder. "You've got a good friend there, Annika." She winked as she directed her small group forward.

My eyes shifted quickly to Mari's face to see if she heard what Maren had whispered. Thankfully, she'd already moved towards the windows. My exhale came louder than planned, but gratefully, I didn't need to wiggle my way out of another mess.

"Oh, Ella, come here. Look at the view."

I hardly peeked the last time, anxious to get my feet solidly back on the ground below. She led me around the circular space, and in every direction I found a familiar landmark. I settled on the border near Bernauer. The enormous pile of rubble once known as the Church of Reconciliation wrenched at my heart and drove me to cry aloud. Immersed in the moment, my original reason for being here nearly went unnoticed. I wiped the moisture from under my eyes and glanced around, searching for my target.

The tour guide, not far away, continued to entertain her guests with stories. Managing to get closer, I overheard bits and pieces of their conversation. The way she interacted captivated all around her. Every word out of her perfect mouth entranced her audience.

I dawdled nearby for the next fifteen minutes, and when she made the motion to leave, I did too. I needed to be in the lift when she went down—for my own conscience.

Again, no elderly man, only the younger, flirtatious employee. I led Mari towards the very back, listening to and watching their playful interchange. Then it happened. The slightest shift, but my eyes did not deceive. She sidled up close enough to touch his jacket and in doing so, slipped a paper into his pocket. I glanced away the moment the action ended and tried to keep my countenance from revealing my true feelings. While she continued to laugh and giggle with her guests, my spirit sank from the notion this extraordinary woman dabbled in espionage.

I took a good look at her contact, the lift operator, on our way out. Brown hair, green eyes, the scruff on his chin, scar on his brow, and dimple on his upper cheekbone when he chuckled. *Will I remember everything?* Once we reached the walk, I quickly grabbed a piece of paper from my purse and jotted some notes.

"Are you okay?" Mari's concern evident in her voice.

"Yes." I scribbled.

"You're acting weird."

"I remembered something I needed to do for work, and if I forgot, it might get me in trouble."

"What exactly do you do? You know, for work." I could feel the weight of her eyes on me while I penned my thoughts. "I know you've told me about the errands and such, but like a delivery girl or what?"

"Yes, something like that. You know, Mari, I'm kind of dizzy. Do you think we can go home?"

"Sure."

"I'm sorry. I know we talked about going to a café, but I feel a bit weak."

"Yes, yes of course. Will you be well enough to walk, or should I hire a ride?"

"I can walk, but thank you."

Later, after Mari left with Cade, I retrieved my sketch book. It wasn't always easy to sketch a target without the person in front of me, but between the notes and my memory, I drew them. Once completed, satisfaction developed with their true likenesses, and now, after witnessing the exchange with my own eyes, I no longer felt the tug of guilt on my heart strings. If Maren sold secrets to the Stasi and the man is involved, they deserved to be exposed.

*****

"And Darek, the lift operator didn't get his information directly from the patrons," I cried excitedly, trying hard to keep my voice down in the back room. "It was her, the beautiful tour guide."

"Interesting." He glanced over my sketches.

"I didn't realize until the second day that there was no way he collected secrets in thirty seconds, but then I watched her and her interaction with the guests. They trusted her. They opened up and many divulged their reasons for being in the West. Some had family here, others only acquaintances. *She* was the one who gave up names. The lift operator, or more likely operators, were the go-between."

Darek stared at me with unusual admiration. "Heaven forbid you ever work for the wrong side," he exclaimed. "You're lethal." He placed the sketch in a folder. "Nothing ever seems to get past you."

"I don't like people who are willing to turn in others for money, satisfaction, gifts, status, whatever. We should be helping each other against the bad guys, not sacrificing our brothers, sisters, families."

"You're a jewel, Annika. This will go in the Grenzfall by Thursday."

"Grenzfall?"

"Yes. It's the new name for the magazine. *Border case.* Do you like it?"

"Yeah." I let the words sink in. "It's good."

This exchange between Darek and I appeared quite different from the one we had after the concert, as if his mistrust had been forgotten, because he sang my praises to anyone within earshot for days.

The published article was mass produced. The magazine developed quite the underground following in its previous form, but now with the new identity, it had a greater reach. I never read the article. Determined not to think of what might happen to the targets afterward, I kept my distance. Whether their justice came from other spies, the government, or angry victims, I justified my conscience with thoughts of the families who fell victim to their deceit.

Twenty-three

I SENTENCE PEOPLE TO DEATH

11ᵗʰ June 1986

"Ella!"

Ghastly screams met me from the kitchen the moment I opened the front door. I left early for a morning walk, and the coffee in my hand splashed my fingers.

"What?" I cried, running inside.

"Ella!" Mari repeated my name, but failed to elaborate. I tossed the coffee into the sink and rushed to her side, expecting to see a giant spider cornering her. I'd never seen her countenance this pale or her hands shake so violently. A folded newspaper, clenched in her grasp, rattled loudly against her thigh.

"Mari, calm down. What's upset you?"

"Oh . . ." She leaned against the counter. I reached for her arms to steady her. "We saw . . . we saw her."

"Saw who? What are you talking about?"

"The woman . . ."

"What woman?" Now she had me quite concerned. Mari had never struggled to speak before.

"Her!" She lifted the crumpled paper, although I couldn't see anything. "The woman you talked to at the tower."

"The tower?"

"Remember, two months ago? Th . . . the television tower. The woman with the curly hair and bright smile."

I suddenly realized she referred to the tour guide. My eyes glanced to the paper still crumpled in her tiny hand, *Morgenpost* printed at the top. My teeth clenched. This had to be bad.

"Sh-she . . ." Mari whimpered as she braced herself. The tea kettle began a high-pitched squeal. I reached for the knob on the stove and flipped it off. I didn't want to talk about this.

"Sh-she . . ."

"Stop. I . . .I don't want to know."

"Ella, it's dreadful! Sh-she—"

"DON'T!" It was the first time I ever raised my voice to Mari. It surprised me as much as it did her. "I'm sorry," I apologized swiftly, although my voice remained brisk. "I don't want to hear this."

Her eyes remained wide and injured.

"I'm sorry." I fled to the bathroom and locked the door. On the toilet, I buried my head in my hands and sobbed. This was not supposed to make me feel bad. *She* hurt people, not me! *She* made the choice to inform, not me!

I couldn't move for nearly an hour, despite Mari's attempts to get me to come out. I finally showered and tried to eliminate any trace of tears, but my cheeks swelled underneath my puffy eyelids.

By the time I exited the bathroom, Mari was gone. Though I regretted the way I acted, her presence would have only enflamed my guilt. I could not look her in the face and lie.

In the kitchen, the crinkled paper lay on the floor, like a curse shadowed its pages. I carefully stepped around it, determined not to touch it or let it touch me. At the door, I glanced back, rage instantly filling my mind. *How did I let this happen? I should've known Mari would read the paper. I myself avoided it for this very reason. Why did I take her to the tower and allow her to get caught up in my mess?*

Once outside, my lungs drew a long inhale, as if the clean air could purify my soul. *You are not a good person,* an evil voice echoed in my head. *You sentence people to death or worse . . . what could be worse than death? Torture?* I turned away from the flat, though I had no control over where I walked. An urgency propelled me away from the building and especially away from the paper.

I passed a children's park, the playground empty at this time of day. I found my way to the seesaw and sat in the middle. I glanced to my right, the seat lay flat against the cement. To the left, the seat rose high above the ground. How ironic I chose to sit here. Many times my choices took me up, and other times my choices brought me down. How is it, though, that my actions gravitated to the down position more often than not?

After hours of wandering the neighborhood, I arrived at the flat a good hour after Mari returned from work. The paper was nowhere in sight. Neither she nor I brought up the earlier conversation. At dinner, I struggled to repair the damage.

"How was work?" I inquired with a forced lightness.

"Good." She toyed with her noodles.

"How's Cade?"

"Good."

I wanted to cry. Of all the people in my life, I never wanted to hurt Mari. I kept trying. "When will you go out again?"

"Sunday."

"To dinner?"

"Yes, but with his friends."

"From KvU?"

Mari glanced at her hands. "Yes."

"You never talked to him? About how you feel?"

"Yes. Yes, I did." She came alive. Her eyes actually lifted and met mine. I grinned with this small progress. "We came up with a compromise. I'll go with him once a week, and he'll do something I want to do once a week."

"Compromise is good. If you're okay with it."

"Yes." She reached for my hand. "Will you come?"

"Come to what?"

"To dinner with us on Sunday?"

"Why me?"

"Because you're *my* friend, Ella. I don't want to be alone."

I thought about how I'd treated her earlier. How I snapped at her when she neither deserved it or understood why. If I was really committed to being a better person, there was no better place than to start here with her. I squeezed her hand back. "Anything for you, Mari. What time and where?"

"Cade will come get us at 6. We can all walk together."

I couldn't believe I had agreed, but Mari's involvement with KvU concerned me. Her innocence and naivety were genuine. It frightened me to think of what she might be getting herself involved in.

The next day, my long-awaited appointment with Herr Wagner finally arrived. I still hadn't mentioned any of this to Mari, being that everything the notary and I had discussed progressed slowly.

I arrived at his office a few minutes before 10 am, and he ushered me inside with his usual happy self. I hoped this welcome was a precursor to his news. If bad, I believed he might not be so jovial.

"Ella, have a seat." He stepped around to the other side and sat down. Opening my file, a small wrinkle appeared on his forehead. I watched him. His lips pulled into a straight line, and I knew my answer.

"I received word from an associate at the Stasi headquarters . . ."

My fingers gripped the armrests on the chair. If I felt faint, at least I wouldn't fall. "Yes?"

"It is what we feared." He sighed heavily. "Your name has been flagged as 'unable to travel'."

Clenching my teeth, I fought the tears that desperately wanted to break free. "Is it . . . is it because of the incident I told you about?"

Herr Wagner licked his lips but never lifted his head. His eyes remained on his paperwork in the folder. "Yes, the one in 1963."

The tears won. They trickled down my cheeks, though I kept my cry stifled. "Please, you mustn't tell Josef."

"I promised you I wouldn't, but I feel he should know the truth. He'll want to know why I couldn't help you get across."

"It's been delayed this long, tell him it's still delayed. He's not here. He won't know."

He placed the folder down and stood up. His eyes finally fell upon me as he approached from the side. "Dear Ella, I'm sorry. I really thought I could help you."

I sniffled. "Thank you for trying." I glanced up. "I'm not sure I could've left Mari anyway."

He placed a hand on my shoulder. "I will keep my promise to you and tell Josef nothing has progressed, but this will only bide him for a short time. He's a smart man, and he knows the law. I suggest you tell him the truth soon. He loves you no matter what."

I shook his hand and thanked him for all his hard work. In the two years since I met him, he had only been honest with me. Ultimately, my own actions were responsible for my continued captivity. With Colonel Anker dead, Captain Sharp absent, and Stefan missing, there were no witnesses to my innocence. My only hope now lay in the voice of the opposition growing loud enough to break the wall.

The following Sunday night, Cade, Mari, and I joined a half dozen people at a new restaurant in Mitte. It had been awhile since I socialized in a bar and didn't drink. It took every ounce of strength to focus on the conversation and not the pints in their hands. Mari and I conversed quietly about other matters while much of the group talked business. Particularly grateful the music played loud enough to muffle the risky conversation, I relaxed but kept a keen eye on our surroundings anyway.

"Annika!" The word reached my ears quickly. My body froze in response. My mind whirled for a speedy solution. *I cannot answer to that name with Mari and Cade here.*

"Annika!" Persistent, the man jockeyed for my eye.

I turned his direction and glared. A barman from Darek's new place stared back at me. Having only seen me twice, our interaction totaled less than three minutes both times. *Doesn't he know?* Hadn't it ever been explained to him the purpose of our anonymity?

"I'm sorry." My expression softened when Mari shifted my direction. All eyes in the company watched with sudden interest. "You must have me confused with someone else."

The man's eyebrows curved inward. "Uh . . ." He realized his actions had brought undue attention to us both. "Uh . . . yeah. You look like someone else I know. Sorry."

The perspiration on my neck—thankfully covered by my collar— trailed uncomfortably down my back. I turned back to the group of *friends* I met less than an hour ago. Most returned to previous conversations, except the woman towards the other end of the table. She hadn't stopped staring since the barman left.

"Ella, *right?*"

"Yes, Ella." I confirmed loudly for everyone.

"What *was* it you said you did for *employment?*" I forgot how skeptical people can be when working underground. This little interchange lost some credibility for me. I knew it would take some time to divert the attention off of me.

"Actually, I never said." I took a sip of my mint tea. "I make deliveries."

"*Really?*" She faked fascination. "What *kind?*" She showed no intention of letting this go.

"Anything really. I check in with my boss, he gives me an assignment, and I deliver a product. Nothing glamorous."

"Hmmm," she sighed. "You're right, *not* glamourous at all. Just *curious* . . ." she added, her eyes studying me, "what's the *most* unusual thing you've *delivered*?"

Mari stopped to listen.

"A cat, actually." The first thing to enter my mind, I thought of Dotzi and how much I disliked that feline at Anklamer. "It was a gift for a child."

"*How* unusual." Her emphasis on certain words grew irritating.

"And what is your name again?" I deflected it back to her.

"Karin."

"Oh yes. Karin Lenz, right?"

"Yes. *Good* memory."

"Well, that's one thing you must have in my job." I laughed, and the others followed suit—everyone except Karin. She turned back to her drink, her doubt evident. I grinned.

Once the night came to a close and we said our goodbyes, Cade walked us home to make sure we arrived safely.

"Your friends are interesting, Cade." I mostly referred to Karin, but the others appeared ambitious as well.

"Yes, they're passionate about their cause."

"Is it your cause as well?"

"Yes, Ella, and it should be yours too."

I didn't argue with him. I had too much respect for Mari to embarrass her, but I sulked silently. Yes, my involvement in the underground went much deeper than ever intended, but I kept it carefully concealed. Too many people were being open about their dissent and disagreements with the government, and that's when things get far more dangerous.

As we arrived at the flat, Mari flew in to put the kettle on. I took advantage of the moment Cade and I were briefly alone.

"Do not put her in danger, Cade." My threat surfaced in bold tones. "She mustn't be seen with those people anymore. You might have already been exposed."

"What do you mean? They only talk. Nothing has happened beyond chatter."

"I'm telling you, I know Karin is not on the up and up. There's something wrong there."

"She's fine, Ella. She's actually more involved with the women's peace group anyway. We hardly see her."

"She's trouble."

"People are too mistrusting in this world."

"For good reason." I attempted to keep my voice down, but his ignorance irritated me. "Are you telling me you haven't seen the fear the Stasi generate—the arrests, the intimidation?"

"I've seen it, but when will people start trusting again? It has to start somewhere."

"Yes, but I can promise you it's not with Karin. I've experienced too much in my past to know when something isn't right. Just promise me you'll keep Mari away from her."

Cade shifted awkwardly to his other foot.

"Hey, you two. Come in here. Get some tea," Mari called from the kitchen.

I grabbed Cade's sleeve. "Promise me!"

"Okay, I promise."

Twenty-four

LENA

15 June 1986

"We found him, Ella," Darek announced as he slid into the seat across from me. His upper lip lifted with pleasure. "We got several pictures of the informant, but only from your last few jobs. My mates, however, are certain this man has been watching you long before."

"Really?" My brows pinched together. "I haven't seen him since the concert."

"He's careful." Darek reached for some papers. "He's definitely trained—meticulous in his position and your proximity."

My mind wandered to the times I'd seen him before. He didn't seem cautious then. "Do you know who he is or anything about him?"

"Not yet, but the photographs are being developed."

"Photos? I don't recall seeing anyone with a camera nearby."

"We're discreet."

"Why don't you use the camera for the initial contacts instead of art?"

"Sometimes we do, but artists are rarely noticed. They're all over the city. I guess I'm old fashioned that way."

"Lay low for this week. The photos should be in by next Monday, and we can talk then."

I nodded.

"Lukas," Darek motioned to a man who entered the pub, clearly ending our business. "What do we have on Heinz Kessler?"

"Quite a bit." The man edged past me and towards Darek. "The Defense Minister has been busy."

"Did we get his orders in print?"

"A copy of his shoot-to-kill orders is right here. We can have it in the next issue."

I pretended not to hear all this, but Darek seemed to have no problem being open about his activities when no patrons were present. "I'll see you next week." My goodbye wasn't acknowledged by either one, their focus heavily on the papers before them.

Shoot to kill order, still? Certain they referred to the wall, I mumbled internally. That's practically all we focused on besides the Stasi, but the Stasi never had an open murder policy ... everything was accomplished in secret. The wall, however, was different.

By the time I reached my flat, the afternoon had barely begun— plenty of time to do what I toyed with on my walk home. Fumbling through the letters on the shelf, I found the envelope of an old letter ... Lena's. I pulled out a street map and located her address. She lived in Prenzlauer Berg. If I caught the bus, I could be at her home in a couple hours. If she didn't answer, did I have the courage to wait?

Once I located the correct apartment, my fingers traced the buttons at the door until I found the right bell. I pressed it, quite certain she may not answer if she knew who rang.

"Hello?" Her voice came through as sweet as I remembered.

I debated answering. She could be angry, hurt, or resentful.

"Hello?" she repeated.

"Uh, yes, Lena?"

"Yes? Who is this?"

"It's . . . it's me, Ella."

"Ella? My friend, Ella?" Her cry nearly shattered the glass next to the door.

"Yes, your terrible friend." I admitted.

She didn't respond. The loud buzz indicated entry into the building. My hand barely reached the handle when she appeared and flung both her arms around my neck, tears streaking her cheeks. "Oh, my dear Ella." She released and towed me up to her flat. "Come, sit." She pointed to her couch and put a kettle on. A toddler played with some toys on the nearby rug.

"Oh," I cried. "Is she yours?"

"Yes. Oh yes, I have two girls. Can you believe it? I'm a mother!"

I smiled. The beautiful child only glanced up briefly with an enchanting smile of her own and then continued to play.

"How old is the other one?"

"Clara is eight and will be home from school soon. Grace here is three. We only planned on one. She was a bit of a surprise."

"You hardly look as if you've aged at all." I pointed out her youthful complexion.

"Oh," she laughed. "The wrinkles are there, I promise." Lena moved next to me and threw her arms around me a second time. "I've missed you. Thank you for the letter. It was such a blessing to know you're alive."

"I have no excuse, Lena. I should've never treated you badly. You've always been good to me."

She held one arm tight around my shoulders. "I'm quite relieved you're recovering. I've seen how alcohol can destroy lives." She jumped to her feet. "Oh, I'm an awful hostess. I almost forgot the tea. How's black?"

"Sure, tea would be nice."

After she returned with two cups, the questions began. I knew they might be hard, but it was only fair. She knew most everything about me up until I started drinking.

"Stefan? Is he—"

"No," I cut her off. Not to be rude, but I didn't want to talk about him. "Tell me about motherhood, Freddy, the neon bar?" I shifted the conversation back to her. "I want to hear all about it."

We immediately fell into our old selves. Chatting had always been easy with her and continued until late in the night. She invited me to stay for dinner, and I met her oldest daughter whose beauty emulated her mother's. Freddy was working unfortunately, but before I departed, we made plans to meet again soon.

At the door, she embraced me snuggly. "Ella, no matter what the future holds, please remember I'm your friend. Not only in the good times but the hard times too."

I kissed her on the cheek. "I know. I promise to stay in touch."

Reflecting on the day while returning home, a strong, healthy, confidence filled my soul and allowed me to settle to a good place. My reconnection with family and friends, specifically Josef, Anton, Mari, and Lena was the reason my heart showed signs of healing. Despite the absence of others, the chasm that existed for so long began to have some closure for once.

Twenty-five

IT'S NOT HIM

21 June 1986

"Nikolaus, get Annika a glass of wasser please," Darek announced the moment I stepped inside. "Come, join me here." He patted the stool next to him. Anxious to put an end to this, I conceded quickly. He let go of an envelope to hold his glass up for a refill. Nikolaus set the water in front of me. My eyes shifted back to the envelope.

Darek tapped the bar. "I have the photographs."

"Are we sure its him?"

"No question." His fingers fumbled long enough for the sweat to pool above my brows. He retrieved three small black-and-white photos.

I inched forward, leaning closer against the bar. A coat and cap materialized in the image. I squinted. Instantly, all oxygen evaporated, and I gasped for air. When the words came, I wasn't even sure they were mine. "No . . . no . . . no." The whisper graduated to loud unfiltered cries. "NO! NO!"

"What?" he questioned.

"No, no, that's not right. Where's the sketch I gave you?" My hands shook as I held the photographs up for closer inspection. Leaning against a tree, one behind a lamp post, the last sitting on a bench—same form and profile. My illusions now developed on paper. How could he be there? *He* wasn't real!

"Annika, what's wrong?" Darek faced me

"It's—" my head spun wildly "—It's not him." I stuttered childishly. "Th-the man who w-watched me is not him!" My finger pressed onto the image.

Darek folded his arms across his chest. I could feel the weight of his eyes upon me. "I forwarded the sketch. This is him: the coat, hat, long hair . . . this is the man who's been following you."

The lump in my throat made it hard for me to swallow. In fact, my whole face seemed to swell as if I developed an allergy. "I'm telling you, it's not him. He's the wrong man."

"Nikolaus!" Darek demanded. "Where's Jakob?"

"In the back."

"Tell him to come here."

"It's interesting you would say this, Annika."

"Why?"

He uttered with unmistaken misgivings, "He said you would say this."

My mind labored to interpret his words or their meaning. "Wh-what do you mean?" I continued to stumble, "You spoke to him?"

"No, my informant. The one I sent to keep an eye on you and identify the source."

My eyes glanced back to the photographs and then burrowed into Darek. "Why would anyone say that? Was it Nikolaus?"

The storeroom door creaked open. My eyes narrowed in on a hand, and then the arm, and finally a full body entered. My fingers gripped the edge of the bar with an instant need to steady myself.

Despite my desperate appeal for air, nothing came. Paralysis bled through my entire form as the man approached.

His deep gurgling laugh began from his stomach and rolled all the way up his throat to his curled lips. I scanned his face, the scar no longer visible. Replaced with black ink, a detailed profile of a skull tattoo covered his right side, and precisely where his charred cheek should have been, a skeletal jawbone materialized. His eyes scrutinized me with hate and loathing, much like a hungry wolf eyeing prey. I teetered towards losing my balance.

"H-how? Wh-what . . ." Nothing legible came out. His laugh echoed in my ears, but I couldn't process anything. I only saw the wood slats of the floor get closer and closer.

Darek grabbed my arm and held me up. "What's wrong?"

I pointed to Jurek, the last person in the world I hoped to ever see again. I tried to mentally identify the last whereabouts of my knife. The devil himself stood before me, and I did not believe Darek could stop him from harming me.

"Why? Why is he here?" I finally spit out.

"Why shouldn't he be?" Darek's forehead twisted in confusion.

My eyes shifted between the men and the exit, calculating my chances for escape. I knew Jurek could fight, and I questioned my ability to outrun him, but where would Darek fit into my plan?

"What's going on here?" He physically lifted me to my feet and thrust me through the open door Jurek entered from. My neck stretched back, my eyes locked on Jurek, expecting him to attack from behind. Darek pulled me into the small room and then harshly forward to face him, both hands gripping my forearms tightly. He shook my torso with unfamiliar coarseness. "What is going on?"

I swallowed hard. *What can I say?* Obviously, he trusted Jurek or he wouldn't be here.

"Yes, Annika," Jurek's tone dripped with sarcasm as he appeared next to us. "What's the problem?" His confidence surged.

My eyes fearfully glanced between the two. I suddenly felt more fearful for my life than ever before. I suspected the possibility Darek could be dangerous, but I had no doubts about Jurek. If we were left alone, I might not survive.

"Jurek—or Jakob, whatever you call him—we have a past." My whisper was intended only for him.

"Is that what you call it?" Jurek sneered and moved closer to intimidate me.

Darek put up his hand to stop him. "Back off," he commanded. "Let her speak."

I knew Darek could feel my body tremble under his grip. Maybe this warranted his compassion, or maybe it increased his suspicion.

"We've crossed paths before." My eyes only met Darek's, but in my sideview I could see the tattoo tighten under strain. I continued, "My friend Anton lived on the streets with Jurek. They fought, and Jurek wanted his revenge. He attacked me." Those final words came out in desperation.

"Your Soldat junge assaulted *me!*" Jurek's voice rose heatedly. "She doesn't belong here!"

Immediately, Darek whipped around, jabbing his finger against Jurek's chest. "You do NOT tell me who does and does not belong here!" Jurek's eyes widened like never before. "You will learn your place!"

Jurek's lips sealed into a thin line. The bones in his jaw protruded, but he remained silent.

"Now, whether what she says is true or not, we are in this cause together. This is over. Whatever history you have, it's done!" Darek spoke to us like children fighting in a play yard.

"Darek, can I please speak to you alone?"

"No," he snapped. "We all work together. Say what you need to here."

I glanced at Jurek. His countenance seethed in repulsion.

"The man in the picture—" I exhaled quickly "—he's not the one I believed to be following me. He . . . this man is my former fiancé."

"Former?"

188

"Yes." I took another deep breath, thankful Jurek remained silent. "We were engaged, but he disappeared."

"Is he the soldier Jurek referred to?"

"Yes, but forced into conscript for ten years . . . NVA."

"Where?"

My chest rose and fell a full minute before I answered. "All over . . . then the border."

"Scheisse, Ella!" Darek's cry reverberated throughout the small space. His hands flew to his head. "Why didn't you tell me?"

Jurek's lips curved into a sneer, but again he didn't speak.

"He left me fifteen years ago. I didn't think it was necessary."

"Yet now he's here, following you, and you think it's a coincidence?"

"He's not the one I told you about. He has black hair, not blond! The man I saw was not Stefan!"

"Stefan? What's his family name?"

My whole body went rigid. I reached for Darek's arm with both hands. "He's not the threat."

"How can you know?"

"Because he saved my life three times."

"Jakob, do you know where he lives?"

My mouth flew open. "No!" I cried. "Please . . . don't." My grip tightened.

"We can't take any chances, Annika. Jakob?"

Jurek's lip raised on one side. He stared at me with an immediate satisfying snarl. "No, but we are close. We know the neighborhood."

"Darek, please . . ." Tears formed at the corner of my eyes. I didn't care if I made a fool of myself. "Please, he would never hurt me . . . or you."

He fell silent, deep in thought. He didn't look at either one of us directly. Jurek leaned forward, positioned for a full sprint the moment he got the okay from Darek, a predator ready to strike.

"Darek," I pleaded. "I still love him." My confession was as much for me as it was anyone else.

Several minutes passed, but it could've been hours. I hung onto every hope I had to change his mind.

"Alright—"

"Verdammit!" Jurek slammed his fist against the wall and immediately Darek's hand went for his throat, pinning him tightly. I had never seen such exertion from him.

"If you ever question me again, I will kill you."

I couldn't see Darek's countenance from my angle, but Jurek's expression revealed much. His eyes expanded with each passing second, and though he remained silent, his lip twitched sporadically. Once Darek released his grip, Jurek fled the room.

Darek pressed his fingers against his forehead. When he brought them back down, his hands shuddered at his sides. "I'm giving you one week to let this Stefan know to stay away from you and anyone else involved in the cause, or he'll regret it."

"I . . . I don't know if I can find him."

One hand flew towards my face but never reached it. A sole finger pointed at me forcefully. "One week, Annika!"

Twenty-six

RALF?

29 June 1986

Bam, bam, bam! Waiting only a second in between knocks, I kept my hand fisted against the ornate wooden door. *Oh please, oh please, be here.* The images of Stefan materialized. His long hair, his scruffy, unkept appearance, and his cautious demeanor, all developed on the film that Darek shared only yesterday. Everything about my carefully-constructed recovery came crashing down in a matter of minutes.

Edmund opened the door. "Ella?" His irritated scowl softened upon recognition. "What are you doing here?"

"I need to see Katharina, right now."

"Come in, are you well?"

"Yes. If you're asking if I'm sober, I am." Immediately I regretted my quick, biting response. Seeing him in his doctor's coat brought emotions I thought were long extinguished. He didn't deserve that. I stumbled in my backtrack. "I . . . I'm sorry, Edmund. I didn't mean that."

He shrugged his shoulders and pointed to the hallway. "Have a seat. I'll get Katharina."

"Ella?" She ran down the hall. With one hand she ripped off her apron, and with the other she brushed her hair behind her ear. "Oh my goodness." She launched into me and held tight for several minutes.

"Are you alright?" she cried and held my hands tightly while we moved to sit. "Where have you been? What's been going on?"

I glanced at her, confused. "Edmund didn't tell you?"

Her eyelashes fluttered downward as she spoke. "He was vague. He thought you should tell me."

"I wrote you a letter."

"Yes, I received the letter, but it would've been better in person."

My heart wanted to wilt in humiliation, though I hardly had the time. "I'm sorry, Katharina. You deserve better. The letter was meant to explain my stupid decisions over the last ten years. I hoped it would make it easier when I faced you."

Her expression was hard to read, almost wounded.

"I don't deserve your friendship or" —I peeked down the empty hallway he'd disappeared into— "Edmund's rescue."

"Rescue?"

"He saved me at the hospital. I suffered from alcohol poisoning."

"Oh no." She cupped my cheek and kissed the other one. "That's awful. What can we do to help?"

I cringed knowing what needed to come forth. "I hate to say this. You might think it's selfish of me, but . . ."

Her nose pinched in confusion. "What?"

"I need to reach Stefan."

"Stefan?" Her wide eyes told me she didn't expect this. "I . . . I don't know where he is."

I inhaled deeply then let my words roll out. "He's here, somewhere in Berlin. I . . ." *Oh how am I going to explain this?* "Recently,

192

a photograph was taken of me, and . . . well, . . . Stefan was behind me. He's been following me."

"No!" She stood. "Is this true?"

Her cry brought Edmund running. "What happened?"

"Nothing . . . nothing. I'm fine, just confused." Katharina reached for her husband's hand.

"Me too," I added, "but I need to find him."

"Oh, El, he hasn't been here. We haven't heard from him . . . at all. Are you sure it was him?"

"Yes, I'm positive."

"I can't believe he's here." Katharina's cheeks went pale. "He never approached you? Or spoke to you at all?"

"No." My chin tilted downward, "and I don't think he ever will."

"Why do you suppose he hasn't come here, to his home?"

"I don't know," I answered truthfully.

"Why are people taking photographs of you? Are you in trouble?" Edmund asked, his interest in my strange behavior piqued. The doctor in him poised and ready.

"No, I'm not. It was a friend's camera, but I'm afraid *he* might be."

"Why?" Katharina asked.

"There's details about the photo I'm not free to share. I have a bad feeling, only I don't know where to find him to warn him. That's why I came here."

Katharina peered over at Edmund. Her stare was subtle but not missed. "You're the second person to come looking for him."

"Second?" The lump in my throat swelled.

"Yes. Ralf came over a year ago."

"Ralf?" My mind spun, attempting to place that name.

"Ralf was his childhood friend. They spent a lot of time together before Stefan and he got in trouble in Czechoslovakia. Then we never saw Ralf again."

Ralf? The parlor. The secret ski holiday. The connection came together. "Katharina . . . you don't know?"

193

"Know what?"

"Ralf didn't get released when Stefan did."

"He didn't?"

"No." Questions flooded my thoughts. *Why is Ralf looking for Stefan? Is it reconnection or revenge?*

Katharina's hand covered her mouth. Her head didn't move, but her eyes did. "That explains his behavior," she whispered. "It was strange."

"Like what?"

"Odd. Not the way I remembered him as a child. His expression revealed nothing, but his body twitched in agitation. Even through his black coat he shook."

Unsure whether my chest or my cheeks enflamed first, I stumbled to a chair and caught myself before I collapsed. My head weighed heavy in my hands. *Black coat?*

"Ella?"

A minute passed before I lifted my head to meet their eyes. "What did Ralf look like when he came over?"

Katharina's brows rose. "There were similarities to when he was younger, only his hair was darker, black. Tall and very thin."

"Did he wear a gold chain and have a scar above his lip?"

"Yes. How did you know?"

All the air around me evaporated. I struggled to breathe much less think. *It's him! The black-coat man is Ralf!*

"You're pale," Edmund cried. "Let me get you a glass of water."

"Did you . . ." I mumbled, "did you happen to mention anything about me to Ralf?"

"Some." Katharina sat next to me. "He asked about Stefan of course, but then asked if he had a loved one. You're the only one he's ever loved."

The palpitations in my chest were deafening. I knew Katharina was still next to me, but my head spun so fast I could no longer see her.

An arm reached around my shoulders and pulled me close. Katharina's voice tremored against my ear. "Why is this upsetting you?"

When I didn't answer, she brushed my hair tenderly with her fingers. Any other time this would have been soothing, but my thoughts raced fiercely. *Does Stefan know?*

Edmund returned with the water, but I hardly felt like drinking. "Here." His tone did not give me a choice. His hand went to my neck. "You're warm."

I lifted the cup to my lips, but it shook until Katharina assisted. "Stay here," she whispered. "Let us help you."

I took one sip before my head swung backward. I would only be putting their little family in danger. Even now, as I lingered, someone may have already followed me. *Why did Ralf need to know about me? What are his intentions?*

"I can't." I sprang to my feet, almost too quickly. The cup slipped out of her hands to the floor.

Edmund held me steady. "She's right, Ella, you need to stay."

I gripped both his arms and glanced between him and Katharina who joined him. "Just promise me, if Stefan reaches out to you, you must tell him to keep away from me."

"Keep away?" Katharina cried.

My eyelids couldn't stop the tears despite how hard I pressed them closed. "Yes." I opened my eyes again. "He can never come around me again." Rushing to the door, I ignored their calls and ran until out of sight.

I envisioned the reconnection with Katharina so differently. It hurt to imagine the additional heartache I caused, but I couldn't explain my reasons. The opposition, the SED, and now Darek and Ralf watching me, all of these reasons kept my loved ones at a distance. I needed time—time to process my next course. Frustrated, I found a bench. Sitting seemed so passive, but sometimes that was the only way clarity emerged. The leaves on the linden tree above me danced in random order. There's always been something mystical about the way the wind moves—an unseen interchange until it crosses another object's path, then magically you see its effect. When the wind reached my cheeks, its gentle kiss washed over me, bringing a much-needed calming.

With my spirit restored, a new plan formed. I made my way towards Prenzlauer and Darek. The smoke-filled pub was filled to capacity. Deafening cheers shook the walls, tables, and me the farther I dared to enter. A small black and white television rested on the bar next to a pyramid of empty beer steins and a platter of half-eaten Brats. On the tube, a futbol match aired. Never interested in sports, I knew little of its popularity, but this particular game somehow drew a large crowd.

I glanced around the room. Darek noticed me and pointed to the storeroom where we met behind the closed door.

"Make this quick, there's only a few minutes left, and the match is tied."

"Who's playing?" My question relayed innocence, but it might as well have been an insult.

The upper part of his nose and forehead crinkled. "Are you joking?"

"No . . ." Instantly self-conscious, I glanced away.

"West Germany, Annika . . . in the World Cup finals."

I shrugged my shoulders, which added offense to the injury. "I don't follow sports at all."

"The World Cup!" he cried then opened the door to a raucous cheer. "Kurt, what happened?"

A voice hollered. "Enrique yellow card. Argentina's wasting time."

"Verdammit. What do you need?" His voice rose with irritation. "I want to finish the match."

I inhaled. My speech had been rehearsed on the walk here, but now I grappled to find the right words. "I . . . I searched for him, Darek. I really tried, but I can't find him."

"Who?" he questioned. The wrinkle on the bridge of his nose matched the one on his forehead; his thoughts must've remained on the futbol game.

"My friend Stefan."

"Oh, the soldier."

"Yes, Darek. Please understand. He's not in my life now, and he would never hurt me. If anything, he probably feels compelled to make sure I'm safe."

"He can't lurk around. We can't take any chances." A loud roar came from the bar. Darek reached for the door again and stuck his head out.

"A missed goal," Kurt yelled his direction.

He turned back to me but his mouth pulled against his teeth as he spoke. "Are you finished?"

"Darek, please. You trust me, right?"

"Yes."

"Please believe me when I tell you he won't cause trouble. He's a ghost."

He thought about what I said. Another roar came from the room.

Darek placed his hand on the handle and glanced back at me. "I will let it go for now, but if I even *sense* a problem, it'll be taken care of."

"There won't be a problem," I promised, but he already disappeared into the crowd.

Slipping out of the noisy, foul-smelling room, not one face peeked my direction. I drew a clean breath outside. *Did Darek truly understand?* I could thank the futbol match for his partial inattentiveness, but I promised him Stefan wouldn't be a problem. Only that was a promise I was in no position to make.

Positive Stefan would never approach me, I had to figure out a way to warn him or make myself more invisible. With each new assignment, I decided to scramble my routine, even my appearance if possible, like Stefan did to lose his mother's spy and get to me, years ago. Memory of that time, a time I took for granted, surfaced. How I would give anything to sit across from Stefan now, even in borrowed obdachlos clothing in a dark corner of a pub.

Brushing the moisture beneath my eyes, I swept old desires aside and ignited my resolve to control this. If I can prevent Stefan from following me, he won't be seen by Darek . . . or Ralf. *It's up to me now.*

Twenty-seven

A SPY AND HER HANDLER

April 1987

"Ella!"

"Heidi told me to call back when you got home from work, Josef. She made it sound urgent. Is everything okay?"

"I spoke to Paul yesterday."

"Paul?" The name evaded me momentarily.

"Paul Wagner."

"Wagner, yes, Herr Wagner." I bit the inside of my cheek, waiting for him to proceed. Unsure whether Herr Wagner lived up to his promise or if Josef figured things out on his own, I braced for the outcome.

"He said your situation is still delayed. I don't believe it!" His tone increased with each syllable. "Nobody I've sent to him has taken this long. The man is a miracle worker."

I'd thought of a dozen different scenarios leading up to this day, yet none of them came to mind. I babbled mindlessly, "It's the East, Josef. You know how difficult it is over here. They change the laws like they change their clothes. Every time a different leader takes over, the old rules go out the window."

"It doesn't make sense. Their laws have become more lenient. They're losing their grip on the people. Herr Wagner has a government connection for heaven's sake!" A loud slam echoed through the receiver. I pulled the handset away from my ear, and even with the short distance, I still heard every word. "Ella, are you there?"

"Don't yell, and please be mindful of the conversation. I don't want to be disconnected."

His sigh was loud and exhaustive. "I'm sorry. I just don't know what's taking so long, and Herr Wagner was acting strange. Is there something I don't know?"

"No!" My reply was almost too quick. "No, brother. We're still trying. Please don't give up on me."

"I'm not. I would never. I just think after twenty-six years it would have happened by now."

"Me too." Even though I generally spoke to Josef twice a month, I never wanted to part in frustration. "How was your Easter?" My attempt to swing the conversation seemed forced, but he obliged. His belief in the recent religious holiday made for an easier subject.

"It was nice. We all spent it on holiday in Denmark. Anton and his two kids with us five. We hadn't been there since my 16th birthday, if you remember."

"Yes," I chuckled. "I remember you telling me in a letter. What a wonderful way to spend a holiday. I hope to see Denmark one day."

"You will, I promise."

"How's Heidi and the children?"

"They're well. The change of scenery was good for us all. Oh, by the way, Cade called this morning and told Heidi he's dating Mari. Have you heard?"

"Yes, but very little." Shocked that my brother from the West was sharing news about the person I shared a room with, I elaborated. "I know they see each other often, but I didn't know it became official. Cade is a good man; he'll make her happy"

"Well, it's made Heidi's heart swell with happiness, knowing her little brother might wed someday and have a family of his own."

"Don't jump ahead too fast. Cade dragged his feet getting this far, but yes, that's my wish too. Thanks for telling me. How's Anton and his family? I haven't talked to him in months. Tell him I'm sorry. I've just been really busy."

"He's doing well. His business is growing. He's a fine businessman. And how is your delivery job?"

"Good, really good." While I knew this was my brother, and our conversations in the past were generally simple, for some reason this whole exchange felt strained—starting with the emigration lies and now talking about another false part of my life.

"Listen, Josef, I need to go and get to work." *Another lie.* "Don't worry about me or the papers. It will all work out soon. Love you. Give my love to your family as well."

"I will, sister, and I'll keep searching on my end. This is not over."

"I know."

I left the telephone booth feeling guilty. Not only did I lie about my real job, I also told him we were still working on the papers—which we weren't. In fact, I hadn't spoken to Herr Wagner since the day I left his office with the bad news. Why did I continually lie to everyone in my life?

Not due to check in with Darek until tomorrow, I decided to walk towards Zur. It had been quite some time since I'd seen Conrad and Angelika. Surely, they'd see the transformation, but if he stopped me at the door once more, the humiliation would be devastating. Strolling the direction of the restaurant I loved and missed so much, I made my way down the cobblestone alley. The divine grandeur of the *Parokialkirche,* positioned on my right, vaulted upward in intimidation. Though its size had been noted in the past, I dawdled in its presence before I wound around back towards the cemetery. The full foliage of the sycamore trees offered a comfortable place to relax . . . and hide. The stone steps that led to the church's private entrance were an appealing place to rest and still relish the colorful front of Zur Letzen.

The green shutters with brown trim matched the boxes of vine that hung from the upstairs windows. Random splashes of yellow and blue petals brought a recollection of how I loved to serve near those windows, at times left open to draw the floral scent amidst the patrons. I watched as several customers stepped in and out and unfamiliar waitresses served from both the bar and out to the biergarten—my favorite place to work, the garden patio. Many good memories began there, and although Angelika and I had a bumpy friendship at times, she was one of a kind. She knew how to lift one's spirit like no one else. I hoped she too had not disappeared entirely.

With gentle observation, I couldn't imagine a more peaceful way to spend my afternoon. I had become a people watcher after all. The only difference here was that I didn't have to sketch anyone in particular. Today was for pleasure.

Leaning back on my elbows, I allowed the sun's beam through the trees above to fall directly upon me. Nothing rejuvenated the spirit like sunshine. After a considerable time, I sat up. Debating once again if I should approach the restaurant, I noticed something unusual. A woman in the top left corner window looked vaguely familiar. *How do I know her?* Pulling my torso upright, I narrowed my sights. She conversed with one or possibly multiple people, but I couldn't see who her party included. This woman could be anyone, though. After forty-one years, many people had passed through my life. Maybe a friend of a friend. *That's it!* The short dark hair, long bangs, high cheekbones, and if I could get closer, I might see the small gap between her two front teeth. *Karin Lenz, the woman from the KvU dinner.* The lady I warned Cade about—something about her felt off then, and now, here she is.

Why did this bother me? Nothing about socializing and eating out with friends is unusual—except those second-floor tables were generally occupied for business. That's where Herr Franke, Mielke, and Wolf often ate. It's also where other SED or Stasi members met, because it provided the most privacy and seclusion in the establishment.

If only I could see who her companion is. Knowing there was only one way in and out, I devised a plan. If I waited long enough, they would be exposed upon their exit—unless they left at different times. I needed to see them at the table, but if I tried to get any closer, she might see me through the window. Even the spiral stairs leading up to the second floor provided no protection. Anyone can be seen upon approach.

Scheisse, Ella! I reprimanded myself. *Here I thought it was going to be an uneventful afternoon and you have to go and get curious!* It really could be nothing at all, but if she was up to something, Cade needed to know about it, especially if he and Mari are now getting serious.

Biting my nails, I knew my decision time was limited. I had no resources other than a hat on my head to hide my appearance. I glanced around and spotted a rubbish can sitting near the back corridor of the church. It might contain something suitable, at least to get me past the window. I rummaged through the garbage like obdachlose. *What has my inquisitive nosiness led me to now?* Finding a crumpled newspaper, I flattened the wrinkles and spread the pages open. Walking towards the front of the restaurant, I pretended to be so involved with the news that it covered my entire face. At the door, I peeked in warily to make sure Conrad wasn't present before I stepped inside. A waitress I didn't recognize met me immediately. Folding up the paper, I placed it under my arm.

"May I find you a seat? How many in your party?"

"Actually, might I use your water closet?"

"Yes, absolutely. It's back there." She pointed past the stairs and towards a small niche. Of course, I knew where the water closet was. I knew this building better than the one I currently lived in, but my intent was to somehow get up those stairs without being identified. Karin would surely know me if she saw me.

"Oh, fräulein?" I waved her down.

"Yes?" She stopped and turned.

"I thought I saw an old friend enter earlier, my friend Karin. She has short dark hair, brown eyes . . ."

"Yes, Frau Lenz. She's upstairs. You're welcome to go up."

"Oh, I don't want to bother her if she's with someone. Is she dining alone?"

"No, she's with a gentleman. Herr Becker, I believe."

"Thank you, I appreciate it. They might be here for a romantic lunch; I don't want to interrupt."

"No, ma'am. They aren't—"

"Ella?"

"Angelika!" I swallowed hard as she walked through the front door. I smiled at the other waitress and thanked her again. Waiting for her to disappear, I stepped closer to my old friend.

"I . . . I was just asking about you. I didn't know if you still worked here or not."

She chuckled, "I've tried to get fired so many times."

I smiled at her sorely-missed humor.

"Um, were you headed somewhere?" She pointed to the side of the restaurant I came from.

"I was actually just going to the bathroom."

"Oh, don't let me stop you. I'll wait until you come out."

I grinned nervously, stepped into the water closet, and locked the door. *Okay, now what?* Small beads of sweat rolled down my cheeks, and perspiration filled my blouse. *Think fast.* I needed to abort my original plan and come up with a new one, not knowing where Karin might be when I walked out. *Whatever happens, I'm Ella.* Both Angelika and Karin knew me as Ella in my real life. This sneaking around trying to find out who she was with . . . that was my pretend life.

I unlocked the door and walked out. Angelika stood behind the bar tying an apron on. When I met her again, my arms immediately reached around and gave her a tight hug. "I've missed you, Angelika."

She hugged back. "The place is definitely not the same without you." When she released, she retrieved two glasses and filled them both with water. I didn't even ask her to. "You look good, Ella. How are you doing?"

I knew she referred to the alcohol. "I'm actually clean. Three and a half years. Not a drop since I saw you last, either."

"Really? That's wonderful," she cried and handed me one glass and clinked her own with mine as if we were toasting. "I've thought of you often. What are you doing for work?"

"*She's* a delivery *girl*, right?" I turned around to find Karin standing behind me. Unwelcome goosebumps ran up the back of my neck.

"Karin?" I forced a smile and silently demanded my heart to slow down. "It's good to see you again."

"Yes," —although the words were friendly, the tone hinted otherwise— "you *too*."

"Are you here alone?" I glanced past her and saw no one.

"I had *lunch* with a friend, an old schoolmate *actually*."

"Oh, and where is he?"

"What makes *you* assume it was a *he*?"

"Um . . ." I pulled my lips tight. Then lied, "I assumed a woman as attractive as you would be with a man. I'm sorry. Is *she* gone?"

"Yes, *she* had to leave early. *Good* to see you, Ella, or was it . . . *Annika*?"

There it was. Her first strike. I smiled before I answered, "Ella, only Ella. Goodbye, Karin."

Once she departed, Angelika flashed a confused gaze my direction. "Is she a friend?"

"No," I responded curtly, "not a friend at all. Just someone I met through someone else."

"She's a bit . . . oh forget it. I don't want to talk about her anyway." Angelika laughed and took another sip. "How's your love life? Anyone new?" She smacked her lips together hoping for some juicy girl talk, but I had nothing.

"Sorry, I'm going to be a nun."

"You liar," she groaned. "You're not even religious."

I laughed out loud. "Who are you with nowadays?"

"Umm." She scanned the empty room and then peeked outside. "See that tasty piece of arse right there?" She pointed to the street sweeper. I hooted even louder this time. "Oh, Angelika, I think you're running out of options."

She snickered playfully.

"I've got to go," —I kissed her on the cheek— "but I promise to come by more often." I circled towards the door and inadvertently bumped into a man trying to exit at the same time.

"My apologies." The middle-aged man with a receding hairline and thick brows waved his hand. "Ladies first."

"Oh, um . . . that's okay. Go ahead."

He nodded his head and stepped out alone. I threw a playful smile Angelika's direction and whispered, "he might be available."

"Herr Becker?" The red-headed waitress I met earlier came rushing down the stairs behind me. "Herr Becker?"

Recalling the name, I sprang towards the open door just as he passed the garden. The waitress flew past me with a man's hat clutched in her hands.

"You left this on the table." She handed it to him the moment he turned around. His eyes lifted and sailed past her, meeting mine with bewilderment. I hadn't recognized my audacity—standing near the door, gawking at their interchange.

The waitress followed his gape and turned to me. "Do you need something?" Her sweet voice became brusque. I mumbled a no and scrambled back inside.

Though I no longer saw the man or the waitress, my mind mentally made a list of his features. I reached for the pen and paper on the bar and aggressively jotted down notes.

When I peered back up, Angelika's hands rested assertively on her hips like they used to, before she started in on someone. "What was that all about?"

"Nothing, really."

"Don't lie. I can always tell when you're lying. I can actually tell when anyone is lying—I've been around men too long."

I grinned. "Then you knew Karin was lying when she said she was dining with a woman?"

"Of course. She's been here several times and only with that man, but he's not a lover—or she's the coldest woman I know."

"I think she's an informant." The words fell out quickly. I studied Angelika before she responded.

"That doesn't surprise me," she muttered. "Ella, you know meetings happen here all the time, but what does she have to do with you?"

"Not me. One of my dearest friends."

"So, you do have friends?" Her comment stung, though it was much deserved.

"I'm sorry I haven't stayed in touch better. My recovery has been challenging. I wanted to see you and Conrad when I reached a healthy place again. You saw me at my worst, and I wanted you to see me healed."

"I understand, love." She gave me another hug, only this time she hung on for longer. "Just come back soon. I really miss you."

"Thank you. I promise. Say hello to Conrad as well."

"I will."

At home, in the quietness of my apartment, I sketched Karin and the mysterious Herr Becker. My interaction with him was brief, but close enough to get some pointed details. Karin, on the other hand was easier . . . even down to the chip on her tainted reptilian shoulder.

Twenty-eight

CONFESSIONS

24 May 1987

I crossed my legs at the ankles and shifted my aching hips on the small dirt patch next to a full bush of Bishop's weed. The light jacket I wore came with a hood that covered most of my head and parts of my face. For thirteen months now, extra precautions were taken in my assignments. I left through the back door of my apartment building, sometimes riding the bus or tram for only one stop and then taking the subway. I even went as far as getting my tasks from different locations, anything to lose a follower if one was near. It may have worked. Ralf became invisible after the concert, and to my great relief, there was no sign of Stefan either. If he was watching, neither myself nor Darek was aware of it.

Today I left before the sun rose, rode the train through Mitte, and circled back to Friedrichshain before arriving here by late morning. When I first opened the instructions yesterday, my brief scan stumbled upon one word . . . *one word*. The letters magnified as if they reached out and clutched my throat. It took everything I had to not refuse it, convincing myself the location was no different than any other park. *It's only a job*, I assured myself, *a means to an end*.

Sketching for nearly an hour, I waited for my target to appear. Darek acted on pure suspicion and speculated that my day could turn up nothing at all, yet I waited. I remained mostly for the fountain. Nine years passed since I'd been to Volkspark and the fairytale fountain. Not that I hadn't thought about it, seen it in my dreams, or wished to find peace here, but avoiding it seemed much simpler. I wouldn't have to think of the memories, good or bad.

I pulled my jacket tighter towards my chin. The wind picked up, and despite the unusually cool temperature for May, a decent crowd converged on nature that day—several mothers with layered babes in strollers, a primary school of children and their instructors, and a handful of couples wandering the grounds hand in hand. None of them notice me seated in the brush, which was precisely the way I liked to work . . . no distractions.

My detailed sketch already included a full-length *Rübezahl* statue and a partial Gretel when a man in a brown leather jacket appeared. He leaned against the column supporting the left stone arch. It had to be him, too nervous to be a casual visitor. His hands fidgeted as they slipped in and out of his pockets and up to adjust his hat, his eyes shifting past the growing visitors, here to enjoy the late spring bloom. When he scanned my direction, I quickly focused on my sketches once again. It actually wasn't him Darek showed interested in. I needed to identify the person he met, but I drew him anyway. He continued to pace nervously for another ten minutes when I swung back to work on Hansel, Gretel's companion.

Two elderly women, either sightseeing or on a simple stroll, chatted loudly about their grandchildren and then stood directly between me and the man, known only as Thomas. Although irritated, my murmur was minimal as I scooted to the right for a clearer view, but in adjusting my sights, something else materialized. My pencil slowed and stopped.

Trembling, my fingers lost grip on the utensil, and it fell to the ground. I rubbed my eyes. *Can it be?* Only steps from Thomas, a man in a familiar green military jacket and gray hat sauntered in slow motion, then paused, seemingly unaware he was being watched. I pulled deeper into the brush, letting the leaves shroud my position. My teeth pressed deep into my lower lip. Waiting and watching to see the man's final destination, I pled, *Please don't talk to Thomas. Don't hand him anything. Please keep walking.* It had been over a year since I convinced Darek of his innocence . . . *was I wrong?*

A wisp of air slipped across my lips when the man passed Thomas without even a nod. *He isn't the contact!* In relief, my head rolled back into a branch. I rested momentarily before I tugged it free. When I focused forward again, he was gone. Yet Thomas remained, and within seconds another man appeared at his side, their interaction absolute. He must be the one, but my mind no longer tarried on either suspect.

Trying to mentally remember as much as possible, I quickly snapped my sketchbook closed and threw it into my side bag. I leapt to my feet and jogged underneath the right-side arches that led to the back where a smaller, simpler fountain stood. *Where did he go?* I spun slowly, my eyes darting all directions. The man in the military jacket was nowhere to be found. The enclosed plaza, behind the fairytales, revealed nothing: no footsteps, no clues, and no trace. "Not another illusion!" I cried, gripping the iron gate that directed guests deeper into the park. The harder I pressed, the more I needed to feel its tangible certainty.

When Darek showed me the photographs of Stefan shadowing me, I was devastated, though relieved. *I'm not crazy!* I really did see him all those times. Only, once again, I'm chasing an apparition. One minute there, the next gone. Glancing back at the targets, huddled in secret, I contemplated my predicament. Time still remained to sketch them, but only seconds to make a decision.

What if he ventured down our path?

Confused, I paced. Nothing led me to believe he would be there except that he vanished. Proceeding, however, meant treading through heartbreaking memories. Even back in 1978, the last time I was here, I dared not go there. The garden's remembrance was sacred.

In careful reverence I entered on tiptoe. The overgrown vegetation kept the rarely-used trail private, and my vision narrowed under the thick foliage as I entered. The hood fell to my shoulders, swallowed by the terrain. The shrieks and giggles of children at the fountain gradually disappeared. Motionless at the entrance of the secret garden, I faltered. The simple beauty of a branch or a petal before me should have been comforting, yet it was what they concealed that intimidated me. I bit the inside of my cheek hard, hard enough to draw blood, but the pain didn't distract me from my motive, and I stepped inside with both of my eyes closed tight. The sudden flutter of wings surfaced all around me. Small flits of air with occasional contact tickled my skin. Once I mustered the courage to open my eyes, they fell upon the man in the green jacket. His proximity was close enough that if I reached out, my hand would brush his clothing.

Desperate to know if my eyes baited this manifestation before me, I rubbed them aggressively. When I finally allowed them to see, although fuzzy, there was no doubt he stood before me. Long locks of blond hair chaotically extended from beneath the cap, where unfamiliar scruff trailed his jaw and above his lips, but it was Stefan's unmistakable pools of deep blue that ultimately confirmed his existence.

My eyelashes flickered in competition with the restless butterflies who danced in-flight and settled on any available appendage. I swiped them away and choked out desperately, "Are you real?"

The question clearly shocked him. One hand wiped his bangs aside and revealed a reticence I'd never seen from him. "What—" his voice cracked "—what are you doing here?"

211

My eyes betrayed me as moisture built in the corners. "What am *I* doing here?"

His jaw stiffened.

A familiar rage-filled emotion began to tunnel out of me. "This is . . ." —my balance teetered— "This is *my* garden. Remember, you shared it with me." I reached for a nearby branch to steady myself, but the twig collapsed in my hand. "Why are *you* here?" My demand came out weaker than intended.

Stefan removed his hat. His long locks flung wildly about until he pushed them behind his ears with an obvious tremor in his fingers.

"Why?" I repeated. My cheeks grew warm, small beads of sweat forming on my nose. He didn't look at me. "Stefan!" The sound of his name slipping through my teeth and lips winded me, but in clear contradiction, his breath elevated. His body rigid, his hands knotted tightly at his sides, when he gazed at me, a troubling mixture of fear and torment surfaced. He stepped passed me.

"NO!" I didn't recognize my own voice. I clutched the sleeve of his jacket and squeezed. "No, Stefan!" My fingers tightened their grip, although if he wanted to release them, the bond could be effortlessly broken with a simple flick of his arm. Barely a step away, the spicy scent radiating off his skin hindered me. My prolonged inhale cluttered my mind with instant lightheadedness. "Please?" I begged, unable to stop the course of easy tears. "Please don't go."

My fingers remained fast, but he twisted his back to me while he spoke. "Ella, don't."

"Don't what?" my voice squeaked childishly. Tears dripped off my chin and pooled at my neck.

"We can't do this," his mumble strained.

"Do what?" I cried. "We've already done the *can't!*" Faint sobs resonated from my throat as he attempted to step away again. Both of my hands reached for his arms and forced him to meet me. His sight shifted over my head, but the moisture that appeared in the corners of his eyes was sure.

"Don't go," I implored. "Please, Stefan, don't leave." Although my touch confirmed his reality, his physical proximity contradicted his emotional presence.

My body swayed hypnotically forward as if an imaginary magnet drew me in. The yearn to be next to him heightened. The longing to feel his heart beating against my chest or the warmth of his skin in an embrace, intensified. I ached for his touch, but his defenses endured.

Despite the strength in my fingers, my knees weakened and buckled beneath me. I slid to the ground, completely immersed in despair. My hands shielded my eyes as the sobs multiplied. His intent to retreat left my fight futile. If he wanted to leave, nothing I could do would stop him.

What seemed like minutes may have only been seconds as my muffled cries carried above the torturous silence. Certain they masked his swift departure, my form continued to sink in the grass. Nothing—nothing mattered now.

A hand fell to my neck. Although light, his caress magnified. The stimulating touch carried the same electrifying intensity from years before. Fearing the cruelty of my imagination, I refused to peek. Its tingle blazed a trail around my neck and up to my chin. Stefan gently pulled my hands from my face as he knelt before me. Without releasing, his fingers stroked my skin lightly. Inches away, I absorbed every detail. Subtle lines appeared in both his forehead and at the edges of his eyes, the softness now visible enough to expose his vulnerability. His hair, although unkept, offered an appealing roughness that validated the fact that he was still breathtakingly handsome. As his thumb brushed my cheek to stop the tears, my lips parted in involuntary awe. After all these years, he left me breathless.

"I never meant to hurt you." The tenderness of his voice nearly incapacitated me.

My chest filled with a sweeping desire to weep. "Don't you know?" I choked, "Don't you know that your absence is my greatest pain?"

Stefan's countenance fell. His forehead pressed softly against mine. Every trace of skin or strand of hair that connected with me sent bursts of stimulus straight to my heart. My hand reached for his and drew it directly to my chest. The pulses speared us both.

"Stefan, I don't care what you've seen or done," I whispered, "*I need you.* I need you in my life. You have to know you're the only one I live for."

His arms glided past my shoulders and took me in a tight embrace, my disbelief melting with his touch. The rapid beat of his pulsing heart thumped in equal rhythm next to my own. *Stefan is holding me!* Fearing this moment would suddenly vanish, I reached beneath his arms and clenched the back of his jacket.

The butterflies continued to flutter fervently around us, but even their tickle couldn't budge me. Immortality in this position would have been a gift. My cheek next to his, I whispered, "Please, please don't leave me."

His silence frightened me. *What if this is goodbye? What if he's doing this only to disappear again?* "Stefan?"

His hold only tightened. When he finally released, my fingers clambered to hang on.

"Ella, I'm not the same person you fell in love with." Years of agony manifested in every line of his face.

"Don't!" My hand reached up and brushed his cheek, his forehead, and hair. "You are the only one I want to be with. Don't do this."

"Ella?"

My hand went to his lips. A burning filled my bosom to remove them and replace them with my own. Yet the fear that surfaced in his eyes held me still. "Please don't, Stefan. Please don't turn me away."

He buried his face in my neck, and although he remained quiet, moisture built on my skin. It was then that I realized the challenge ahead of us—*if* there was to be an us.

As the sun dipped below the trees, the night air grew cold, and the garden went dark. Stefan stood and reached for my hand, drawing me upward. He shifted to let go, but my grip scrambled and held fast. Inching my body closer to his with each step down the blackened path, I yearned for reassurance. With the distant lamplights casting very little light upon us, Stefan's other hand slipped easily around my waist, igniting a dormant charge, it's release effortless and free, as though my entire body levitated above ground.

I refused to pull my eyes away from him until we reached the fountain, where they gradually shifted towards the spot Thomas stood earlier with the short balding man I was tasked to identify. They were long gone. I knew they would be the moment I decided to leave.

As we departed from the fountain of fairytales, my original purpose for being here no longer mattered. I shuddered at the thought of almost not following my intuition. *What if I hadn't accepted this assignment? What if I had missed him?* The thread seemed thinner than ever before.

Under the shroud of night, we meandered towards my apartment without guidance. This confirmed my belief he'd been here before. All of those sightings I believed were imagined, weren't. Stefan kept one arm securely around me, and I clung to his other with all the courage I possessed. The silence between us rumbled louder than the noise on the street, our proximity incited an unprecedented sensation. *Is his skin really next to mine?* My mind struggled to trust its actuality, fearing I'd wake up and find his touch, his face, even his smell to be a dream.

We reached my door too soon. His arm released, but my grip intensified. "Please don't leave me."

He squeezed my waist and leaned in, his lips tickling my ear with his breath. "I promise to return tomorrow."

I sniffled, "You won't." My hands skimmed across his arms to his neck. The desire to pull him in consumed me. "You'll disappear." My whispers intertwined with a whimper. "I'll never see you again."

Stefan loosened my hands and centered them on his chest. Familiar curvatures distracted me. Even at forty-three, he proved strong. "Trust me," he whispered. His eyes met mine. "I just need to work through this."

Work through? His choice of words frightened me. It sounded like more of a task than a desire. *Did he stop loving me? Does he need to consider how he feels about me?* I pinched my eyes momentarily to stop the tears from fogging my sight.

When I opened them, they centered on his mouth as he spoke. "I will see you tomorrow." He squeezed my hands again and opened my door.

I reluctantly entered and cringed as he turned away. "Wait!" My hand flew to stop him, but distance remained. "Promise me again you'll be back tomorrow."

"I promise." Nothing in his eyes contradicted his words, though my own selfish doubts twisted my insides.

He vanished down the stairs before I ran to the window. I stared below until his form became visible. He glanced up, as if he knew I'd be there, his lip lifting in a half-smile for the first time today. My palm touched the window, desperately holding on to his every move, too afraid it was all invented. The stillness in his stance validated the truth before he faded into the darkness.

Did I make the mistake of letting him go? Instantly angry with myself, I paced the room. My hands shook while my mind reeled with regret. *What if he never returns?* Sitting by the window, each passing minute alone persecuted me until Mari returned.

"What happened?" She rushed to my side. My red, swollen eyes revealed my torment.

"I . . . I'm not sure," I stuttered.

She reached for me and led me towards the bed. "Talk to me." Her fingers tenderly soothed my hair.

Over the next few hours, I told her everything, beginning with the day I said goodbye to her—the tunnel, the shooting, and everything that separated me from Stefan. By the time the clock struck midnight, with nothing about my past overlooked, my head fell heavy in her lap.

Twenty-nine

JEALOUSY

The next morning, when I rolled over in bed, my mind grasped the significance of yesterday's events with an accelerated charge to my chest. Each scene unfolded, simultaneous to a brisk heartbeat. *Thu-dump*— the fairytale fountain. *Thu-dump*— the butterfly garden. *Thu-dump*—my confession to Mari.— *Thu-dump*—Stefan. *thu-dump, thu-dump, thu-dump.* My head leaned towards the melodic humming from the kitchen.

"Why so happy?" I mumbled. My head throbbed from the massive amounts of tears shed only hours ago. Piecing things together, I remembered Stefan's promise and shot out of bed. The cold windowpane, chilled from an early rain, should have stunned my warm skin, but I didn't care as I scanned the walkway. Nobody appeared. *Did I dream it?*

"Was it real?" I turned towards Mari who swept the kitchen floor with a wide grin I hadn't seen since Cade's last visit. "Did I really see Stefan?"

She stopped and set the broom against the counter. Meeting me at the window, she reached for my hands lovingly. "I believe so." Her countenance radiated.

"Why are you so cheery?" My eyes narrowed with curiosity.

Mari held her tongue for a brief moment, but her eyes glowed. "I thought you abandoned me." Her clasp on my hands tightened. "I thought you left me because you didn't want me anymore. When you told me what happened last night, it was life-changing."

"Why would you ever think that?" The very idea sent heartbreaking pangs through my chest.

"Because all those years I didn't see you, I thought it was because of me."

"Oh, Mari." My spirit melted with an urgency to explain. "I'm so sorry you felt that way. It isn't true. I couldn't take you with me. To risk your life would have been unforgiveable, especially after what happened." One arm slipped around her shoulders and pulled her in for a hug. "Then Stefan . . . his rejection paralyzed me. I didn't believe I deserved to live, much less care for anyone else."

"I had no idea you'd been through so much. I understand now."

"I never told anyone the whole story, but now you know everything about my past."

Mari beamed. "And it's made all the difference to me." She kissed me on the cheek. "I'm so glad we're together now."

"Me too." As we released, my body pulled to the window once more, a few passers-by but no Stefan. *What if he only said he would come but never really meant it?*

"Ella, now that we're being honest with each other . . ." Mari went to the kitchen to heat a kettle of water.

"Yes . . ." Although I knew there was one very big secret I kept concealed, my job details could never be disclosed to her.

"I have a confession to make." Mari turned around and lowered her head. She appeared legitimately concerned about my response.

"Okay," I encouraged. *What will sweet Mari have to confess that could upset me?*

She fumbled with the hem of her blouse as she spoke. "I . . . I'm actually not sure how to say this."

"Just spit it out." I braced for bad news.

"Okay." She stepped forward, only a metre away. "It was Stefan who brought me to you."

Heat converged on my cheeks, her words floating above me without sinking in. "What?" Unsure if they kindled anger or betrayal, I tried to wrap my head around what she said. "I don't understand." My stare penetrated forcefully, but she still toyed with her hem. "Mari?" She finally glanced up. "Explain."

"Stefan visited me several times in the orphanage, the first being about nine years ago, in 1978. I barely knew him." She took a long breath and continued, "He explained who he was, and though I faintly remembered him the day we met, I recalled the stories you told me. Often times he paid for some new clothes and school supplies. He even bought me a sketchbook and paints." She finally found her confidence. "Ella, he was kind to me at a very lonely time in my life. He told me you were sick and assured me you would visit as soon as you were better. I believed him."

"Oh." Blood rushed to my head and pulsated in tiny spasms. My hand wiped my bangs aside and rubbed my forehead for relief. *Stefan cared for her when I couldn't. Why did I let it go that far?*

She went on. "He showed up a week before I got here. He told me you were in the hospital and that you needed me." She stole a quick breath "Stefan's timing was miraculous. The orphanage had just notified me of the need for my bed. He saved me . . . he saved us both." The last sentence rose barely above a whisper.

I slumped to Mama's chair, overwhelmed from the information, much like I imagined Mari felt the night before, when a decade of wrongs reached confession.

Mari came and knelt before me. "Please don't be upset with me . . . or Stefan," she begged.

Though anger reeled wildly as a possibility, countless questions mounted. *How did he know I was sick? How did he know about the hospital?*

"I'm more confused than upset. I don't know how he knew all this. We haven't spoken since the shooting."

She patted my hands tenderly. "He told me he watched over you, and he would me as well."

Watched over me? My pulse accelerated. *When did his observations turn to action?* My mouth dropped with instant realization. *It was he who took me to the hospital and paid my rent. Then brought Mari to me.*

"Are you disappointed?" Her anxious eyes studied me carefully. I hadn't spoken, unsure of what to say.

The kettle whistled, and she quickly jumped up to retrieve it. Numbness spread from my limbs to my torso, affecting my breathing, as well. *How long had he been watching? How many times did he see me walk home so inebriated it took a dozen attempts just to unlock my door?*

Mari handed me a warm mug of chamomile tea. The heat seeped into both hands as I contemplated without drinking *How many times did he intervene when I stumbled upon something dangerous? Why didn't he show himself? Could it have been him at the concert?*

"Please tell me you're not angry." She sat back down in front of me. I'd forgotten that my answer never came the first time she asked.

"No, not at all." My hand wiped my forehead. "I'm embarrassed. I failed you. I deserted you when you needed me most, and if it weren't for Stefan you would . . . I don't know, but it could've been bad."

She placed both hands on my knees. "I didn't know you'd been through such difficulty. I'm glad you shared it with me last night, or I still wouldn't know. I don't blame you for pulling away. You were in pain."

"What did Stefan say about me?" She may have already told me, but I needed to hear it again.

"He said you were struggling, that you were sick and needed help." She let go of me and reached for her tea. Her next words came slowly. "When he came the last time with your address, he seemed sad, more than I'd ever seen before."

I tried to absorb all this. It just didn't make sense. Why care so much from afar? "I wonder why he kept his involvement hidden. If Stefan felt something for me, even the slightest bit of protection, why couldn't he face me?" The questions developed slowly in my mind yet exploded out loud.

Mari answered, although she seemed to know the question wasn't directed to her. "There seems to be a lot of pain going around," —she took a sip— "a lot of confusion and maybe the need for a lot of forgiveness." There was much wisdom in her words, more than I understood at this moment.

When the knock finally came, my nerves rattled on cue. *What if it isn't him?*

My chest caving slightly, I reached for the door. The inhale that followed soothed my apprehension. The door cracked open, and I wanted to pinch myself. *Stefan! Here and real! He fulfilled his promise to return.* My stare lasted longer than expected. He shifted his weight and waited for an invitation.

I shook my head to enter reality again. A thin layer of perspiration bubbled on my upper lip. I motioned for him to enter, my eyes never leaving him. The long blond strands of our early years, touched with a hint of grey, fell gently against his freshly-shaven jaw. No more beard, only a trimmed mustache remained. Long or short, facial hair or not, nothing mattered except that he stood before me. With the absence of his hat, his eyes no longer remained hidden. They peered cautiously my direction as he stepped past me and into the apartment. His black button-down shirt and light-colored slacks were neatly pressed. He appeared as if he stepped directly out of my dreams.

Not knowing what to expect or if he really would return, I'd been dressed up since breakfast. Although I wore denim jeans more often now, I craved this opportunity to wear a dress. My pleated blue skirt

221

went barely above my knees, accented with a cream-colored blouse and cardigan. My hair, shorter than when we dated so long ago, spiked outward at the nape of my neck, and my long bangs were held back with a barrette, but he didn't seem to notice the length of my hair or the color of my skirt.

Stefan paused barely inside the door and smiled. "Well, hello, Miss Mari." She ran to him and embraced him warmly. Their tender interchange showed a bond never witnessed before. I watched with captivation as a small sting arose, wondering why he couldn't come to me that way.

Mari kissed him on the cheek before she reached for her jacket.

"I must go." She giggled. "But I told her our plan. You know . . . how this all came about. I hope you don't mind."

He glanced at my countenance for confirmation, as if he searched for the same anger she did. "No, I don't mind."

"Well, I have to run. Work begins in fifteen minutes. Good to see you, Stefan. Really good to see you." She hugged him again and walked out.

"Not much has changed." I pointed around the room. "I don't really have a place to sit or visit. We've been searching for a table and chairs." Our little flat still only held Mama's chair and the bed Mari and I shared.

"Do you want to take a walk?" Stefan's calm left with Mari. He was much more unsettled with me than I remembered, at least since before the shooting.

"Yes, that's a good idea. Let's walk."

Upon reaching the sidewalk, he glanced around. Finally, he pointed right, and we fell into a slow saunter. After a few miserable minutes, I let my hand fall to my side, hoping Stefan would reach for it. Nothing . . . not even a muscle twitch my direction. We were two "strangers" walking the same direction down the same sidewalk, sharing the same air. Frustrated, I stopped. *Is it unrealistic to believe we can fall back into a familiar place, or am I desiring the impossible?*

"Stefan," —my halt forced him my direction— "I have so many questions, I don't know where to begin. Some I'm afraid to ask." Obscured by angst, my words tangled.

Silent for an uncomfortable minute, he answered. "I know." His fingers grazed my arm, the tingle sending a current through my skin. "Please be patient with me. So much has happened since that morning I left you. I'm not sure it can all be shared at once. Even so, you may not understand my reasons."

My lips pulled into a thin line, fighting to keep my emotion contained. Little did I know *that* particular goodbye would span decades. I nodded, although patience challenged me.

"I will, however, promise to be honest." His fingers slid from my arm to my hand. When his fingers reached my own and interlocked, a subtle sigh of relief escaped my lips. "But Ella, please understand. If I can't talk about something, I just can't."

My mind instantly converged on Vietnam and Herr Weitzner's reaction to my questions—him being a prisoner and seeing his comrades die. The next breath I took was forcibly quiet. We continued down the street in complete silence again.

I mustered the courage to speak. "It's possible you have questions about me, as well." Although I wondered if this was trivial since learning about his familiarity with my actions. How much of my spiral did he witness from the shadows? I tried not to dwell on the possibility that he observed my senseless behavior often. As my head tilted downward in shame, he jockeyed to keep my eyes locked on his and then smiled halfway. "There's plenty of time to figure it all out."

"What if you disappear again?" The desperation in my voice was muttered so lightly its recognition was barely heard, yet he responded clearly.

"I'm not going anywhere." My heart tapped in double time, but I remained still as he repeated himself. "Ella, I'm not going anywhere."

I squeezed his hand, wishing to freeze this moment forever.

Crossing the street, I shifted to a lighter subject. "Do you see your family?"

"Yes, only recently—six months ago."

"Katharina?"

"Yes. Especially after Edmund— uh," He caught himself.

"Saved me," I whispered.

He nodded. "I felt obligated to thank him years ago, but didn't know how."

"Obligated?" Unsure of the image that word rendered, I added. "That sounds like more of a chore." I couldn't stop the irritation in my expression, and he couldn't seem to stop the exasperation in his voice.

"No," he backtracked quickly. "That's not what I meant."

"Stefan, why do you feel so responsible for me?" I undoubtedly launched into a tough question too early. My mind wrestled my body with an innate need to obtain answers.

His jaw grew rigid. His stance wavered.

"I don't understand why you felt the need to rescue me but wouldn't talk to me. Hiding, sneaking around . . . avoiding me." My voice elevated to a higher octave.

He stared forward, meeting nothing but a brick wall. We wandered aimlessly into an alleyway.

"Why? Why did you take me to the hospital, pay my rent, and bring Mari to fix me? Why, after staying away for so long?" My voice continued to range from high to low, the tone sliding easily into distress. "Why?"

No longer gentle, his own voice carried above us and filled the space with tension. "Why do you have to know these things now!" He rubbed his head with his free hand.

"I just do!" I matched his shout.

Letting go of my hand, Stefan paced with growing agitation. His arm muscles expanded as he tightened his fists and pressed them against his forehead. "Th-this is—"

I cut him off, "Please, tell me why."

His hands flung down with one finger spearing his own chest. "It's because of me that you drank!" His cry came with deep lines around his eyes. When he moved closer, I could see his cheeks had turned ruddy. "It was all my fault!" Tears filled the bottom half of his eyes.

My lips parted with an unsettling gasp. Gripping the edge of my sweater, my own fists held tight. Stefan sensed my imbalance and quickly reached for me. He led me to the wall where my knees buckled, and I slipped to the ground. Landing on paper and rubbish barely phased me. The only thing on my mind was Stefan's confession. *He feels responsible for my stupid, selfish decisions!* This man who'd been through hell and back because of *me* continued to claim accountability.

When he sat down next to me, I grappled for the right words. "Stefan, I . . ." Extreme heaviness surged through my chest. "Yes, I drank . . . a lot."

His head lowered. The dense air seemed to smother me until I forced an explanation out. "I wanted to take away the pain of loneliness, the pain of memories, the pain of you . . ." He avoided my eyes. "but" —my fingers lifted his chin my direction— "it was entirely my fault, not yours. I'm the one who put the glass to my lips, not you."

He reached for my hand again, now cold. The warmth vanished with the simplicity of our former life. I suddenly realized that nothing would be sorted out quickly. So many misunderstandings, so much guilt, blame, and confusion. "This isn't going to be easy is it?" Filled with trepidation, I breathed a substantial sigh.

His thumb rubbed the back of my hand until our eyes finally collided. He nodded his head in agreement and added. "It will be worth it, though."

Every syllable of that sentence sparked hope, but I hungered for the truth.

He helped me to my feet, and we headed back towards my flat. The silent strain was evidence our initial time together required gradual strides. When we reached the steps, I wanted to grab him and hug him the way Mari did earlier—the way I used to wrap my arms around his neck and pull him so close the scent off his skin became part of me. A twinge of jealousy gnawed at me with the reminder I no longer retained the right.

"Where do we go from here?" Discouragement filled my words.

"Where do you want it to go?" he queried, apprehension evident in his eyes.

I thought about his question. Never before had there been any doubt of what I wanted. I yearned for our past, but was it even attainable anymore? Had we changed so significantly that we could never have that again? Would it be better to leave it buried? My mind spun with confusion, but truth prevailed. "I want you in my life. It's the only thing I have ever wanted."

Stefan's smile lifted on one side. He brushed his bangs aside, and the blue in his eyes glistened.

"Just be patient with me, Ella Kühn." He raised my hand to his lips, the heat from his breath warming my skin the moment he pressed. A tickle surfaced when he spoke. "Please?"

With a conflicting goodbye, I stepped inside and naturally walked to the window. Stefan paused below. My heart thumped at the sight of him. *Stefan is alive and real!* These words repeated over and over while actuality wrestled my underlying fears. I studied him carefully. His wary stance resembled a guard dog, cautious and careful.

I tried to make sense of it all: his arrival, his protectiveness—his reservation. My hand shot to my forehead with discouragement. In the confusion of seeing him again, between the questions and misunderstandings, I forgot to talk to him about Darek and the threats. Even though I'd given Darek reason to drop it in the past, if Stefan showed up again and was somehow reported, it would only raise suspicion. Jurek and I rarely crossed paths, but when we did, his hatred for me was more than evident. He only needed the okay, and his vengeance would be with Darek's blessing.

I fumbled for the clasp on the window. My fingers opened it a thousand times, but right now, when I needed them to in a moment's notice, they failed. By the time I pushed the window open, Stefan had disappeared down the street. Daunted, I weighed the idea of chasing after him but couldn't get my legs to budge. Our goodbye had been so ordinary, nothing reminiscent of the past—the nights I forced my fingers to unlock or my lips to release and draw breath. That same driving desire and craving I experienced for years remained suppressed. Would it ever come back? I dreamt of this moment for so long, and now that it was here, I could barely identify the emotion. It was as foreign to me as freedom had been for over twenty-six years.

That night, when Mari came home, she found me unmoved at the windowsill, my legs pulled up to my chest and my knees wet from a half day's worth of tears. She immediately appeared at my side, but once again, I fought the darkness that crept over me in the guise of envy. Mari now shared the affection I thought was exclusively mine. Stefan's countenance instantly lightened in her presence, while my existence burdened him. She held me and the cries multiplied. I could never tell her the source of my pain. Jealousy must remain deeply buried.

Thirty

WHY?

The next day brought as much uncertainty as the previous. An unexplained encumbrance hung around my neck and dampened my mood all morning. Mari departed for work long before I shuffled to the kitchen for tea and biscuits. Staring at the can of wafers, my appetite waned. With my mug in hand, a stupor immobilized me. Unsure of what to do next, I paced irritably from the kitchen to the bathroom to the bed. A triangle shape could have easily worn into the floor. *Should I get ready? Is Stefan coming? Did our conversation yesterday scare him off?*

Memories of another time I waited for him to arrive flooded my thoughts. Stefan's last day of leave and he'd been at his mother's for brunch. Agonizing ticks of my antiquated clock pulsated over and over as I counted objects and people outside the window. Though I didn't stare longingly out my window this time, the unknown nearly drove me mad. After two hours, nothing led me to believe I'd find answers by remaining in the flat. I dressed quickly and departed without a clue as to where I headed.

In my wanderings, I meandered north toward *Do Nothing*. Jörg was always full of advice and necessary comfort. Sauntering slowly down Invaliden, I reached the front of his bar. Since the hospital, I'd been here a half dozen times, and each instance my body craved a drink. Similar to a cat entering a room filled with mice, temptation heightened the very moment my nose filled with the acrid scent of liquor. I would have to resist. Stretching for the knob, a hand quickly shot over mine, preventing me from opening. My eyes flashed to its owner.

"Stefan!"

"Don't, Ella. Please."

"Don't what?" A fire quickly rose from the pit of my stomach through my entire body, awakening a harshness in my voice.

"Don't go in."

"Why are you following me?" Every carefully concealed emotion cracked. I reached for him and, with a fistful of shirt, led him away from the door. Stefan complied under the coarseness of my touch. "Why?" My demand necessitated answers. I refused to mask the reality of my frustration.

"I . . . I just . . ." —he ran both hands through his hair, forcing my fingers to release his clothes, and attempted to turn away— "It . . . its habit. I'm sorry."

I gripped his arm, bringing him back towards me. "Stefan!" His jaw grew rigged. "Stefan, look at me!" My cries were knotted between rage and fear. His eyes made their way from the ground, and when they finally locked, the gaze terrified me. The desire surfaced to reach for him and hold him until all of the harrowing past melted away, but he was a stranger to me—a shell of the man I loved.

Irregular breaths drew air quickly to my lungs. I scrambled for the nearby bench and lowered my head between my knees, grasping my head and pressing as quiet sobs increased. "If we can't be together, if you can't walk with me on the street or talk, it's never going to be okay." My voice professed assurance but inside, my soul crumbled. *What if he agrees? What if we will never work?* My mind begged for him to disagree, not realizing I held my breath until he spoke.

"We can." The weight of his body bumped next to me. One arm slid across my back to my opposite shoulder, the touch skimming softly. "It's tough right now." The other hand slid to my chin and gently drew it his direction. His thumb brushed my tears as our eyes met once more. "I see you, Ella, and the desire to have you is unquestionable." He leaned forward. "I want to forget about everything terrible in the past and be with you." The blue in his eyes darkened. "And then I remember the reasons we're apart and what I did to you."

My hand pressed against my chest with an unyielding strain on my heart. Impenetrable obstacles hung in the balance, making the mere centimetres between us multiply into kilometres.

"I'm sorry." My body twisted toward him. His muscles fixed as if chains bound and held him prisoner. Caressing his frigid fingers, I brought them from my cheek to my lips for added warmth. "I believed it was my fault."

"No, it's not. I *want* to be around people, and live a normal life again—" he bit his bottom lip and sighed "—but mostly I want to be with you."

I kissed his palm, drawing in the scent of nature on his skin. "Then walk next to me, Stefan. Don't *follow* me."

His stare, sharpened by the sun's reflection, captured me. "These habits will take time to break, but please" —his voice cracked— "please don't go into a bar. I can't watch you go down that path again."

A grin broke through before I could prevent it. The lowering of his chin and eyes spurned a quick response. "Oh no, this isn't one of those places. This is different."

His eyebrows curved skeptically.

"No, it is a bar, but it's my friend Jörg's place." My hand squeezed his with assurance, the softness of our touch calmed me. "He's helped me through some difficult times." I paused for a brief second. "I would love for you to meet him. Actually, he'll be quite surprised to find out the mysterious Stefan is real and not a figment of my imagination."

"Isn't it hard to be around all the alcohol?"

"Yeah. Truthfully, it's really hard. Jörg helps me. He knows I'm recovering."

"But why do you do it?"

I thought about his question. *Why would an alcoholic go to a place filled with alcohol?*

"I guess seeking the advice and friendship is worth the risk, despite the temptation. Jörg has been a true friend over the years, and maybe I want to prove I'm not weak. That I can overcome the lure, and it won't continue to torment me."

With those words, I released my grip and held his stare. "If you want to, I would love for you to join me . . . by my side." My lips curved softly.

Stefan reached for my hand and led me back to the door but hesitated. "Please understand, the time will come when I can meet your friends, but it isn't today." If his countenance hadn't radiated sincerity, I would've felt more disappointed. He reached for the handle and continued, "I'll be here waiting for you. I promise." Then he cracked open the door.

My smile grew wide when I stepped inside and found Jörg behind the bar.

"Hello, Ella, my dear."

"Guten morgen, Jörg." Within seconds a glass of water appeared in front of me.

"How is my delightful friend doing today?"

"You might not believe me if I told you."

He stopped working and appeared at my side. After sharing the events of the last few days, Jörg—as always—had many wise words to say.

"Is he worth waiting for?" Without a doubt, I nodded fervently. "Then give him the time he needs. If he has assured you he is here to stay, then you must convey a similar belief to him. Take one step . . . one moment at a time."

With a parting hug, I walked towards the door. The insecurity in me wondered if Stefan would be there an hour later, waiting outside as promised. As I stood at the exit, I contemplated Jörg's wise words, *take one step, one moment at a time.* If we truly were meant to be together forever, there was no rush to force everything to fall into place today. *He* is *worth the wait.* Of that I was certain.

I waved one last goodbye and stepped into the sunshine. On the bench I met Jörg those many years ago, my desire—my future—sat patiently waiting for me. He stood to his feet, and I joined him.

"Stefan." My countenance, cleansed with a peace that had been misplaced for ages, signaled a change.

"Are you well?" He reached for both my hands and waited.

"Yes. I'm good.". Reassurance, in the form of patience, filled my soul. Stefan needed time, and with Jörg's advice fresh on my mind, I kept my response simple.

With fortitude evident in his reaction, he embraced me. His cheek nudged deep into the nape of my neck, his breath warming my skin as he spoke. "You're more than good. You're everything."

The walk home had a renewed ambiance. Not back to the way things were, but a refreshing sense of possibility that lacked earlier. Conversation came easier.

"What was it like seeing Katharina after all this time?" My questions were deliberately lightened. "I can only imagine her joy when she laid eyes on you the first time." I grinned. "And you're an uncle too!"

He chuckled. "Yes, I have a nephew and a niece. Katharina is an angel; she never ceases to amaze me."

I nodded in agreement. "How is she managing . . . with the mortuary?"

"Unlike me, she never questioned her role. She stepped in and picked up where father left off."

"She's on her own? Your father doesn't help?"

"No, he is . . . um." Stefan's words did not come easily.

"Aged?"

"Yes, he's slowed down considerably and unable to assist her."

"And the death of your mother? Did you know?"

"Yes, I knew." His forehead creased. "I've made my peace with her in the cemetery. I wish I'd seen her before she passed." The deep lines near his eyes revealed his personal torment. Though I would never find anything kind to say about that woman, she was Stefan's mother, and he cared for her.

"Where are you living?"

"I have a flat in Pankow, not far from the house."

Recalling the conversation with Darek and Jurek over Stefan's photograph, Jurek knew the neighborhood. Did he find the flat, as well? I avoided the idea of turning our conversation serious.

"Will you go back home?"

"I'm not sure. A lot has happened at once. I need to think things through. With Edmund busy at the hospital, it seems a logical choice, but I'm not sure I'm ready yet."

"Katharina has a lot to handle on her own, especially as a mother."

"I've hired someone to help."

I reached for a mint branch from a nearby bush and pressed the fragile purple petals to my nose. The zesty scent filled my nostrils and created a charming image. "Do you paint?"

Stefan watched me with a grin. "Not really. There are times I've sketched, to remember the happier things in my life but not much more. I saw you sketch, though; you must be painting again."

"Me?" A nervous pang swirled in my chest; my current job came to mind. Fairly sure Stefan wouldn't be too excited with my occupation, I bit my inner cheek and waited.

"Yes, several months after Mari arrived, I followed you to the station. I wasn't sure what you were drawing, especially since several trains came and went, but you were hard at work."

I remembered the assignment, the first one given after my skills were evaluated at the concert. Darek sent me to sketch several Stasi members in transit at the station closest to their headquarters. "Where were you? How did you see me?"

"I sat on the platform behind you and again at the Spree across from the Reichstag a week later, but it wasn't until you sketched a Priest that I realized you weren't painting for fun. You were working. Then I followed you to the pub. That's where you go for instructions, don't you?"

My teeth clenched. Though the discussion needed to happen, an uncomfortable pressure rose from the pit of my stomach. "It's complicated."

"I don't fault you, Ella. Only I don't think you understand how dangerous your role is."

I comprehend it better than he thinks I do. "Were you the one who warned me at the last concert?"

His eyes wandered.

"In the confession stall? Was it you who told me to leave?"

He nodded.

My cheeks heated. I honestly believed I had it all under control, nevertheless, my inexperience exposed a lack of common sense. Despite my embarrassment, I owed him my gratitude. "Thank you," I whispered, the words insignificant considering what he possibly prevented from happening.

A street away from my flat, I pointed to a nearby bench, and we sat. With much to say, I delayed the end of our short visit. Regardless of longing to be with him every moment from here on out, realistically, we needed to proceed slowly. Reconstructing a lifetime together would be comparable to restoring a shattered vase . . . requiring patience and finesse.

Stefan held my hand. Moisture built easily between us. Now with some truth about my job exposed, he opened the door for further discussion, though difficult to share.

"About my job, Stefan." Twinges pinched my chest, fearing the course of this conversation. "I need you to not follow me." My eyes met his with trepidation.

"Katharina told me that. Why?"

"You've already been linked to me. They've seen your face; they have photos of you and—"

"—And what?" The rise in his tone, lowered mine. His hand released mine as his fingers slipped to his knees and gripped until his knuckles turned white.

My throat constricted. "I can't lose you, Stefan."

"So, you're aware of what they do." His hands curled into fists.

"I have assumptions."

"And you stay involved?"

"It's not that easy. I have no place to go." My voice grew defensive. "Recovering and sick, I needed work. They were the only ones who offered me employment."

"But now you're well. You need to get away from them. It's treacherous and unpredictable, but you already know that. It's why you change your appearance and alter your routes."

"You know?"

Stefan stood and ran his fingers through his hair like he used to when frustrated "Many opposition groups have been targeted by the Stasi. Their informers have infiltrated several already."

"How do you know all this?"

He ignored my question and turned his back on me. "In fact, if *I* know what you do, they're probably aware of it too. It's not safe."

I gazed at my hands twisted together in my lap and muttered, "I think they are." It was the first time I said those words out loud to someone other than Darek.

Stefan whirled towards me. I peeked up to see the color drain from his cheeks. "You can't go back! Promise me you won't go back!"

My sight shifted to the nearby tree and followed the vine from its roots to the highest branch. Tears simmered on my bottom lashes, but I hoped they would dissipate before Stefan saw them fall. "I know, but it's hard."

"Why?" he pushed.

"I can't simply stop without a reason. I need to explain myself."

"So, you are planning on leaving soon?" He sat down next to me.

"Yes, I think so."

"Think so?"

"Well I . . . I don't know. I'm not sure of anything anymore. Mari's job can't cover our expenses. It's only enough to pay the rent. I've saved some, but Stefan what if . . . what if . . ."

"What if what?"

I shook my head.

"What if we don't work out?" Stefan finished my sentence although his words were more devastating than mine.

"I was going to say . . . what if nobody hires me." My heart physically ached. *Even with my resolve to make things right with Stefan, did he think we might not make it?* An irresistible yearning to run and hide surfaced.

He grabbed my hands again, and the force of his grasp brought me close enough to see the wrinkle between his brows deepen. "Ella, I have to know you're safe. You can't imagine how hard it was to see you vulnerable and broken all those years."

The depth of those provoking words lurked in the crevices of my mind. *He watched me for years.* "Why?" my voice remained eerily calm, while the repetition of this inquiry ascended, unresolved. "Stefan, why did you watch me hurt myself and not intervene?"

His jaw set firm, and the way his lashes brushed his bottom ones a dozen times relayed an anxiousness I was not accustomed to. "I couldn't," he whispered. When his hold released, he took part of me with him. "I didn't feel I deserved to be with you again, not even

236

speak to you. I hurt you . . . For heaven's sake, El. I shot you! Why would you *ever* want to see me?"

"You shot me to save my life! I know that. *You* know that! The soldier would have killed me. His rifle was aimed only a half metre from my chest. He already reached for the trigger."

"Why were you leaving?" he asked, low and muffled. Replaying the words in my head, a quick interpretation of his question dawned on me. We went from simple dialogue to the deepest root of our questions.

"Stefan," —tears dipped over the edges of my lashes— "I thought you didn't want me anymore." Despite the security his presence provided, it wasn't enough. I clasped onto his wrists. "When I didn't hear from you again, no letters, no contact, I thought you no longer wanted me in your life. I thought you changed your mind and no longer loved me."

He stood up quickly, his pacing burst with agitation.

"See, Ella. Verdammit!" His fists balled up at his sides then slammed hard against the post. I wobbled at his explosion. "I hurt you! What are we trying to do here? This is too hard."

I panicked; I was losing him. We were pushing too hard.

"Were you going to Anton?" The question rolled out without him glancing my direction.

That wasn't my intention, though I struggled to find words after his abrupt reaction. I knew Stefan worried about my relationship with Anton, but I thought we'd moved past this.

"Were you?" he repeated, his restless stance indicating a desire to leave.

"No," I muttered, confused. "Why would you think that?" I jumped to my feet and closed the gap. The ire in my words matched his expression. "I told you. I've said it a hundred times. It was always *you*! I tried leaving because there was nothing for me here."

"What about Hans?" he shot back.

It was inevitable Hans would come up at some point, I simply didn't realize it would be this soon. Stefan's legs stood strong, but his torso shook while he waited for my answer. I suspected each day would be difficult, but this conversation teetered towards unbearable. There was nothing calm about the silence that drifted between us. The dense space resembled more of an ambiguous quiet prior to upheaval than a resulting comfort. Each of us shouldered wounds at varying stages—some hardened over time, turning to scars; others attempted to heal; and clearly, wounds that remained open and raw. Those were the ones that make or break our survival. I watched this man, who'd become everything to me over the years, struggle with his own demons and still attempt to bear mine. This moment suddenly became a critical turning point, one direction or the other.

"Stefan—" Moving in front of him, I placed my hands gently around his wrists. His eyes averted my sight. "— please look at me." I lifted one palm to his jaw and cupped the sculpted curves with all the tenderness I had. "This is going to be difficult, much harder than ever imagined, but you have to believe me when I say, I did *not* love Hans. In fact, I'm ashamed to say it, but I used him. My goal was to gain knowledge about the border patrol, about the changes *you* made . . . all for our escape." My thumb glided across the new stubble on his chin. "I'm not going to lie to you, Stefan. It felt good to be wanted again, to be held." His muscles remained tense under my touch. "But the only person I truly wanted to be held by was you—only you."

His tempest-blue eyes diminished to a calmer shade, but his suffering remained. We'd reached our limit for one day. Despite my desire to cling with every fiber of my being and soul, I understood now more than ever that living a lifetime apart, it would take a lifetime to learn about each other again. My needs were no longer the priority.

"Let's walk back," I suggested softly. I slid my other hand from his wrist to his fingers, which he willingly accepted.

When we reached my door, I didn't invite him up. He appeared spent. Fine lines on his forehead and above his nose exaggerated with thought. If I could see his mind, I knew it would be spinning. I feared that every moment together could be our last. Although my pleadings

238

over avoiding Darek were expressed without question, one more difficult thing needed to be said.

"Stefan?" His eyes cast downward, I nudged him for his full attention. "Ralf is searching for you."

His eyes, although visibly drained, narrowed with skepticism. "What do you know of Ralf?"

"I know he followed me, up until a year ago. I believed he worked for Stasi. Truthfully, I still don't know."

"You've seen him?" His interest piqued.

"Yes. Long black hair, thick coat." I wondered if it would help if I grabbed my sketchbook and attempted to recreate his image. "He went to the mortuary asking for you. Katharina inadvertently told him about us. I don't understand why he believed you would be with me, but he followed me."

Although nothing about Stefan's stance changed, his eyes steered far away.

"I'm telling you because I don't know if he means you harm."

He remained quiet.

"Did you ever see him? When you followed me all those times? At the Spree or the concert, the one where you warned me. He was there."

His lips pulled into a thin line, and my gut told me he was holding back.

"Stefan? I'm worried he's angry with you."

His lips relaxed. "You don't need to worry about Ralf."

"I fear *anything* that may take you away from me again."

He leaned in and kissed my cheek, much like a father would a daughter. I wrestled more tears from reaching the surface. "Promise me you'll come back tomorrow." Everything in my body halted, awaiting his answer. More than anything I wished we could fall hopelessly into each other's arms, forget the agony of our separation, and move on, but it was unrealistic. As much as I wanted to be with him, we'd changed—as if we were practically strangers now.

My palm went to his cheek once more. His head leaned into my hand, his bangs falling loosely and hiding his eyes. What shade of blue were they? *Is he happy? Scared? Angry?*

"Please, Stefan, can I see you tomorrow?"

He nodded and placed his hand over mine, pulling it to his chest. His heart beat rapidly. I longed for his arms, his embrace, his warmth, but I needed him to offer it.

"I'll see you tomorrow," he said and walked away.

Why am I so foolish? I chided all the way up to my apartment. *Am I incapable of being patient or understanding? Stefan is injured . . . the wounds right in front of me. His spirit, his eyes, his actions. Why was I determined to escape, to leave? Couldn't I have waited? What if we can't heal from the past? What if he doesn't believe me? What if he doesn't trust me now or ever?*

After all these years, could we be at the end of our story?

Thirty-one

"TEAR DOWN THIS WALL"

12 June 1987

"Mr. Gorbachev, open this gate! Mr. Gorbachev, tear down this wall!" The West Berlin crowd at Brandenburg Tor roared their approval. Had I been any closer, I might've heard the words from the American President in person.

I entered the pub a few minutes earlier where a small crowd gathered around the television.

"*An den Präsidenten Reagan!*" A tall thin man holding a stein nearly twice his body weight ignited a boisterous cheer. There had been a lot of chatter in the last week about the politician's second visit to the West.

"*Nach Amerika!*" Another man hollered, but it was the third man's words that caused the greatest commotion.

His gray hair matched his speckled beard and when he spoke of a united Germany, his other hand wiped moisture from his eyes. *"Nach Deutschland ein vereinigtes, Deutschland!"*

The group roared. I watched the screen with curiosity as President Reagan's speech was translated into our language. His confident, strong, and persistent demands to the Soviet leader, Mikhail Gorbachev, showed concern and compassion for a people not of his own and were exactly what we lacked in our own government. It was an inspiring twist.

Two full weeks passed since I spoke to Darek. Stefan came every morning as promised, and every afternoon we said goodbye like acquaintances. As difficult as it proved to be, finding our place took precedence. Each day we tried again, our questions deliberately light and marginal, deployed with caution. Nothing more was mentioned about the escape attempt, the shooting, Anton, or Hans. Casual and considerate, we spoke mostly of family, food, and the weather.

The President's speech concluded to another aggressive applause and a round of pats on the back. I scanned the group for Darek but didn't find him. Certain by now he questioned my safety, loyalty—or both, I packed an *apfelkuchen* in a paper sack as consolation, hoping the apple tart might soften the blow.

"Well, look who decided to finally show up." Nikolaus's scoff materialized from behind. Despite my individual contributions to the cause, he continued to harass.

"Is Darek here?" I rose above his petty taunts.

"No, you just missed him. He's been quite occupied lately, since he's covering another's workload. Someone got lazy."

Not today. I'm hardly in the mood. "I've been busy."

"With what? You barely work!"

"Verdammit, Nikolaus! I work harder than you ever have or ever pretend to! Tell me where he is."

His jaw tightened, and he slapped a paper on the bar. "He said if you ever showed up, to send you to this address, although I can't understand why he tolerates you."

242

I snatched the paper from under his palm and stomped out. Reaching the walk briskly, I grunted in frustration. *Why do I let him get under my skin? He's merely a kid, an ignorant child.* I peered at the paper. The address led me back to a vaguely familiar location in Mitte.

I told Stefan I owed Darek a direct explanation. He deserved my honesty since his employment helped prevent our destitution. Although Stefan tried to convince me multiple times in the last week that he should be with me when we met, I refused. I didn't want Darek, Nikolaus, or Jurek to see him, follow him, or know anything more about him. The risk was too great. With Stefan back in my life—even if it was only part of him—I'd do anything to protect him.

Zionskirche, the Zion Church. Its columned, brick façade stood daunting and empowering. From my approach on the south embankment, its crowning steeple sloped upward past the trees and appeared to puncture heaven. Previously when passed, I never went in. The arched entrance shrouded hefty doors that brimmed with intimidation. *Why here?* Darek didn't come across as a spiritual man. He used churches for the concerts, but I believed its purpose fell solely on safety. Maybe protection was his intent here as well.

Met by the large congregation room, like an ant in a tomb, I sensed its conflicting force. Elongated windows, carved archways, and an exquisite balcony peered down on a cross, larger than my body. I fidgeted nervously.

"Frau?"

I whipped around and found myself standing in front of a priest. Draped in a plain, black frock with a white collar, his dress was far from the elaborate costumes I'd envisioned. When he bowed my direction in simple acknowledgement, he radiated a peace I hungered for.

"Wie kann ich Ihnen behilflich sein?" The cleric kindly offered his help.

"I'm here for Darek Mayer. He sent for me."

He nodded and disappeared through one of the side arches. I waited. There was a time I sought solace in a house of God, but now, conflicting emotions stirred.

"Well, Annika, I'm glad to see you're well and without harm." Darek appeared under the arch. I fiddled with the zipper on my jacket.

"Yes. Yes, I am."

"Did you find it difficult to notify me of your absence? Your delay?" Though very few years separated our ages, he scrutinized me similar to a disappointed Nurse Gitta when I was a child in the Waisenhaus.

"I'm sorry, Darek. I don't have any excuse. A close friend needed me, and I was . . . I became sidetracked." I recalled the paper sack stuffed in my jacket pocket and handed him the pastry.

Though he accepted the bag, his stare never wavered. "Are you done?"

"Done?" I choked. "With the person?"

"Or the cause?" he added.

I shifted weight to my other foot. "The job."

"Why?"

"I'm not certain. I feel I'm needed elsewhere."

"Women for Peace?"

"No, no other opposition groups."

"What could be more important than freedom?"

I let his question sink in and answered. "From fifteen years of age, free-will became my only objective. My whole life I've searched for the means to leave the East and be reunited with my family. Though still important, it's no longer the central goal in my life."

"Why not?"

"I'm not sure I can explain it very well."

"Try." Darek's deep-set eyes resembled a magnifying glass as he examined me inch by inch. I needed to be careful and not give away more than necessary.

"I've always believed in causes that prevent oppression and control." I wanted to be honest with him since he'd done a great deal for me. "Like what you do with IFM. There's a need for it and the other organizations. Change needs to happen, and it requires leaders like you to facilitate it." He waited for me to continue. Patience was always his virtue. "The loss and separation I've experienced has driven my anger. I hate those who forced my future, but right now, things are happening that require my full attention. My diversion is unfair to you and the cause."

He set the bag aside as his hands slipped into his pant pockets. "Well, I'm glad you came to me in person." Expanded silence followed.

"Darek?" A man with a thick, heavy beard entered from a side room. "I'm sorry to interrupt, but I need you to review this." He held a paper in his hand.

"Review what?" Darek's attention was pulled temporarily.

The man glanced at me, but Darek repeated himself sternly. "What?"

"The leaflet for the Olof Palme march and the flyer campaign."

Darek said nothing in response and turned back to me. "Is your leave temporary or permanent?"

"Permanent." I may have answered too quickly, but there was no doubt.

He mulled this over and then faced the man who waited patiently. "Make sure the Olaf Palme paper gives the date in Dresden, and it will be fine. I saw it this morning. And for the campaign, we're waiting for Roland to bring more ink." Darek waved him off.

"Well, I'm disappointed we're losing someone with your experience and qualifications, Annika. You've made a significant contribution to our work."

"I've learned a lot, and I appreciate what you've done for me. I'm sorry I can't continue."

He took a deep breath. "As am I."

He continued to stare for another uncomfortable minute until he spoke again, "I have a particularly unique assignment coming up." He never blinked as he continued, "I believe it necessitates your talent. Would you be able to do one more job?"

I gnawed on the inside of my cheek, trying to make a quick decision. *One more job shouldn't hurt.* "Yes," I nodded. "I think it would be okay."

He placed an arm around me as he motioned us towards the door. Although light, its pressure remained consistent through the foyer and only released when his hand reached for the handle. I wasn't the only one anxious for our conversation to be over.

"Oh, one more thing, Darek." When I recognized our meeting wasn't as difficult as I invented it to be, I took advantage of the moment. Opening my handbag, I retrieved the picture of Karin Lenz I drew from memory after the event at Zur Letzen Instanz two months ago. "Could you take a look at these sketches, and see if you recognize them? I met this woman at a KvU dinner a year ago."

"Yes, I'm familiar with Karin. She's been to several of our events. She mostly works with Women for Peace, though." His eyebrows met. "Why did you sketch her?"

"She dined with this man for lunch." I pulled out the other sketch. "I used to work at Zur and recently went to visit a friend when she happened to be there. They left separately, and when we briefly spoke on her way out, she said she dined with a woman."

His expression revealed nothing, though he spent a lengthy amount of time studying the man's drawing. "What should it matter who she ate with?"

"I'm only telling you because I think she's up to something. It doesn't seem right. I worked there for twelve years, remember. A lot of meetings took place between agents and informers, and they all arrived and left separately."

He pressed his lips together, and after a few seconds he finally spoke, "Do you mind if I keep these?"

"No, it's fine."

246

He opened the door and hesitated. "By the way, whatever happened to that man, the *former* fiancé?"

"Oh . . . uh." I stuttered, taken aback by his question. *Could he know?* This was one truth I needed to protect. "Nothing. He's gone."

"That's a good thing, right?"

I glanced anywhere but him. "Yeah, oh yeah," I waffled in place, "nothing to worry about."

He reached out to shake my hand; I knew if I met it, he would feel me trembling.

I leaned in and kissed him on the cheek. This surprised us both. "I appreciate you giving me hope when there was none."

"Come to the bar next Tuesday, Annika, and your assignment will be ready." He dipped his chin in quiet acknowledgement and closed the door.

Motionless, the thick wooden door with its black iron hinges stared back at me, though its presence intimidated me for different reasons than before. A fine layer of moisture coated my skin and built with the recap of our final words, centered on Stefan. *Does Darek know? Did he sense my deceit?* I slowly circled about, my thumbnail securely between my teeth as I gnawed for answers. *I can't tell Stefan I have one final assignment.* He'd only worry, possibly arrive and complicate things. No, this task must be entirely on my own.

Thirty-two

TWO FOR THE PRICE OF ONE

July 1987

The paper, folded in half, felt damp and sticky between my fingers. Dank moisture in the air hung thick around my neck and pasted my clothes against my body. The leather strap on my bag slid effortlessly down my clammy, bare shoulder twice while I walked. As dusk lingered, the humidity sagged, unchanged. I wiped my upper lip and scanned the street name, *Feuersteiner.* Koepnick had always been foreign to me, but the hollowness of this particular neighborhood brought an additional layer of uncertainty. *Why did Darek send me here?*

My eyes shifted down the nearly-deserted street. One man swept the sidewalk in front of his shoe repair store. Three vacant buildings adjacent to his crumbled in varying degrees. One didn't even have a front window; the shattered glass remained littered below it. The elderly man glanced up at me, his two eyebrows merged into one. An unnerving stare preceded a slow shake of his head as he hustled inside his shop, slamming the door behind him.

I peered around and then back at the paper, unfolding it and reading it for the fifth time.

Corner of Deutschhofer and Feuersteiner. Older man mid-sixties, gray hair, glasses, walks with a limp, occasionally uses a walking cane. Meeting a younger man, thirty range, black hair, mustache, shifty eyes and carries a briefcase. Get as much information about both then report in two days.

Nothing unusual about the directions except the fact that I've always worked in busy areas, making it easier to blend in. Although, Darek did mention a *unique* assignment. It's possible this contact avoided the more public scene, but at what risk for me?

I'm too exposed.

If Ralf really did work for Stasi and was scheming a way to incite vengeance on me or Stefan, this would be a prime place to find me alone. The only thing I did to disguise my routine today was not tell Stefan my whereabouts. My departure, transportation, even my appearance remained the same. With it being my last job, I rebuked myself for being careless.

Finding the closest bench, I sat down and retrieved my sketch book. With short-lived chastising, I justified the fact that it would be over soon. Once the targets were identified, I would be in and out in less than thirty minutes.

Glancing about, nothing nearby emerged art-worthy. Besides the shoe repair and appliance shop across the street, a letter box, water hydrant, and two streetlamps on each side of the road, the area appeared vacant. It was a dying part of the city, a common characteristic over time.

I started to pencil the profile of the buildings under the setting sun. The glow reflected off the brick in an unusually magical way. The developing sketch captured the deep contrast between the streaks of radiant beams and the gloomy shadows below.

A mother holding the hand of a child hustled down the walk. Her eyes met mine momentarily and veered from a gentle calm to sudden alarm as she pulled her child closer and swung the opposite direction. I paused at her unusual reaction.

A breeze blew from behind. The sweat coating my skin cooled. A tickle followed, and my free hand slapped the base of my neck as if a fly crawled on it. A deep mumble surfaced. "Well, hello, Annika."

I didn't need to turn around to know who it was. Every muscle in my body tightened to the taunting voice. My eyes darted to the woman as she disappeared and then fell to my sketch pad, calculating a way to write the word *HELP* and have it seen by anyone but him. I stared forward. The desolate scene played out, not one soul to hear my screams.

His signature cackle traveled from behind me with one swift leap over the backside of the bench. My eyes remained fixed frontward, but my sideview confirmed, without a doubt, that Jurek now sidled up next to me. His arm lifted to rest on the bench behind, and a rotten smell entered my nostrils. It was possible he hadn't bathed in weeks. My jaw tightened, refusing to turn his direction.

He leaned in. "Funny finding you here" —he licked his lips with a sloppy smack— "alone." His left hand pressed against his leather pants, wiping the growing sweat off. Had his top been anything other than a matching leather vest, he would have overheated in the sweltering heat. His fingers slid to the silver spikes squeezing his neck and adjusted the band.

My thoughts flashed to the time he rose from the shadows when I searched for Fritz and Klaus years ago. Border Patrol scared him off. It was Hans who ultimately saved me. Similarly, I found myself alone with him. "Let me do my job, Jurek." Confidence flamed, but the thump of my heart worked overtime.

He pulled one knee up to rest on the other and clasped his hands together. "By all means," —still linked, his fingers pointed to the deserted scene before us— "please, do your job." In my peripheral vision, it appeared as though the skeletal jaw, which covered his own, laughed at me. The momentary silence swelled until he uttered, "And I will do mine."

My face flipped his direction the moment his hands went for my throat. My sketchbook flew as I hurled both arms up defensively. My pencil stabbed into his bare shoulder but only slowed him for a brief second before he shoved me to the ground. My head smacked hard against the curb. Piercing pain streaked from the back of my skull, attacking my senses. My ears pulsated in agony, and my sight dimmed. Three forms hovered above me until I squinted them back into one. Jurek stood, his boots clamped on each side of my body, pinching my hips in place. Blood began to pool underneath the surface of the wound until he yanked the pencil out of his skin, tossing it aside. The slow and methodical curl of his lips taunted. "Is that all you got?" The blood trailed down his arm and dripped on my shirt.

My eyes flickered in bewilderment. *My knife! If I can just get to my knife.* Stretching towards my knapsack at the base of the bench, pain from my head shot down my side, but I ignored it. Jurek snorted and stomped on my extended arm on his way to the bag. I yelped under his excruciating weight and then watched him kick the sack farther away. Scrambling in my momentary freedom, I tried to scoot backward, but his next kick knocked my arms flat. He circled around, like a bird of prey. My throbbing head followed his movements, desperate to stay cognizant and alert.

"D-Darek, will not b-be happy when he hears about this." My frantic attempt at logic squeaked out. Jurek's head tilted back in a full laugh, the bones from the tattoo flexed with his muscles as he cackled.

"I'm sure Darek will be fine."

"N-no he said to l-leave me a-lone, remember?"

Jurek's hand thrust forward and squeezed my lower jaw. Pain streaked down my neck from the grip. My eyes blurred with tears. He tilted his head, a smug expression plastered across his face. The foul stench of tobacco stung my nose the moment he opened his mouth. "Darek's the one who sent me."

Air from my lungs hit the top of my throat and stalled. The lump literally cut off all circulation. I tried to wiggle free of his hold, afraid I might faint. Instantly, Jurek's grip released with the flash of a fist. It came out of nowhere and connected brutally with Jurek's cheek. Although the attack came abruptly, his fall materialized in segments, as if all time slowed down. His head whipped backward right as his body hit the metal end of the bench.

Two hands reached underneath my arms from behind and dragged my stiff legs across the cobblestone to the other side of the road. Jurek stumbled to his feet and yanked the chains off his waist. Dropped to the ground, I pushed up to see a man's back a couple metres in front of me—his feet shoulder-width apart, arms curved at his sides, with his hands rolled into fists, no doubt the stance of one braced and ready to fight. He never turned around as I leaned weakly on one arm.

"Stefan?" I questioned, my understanding hazy. "Stefan, no," I cried with as much exertion as my still-throbbing head allowed. Jurek launched into a dead run. With both arms he tackled Stefan, and they landed at my feet. I drew my knees firmly against my chest. The men rolled harshly on the unforgiving road. The chain, clutched in Jurek's fist, wrapped around Stefan's throat.

My own throat blazed as my scream clawed for air.

Jurek yanked but Stefan wriggled and rolled free, landing several blows to Jurek's gut. Within seconds, Jurek headbutted Stefan squarely in the nose. The blow knocked him backwards. Blood and sweat exploded from Stefan's face as Jurek straddled him. Dazed, I scanned the ground around me. *What can I do?* My fingers stretched for a scattering of crumbled cement. I grabbed the biggest chunk and aimed right for Jurek. *I missed!* A second time I hurled a handful, hitting him solidly on the side of his head, striking him down. Stefan shoved him aside and jumped to his feet.

252

The fear in Stefan's eyes as he glanced towards me told me his concern centered more on *my* welfare than his own. He sprinted over and clutched one of my arms. His strength outmatched mine as he yanked on my limb. The pull tore, but the burn that ignited between my skin and the sidewalk as he dragged me farther away stung like my thigh was actually on fire.

Dropping me to the dirt, Stefan's eyes held Jurek without peering my direction, and he demanded, "Ella, get out of here! Go, please!"

Jurek located his knife. Wiping the trickling blood off his cheek, he sneered. "Two . . . for the price of one."

Grabbing my shirt, Stefan tugged. The material tore in his hands. Sharp pains from my side to the back of the head paralyzed me. Stefan crouched behind and slid his arms underneath once more. His torso shook from the strain on his muscles. "Please," he cried. I tried to absorb his words but the fog that smothered my thoughts since my head hit the curb prevented me from organizing an escape plan.

Jurek paced—his chin lowered, eyes glaring, dagger pointed outward.

My knees bent but wobbled, unable to lift. I covered Stefan's hands against my chest. "I can't!" I cried. "I can't." Jurek stalked closer, and I shrieked, "Jurek! Get out of here. Leave us alone!"

He scoffed, "I'm here on official business, and I'm not leaving til it's done."

I squeezed Stefan's arm and pulled him around to my side. "You don't have to do this."

His eyes remained fixed on Jurek. "I don't think we have a choice, Ella."

"Ya . . . El-la . . . or is it An-nika." Jurek hissed, pacing. "You *don't* have a choice."

My body trembled hard, but I wrapped my arms around my legs to force it still. "Stefan, I'll be okay."

Stefan stepped to the right, giving me a slight nudge with his left hand. His brief glance and nod my direction communicated this fight was his. He drew Jurek's eyes from me to him. Jurek smirked and lunged. Stefan rotated easily, and Jurek missed, skidding to his knees. He shot to his feet and flipped around. Again, he charged. Stefan's agility prevailed as Jurek swiped midair. With swift turns, the men faced each other, their hands raised chest high, and steps orbiting an imaginary circle. Jurek peered my direction. His vile titter should have clued me to his intent. In less than a second he tore off my direction. Stefan launched and caught his leg, landing Jurek on his stomach. His arm extended, and the tip of the knife grazed my ankle as I scurried backwards. More blood, more screams erupted. Stefan scrambled to his knees still clutching Jurek's pantleg as he lifted the knife again for another stab. I dove the opposite direction while Stefan clambered onto Jurek's back.

Pressed flat to the ground, Jurek wrestled to turn. Stefan pounded his arm until the knife released. Despite my fear, I snatched the blade. My hand, dwarfed against the cold steel, lifted it. The reflection of my face flashed in the blade, bigger and sharper than mine. I gripped the handle. *This was brought to kill me!*

Snarled together, the brawl continued. I held the weapon high and tight but feared I might strike Stefan. Flesh merged through violent, indistinct twists. Stefan managed to get Jurek by the throat above the spikes. He straddled his form. The muscles in his forearms expanded the tighter he clenched. Jurek's skin turned a cherry red and slowly shaded to nearly purple.

"Stop—Stefan—stop!" My cries lurched in broken segments until my body collapsed in a full sob at my contradiction. *It's okay for me to kill Jurek but not Stefan. It would destroy him.*

Stefan's eyes glazed over. The veins in his neck protruded until he finally let go of Jurek, who gasped for air. Jurek's hands fell to his throat as he slumped to his side.

Stefan stood and, bending over him, shoved his finger with a vengeance into Jurek's chest as he struggled for oxygen. "Never, EVER come around us again, or I *will* kill you!"

His glare softened as he stumbled my direction, taking several deep breaths while reaching for my arms and lifting me upright. His hand folded over mine and released my grasp on the knife. Numbness masked the pain from my injuries as he wrapped one arm around my waist and brought my body next to his, my arm up over his shoulder. Secure, he led me down the street.

The crunch of rocks and subsequent hiss surfaced so quickly I barely comprehended it. Stefan shoved me to the ground the moment Jurek pounced. His arms clinched tightly around Stefan's neck, pressing the air out of him. Stefan stabbed Jurek's arm, forcing a release. He fell backwards to the ground, and Stefan bent over, gasping for breath. Jurek yanked the weapon from his skin, blood snaking down his arm as he raised the knife and charged again, without blinking.

"Stefan!" My warning came too late. Jurek's leap caught Stefan's defensive hand and sliced, but Stefan's other fist knocked Jurek in the ribs. He gasped as they both went down. Tangled against the brick, they tussled through the shadows, blending their identities in the growing darkness. *Who has the knife? Which one's Stefan?*. Twice the blade caught the reflection of the lamplight in the twist and flashed briefly then disappeared. I squinted hard trying to follow the chaos when suddenly their bodies stopped.

"Stefan?" I jockeyed to my knees. The clump lay motionless. Tears burst easily as I crawled forward, terrified at what I might find. "Stefan?" My whisper elevated to a scream. "Stefan!"

The neck spikes reflected off the lamplight and glistened as they moved.

"No!" I shrieked. "Oh, please God. No!" My heart raced. Jurek's body curved upward. His shoulders and back raised. Bile filled my throat. He tumbled to the side, the knife protruding from *his* chest. Stefan lay underneath. Jurek's limp and unresponsive body rolled to a stop where it hit the curb. His frozen eyes stared hauntingly forward.

I frantically crawled backwards to create distance from the body, scraping hard against the surface. A short distance away, I turned to vomit, my own body jerking wildly. Stefan clambered to my side.

255

Even with blood soaking on his clothes, he held my shoulders until I fell back to the concrete.

Darkness now penetrated the neighborhood. In the flurry, the sun and heat disappeared, but layers of sweat, mixed with filth, covered my skin. Incapable of grasping the event, I whimpered in agony. Stefan slid both his hands underneath me and lifted me up. My head fell limp against his chest. Unable to speak or even think, a fog blanketed me with each step.

It wasn't until we reached my flat that I realized Stefan carried me the entire distance home and didn't let go until we reached my bathroom. Silence and darkness indicated our solitude. I sighed with relief at not having to explain the injuries to Mari, but most of all the splatter of blood covering our clothes.

Stefan sat me on the edge of the bathtub. He twisted the knobs, testing the temperature and letting the warm water immerse his battered hand. He hadn't looked at me since the fight. His shoulders curved inward while his sunken eyes never lifted. I knew there was no other way, but the life he had taken would grate at his soul. He reached for a towel and hung it on a nearby hook. I grabbed his arm and forced him to stop.

"Stefan," I whispered above the water flow. "Please, look at me."

His head turned barely enough for me to see the path of tears that slid through the dirt marks towards his chin. I pulled him towards me, and he knelt to my level. My palms went to his cheeks. "Stefan, if you didn't kill Jurek, one or both of us would be dead right now." His face slumped, heavy in my hands. "You *know* that, right?" I pleaded for him to answer. He tried to turn his head, but I held fast. "You are *not* a killer." I leaned in; our eyes so close I could see his bloodshot veins expanding. "You are a good man. You saved my life . . . again." Tears filled my own eyes as my forehead tilted and rested against his.

Once the tub filled, he shut the water off. His hands slid to my ankle and lifted it to examine the cut. A ragged trail of dried blood camouflaged the gap. "I will bandage it after your bath. Take as long as you need; I'm not going to leave you." Stefan kissed the top of my head and then closed the door behind him. Even in his own time of need, my care was his first thought.

The hot water bestowed a healing effect for both body and soul. After scrubbing the dirt and blood off, I quickly drained the brown water. I wrapped the provided towel around me and allowed my wet locks to fall on my shoulders, untouched. Stepping over the pile of soiled clothes, I opened the door to a single light in the room.

The lamp next to Mama's chair created a soft glow, illuminating Stefan. His form filled the seat, his bare, sculpted chest discolored from multiple injuries sustained in the attack. "I'm sorry," he said, noticing the direction of my gaze. "I don't have another shirt." He jumped to his feet, his eyes lifting and following the length of my form. Although the towel covered the intimate parts, it suddenly confined me. He darted towards the kitchen and retrieved a cup from the counter.

"I made you some tea." He approached cautiously. I smiled, but the sag in his cheeks could not be ignored.

"Stefan?" I touched his arm. "Please, stop." He bore the weight of the night on his shoulders.

"Come sit down" He brushed my plea aside and placed his hand at my lower back. "Let me bandage your ankle." Guiding me to the bed, he positioned me on the edge. As he knelt, his eyes trailed my legs downward. His fingers gently grazed the burns on my thigh, but instead of inciting pain, his touch magnified my desire. I wanted him . . . needed him.

"I'm sorry I dragged you." His torment was evident in the downward pull of his mouth.

"I'm sorry I didn't move faster."

His hands tenderly cupped my foot, and he examined the cut. Mostly superficial, the slice barely reached the length of a thumb and the depth of a fingernail.

"I don't think you need stitches." He remained on one knee and reached for the bandage and tape he placed on the bedside table. His touch was slow and gentle as he nursed the wound.

257

I patted the bed next to me. "Please sit, Stefan."

He came to my side. The sight of his wounds forced me to my feet. I took my tea to the kitchen, retrieved a cloth, ran it under warm water, and returned. Standing before him, I pressed it softly against his skin, brushing over the ugly bruise that flanked his right eye, down his split cheek, and across his swollen lip. Although the injuries surely stung, Stefan didn't flinch. I reached for his hand and carefully tended to the slash between his two fingers. He watched the cloth and shifted his gaze to me when it glided up his arm and across his neck to where the chains imprinted and bruised. I skimmed down his chest to the deep scratches on his ribs. The stir his naked skin provoked sent pulsations through my hand like a conduit.

His eyes scanned past my face and down my neck. He motioned to the scar on my chest near my right shoulder. "Does it hurt?"

"Not anymore," I said with honesty, having grown used to it. When I sat down next to him, I angled my body slightly to the left, pulled my hair aside, and brought the back of my right shoulder in full view. The butterfly tattoo, with its injured wing, became fully exposed. "Edmund retrieved the bullet through the back. Do you see the hole?"

Stefan's fingers grazed my skin, his touch tingling every nerve and more so throughout my shoulder. The soft touch of his lips swept across my shoulder, caressing the butterfly that symbolized our separation. Each stroke singed me; his breath heated and calmed simultaneously, amplifying at the scar. "I'm sorry, El."

Unable to move, I yearned to feel his body against me. The ache in his voice gripped my heart. I leaned back against his chest and let his head fall over my shoulder, cheek to cheek. "Stefan, everything that has happened in our lives has brought us here. We are together now, and that's the only thing that matters."

The door handle clicked and opened. Mari entered and froze with wide eyes. Stefan's arms wrapped around my towel-clad body.

"I'm sorry," she cried. Her hands flew to her eyes, although Stefan's nakedness remained above the waist. "I can leave."

"No, Mari." I stood. "It's fine, we're only talking."

Her brows furrowed with alarm. "What happened to you, Stefan?" I could see her trying to comprehend his condition.

I reached for her hand and squeezed in assurance. "An old enemy confronted us, but" —I exchanged looks with Stefan— "it's over now." The words were for his benefit as much as Mari's.

"Oh," she gasped, "and your leg."

"I'm fine, Mari. I promise." I went to my closet. "Stefan, let me see if I can find something for you to wear."

Mari's eyes studied his appearance again. She bit her lip. "I have some things of Cade's here. Let me get them."

"You do?" I whirled around, surprised. Mari smiled without response and walked to the drawers. She pulled out a t-shirt and a pair of slacks. "These should work."

I led Stefan to the bathroom. His countenance crushed, "I know you feel responsible for everything, Stefan. How can I assure you that you're not."

"Most everything," he mumbled.

"No, not most."

"Our separation, your attempted escape, your scar, Darek's vengeance, blood on my hands—"

"Stop!" My hand pressed against his rapidly beating heart. "Please stop. You're the only reason I'm alive right now. Don't take that away from me." My fingers slid upward and rested on his cheek. "Thank you." These words seemed insufficient for the man I owed much more to.

He placed his hand over mine and glided it from his jaw to his mouth. His warm breath filled my palm before his lips skimmed across my inner wrist. My longing amplified the farther it traveled up the length of my arm. When he let go, his hands fell to my waist. With one quick boost, he lifted me onto the edge of the sink, my legs wrapping securely around him. The closer he came, the more we shared. Sliding along the contours of his bare chest, my hands parted to his shoulders once his determined lips reached my neck. His body

259

met mine with every ounce of suppressed passion we possessed. My head rolled back and exposed my skin to the intensity of a touch that instantly weakened me. A soft moan escaped my lips.

Skimming the length of my chest, from one shoulder to the other, his lips left a scorching trail until my fingers drew him in. Our lips connected so powerfully it melted any doubt I ever had about his feelings for me. Stealing a breath, his whisper wielded a fervency missing prior to today, "You are my everything, Ella." The next kiss tinged as light as a butterfly's wing and followed with a whisper. "I love you."

This man is my life and my future. I never wanted to let go again. Stefan's forehead rested against mine, and he gently brought me down to earth with a simple kiss on my cheek. Despite the temptation of letting my towel fall to the floor, I kept it intact. I no longer felt our love was an *if* but a *when,* and for the first time in years, the notion brought forth immense comfort.

While he showered, I changed into some lounge clothes and Mari cooked. Well past ten o'clock when we dined, my hearty appetite returned. I devoured the *kartoffelpuffer* in very few bites. The potato pancake melted in my mouth. Stefan hardly ate.

After we washed the dishes, exhaustion set in. "Stefan, are you staying the night?" Mari asked with the last of the dishes finally put away.

"Just tonight, Mari. I want to make sure Ella is well."

"You must take the bed then."

"No, I'll sleep in the chair. I probably won't sleep much anyway."

She kissed him on the cheek, beneath the bandaged cut. "Oh, Stefan. Always the protector." Then she crawled into bed, turned over, and within minutes a steady breath indicated she slept.

Stefan pointed to the other side of the bed. "Here, let me tuck you in. It's been quite some time since I've done that." He forced a subtle grin.

"May I sit with you a bit?" I indicated the chair. His smile lifted fully on one side. He nodded and sat down. I curled up on his lap and rested my head against his chest. The beats came at a much slower pace. He placed one hand securely around me and with the other stroked my hair tenderly. His arms encircled me with peace, the kind that lulled me to sleep without effort.

Thirty-three

TINNIE PIN

A gentle breeze kissed my face as my eyelids opened to the brightness in the room. Stretching, my muscles groaned at the movement. Rolling to the right, my inflamed skin bristled, pressed against the bed. I suddenly recalled the night's events: Jurek, the knife, blood, Stefan! My eyes flashed towards the chair, its vacancy shot a spear of terror through me. I scrambled to my feet and in the process rubbed my ankle against the blanket while I moved, its sting failed in comparison to the panic that rose from my chest.

When my knees hit the floor with a thud, Stefan arrived at my side. "Ella, did you fall?"

I glanced around and immediately felt foolish. "I thought you left." I wiped my nose.

Stefan lifted me up and back to the bed. "I said I wouldn't leave." He brushed my hair from my cheek and secured it behind my ear. His wounds took on a different form in the daylight. Deep purple bruising encased a swollen eye. The removed bandage revealed a gash the length of his cheekbone, its edges crusted. I touched his lips, the top one puffy and flushed on one side. Stefan closed his eyes as my fingers traced them.

"How did you sleep?" I inspected his eyes again, the blue mingled with red. "You didn't sleep, did you?"

"Good enough," he mumbled.

I folded my legs on the bed and patted the empty space. "Sit with me?" I pressed, wanting him near. He complied but left a gap between us.

"Your Linden trees are in full bloom." He pointed towards the cracked window. They weren't really mine per se, though I claimed the two on the street that bordered my building.

I took a deep breath. Even from this distance the scent filled me. "It's my favorite time of year, their fragrance permeates the flat nicely."

"Can I get you a cup of tea?" Stefan asked. His hands toyed with the crumpled blanket nearby.

I took a deep breath, wondering if we were back to talking about the weather again.

"Stefan," I hesitated to proceed. *But if not now . . . when?* "I can't begin to understand what you went through during our separation," I whispered. "I've never experienced the atrocities that you have with war and imprisonment. I only know how much you helped me through my own traumatic experience." Stefan's eyes fell upon me for the first time since he sat down. The intense blue flowed.

One of his hands went to my arm. His fingers traced my skin up to my shoulder, and though my scar was covered by fabric, he touched it again. "I don't know if I can ever forgive myself for hurting you."

I allowed his words to sink in before I spoke. "Stefan, you speak as though I didn't bring pain upon myself, which I did. Consequences surround me for decisions I made *alone*. But you must understand—"

I reached for both of his hands. "—Remember our night together, the last one from your leave?"

He nodded.

"I wanted to be with you . . . to be next to you." I bit my lip. "You loved me, Stefan, even when I didn't love myself."

His eyes fell to our conjoined hands until one of my hands broke free and tugged his chin gently upward. His pain reflected in his deep-blue eyes immobilized me. My heart physically ached for the burden I imagined he carried. "Please . . . please let me do the same for you."

The silence settled as a calm before the storm. *Tick, tick, tick.* That blasted clock in the kitchen echoed each passing second until his whisper interrupted it. "When I got my orders to go to Vietnam, I wrote you."

My brows arched. "You did?"

Small beads of sweat built on his temples and along his cheekbones, but he didn't wipe them away. "I tried to send it, but they confiscated it, insisting no one could know anything."

"They?"

"My Soviet Commanders."

I nodded as he continued. "It was my greatest fear . . . not death or prison."

I brought his hands to my lips and tenderly kissed each of his fingers. "What was?"

His eyes travelled back to mine. "That you'd believe I deserted you." The intensity quite clear, his confession stopped me. Stefan hoped I would believe even when I had nothing to hold on to. My eyelashes fell, heavy. *I failed him.* Then words failed me. *What can I possibly say?* He had no way of reaching me, and all I could do was think of my own depressing circumstances.

"I should've had more faith."

"I don't blame you for trying to leave. You didn't know."

"I should've waited."

"To be honest, Ella, I doubted my own return."

"Why?"

"Everything I saw, experienced. It was as if I played a game of chance. One hour I'm alive . . . the next, maybe not. Men died in my arms. Men I stood next to minutes before. Then after we were captured—" His teeth clenched. His eyes glazed over. I rested my head against his shoulder. "Do you want to visit Herr Weitzner? I could go with you."

His tightened muscles relaxed next to my cheek. "I think my first visit needs to be alone, but yes, I would like that very much. He's part of the reason I survived."

"I know. He feels the same way about you."

Stefan's hands slid from mine down to my hips. He pulled me gently atop his lap and wrapped his arms around me. My arms wound comfortably over his shoulders. Every part of me fit him perfectly, as if we were made to match.

"Right now, though, I need to keep you safe." His whisper tickled my ear. "If Darek sent Jurek, he might proceed with others."

My body drew back slightly. "I can't believe it's Darek. He's been good to me for a long time."

"Good people make bad choices too."

I eyed him carefully. Were his words meant for him or me? "Yes. Yes, they do." I laid my head back on his shoulder, and although I could no longer see his face, his heartbeat increased. "Maybe we should move you and Mari to the house"

"In Pankow?" My cry launched my head backward.

Stefan flinched.

"Sorry," I untangled myself from his grasp and stepped to the window. My eyes flashed below. Nobody suspicious appeared, but I half expected someone to be watching us. "Do you really feel we're in danger?"

"Yes."

"I don't know. Your . . . your dad . . . he won't approve."

"He's not the man he used to be," Stefan said this in passing and continued, "Katharina and Edmund run the house and mortuary. I would need to speak with them, but you and Mari can't stay here. I'm sure they already know where you live." He joined me at the window and gently guided me back to the bed.

I scanned the room. "Where's Mari?"

"She went to work, but I already spoke to her about my concerns. She's willing to do whatever's necessary."

I felt silly. *I should be the one who's willing. Stefan wants me to be safe. I shouldn't fight him on this.* "Okay, I'll go wherever you want me to, on one condition—"

He braced for bad news. "What's the condition?"

"We stay together."

His lips slid into a grin. Squeezing my hand, he kissed me on the cheek before he added, "Let's catch the next bus to Pankow. Pack a few things to take with us for now. I can come back for anything else and to meet up with Mari."

In a hurried glance, my eyes went to the shelf. Everything that mattered to me, besides Stefan, sat atop that ledge.

He noticed my hesitation and reached for Anton's tinnie pin. "Tell me about this." It balanced on his fingers and not for the first time. Years ago, in the mortuary, it poked him during our embrace. He held it briefly then too. Shortly after, it became the source of bitter jealousy and disappeared, only to end up in his mother's possession. What followed, led to our near destruction.

With the previous experience triggered, my first reaction sparked panic. I gazed nervously at him, though nothing but genuine compassion met me. I retrieved it from his grasp and examined the front of the shield. I peered over to Stefan. He urged. "It's okay. I want to know."

"It belonged to Anton." My fingers brushed across the jewel in the center. "He wore it every day on his collar. It was the only thing Anton owned from his family. When the Kühns adopted me, he ran away from the orphanage and lived on the street."

"What happened to his family? How did he become an orphan?"

"He never told me, and I never asked."

"Living on the street must've been hard for him."

266

I nodded. "He had some friends, even Jurek at first, but it was a tough life. The night I met Jurek, they fought . . . because of me." My mind briefly flashed to yesterday and how Jurek will never have the chance to hurt the people I love again.

"Why? What happened?"

"Anton defended me from Jurek's insults over my skin color."

"Sounds like Anton cares for you."

"We had only each other for a long time. He gave me the pin the night the wire was rolled out—the night he and Josef ran to freedom." My nose stung. "He wanted me to have it so I wouldn't forget him." Saying this out loud frightened me, but Stefan's calm comforted. He even smiled.

Lifting it out of my hand, he opened the clasp. His fingers brushed my neckline lightly as he pinned it to my shirt. "Don't forget it then."

I wrapped my arms around him and kissed his cheek. "Thank you."

When I stepped into the closet to retrieve the suitcase, I paused. Every reminder of Stefan had been stashed in here: his letters, the painting, even the ring. He walked up behind me and casually transferred the suitcase handle to his hand and never said a word about what else he might've seen.

I packed a few pairs of slacks, shirts, and my memories. For a brief moment I found myself at Bernauer again saying goodbye. The same suitcase held the same mementos, and I was leaving. Only this time, Stefan's touch reassured me I wouldn't be leaving alone.

Katharina didn't hesitate to welcome me, even before Stefan gave her the abbreviated version of why Mari and I needed to be there. She cleaved unto me like a lost puppy. I should've never doubted. Between Stefan, Edmund, and Katharina, anyone would be hard-pressed to reach me.

Once settled into the guest room Mari and I would share, Stefan's goodbye followed promises of a temporary separation. He would go back to my flat and retrieve Mari and any other possessions I requested.

"I'll have Mama G's chair delivered tomorrow."

"Here?" The suggestion warmed my heart.

"Of course, we can't leave that behind, and if you happen to see my father," —Stefan glanced my direction— "you might want to leave the explanation to me."

"Wh-what if he asks or insists?" A tremor in my voice arose. Even as a grown woman, he terrified me.

"He won't."

It wasn't until nearly eight o'clock in the evening that Stefan returned with Mari by his side. Even under the stressful circumstances, she beamed. "Oh, Ella, I'm glad you're safe."

"I'm sorry you have to relocate because of me."

"You make it sound like a chore." She laughed. "I have more family now than I've ever had. How can that be a bad thing?"

I joined her laugh. I'd never thought of it that way. Although I knew exactly how it felt to have no family, those feelings disappeared long ago. "Yes, we are family, and we are finally together."

Thirty-four

WAITING

The next morning, when I arrived in the kitchen for breakfast, a familiar woman pulled a fresh loaf of bread from the oven.

"Lena!" I cried and nearly tripped over my feet getting to her. "What are you doing here?"

She quickly set the bread down on a warming rack and met my arms as they swung anxiously around her.

"Why would my being her be such a surprise?" She laughed. "I've worked here most of my life."

"Yes, but you're a mother now. You have a family."

"A family who must eat."

"Of course." Had I really been so distant from everything I'd forgotten that most of the country was still starving? "And Freddy, how is he?"

"He's well. He watches Grace during the day while I work. Katharina allows me to leave by 3, in time to be home before his shift at the pub begins."

"When do you see each other?" My lips pouted.

"On the weekends. We spend our Saturdays and Sundays together, all day, which at times is quite enough." She giggled like the Lena of my past. Now, a wife and mother and beautiful as ever.

"Sit, Ella. Here, let me get you some juice or tea. Which would you prefer?"

"Juice is fine, but sit with me."

"Yes, it seems quite a lot has occurred since we saw each other last."

I grinned sheepishly. When I visited her, Stefan was a tragic memory, and now he was the center of my universe.

"Where's Johann? I haven't seen him nosing about." I chuckled until I noticed Lena's countenance plummet. "What happened? Where is he?"

"He passed away a year ago from cancer."

"Oh, how awful. I'm sorry." The thought of Johann not marching through the halls or barking orders brought a sadness to our morning.

"Yes, it's a lot quieter now, and Herr Franke has refused to replace him. Katharina and Edmund do more than their fair share of everything here."

Mari joined us ten minutes later, and the three of us gossiped for over an hour. When Stefan never showed, I grew concerned.

"Did you see Stefan this morning?" I asked Lena, interrupting the fun.

"Yes. He left the house quite early, right after I arrived."

"Did he say why?"

"No, only that he would be back later. He didn't want to wake you."

I didn't let on that this concerned me and went about, falling into my new jobless routine. To keep busy, I unpacked the two boxes Stefan brought back with him when he returned with Mari the night before. They contained the rest of my clothes, the phonograph, my records, and all of his letters. So, he had seen them. Slightly embarrassed, yet grateful, I settled into a chair in my old favorite room—the library—and began to read each one.

By three in the afternoon, Stefan still hadn't returned. I paced the floor, attempting to find a new beloved read but struggled to find the same joy in them from before, my thoughts centered only on Stefan. *Where could he be? Maybe he took my advice and went to visit Edgar. He did mention his desire to go alone the first time. I'm sure there were many personal things to discuss.*

Five o'clock . . . nothing.

When Mari and I started to prepare dinner and Stefan still hadn't returned, I couldn't keep my concern hidden. *CHOP! CHOP! CHOP!* I dismembered the cabbage.

"Ella, Stefan will be home soon, don't worry."

"I'm not worried." *CHOP! CHOP!*

"Uh huh." She smiled as she scooped the potatoes and dropped them into the pot. "You know, he's quite good at staying undetected when he wants to, right?"

I thought about how she worded this—"when he wants to". For three years I worked for Darek and never saw him watching me, but out of the blue I spotted him at the fairytale fountain. *Is it possible he wanted me to see him? Although . . . he seemed surprised . . . or did I imagine that?*

"Okay, I know that look. What are you thinking?"

"Nothing."

"You're not a good liar."

"Sometimes I am," I teased.

Mari wrinkled her nose.

"Do you know why we left the flat?"

"I think so." She added seasoning to the soup. "Stefan hinted a bit, but I had my suspicions. It involved your job didn't it?"

"Wait. You suspected something? Really? When?"

"When you never talked about it, . . . and when you hid your sketch bag from me, . . . when you came home reeking like a smokestack, . . . and of course, when people called you Annika."

"Oh." I frowned. "You heard that?"

She nodded. "And your reaction to the tour guide's death."

I lowered my eyes.

"Look, I know you faced challenges getting a job after the restaurant and the alcohol, but we're friends. I mean, we're family. The only thing that matters to me is that you're safe, and Stefan said this move would make you safe."

I wrapped my arms around her for a quick hug and returned to chopping the celery and onion.

"Dinner smells wonderful, Lena—" An aged voice entered the room. With very little hair left on his head, and all that remained as white as snow, I barely recognized Herr Franke. When our eyes met, his jaw and cheeks sagged downward into a permanent frown.

"L-Lena . . ." I stuttered, "Lena has gone home. Mari and I made dinner tonight."

His lips pulled tight as he glanced between the two of us and immediately turned on his heels and left the room. Mari's one eyebrow rose curiously.

"It's a long story." I shook my head.

We set the table and called Katharina's family to dine with us.

"Finally, my children will have a warm meal." She clapped her hands together and removed her lab coat.

I grinned at her reaction. Though Lena was employed throughout the day, she left well before dinner time. Her response did not surprise me.

"Oh, and Katharina, your father, he—"

She glanced up fairly alarmed. "Is something the matter?"

"He came down but left when he saw me."

She patted my arm. "It's not you, Ella. He is . . . well, he's getting old and can be difficult with change." She reached for a bowl and

272

poured him some cabbage soup, added a couple of biscuits, and slipped out.

"Any word from Stefan?" I asked when she returned, as if he might have called her at some point to explain his delay.

"Actually, I didn't know he left." Katharina chuckled, until she saw my expression. "He's fine, Ella. I guess I'm just used to his disappearances."

I grimaced. She made it sound like accepting this part of his behavior was necessary, but I agreed to come only if we would be together. If not together, at least I should know his plans. My sulking resembled an old married woman, and I'd only been here one day.

Shortly after midnight, I made my way up the stairs for the night. The front door clicked open. Hustling back down, I arrived in time to see Stefan hang his jacket. When he turned to find me on the bottom stair, he immediately met me with a long embrace. Something in his touch confirmed he'd seen Edgar. His cheek pressed against my chest and made no move to pull away. My fingers gently raked through the hair on the back of his head. Consumed in my own needs all this time, I failed to recognize how difficult these changes were for him. We remained in place for several minutes until he finally broke off.

"Can I get you anything before bed, Stefan?"

He shook his head and kissed my cheek before he left me.

I slumped to the bottom step. My fist held my chin in thought. *What can I do to help him?*

Thirty-five

NEW MEMORIES

Immensely troubled over Stefan's well-being, I wandered my bedroom quietly for almost an hour. Fearing I might awaken Mari, I slipped into the hall and down to the art room. Closing the door, I turned on the light and instantly my spirit soared. Though the room offered no traces of fresh paint, the smell settled into the floor and walls. Even the scent of my beloved chalk seeped through. Immense happiness occurred here. If only it could be bottled and carried.

The infectious atmosphere created a whirlwind of ideas that suddenly awakened my soul. All this time I'd been trying to force us back into a life we no longer lived instead of recognizing the good that came from change. We'd aged, but growth and experience weren't negative things. Our past shaped us and became part of who we were. With this as our starting point, we could make our own path, create new experiences, and generate new memories.

By morning I could barely contain the excitement this newfound knowledge produced. In the kitchen, I waited for Stefan like a child waited for St. Nicholas Day—impatiently. By the time he arrived shortly after nine, breakfast was over, the dishes washed, and I had already started Lena's regular tasks as well, just to pass the time.

"Good morning, Stefan." I handed him a mug of coffee.

He glanced around and peeked at his watch. "Where is everyone?"

"Off to work or play, I suppose."

"I didn't realize I'd slept this long. I'm sorry."

"It's fine. Did you sleep well?"

"Much better, thank you." He lifted the mug to his lips but stopped. His eyes narrowed. "What are you up to?"

I grinned widely. He knew me too well. "There are some things I need to do today, but you must come with me."

"Me?"

"Of course." I cinched up next to him. Still adjusting to our proximity, my heart pounded faster. "I knew you wouldn't let me do it alone."

"You probably shouldn't be out at all." Stefan placed his cup down and reached for my arms. His hands glided from my elbows, down past my wrists, to fit securely in my palms.

"It'll be safe, we'll stay in public places."

"I don't know—"

I stepped closer, my nose nuzzling his neck. "Please," I whispered, inhaling his aftershave. "It'll be nice to get out." I rested my cheek next to his. The swelling, both on his eye and lip had shrunk considerably, and despite the several days growth on his chin, the scratch didn't bother me.

"Alright but only a couple of hours."

My fingers celebrated his answer with a squeeze. I let go and reached for my sweater, which already happened to be downstairs, draped over a chair. I hoped he didn't pick up on this, but not much got past him.

"Do we need the car?" Stefan asked. The offer tempted me; it had been quite some time since I'd been in one.

"No, the bus will take us where we need to go." One of his eyebrows arched. He already suspected something. I smiled big in response to his silence.

We caught the bus to Friedrichshain and stepped off about a block west of Karl Marx Allee. Stefan's eyes twitched slightly as we approached the wide street. The parade here, back in 1966, evoked fond memories. Stepping up on the same bench I stood on that fateful day with Lena, I waved him over. "This is where I watched for you. I searched as best as possible." He jumped up next to me and pointed across the street. "I was closer to the opposite side, my platoon marched last, before the tanks." I followed his hand. His expression lightened; it must've been a good memory for him as well.

"There were so many people in the streets that day, all happy and excited."

"Yes," he reached for my hand, the motion becoming natural now. "I feared I would never find you."

"Lucky for me you did." I kissed his cheek before we stepped off the bench. Two blocks later, I led him towards the bookstore, the one I bought the book *nakt unter Wölfen* at. "This exact place was where I awaited the news."

"What news and when?"

"I hadn't heard from you for a long time, and Hilde, the one who ran the café down by Checkpoint Charlie—if you remember— arranged for soldiers who worked in records to search for you."

"They didn't find anything did they?"

I couldn't stop the way my countenance fell, recalling our conversation and what the soldiers discovered.

"Ella," —Stefan drew his free hand to my neck and rubbed gently— "what happened?"

"They said your record showed a red line," my voice cracked with the memory.

"You thought I'd been killed?" His eyes widened with the idea.

I nodded. "When I left Hilde's, I was a wreck. I didn't even remember how I got home. In fact, there are several days I have no memory of."

"Was this before the incident at the wall? The drunk man?"

"Yes, only a few weeks."

"That explains your expression."

"My expression?"

"When you saw me at the wall—like you'd seen a ghost."

My thoughts reflected back. I shuttered from the memory. "That night . . . when I heard your voice . . . and saw your profile, I . . ."

Stefan's arms wrapped around me and pulled me in. My body melted into him. "I didn't know you thought I was dead," he whispered.

My eyes lifted towards him. "Seeing you alive—" a tear descended rapidly "—it was difficult but reassuring at the same time."

He leaned in. His lips brushed the wetness away and left a soothing impression. "It doesn't matter now, love," he encouraged. "It's over. It's all over."

Releasing our embrace, we stepped inside the bookstore, and the dusty smell of old pages filled my nose and enhanced my step. Only yesterday I held a leather-bound book in my hands, but today it felt different. Stefan held my hand as we moved around the bookshelves, each with nearly the same inventory as before.

"So, what are you reading these days?"

I smiled, recalling my shelf of books I'd reread a dozen times or so. "Same as always," I chuckled.

His free hand traced the spines slowly until it stopped, and he pulled one out. He let go of my hand momentarily to flip through his new find. I leaned over his shoulder and peeked. At the top of one page, the name Aleksandr Solzhenitsyn appeared. Stefan noticed my interest and spoke with reverence. "I read this once in the Soviet Union. My comrade owned it."

"What's it called?"

"One Day In The Life of Ivan Denisovich."

When he closed the book, I reached for it. The cover showed a man behind barbed wire. "What's it about?"

"Stalin oppression, actually." Stefan smirked.

"Did you like it?"

"Yes." He nodded. "Very much."

I kissed him on the cheek— "My treat." —and walked to the counter to pay.

Stefan's expression revealed confusion and conflict, his brow curving inward. "I should be paying," he said, one hand rubbing his forehead.

I winked. "Not today, love."

When I placed the paper sack in his hands upon exiting, I elaborated. "You've always been good to me, so thoughtful and giving, please let me do this for you."

He wrapped one arm around me as we continued walking. A cool breeze blew the sticky summer heat aside and created a practically perfect afternoon. At this point, Stefan most likely knew I invented our itinerary as we went along, but I appreciated his quiet conciliation.

Half a street later, we passed a sign, *Café Sybille,* in large gold letters. Its brightness contradicted the drab gray concrete on the rest of the building. It called for us to enter.

"Have you been here before?" I questioned. He shook his head. My heart swelled—precisely the place to generate new memories.

We entered and were directed to a seat near the corner with an incompletely-decorated wall. Different than any place we'd been, yet filled nearly to capacity. A narrow, checkered tablecloth covered the table where a sole vase with a sunflower stood atop the otherwise plain wood ambiance. A long floor lamp with four hanging sconces provided minimal light next to the ceiling-to-floor windows. Stefan pulled out my chair before he sat in his.

"Anything to drink?" The waitress' high ratted hair matched her enormous, hooped earrings.

"Yes, please," I spoke first. "May I get black tea?"

"Coffee please," Stefan added. He couldn't pull his eyes from her earlobes. I bit my lip to avoid giggling.

"I'll return for your order."

I glanced at Stefan and noticed his struggle to hold back his astonishment, until we both relinquished and laughed aloud.

"I have never seen . . ." I didn't even finish.

"Me neither." He chuckled and flashed his first genuine smile in days as he laid his hands across the top of the table and motioned for me to join him.

We ordered lunch and talked about his mission to Poland, the one I didn't know he deployed for before Vietnam. By dessert we reached his training in Russia, and there, the conversation stopped. I never pushed.

"How is Edgar?" I hesitated to ask but hoped the lightheartedness of the conversation would make it simpler. Stefan pushed his bangs behind his ear and delayed his response. "You don't have to talk about it if you don't want to."

Stefan nodded. "He's good, happy."

"How old is his son?"

"Oh my, I'm such a bad judge of children. The oldest is seventeen, I believe."

"Oldest?" I didn't know he had more children.

"Yes, he has two more boys. One is early teens and a six or seven-year-old."

"Seventeen? Unbelievable. I saw him as a toddler. Does Edgar live in the same neighborhood?"

"The same flat." Stefan beamed. "He asked about you."

"Why me?" I only met him once. I couldn't have made a notable impression.

"He thinks very highly of you."

"I can't imagine why"

Stefan rolled his eyes. "He said you came to him determined to get answers. He respects you."

I watched his reaction carefully, not wanting to go down this road if it caused him pain.

"I needed to know if you were safe."

"I know." He toyed with his food. The quiet, reserved Stefan surfaced.

I waved the waitress over. "Bring us the sweetest dessert you have."

"We have some fresh *Beinenstich*."

"Yes." My cheeks lifted in delight. We made it several times at the Franke's for their guests, only we called it Bee-sting cake. "Please, with two spoons and a small dash of sugar."

Stefan glanced up; his pinched mouth dissolved into a grin.

Upon its arrival, he sprinkled the sweetener on top even though the honey custard cake already dripped with pleasing confections. To hear his laugh as we devoured it was worth every penny.

Afterward, I paid the bill. Once again, Stefan struggled with the notion. "It should be I who pays."

I brushed it off. "I'm out doing what I would've done anyway. You just happen to be my escort." Winking, I slipped my arm through his.

"Where to now?" he asked. My insides burst with his question. The two-hour rule he initially set had passed by thirty minutes.

"The Volksbühne."

"On Rosa?"

"Yes, near my old flat." I hesitated to add, "Have you been there before?"

"I went there as a child." The boost in his step was obvious when we boarded the tram to take us to the opposite end of Mitte. The Volksbühne was only a street from Max-Beer and a street from the Babylon, but we wouldn't be going to either one.

Unfamiliar with the process of a live show, I didn't know what to expect. The advertisement in the newspaper intrigued me. Real actors, instruments, and props. What a concept. With his hand in mine, he gladly acknowledged the next portion of our adventure.

"Le Nozze de Figaro?" Stefan stepped past the colonnades to open the doors for me. "Is that what we're going to see?"

I nodded happily. "If you'd like to. Today is the only matinee . . . and I've never been to one." I grinned sheepishly naïve.

He squeezed my hands. Like a child again, his smile reached both cheekbones. "It's the marriage of Figaro. The music from Mozart, Ella, it—" his arms wound around me as we waited in a short line to enter the hall "—it inspired me to draw."

Inside the theater, we fell into another world. The world of oppression, pain, war, separation, loneliness, and anger remained outside, but here for several hours, we drifted into love, beauty, song, and happiness. My eyes toggled between him and the stage. I tried hard to recall a time when Stefan's countenance revealed so much peace.

At the close of the performance, Stefan launched upright into an insistent standing ovation. I swiftly joined him. The show moved me in ways I never understood before, and as we exited the building, a miraculous transformation developed.

The entire walk to the bus and ride back to Pankow I barely spoke. Stefan chatted nearly nonstop, mostly of his childhood, the art training he received in Dresden, how his instructor lost his home and all of his family during the war, but how painting healed him. Stefan spoke of his first love of music and his collection of Mozart works and the dream he once had of opening a discotheque.

"When we get home, can I show you?"

"The records?"

"Yes, they're in the art room."

My heart sprung into somersaults. Stefan and I in the art room listening to music? I couldn't imagine a more perfect end to a perfect day.

Once we returned the phonograph to its shelf in the cupboard, Stefan pulled out album after album and played one song after another. Listening, I reached for a canvas and removed the dusty butterfly collage. Though its presence brought happy memories, today was about new beginnings. I positioned the easel near the window and searched for a brush.

"Would you paint for me?"

His head shot upward from the stack of album covers in his arms. A momentary flash of panic appeared and then evaporated. He changed the record on the phonograph, set the needle, and stepped next to me. I recognized the music from the play . . . Mozart.

Standing before me, his hand wrapped over mine and held for several seconds, the paintbrush centered within our touch. His other hand slid to my waist, his fingers caressing my blouse. The tickle his touch created vanished the moment he leaned in. His closeness always left me wanting. The sensation of his lips on my neck lingered long after his mouth withdrew.

Breathless, my quickened pulse decelerated the farther he stepped away towards the paint cupboards. He scanned the supplies and pulled several colors from the rack. After he mixed them with oils to moisten again, he stepped to the canvas. It had been well over two decades since I witnessed Stefan's talent on a backdrop, but as he made his first brush strokes, it was obvious his skills endured. I pulled up a stool and watched as he worked. Within minutes I recognized the distinct profile of the Volksbühne. Today made quite a powerful impression on him.

He worked for an hour before Mari found us and announced dinner. In her quick assessment of the room, she winked my direction and quickly vacated the space.

Stefan continued for another thirty minutes and, short of a finishing touch, the portrait neared completion. By the time he turned back to me, fatigue set in, but without a doubt, his result brandished a long-absent joy.

He replaced the brush and paint and reached for me. In an instant, my body pressed next to him, his skin coated with a light layer of sweat. His arms wrapped fully around me, his chin resting in the hollow of my neck. When the record ended, the only sound came in the slow hum of his breath. Stefan made no motion to let go, and I willingly surrendered.

That night, when Stefan tucked me into bed, he sat on the edge like before. His fingers tenderly tickled my ear and settled on my cheek. Since we left the art room, silence consumed him. When he leaned down to kiss me goodnight, words would have spoiled the sensation. His lips arrived lightly, but induced intensity the more he pursued. There was no doubt Stefan's kisses weakened me, but tonight my whole body went numb. Relishing in the sensation, I peered over to confirm Mari had not awakened to our affection. Drawn to him, and everything about him, I cherished the idea that we were entering uncommon ground—that today became the first day of the rest of our lives.

Thirty-six

ZIONSKIRCHE

October 1987

"Ella, could you get the door?" Lena cried from the hallway. A large plate of warm biscuits filled her hands as she waited at the mortuary door. "I made these for Edmund and Katharina. There are more in the kitchen if you want one." Flour covered her arms up to her elbows. I quickly rushed forward and propped the heavy door open.

"Oh, Lena, there are times I miss this."

"Miss what?" Her back held the door as she waited for me.

"Working in a restaurant. Like when I worked for Hilde and Gus at the cafe. I miss serving and making people happy."

Lena's brow raised. "You can join me in the kitchen anytime."

I smiled at her playfulness. "I just want to feel useful again."

She leaned in and kissed my cheek. "Your time will come. You'll find your place once more. For today, enjoy the peace." She tipped her chin with gratitude, and I let the door fall closed as she greeted someone on the other side.

Curious, I cracked the door to peek. My eyes briefly scanned the backside of a stranger in a white lab coat before he disappeared through the office doorway. Business never slowed or stopped for the Frankes, and it wouldn't surprise me if they brought in more help. Maybe he was a colleague of Edmunds. I shut the door with an urgency. The less I became reacquainted with the mortuary responsibilities, the better. Despite Katharina's pure heart, I knew the DDR and their requirements for a continued relationship.

Being in the Franke home once again, after all this time, I needed to find a way to look beyond it or accept it.

"Ella!" Stefan's alarmed voice called from behind.

That tone never delivered good news. "Yes?" I glanced at a newspaper rolled in his fist, his fingers white from the grip. "What's wrong, Stefan?" Josef and Anton immediately entered my thoughts. Terrorist acts continued to increase against the foreign militaries in the West, and many innocent bystanders were continuously caught in the fray.

"An incident occurred two nights ago."

"Where?" Instantly at his side, I feared the worst. He rolled out the paper and laid it flat on a table. A picture of the Zion church covered the front page. My eyes squinted to read as fast as possible. "Darek?"

"I don't know." He rubbed his chin. "The article describes a raid at the church, but also insists no government involvement. A group of skinheads attacked and injured the concert attendees."

"Skinheads?" I questioned. More than a few punk and hippie vagabond could be described as a *skinhead*. Why were they targeting their own? I mulled over this knowledge for several seconds. "Stasi has to be behind it."

My eyes continued to scan for details. There were hundreds of people listening to a western punk band called *Element of Crime*. The People's police official statement claims they were unaware of the attack. My nose stung. *No way they were unaware.* They watched the building daily but especially concert nights. They'd even been known to arrest the patrons before they entered. "They let this happen, Stefan."

"Yes, Ella. I'm sure of it. And to think . . . you could have been there."

His words rang true. If we hadn't come together, I would've been sketching the concert. "It doesn't say how many are injured."

"It won't. You'll have to get more information elsewhere."

Agitated, I couldn't settle my mind the rest of the day. Although wounded by Darek's betrayal and his decision to send Jurek after us, a small part of me took this attack personally, despite not being present when it happened. The movement and its people were a central part of my life for three-and-a-half years.

The next morning, I slipped downstairs before the sun came up. If I didn't, I knew Stefan would try to stop me. On my way to the servant's exit I bumped into Lena.

"Where are you off to so early?" she asked, tying her apron.

"I have some errands to see to; I'll be back soon."

"By yourself?" She eyed me warily.

"Yes, I'll be fine." I kissed her on the cheek and quickly fled the house. There was little doubt in my mind as to where I was headed. My restlessness in the last twenty-four hours needed resolution. The bus ride to Mitte dragged longer than previously. Every building, streetlamp, or tree we passed prolonged my insecurity and what I'd say once I arrived.

Nothing about the Zionskirche's superior appearance had changed. This time, however, when I entered I didn't linger or wait for the Priest. I led myself through the arches, located the stairs, and descended. The environmental library where IFM conducted their business was rumored to be in the basement.

Over a year ago, changes took place within Darek's group. Although I kept myself clear of the details on purpose, some adjustments were hard to ignore. The formation of a new opposition group called Initiative for Peace and Human Rights (IFM) came forth, and judging by the size, this one absorbed many smaller factions. Its creation, meant to force political reform and establish democracy—though still in the infant stages—became one of Darek's biggest ambitions, along with his continued involvement in *The Grenzfall*. Its literary success defied everything the DDR stood for. Despite the pressure churches were under for protecting the "dissenters", the environmental library in the Zionskirche was where the IFM operated.

I hesitated briefly before pushing the door open and entering the room uninvited. A tall man with a buzz cut and wiry glasses tried to stop me until I spied Darek behind him.

"Darek!" I called.

"Annika?" He waved the man aside and stepped into full view. I gasped. The entire right side of his head bulged, black and blue.

With disbelief, I could hardly find the words. I averted his gaze by briefly peering around the room. Shelves of books and supplies piled high against each wall, and the printing press from the pub sat atop a desk in the center of the small space.

"What are you doing here?" Darek approached me. Again, his mood proved difficult to read.

"I . . . I" My teeth gnawed on the inside of my cheek nervously. He stopped at the edge of the desk when I pointed to his injuries "You were there?"

He ignored my question. "Why are you here?"

Riled, I found my voice. "Look, Darek, I'm not here to inform on you, disrupt your work, or cause issues—"

"Then why?" He crossed his arms over his chest as a couple other men entered the room. Their stances equally defensive as they watched and waited from the other side.

"Because whether you believe me or not, I have always been loyal to this cause and to you!"

His weight shifted. His hand went to his forehead and rubbed for a curiously long time.

"I came to see if you were okay."

Darek had always been good at hiding emotion, but astonishment blanketed him.

"I don't think you realize what you did for me when you hired me . . . and believed in me when no one else did." My eyes searched his for understanding. "I always kept your confidence. I never revealed anything outside of our group and truly hoped we'd find an end to this government's control."

"You changed," he muttered. "Your drive vanished."

I considered his words. "No, Darek. It only shifted."

"I saw potential. I saw someone with nothing to lose . . . then you found something to lose."

My eyes narrowed with confusion. "What are you talking about?"

"The man, the soldier who returned. He changed you."

"The soldier?"

"Stefan, right?" Darek's eyes narrowed my direction.

"H . . .how do you know he came back?"

"He made his intentions quite clear."

"When . . . how?" My mind struggled to keep up. *What is he saying?*

"Why do you think I've left you alone?"

"I disappeared."

"I stopped looking."

"Why?"

"Because you were right . . . and he was right."

"Right about what?"

"Right about your loyalty." His eyes softened. "He clearly didn't care about what we did, simply that you were safe."

"How do you know this?"

Darek's mouth tightened into a thin line. "He's quite persuasive."

"You met?"

"He told me of Jakob's fate." He rubbed his chin. "Is he aware you're here?"

My heart skipped a beat over the odd question. If I said yes, he might recognize I'm lying. Though too risky to say no, I stared at him for a full minute in silence.

"It doesn't matter. You have nothing to fear from me anymore," he added.

My exhale bared relief.

"I'm unfamiliar with Stefan's history, but he knows the system. I have too much to lose to worry about you."

"So, Stefan came here . . . to you?"

Darek glanced at his wristwatch and back at me with tired eyes.

This behavior implied our conversation was over, something I'd learned about him years ago. "I'm sorry, Darek. I'm sorry you were attacked." My eyes lowered briefly. "I just wanted you to know." I extended my hand.

He glanced at me warily. I motioned for him to shake it. He did.

"I'm glad you're still leading the fight. The cause needs someone like you. I wish you well."

He nodded. "Thank you for your concern. Your visit comes as a . . . surprise."

Our hands released, and he turned away. As I walked towards the door, he called to me. "Ella?"

He used my real name.

"By the way, you were right about Karin. Actually, its Monika."

"Karin Lenz?" I hadn't thought of her since the day I left Darek last.

"Yes, and the man . . . he's a Stasi agent named Detlef." He shook his head and handed the sketches back to me. "You were always quite good at your job."

"Thank you, Darek." I placed them in my purse.

"Good luck."

When I stepped outside, I took a deep breath and finally allowed my anxious soul to find reprieve for the first time since arriving. When I opened my eyes, they fell upon another restless form trying hard to stay calm at a nearby bench, his movements too shifty to be enjoying an afternoon in the park. I caught his eye. I should've known he would come.

"Stefan?"

"Ella." He rubbed his hands on his pants before standing. "Everything alright?" His eyes motioned back to the church.

I studied it for a moment and nodded. "Yes, everything's good."

He held out his hand and joined mine. Nothing else was expressed, nothing needed to be. This part of my life was certainly over and soon to be forgotten.

We took our time walking back to the house, but as we approached, a terrifying scream met us.

"Stefan!" The hair on the back of my neck stood straight. "Stefan!" Katharina ran from the back door of the mortuary without shoes, her hair flying wildly.

"Katharina?" Stefan let go of my hand and ran to her side, holding her up. "What happened?"

"It's father."

"What happened?"

"He collapsed. Edmund is attending him. I've called the *krakenwagen*."

"Did he fall? Hit his head? What?"

"I'm not sure. We found him on the floor, and he—" she sobbed into his shoulder "—he's not breathing."

We ran back to the house. By the time we reached the front door, the ambulance pulled onto our street. Breathless, I immediately went upstairs to find the children, sure they'd be scared with the heightened alarm. Thirteen-year-old Jonas held his sister sweetly on the edge of the bed as she whimpered.

I directed the children to the library, the one place capable of diverting attention from the sitting room. I didn't want them to see their grandfather in such a desperate state. Once inside, I closed the door and reached for the first adventure book I could find.

"Come, Jonas and Sofia, have a seat on the couch, and I'll read to you."

"Tante Ella, what's wrong with Papa?"

"He's going to be okay." I said this unapprised of his condition. "He's going to the hospital for help and will come home soon." I held them close and continued to read, trying hard to keep our minds off the emergency.

After an hour, I asked them to help me make dinner, unaware of where Katharina, Edmund, or Stefan might be. We ate alone at the table. Even Mari went missing.

Later that night, after tucking the children into bed, I slipped into the library and grabbed a book with the intent of distracting myself until I received word of Herr Franke's condition. Too difficult to concentrate, I scanned the pages. My mind centered on the night's event. With no love lost between Herr Franke and me, I questioned the time spent worrying. Since I arrived, he carefully avoided me as if I didn't exist. My sole justification for his welfare came in the fact that he *is* the father of two of the most important people in my life.

Well after midnight, Stefan kissed me awake, curled in one of the oversized chairs, the book having slid to the floor.

"Oh, Stefan. How is he? How's your father?" I sat up, searching his puffy red eyes for answers. Stefan knelt at my feet and laid his head in my lap. Although the weeks after our reunion were trying, the distress he currently balanced broke him. "What happened?" My hands smoothed his hair. Expecting the absolute worst, my heart ached for this man.

"He had a stroke," Stefan whispered. His cheek pressed against my leg, moisture soaking through my pants, though I couldn't hear him crying.

"What's a stroke? What does that mean?"

"Half his body is paralyzed."

"Half?" I had never heard of a stroke or its debilitating results.

"His right arm and leg don't move. He'll be in the hospital for a while, but we haven't been told much more." His voice cracked. "He may never come home or be himself again."

"I'm sorry, Stefan." I rubbed his head until he fell asleep. The grandfather clock chimed twice in the hallway signifying the lateness of the hour when I nudged him awake.

"You'll be more comfortable in bed, love." My turn to tuck him in, I guided him to his room.

"Stay," he mumbled. When his head hit the pillow, one hand pulled me near. "Please don't leave."

I kissed him on the cheek and climbed in next to him. Snuggling against his warmth, the weight of his arms around me grew heavier the moment he fell asleep. Whatever happened tonight took a great deal of emotion. My heart suffered for him. *Nothing is harder than seeing a person you love in pain.* I folded my hand in his and closed my eyes.

Thirty-seven

EMPLOYEE OR STASI

1 November 1987

"Stefan . . . .Katharina? Time for dinner." I stuck my head through the morgue door. "Stefan?" No reply. "Katharina?" I called again to no avail. In the last month, Stefan spent nearly as much time as his sister in the mortuary, not only because their workload increased, but the routine took his mind off his father's condition, which progressed quite slowly in the hospital.

"Edmund? Where are you? I made *Sauerbraten* tonight." Chuckling as I stepped inside, I continued, hoping the description would force them to salivate. "The roast was marinated with vinegar, cloves, and juniper berries since yesterday." No answer. "The meat is rather tender; it fell off the bone." I glanced down the darkened hallway. Lights seeped from under several doors. Passing the room with the compartments, I remembered the day I entered and discovered the bodies. Shuddering, I deliberately left it unchecked. Meandering down the hall, I avoided the door to the crematorium as well, which even after decades smelled the same.

"Even your children are washed up and sitting at the table. Where are you?" With my sleeve pressed to my mouth and nose, the question came out muffled. I stood in front of the closed office door. Out of respect I knocked, but with little patience left, quickly entered. Katharina and Edmund sat behind the desk, deep in discussion.

"Hey, you two, dinner's ready. Where's Stefan?" Mari and I continued the dinner duties, and they rarely missed a meal—well, Edmund rarely missed a meal. "Are you okay?"

Katharina glanced up. "Yes, we're fine. Just going through some paperwork. I think Stefan is next door."

I cringed. They referred to the compartment room. "Do you want me to hold dinner for you?"

"No," Edmund answered for them both. "We might be here awhile."

"What's the matter? You look upset."

They glanced at each other solemnly. It really wasn't my business, but in the last few months of living together, we shared more than simply a house.

"Father is coming home soon."

"Oh." My eyes lightened, certain Stefan would be pleased. "That's good news, isn't it?"

"Well," —Katharina teared up— "he's never really recovered from the stroke. Yes, I want him here, but he needs help—lots of help—and . . ." Edmund placed an arm around his wife and kissed her cheek. "I don't know what to do."

"I'm sorry, Katharina." There were few times I'd seen her this emotional. She always lifted everyone else's burden. Even through adulthood she retained her *schmetterling* nickname, floating like a butterfly, bringing happiness wherever she went. Her sadness broke my heart.

"Anything I can do to help?"

"No." She wiped her nose. "You're already doing a lot with the house, dinner, and tutoring. Even my children think you're their mother half the time." She laughed between a sniffle.

I grinned. "Well, as for tonight, I'll feed the children and make sure to warm it up for when you're ready. Please don't worry about rushing in." I turned to give them privacy.

"Oh, Ella." Edmund held up a hand. "Check with Ralf. He might be hungry; he's staying late tonight."

My tongue caught in my throat. "Ralf?"

The way I responded brought both of their faces towards mine. My fingers gripped the door frame, but I still felt the floor roll underneath me. Afraid I'd faint, I quickly sat on the couch. Edmund shot to my side. "What's wrong, Ella?"

"R-Ralf?" I repeated.

"Ralf," Katharina confirmed. "Stefan's friend." Her eyes squinted after she rubbed them again. "Remember? We talked about him the time you were here asking about Stefan."

"I'm aware of who he is," I growled. "Why is he here?"

"Are you upset?" Katharina sprang forward, her hands reaching for mine. "You're shaking," she cried.

"Where is everyone?" Stefan appeared in the doorway. My eyes glanced to him and attested to my panic. "Ella, what's wrong?" Immediately before me, he took over for Katharina. His hands wrapped around mine.

"Ralf?" My eyes pleaded.

"Oh no." His countenance fell. "I . . . I meant to . . . ." He peered up at Katharina and Edmund. Katharina spoke for them both, "We'll leave you two and see to the children."

Stefan nodded as they left the room. Guilt washed over me for interrupting their business and driving them from their office. But I struggled to discern which of my emotions carried the most weight at the moment: guilt, anger, or betrayal.

His fingers rubbed mine tenderly. "Ella—"

"What's he doing here?" I tried to whisper, but my pitch escaped high and shaky. The very man who drove terror into me month after month—every time I arrived for an assignment, I spent half the time scanning the location for Ralf, whose identity at the time stayed unknown. Yet here he was, working in this home!

"I'm sorry. I should have told you."

"Told me what?" My cry sounded flustered.

"I intended to tell you he never meant you harm."

"How can you say that he never meant harm? He followed me, frightened me."

"He waited for me. His intent was only about me."

"What do you mean, you?"

"He was searching for me."

"For revenge?"

"At first, . . . yes." Ralf appeared in the office doorway. My body quivered at his arrival. Stefan moved to the couch next to me and pulled me tightly to his side. His arms fully engulfed me, although I couldn't draw my eyes away from the man before us. The long black coat no longer covered his form, and his black hair was cut short and above his ears, but it was him, the stranger who watched me for over a year.

"Why?"

"The truth is, I wanted vengeance for what happened in Czechoslovakia." Ralf came inside and let the door close. His changed look and confession somehow made him appear less threatening, but I continued to stare.

"Are you hearing this, Stefan?" My eyes widened with his truthfulness.

"I already know, Ella. Let him speak."

"It wasn't until Stefan found *me* and— "

"And what?" I pushed.

"—shared his story . . . his regret."

"It was that easy. He confessed, and you just forgave him?"

"No, not easy at all. Nothing is easy with hate or forgiveness." His hands fidgeted at his sides. "It took a lot of time, arguments, even a fistfight once, but Stefan kept trying. He persisted."

"But why me? Why did you come and frighten me?"

"I couldn't find Stefan. When I came here looking for him, Katharina didn't have any answers. When she told me about you, and how you loved each other, I knew you could lead me to him. If Stefan was in Berlin, he wouldn't be far, and you were easier to locate."

I steamed. I thought I'd been careful, yet now I learn how completely vulnerable I'd been.

He wiped the growing sweat off his neck and swallowed hard before he spoke. "I used you as bait to flush him out. I knew if he lingered nearby and saw me approach you, he would intervene . . . and he did."

"Where?"

"The concert."

My eyes flashed to Stefan. "You were busy that night." The words came out bitter. I turned back to Ralf. "Did you intend to hurt me?"

"No, only scare you. I promise, Ella, I wouldn't have laid a hand on you."

Attempting to digest this news, my mind reeled in recollection. My eyes met Stefan's once more. "That's why you weren't surprised when I told you about Ralf." His eyes lowered. "Why didn't you tell me then?" Betrayal was unequivocally evident in my voice.

"We'd only been together a couple days. I didn't think it was the right time. After you got here and life settled down, I forgot. I never meant for this to come as a surprise."

I recognized that Stefan felt responsible for Ralf's circumstances. I also understood he would never forgive himself until he made it right. As the silence expanded, Stefan's eyes returned to his hands, and Ralf transferred his weight as one hand jiggled an object in his pocket. I glanced between the two, searching for direction while I chewed on my thumb nail. Finally, I spoke.

"You gave him a job?" My question was intended for Stefan, but Ralf answered first.

"No, he gave me a life."

Awkward silence ensued again until Ralf continued. "I'm sorry I frightened you, Ella. It was a stupid plan. Please forgive me."

The words of wisdom sweet Mari shared that first day after Stefan reappeared in my life rang in my ears, ". . . there will need to be a lot of forgiveness." Little did she or I realize how far-reaching those words would extend.

Unsteady, I stood with Stefan's help. He refused to let go, even when I turned towards Ralf. Studying his friend closer, I noted how his black bangs clung to his wet forehead, his tall thin frame bent over, and his eyes lowered to match his sulking jaw. His remorse appeared genuine, but I hardly had the authority to judge. With all the wrongs I'd committed over the years and the compassion I sought, I had no right to hold anything against this man. What if Katharina or Lena chose not to forgive me, and I'd hurt them deeper and longer than his harm ever did against me?

I held out my trembling hand, trying hard to grasp the notion I would touch a man who purposefully terrified me for months. His eyebrows lifted shortly before the edges of his mouth did, and when his hand met mine, it shook as well. I stared at our clasped hands for several seconds, trying to digest the moment.

Upon release, I took a couple steps backward. Stefan's arm still draped my waist. I glanced between the two and swallowed. "Dinner is ready, and you're both welcome to come." The men exchanged faint smiles and followed me out of the mortuary.

At dinner that night, my eyes fluctuated from across the table to both ends. The faces that met mine shared no blood relation to me, but we possessed a greater bond. In some cases, our connection spanned decades, in others a few years, and one, mere minutes. Edmund, Katharina, Jonas and Sofia, Mari and Cade, Stefan, I, and Ralf. With many blessings and much to be thankful for, the conversation was light and cheerful, a stark alternative to only an hour before.

Everyone relocated to the sitting room for tea, and I caught Cade by the sleeve, leading him to the hallway before Mari could recognize his delay.

"Cade, I need to talk to you." We stepped farther into a corner. "Do you know why we needed to leave our flat?"

"Yes. Mari told me."

"Do you see why it's important we keep her safe from that life?"

"My group isn't like that. They only want peace."

"Mine wanted peace too but were willing to go great lengths for it."

"It's different, Ella."

"It's not." I pulled the folded sketches from my pocket and handed them to him. "This is Karin's agent." I pointed to Detlef. "They meet together often."

"Stasi?"

"She's an informant. Her real name is Monika Haeger."

Cade studied the sketches. "You're positive."

I nodded and added, "Is the cause worth losing her?"

"No," he whispered. "No, never." He tried handing them back.

"Keep them. I'm done."

"There you are." Mari bounced towards us and slipped her arm through Cade's just as he placed the pictures inside his jacket pocket. "Everything okay?" She glanced between us both.

"Yes, of course." Cade leaned in and kissed her cheek tenderly. "Everything's great."

She grinned wide. "Let's play Skat. It's been too long."

"Of course, love." He led her to the door. "Join us, Ella."

I smiled with a sigh of relief. "I'd love to."

Thirty-eight

COMPASSION

3 December 1987

The grandfather clock chimed midnight only minutes ago, but the light from the dining room glowed as I entered.

"I thought I'd find you here." This was the first time I caught Stefan and Katharina sitting together since their father arrived a week ago. "May I speak with you both?"

A cold dinner spread before them, and exhaustion draped their faces. Not only did they both work tirelessly in the mortuary, but they took turns caring for their father who lost the use of one complete side of his body.

"Don't stop eating, just listen to me please." They glanced at each other but did as I asked and continued to spoon the lentil soup.

"I've been thinking all day and have concluded that neither one of you can keep this up. The fatigue is going to make you careless or sloppy, and it can be dangerous in your work." Stefan stopped and held his spoon to his lips but didn't eat. "I can take over the duties with your father."

His lips parted slightly. For a moment, I wasn't sure if he choked on the food or waited for me to continue. I quickly followed up, "I can still tutor the children for a couple of hours each day and tend to him for the rest. Your father's needs are a priority, and I can't sit and watch you both wear yourselves out trying to care for him and the responsibilities of the mortuary. Please let me do this."

Katharina's tired eyes shifted between Stefan and me, but his remained fixed on my face. "I can't ask you to do this, Ella. He needs" —He swallowed and put his spoon down— "He needs to be fed and cleaned. It's an unpleasant job."

"Stefan, I did this for my own father for weeks before he passed. I'm not afraid of it."

Katharina smiled through her fatigue. "It's very sweet of you, but he has refused anyone but us. We talked about hiring a nurse, but the suggestion makes him angry."

"I'm not exactly a stranger. Maybe he'll give it a chance." I said this knowing I did not top his favorites list. "Let me at least try. You're sitting here eating dinner at midnight, only to wake up at the crack of dawn to start over again. It can't hurt to try."

Stefan reached for my arm and rubbed. "Are you sure?"

"I'm sure."

"Oh, my sweet sister." Katharina got up from her chair and threw her arms around my neck. After she kissed my cheek, she cried, "You're an angel."

I chuckled, "I am most definitely not an angel."

Stefan laughed out loud. "I think I can attest to that."

I shot him a bristly glance. "Neither are you."

He hooted again. "True, true."

Katharina squeezed and said goodnight, leaving Stefan and I in the kitchen alone. He turned outward on his stool and pulled me to his lap. His chin nestled warmly against my neck. "You are being generous and caring in your offer, but I—"

301

"Stefan," I cut him off. "Why are you saying this like a warning?"

He lifted his head and held my hand against his chest "My father is in pain." He exhaled. "And when a person is in pain, they tend to treat others badly . . . even those they love."

Stefan's concern touched me. I let his words sink in and responded carefully. "No offense, love, but your father has rarely been kind to me," I justified, "so, what will change?"

He chuckled as if I joked, although we both knew I spoke the truth.

"I want to do this."

"Okay." He slid me off his lap and to my feet before placing his dishes in the sink. "Meet me at his bedroom door at seven. Wear something . . . that can get dirty." His parting kiss tasted playful and then he patted my butt on his way out. "If anyone can handle my father, it will be you."

Thirty-nine

POWER OF THE WRITTEN WORD

Recalling the arrangement made the night before, I set out for an early walk to clear my head. Although I meant everything I said to Stefan, the idea of voluntary mistreatment stripped my motivation. Wrapped in additional layers from the cold, I ambled down the same side of his street and back several times. My senses soaked up the crispness of the breaking dawn and the cleansing power of the winter air. On the nearby Schönhausen Palace grounds, the skeletal branches of the oak trees offered a commanding presence, but I missed my Linden trees and their fragrant morning kiss. On the third pass, my watch reflected 6:45 am. Taking deep breaths, Stefan's adoring face replaced Herr Franke's sour expression. Stefan counted on me, and that put a lift in my step and gave me the encouragement I needed for my first day. Losing the coat on my way in, I rushed upstairs in my t-shirt and jeans to meet him by his father's bedroom door by 7.

"Good morning, Love." Stefan kissed my hands. "Were you outside?"

"Only for a bit."

"Look at you; even in work clothes you're beautiful."

"You're such a charmer." I smiled in return.

"Well, you'll need all the charm I can offer today, and I promise to give you more tonight as well."

"In that case let's go. The sooner I complete my chores, the sooner I get to be romanced."

Stefan leaned in to kiss me, and it was if we hadn't enjoyed such an indulgence in days. If our duties hadn't called for us, I would've been perfectly content standing there kissing him all day long.

"Father?" Stefan stepped into the dark room first and waved for me to follow. "Father, I've brought someone to help us." He switched the lamp on next to the bed.

I heard the grunts before I saw the damage. It took every ounce of self-control to not cringe at Herr Franke's appearance since the stroke. A few wisps of white hair separated large bald patches on the sides of his skull. Dark and sunken eyes balanced contradictory cheeks. His left side wrinkled with age but his right sagged heavy and limp from the stroke.

"Grrg, frah whooo?" He managed to say a word I recognized.

"Someone who wants to help you and make you comfortable." Stefan stepped over to his father's drawers and retrieved clean clothing for the day.

Herr Franke's eyes finally focused on me, and his expression curled in disgust. "Nnng."

"What?" Stefan placed the clothes at the end of the bed and leaned in.

"Nnoo." His father bellowed. From his functional left side, a finger rattled my direction.

"Father, it's Ella. She's here to help."

304

He continued to moan and thrash similar to a child's tantrum. Stefan's eyes fell. In his attempts to calm his father, he twisted my direction and whispered, "I'm sorry, Ella. I don't think—"

"No, Stefan," I cried. "We haven't even tried. Don't give up this easily. I'm not a cream puff. I can take a hit once in a while."

His eyes rotated between me and the old man. "Okay," he conceded. "Let's give it a go today. I'm going to change him and clean him up." Stefan pulled the covers off his father's legs. "I'll show you how I shift him to the side to replace his linens, but if he fights you, come and get me. It can be dangerous for you both." I stepped back and watched as Stefan explained his actions to his father loud enough for me to hear. The respect in his voice matched the tenderness in his touch as he rolled his father to one side. Herr Franke moaned but not as loud as when we arrived. Making mental notes on where to touch or what to say, I pretended not to worry, but my stomach swayed. When he finished, he turned my direction. "Do you have any questions?"

I shook my head.

"Would you make him some porridge?"

"Yes, anything to drink?"

"He struggles with a glass. If you put juice in a small teacup, it works easier held up to his mouth."

"Of course. I'll be right back."

In the kitchen, Lena had already started her day. "Hello, stranger," she joked. "When will I get some time to get to know you again?"

"Oh, Lena. I miss you too. I promise one of these nights, for sure." I peered up at the ingredients in the cupboard. "I'm going to help with Herr Franke's needs for now."

"Herr Franke, as in *elder* Herr Franke?" She shot me a quizzical look. I giggled. I'd never thought of Stefan as Herr Franke, but I suppose he was also.

"Yes." I responded confidently and proceeded to heat the ingredients on the stove.

"You know he . . . um . . ."

305

"Yes, I know."

"No, I don't think you do," she insisted. "He drove *me* out of the room with a string of cuss words and the sharp end of his utensils . . . and he's always loved me."

"Lena," I stared hard her direction. "This family has taken me in and protected me, loved me, and provided for me. I can't sit back and watch Katharina and Stefan wear themselves to the bone, trying to do it all by themselves, when I'm here."

Lena left her work and stepped over to me. She draped her arms around me and held me tight. "Love makes people do crazy things." She kissed my cheek. "I'm sorry I doubted. I'll be here for you if you need anything."

"Thank you."

I finished preparing the breakfast and carried it upstairs to the master bedroom. In full light, with the drapes opened, I understood why Herr and Frau Franke spent their evenings here. It was a vision of perfection. The carved canopy bed centered the space, and an elegant gold-plated chandelier with crystal trimmings provided dazzling illumination throughout the room. It was exquisite. I placed the tray on the nightstand as Stefan finished propping his father up against a half dozen pillows for better view. I stood at the end of the bed, directly in his sight, and chewed the inside of my cheek as I waited.

Herr Franke grabbed his son's arm with his left hand and squeezed. "Nnnooo." I worried his attempt to change Stefan's mind might be successful. I inhaled and walked to the side of the bed. Placing my arm around Stefan, I led him to the door. "We'll be fine." I spoke as if my stomach didn't churn. "Don't worry about him or me. Go about your duties and remember you owe me a night's worth of charm." I kissed his cheek and closed the door behind him.

Herr Franke's jaw set tight, like stone . . . possibly marble. His eyes followed me while the rest of him lay completely still. I grabbed one of the sitting chairs by the window and pulled it towards the bed. "Now, Herr Franke, you have a wonderful son." I spoke while positioning closer. My intent was to feed him breakfast. "And he loves you, but he needs to work, and you can't be alone." I picked up the bowl and held it firmly in my hands, dishing out a spoonful and bringing it to his lips. They sealed shut. "Come now." My voice relayed a calmness I lacked within. "You need to eat." He wiggled his head the opposite direction when I tried again. "How do you expect to get stronger if you refuse to eat?"

"Kkkathhhha."

"Katharina must also work, and she's caring for her two children, your grandchildren." I held the spoon close and allowed the sugary cinnamon scent to float to his nostrils. "You can't expect her to work through the night, can you?"

His head jerked against the spoon with my third attempt and catapulted the contents on the floor. "Herr Franke!" I spoke resolutely. "You need to eat regardless of how you feel about me!"

His one good hand popped right out from underneath his covers and slapped the bowl. The porridge splashed all over me and the side of the bed.

"Ahhh! Are you kidding me?" Snarling his direction, I shook the chunks off my hands, back onto the tray. Fuming, I sat there and stared at him, certain one side of his lip curled into a ragged smile. "So, you want to behave like a child?" I leaned forward, appearing as if I climbed out of a rubbish can. I grabbed the spoon again and lifted it towards his airtight mouth. "Alright. Well, I can't force you to eat." I tossed the utensil back into the bowl and went to their bathroom to clean up.

Glancing around the room, I imagined this to be a happy place, its ambiance soothing and enjoyable. *There must be something here that brings this cranky, old man joy!* In the corner I spied his radio. Removing the tray and placing the radio on the nightstand, he watched me curiously. I fumbled with the knobs. A classical-music tune sprang forth from the speakers, though met with a thunderous protest.

"You used to listen to the radio all the time when I worked here." My hands rested firmly on my hips. The frustration Stefan and

Katharina warned me about, festered. *What in the world am I going to do for this man all day if all he does is fight me?* His dissentions grew by the second as I fumbled for another station. This time it was a German folk song. I peered at him with hope yet met again with disapproving grunts, accompanied by unruly kicks from his good leg. The coverings on the bed fell to the floor. Pressing my hand against his knee, I feared he might toss his whole body out of bed.

"Herr Franke, please don't do that. You might hurt yourself." I tried to keep him still, but in a brief moment his strength exceeded mine, and he kicked me square in the gut.

"Uggghhh." I doubled over and shot him a dirty look. "You're awfully strong for an old sick man." Holding my stomach, I sat back down in the chair. His tantrum escalating by the minute, I glanced at my watch. Only forty-five minutes passed since I arrived this morning. Another five hours of this until Katharina arrives, in time for me to tutor the kids for a couple hours. Then Stefan would take his shift later this evening. *Five hours!*

I turned towards the television and flipped a switch. The stubbornness in me surfaced, determined to please him. Knowing television lifted his spirits in the past, I scanned a station he might find appealing. The images piqued my curiosity since I rarely spent any reasonable amount of time around one. A show with dancing puppets came on, and Herr Franke kicked again, the lamp on the nightstand falling to its side.

"Are you serious?" I cried. "What will make you happy?" I checked the lamp for cracks and set it on the floor to avoid its possible use as a weapon.

"Ggggoo wyyy. Shisss," he grumbled, and I was sure it was laced with cuss words. Frustrated, I turned the television off.

"Herr Franke, I think I need to make something very clear here." He stopped long enough to stare me in the eyes, although his contempt remained obvious. "Your son, Stefan, and your daughter, Katharina, are doing everything they can to maintain the mortuary . . . .your mortuary!" I pointed my finger sternly his

308

direction. "Everything you have worked for your entire life is at stake. If you continue to behave this way and force them to leave their duties to see to your childish needs, they could lose the business, and you'll be forced to move or live on the street like . . . obdachlose! Is that what you want?"

I inadvertently stepped closer with each word, within striking distance, but didn't waver. "They love you with all their hearts but cannot take care of you *and* the mortuary at the same time. I know you don't feel well. I know you're unhappy. But I'm willing to do anything possible to ease your pain."

His head swung awkwardly to the side, pulling his view away from me. He might not have cared what I said, but I felt a whole lot better saying it.

Moving back to the radio, I turned it on and found a news station. Curious for updates, I listened, and in doing so, it lulled Herr Franke to sleep. I sighed with relief in my brief respite. My head fell to my hands. Tears built, threatening to break free, but my tenacity kept them in check. *What can I do differently to make this work?* I organized my thoughts before he awoke.

What have I learned about Herr Franke? He loved the news, politics, and social upheaval. He loved entertaining and indulgences. He loved his books . . . that's it. Maybe I could read to him. Combine my own love with his, and we might both survive.

While he slept, I slipped down to the library and selected a variety of different books from his personal bookcase. The shelf had been brought to my attention all those years ago when I cleaned the room. Lena warned me to be extraordinarily careful with his selections and especially to never remove them. *This occasion calls for an exception.* I picked up four random titles and hurried back up to the master suite.

When I closed the door, Herr Franke began to stir. He opened his eyes, and I stood before him, his madness resuming. Despite the loss of use in his right side, his left was more than making up for it. His fist slammed against the headboard repetitively until a small crack appeared. Scanning the nearby objects, I swiftly rearranged anything

309

that could fall, break, or be used as a weapon. His spurts of rage could put him in harm.

"Are you hungry yet?" I sat back down and braced for another round.

"Argggghhh!"

I ignored his outburst and produced a plump orange I'd picked up from the kitchen while I was downstairs. I hoped the sweet juices might soften him up.

"Nnnuuuuh" He slapped the bedspread. Placing the books on the floor, I sat on the chair and proceeded to peel the orange in front of him. As I did, his fit began to subside. I took a bite and glanced his direction.

"Ummm." I exaggerated my moan a bit. "Oh, this is perfectly ripe." I took another bite and allowed the juice to squirt on my shirt.

Drool leaked down one side of his mouth. "Oh, do you want some?" I held the next slice towards him "You must be hungry, having eaten nothing for breakfast." He jostled his head the other direction again.

"Ohhh." I nibbled. "This is sooooo delicious."

He bobbed his head back and with a snarl cried, "Sssummm."

I lifted the next piece up to his lips and placed it between them. He tried to bite and pinched part of my finger between his teeth. I didn't cry out, though the tip of my finger went numb. The expression on his face when the juices slipped through his mouth and down his throat was priceless. His eyes closed while he entered the absorbing realm of taste.

"Another one?"

He nodded clumsily. I repeated the process. This time, he gnawed more of the fruit instead of just the juice, and a small chunk separated past his lips. He gurgled and coughed. I stood to my feet as his cheeks turned red and his mouth curled on one side. "Are you okay?" I leaned in. *What if he's choking?* I stuck my finger in his mouth and past his hostile teeth. Pinching the meaty part of the orange, I drew it back

310

out. Seconds later, his skin relaxed on the left side of his face and his coloring improved.

"Whew," I cried and sat back down, holding the remains of the orange. "I need to be more careful."

"Moooorgggg."

I narrowed my eyes. "Are you asking for more?"

"Unnnoooow"

I glanced at the slices in my lap. "Okay but only the juice, no fruit." Each time I squeezed it through his lips, he savored the moment with a groan or a lick. At least he wasn't throwing it at me. After two more times he closed his mouth again. Though the juice trailed down his chin and neck, the smell of fruit beat the smell of old porridge anytime. I washed my hands at the sink and warmed a washcloth for his mouth. As I placed the damp cloth against his skin, he jerked his head, but eventually allowed me to finish. This small allowance was an enormous victory in my mind, though short lived.

When I settled back in the chair, his eyes fired up, but I ignored it. Picking up one of his books, I began to read. His growls grew so loud he couldn't hear me, but I continued, the book, *Kapitales von Karl Marx* gripped in my fingers. Marx's belief of a socialist world overpowering capitalist greed would not have been one of my chosen favorites. Though our interests differed vastly, I was not one to be close-minded and proceeded in Herr Franke's behalf. I read for three hours straight.

When Katharina showed up later in the afternoon, she stepped inside the room and watched with quiet fascination for a good ten minutes before presenting herself. The peace that emanated from her father was unparalleled. Only when he caught sight of her, he snarled as if his protests never ceased.

"Oh, Papa," she laughed, "you were fine until you saw me. Don't play me to be a fool."

He grumbled. I chuckled at this amusing interchange and placed the book down. Katharina came to hug me and noticed the old food still stuck to my shirt. "Oh my." She winced. "That good, huh?"

"He's been fine, Katharina. A bit cranky..." I turned his direction, "but I think we're going to get along just fine."

"Thank you, Ella." She leaned in and kissed me on the cheek. "I can take it from here. The children are quite happy their studies have been reduced to only the afternoons, and they're waiting for you in the library."

"Wonderful. I think I'll change first." We snickered aloud before I departed.

For the rest of the week, the exact same routine materialized. Breakfast thrown at me, extreme groans and protests to both the radio and the television, different fruits or pastries softened him up by midmorning, and hours upon hours of reading time. The books miraculously calmed his angry soul long enough for Katharina to arrive.

By the end of January, Herr Franke grew quite frail, his countenance paler and his fights weaker. He stopped throwing his food and hollering, though his glare assured me he wished to. I recognized the sullen shadow hanging over him. He was dying. I saw it with my father and now witnessed it with Herr Franke. Memories of those weeks before my Papa passed surfaced with every exchange. While we didn't share the same relationship, my concern for his welfare and quality of life evolved. It didn't matter if he felt the same or changed his feelings about me. The important thing was that *I* no longer hated or blamed him.

"Stefan?" I found him in the mortuary office working late, as usual. He glanced up with tired eyes that brightened the moment they found mine. My soul stirred at seeing his half smile. "I think you should see your father tonight."

His eyes narrowed along with the deepening of his brows. "Really? Do you think it's time?"

"Yes." I wasn't an expert on *after* death, as he was, but the moments *before* death were too familiar, and they lingered at Herr Franke's bedside.

"Alright, have you told Katharina?"

312

"Yes, barely a moment ago."

"Thank you, Ella." He came to me. "Thank you for caring for him these last couple months. We couldn't have done it without you, and I understand it hasn't been easy." He rubbed my cheek; I placed my hand over his.

"I'm sorry, Stefan."

"He'll be much happier in death."

I didn't know what that meant, but anything must be better than the life he lived now.

I went to my room, sat on the bed, and cried. Tonight's events dislodged the buried feelings of my own Papa: the illness, Anton and Josef leaving, caring for him in his final days, and his burial. I sobbed quietly but Mari awoke. She cuddled me and rubbed my head until my eyes were so heavy I couldn't keep them open.

The next morning, I found only Lena in the kitchen. "Oh, sweet Ella." She held my hands. "Every time grief strikes, it brings much to the surface, doesn't it?" My swollen eyes must've given my sorrow away.

I nodded. She knew the feelings too well. Her grandfather and father's deaths, Christoph's disappearance, and her mother's passing last year. Death held no prejudice.

"Did you see Stefan this morning?" I asked.

"Yes, only briefly. They took the body to the mortuary, right when I arrived. He hasn't come out since."

I couldn't imagine processing your own father for burial. Was it an extraordinary experience or difficult to manage? If it was the latter, I hoped Ralf would do it for him. The heaviness in my chest grew two-fold. I ached for my loved ones and their loss, and despite our unusual connection, a part of me would miss him.

I went to the master suite. Though nothing appeared amiss, the smell of death settled into every crack and cranny. I sat in the chair, the one I pulled up to his bedside every day for our traditional squabble followed by hours upon hours of reading. A hollowness lingered, much like it did when I returned to my flat on Bernauer without my father. How ironic it was here, at this location, where I left him twenty-six years ago. Katharina arrived a moment later, sniffling with red, puffy eyes.

"Oh, Ella," she cried and clung to me. "I will miss him so." Her tears moistened my neck, and I rubbed her head. When we released, she glanced about the room. "Though he was cranky in the end, his presence alone brought me comfort. I can't bring myself to remove anything, but I know I must." She pointed to the soiled linens on the bed, the smell overpowering yet overlooked.

"You don't have to do anything until you're ready."

"I don't know if I'll ever be ready."

"If you want, I can wash the linens for you."

She sat at the foot of the bed and buried her head in her hands. "I am around death every day. Why does this hurt so much?"

I sat down and wrapped my arms around her. "I wish I knew the answer to that." She laid her head to my shoulder and quivered in my embrace.

"I'm sorry he passed, Katharina. I hope wherever he is, he's free from the confines of a broken body."

"Yes." She sniffled. "Yes, I believe he is." She stopped crying long enough to speak. "You have no idea how much he appreciated you reading to him."

"What do you mean? He never said anything."

"Not in words, but it was the only time he truly seemed at peace. Every day, after I relieved you, he pushed me to continue, though you never knew. It seemed to be the only thing that consoled him."

I grinned, grateful his final time on earth wasn't completely filled with ire and agitation.

"Yes, Ella, if you don't mind removing the bedding, I would appreciate that." She stood and walked to the window. Folding the drapes in her fingers, she sighed. "I'm not sure how I'll get through it. His scent is everywhere."

I recalled the scent of my papa's pillow and walked over and kissed her on the cheek. "My heart is hoping you might have peace through this sad time."

I gathered the laundry from the bed and left her alone in the room.

It was late evening when Stefan finally entered the kitchen after the family retired. His face to his limbs hung low and heavy in exhaustion. I read a poem once where the author described death as a visitor. As a pilgrim, she traveled from house to house until someone let her in. Though no one knew her true identity, it was often times the kindest of persons who welcomed her. Upon departure, however, she'd take a soul with her. Expressed from the poet's point of view, death also took half the hearts of those who were left behind. That's what I experienced the day I buried my father and how Katharina and Stefan appeared today.

I reached for his hand, cold and trembling. Burying it in my own, I led him to the library. With limited light from a table lamp, he sat on the couch, and I curled up on his lap. Burrowing together, we wrapped ourselves within each other's arms.

Forty

FASCHING

16 February 1988

Walking hand in hand through Mitte, towards Invaliden, my heart and fingers tangled with this man at my side, the reason my spirit soared and wanted to burst with joy. Following the heartbreaking burial of the Patriarch of the family, life in the Franke home found tranquility, a trait I occasionally didn't believe would be possible, but as each member played their role, happiness flourished. Stefan, Katharina, and Ralf attended to the mortuary, Cade and Mari managed the butchery, and I resumed tutoring the children, although my heart still yearned for something more.

Earlier in the morning, Stefan and I were met in the kitchen by a large hairy beast . . . Edmund, all 6' 1" of him, lumbered around as the big bad wolf. If I hadn't been prepared for the possibility of surprises, I might have believed he'd gone crazy.

With a new zest for life in the Franke home, Katharina insisted we celebrate Fasching this year as a family. Preparations had ensued for an entire week.

"What are you doing, Edmund?" Stefan shook his head as if his brother-in-law had lost his mind.

"Katharina insisted we try on our costumes this morning, in case they don't fit."

Glancing around his robust form, Stefan and I struggled to keep our laugh contained.

"You just wait." He pointed a hairy finger our direction. "I'm not the only one she set her sights on."

We settled down with our morning coffee as Katharina and the children entered. I pulled my lips together tightly at the sight of their plump pink bellies and curly tails. Even her teenage son willingly complied with the undertaking.

"Oh . . . I see." Stefan didn't curtail his chortle. "The three little pigs and the big bad wolf."

Edmund removed his long nose and sharp teeth to eat his breakfast while Katharina stood in front of us with both hands on her round hips, ready for a fight. "You may laugh," she charged, "but you really don't think you're coming to dinner without a costume do you?" She walked to the closet and produced matching Hansel and Gretel costumes.

"Uh, no." Stefan waved his hand. "I haven't dressed up in years."

"All the more reason to do it."

"Nope."

"Uncle Stefan," —Sofia turned on her five-year-old charm, and we all watched with fascination— "you have to. Mama said this dinner was important to Papa." She snuggled her little pig body in between his arms. "You can't go without a costume."

Stefan sighed helplessly, and I snickered out loud. He squeezed the piglet until she squealed in delight, and then he reached for me. "Well, I surely won't be doing it alone."

"That's why there's one for each of you." Katharina proudly laid them on the table. I glanced warily at the red dress with the crisscrossed top, decorated apron, and coordinating scarf. Reaching for the pointed feathered hat that complimented Hansel, I placed it on his head. "Your crown, my liege." He bowed, and the whole room erupted with laughter.

"You too, Mari." Katharina retrieved another set of costumes. You and Cade will be joining us as well."

"We are?" Mari's eyes grew wide as she jockeyed to see what Katharina produced for them—a dress with a blue bodice and bright yellow skirt next to a regal suitcoat and stately sash. Snow White and her Prince Charming. It was perfect. Mari beamed, having never celebrated the event outside of the Waisenhaus. She snatched the costume eagerly and danced around the room, the dress flowing from her shoulders.

"Dinner is served at six; do not be late!" Katharina warned.

"Yes, ma'am." Stefan saluted her. She tossed an orange at his head, but he was too quick and caught it firmly with both hands. "We will be there, sis."

An hour later and a couple miles from Katharina's frenzy, we took our time strolling through my favorite neighborhood.

"I'm sorry your father didn't make it to Fasching, Stefan. I know this was always a celebrated time for your family."

"It's okay, the time I spent with him before the stroke and his struggle are the memories I hold onto."

I nodded with understanding. "My father used to dance with my mother every night after supper. It's one of the best memories I have." He squeezed my hand as I added. "It's what helped me through the time he lay sick."

Stefan shook his head. "When we met, you had already lost your parents. Knowing now what that feels like, I'm sorry I wasn't more understanding."

"You can't take fault in that. Until you experience it yourself, it's different."

318

"Looking back, though, you were so courageous. To have lived on your own and survived at such a young age, Ella—you're an incredible woman." His arm slipped to my waist and squeezed.

"I think it's wonderful Katharina wants to carry the Fasching dinner forward. Tonight will be quite special."

"Well, I appreciate your willingness to be involved, given that your previous experiences at our house were shadowed by Colonel Anker."

"Only one, the second time is a favorite memory of mine. Our first 'date' in the art room."

"Yes." He beamed. "Mine too."

We sauntered past a children's park. Giggling squeals added to the happiness of the moment.

"How is it carnival became important to your family? From what I've learned, it was more customary to the western parts of Germany."

"My grandfather started the tradition in our home."

"Your grandfather? Your father's father I assume."

"Yes. Before he took over the responsibility of the mortuary, he attended university in Mainz."

"Where's that?"

"West Germany, south of Frankfurt. He always spoke of carnival there as a religion. The entire city participates. They have their initial kick off on November 11th, 11:11 am at a town square. The parties and celebrations last until Shrove Tuesday, in February. They have music concerts, speeches and parades. My grandfather used to joke about the tradition where women could kiss men at any time."

"Simply come up and kiss them? Randomly?"

"Yes, it was generally on the cheek, but he would get this devilish grin occasionally when he spoke of it . . . always outside of my grandmother's ear of course." He chuckled.

"I wonder why Berlin doesn't carry on the carnival tradition?"

"It's possible that smaller celebrations are held, but nothing comparable to Mainz."

319

"What's the significance of dressing up?"

"I'm not sure; it's gone on for centuries. One year, grandpa dressed as a Mainz man."

"Mainz man?"

"Yeah," he chuckled. "Similar to what a British soldier would look like but different. That was the year he was in the main parade. It lasted for four hours! He showed me photographs. It was like nothing I'd ever seen." He beamed; his memory of his grandfather must've been a good one. "In my heart I believe grandfather would have loved to stay there in Mainz, but when his father called him home to take over the mortuary, I guess tradition in the home took precedence. Then he married my grandmother, who was from here in Berlin."

"I've never heard you speak of them before. Did they have any children besides your father?"

"Yes, another son, four years younger than my father."

"Where is he? Why didn't he take over the mortuary responsibilities instead of you and Katharina?"

"The fate of the hierarchy, I suppose. The eldest gets the inheritance. The youngest gets what's left over. When it was known my father would lead the mortuary, he joined the military and died in the war. I never knew him."

"Oh, I'm sorry."

"Yes, that was a difficult time for my father. He lost his brother in 1943, and then both his parents passed within months of each other in 1952. I was eight at the time."

"I'm glad you and Katharina work well together, with no animosity or competition."

"Honestly, if it weren't for the women in my life, I'd be nothing." He pulled me closer.

"What happened to your other grandfather, your mother's father. The one you spoke of from Russia?"

"He's still alive. I actually saw him when I was there."

"But I thought nobody could know your plans?" The hurt in my voice was evident.

"Nobody knew about Vietnam. But my grandfather, a prominent businessman in Moscow, he knew of my arrival before I did."

"Why couldn't he get you out of Vietnam, or out of fighting?"

"It's an honor to serve in an elite mission. I believed what I was being trained for was the right thing. I had no idea what I was going into."

We found our way to Jörg's but did not go in. We sat on the bench outside, and Stefan took a deep breath, as if his head spun wildly, but the nine months reunited taught me patience like none other.

"I'd been well-trained in recognizance. My comrades nicknamed me *die Ratte*."

"The rat? Why?"

"I could sense things others couldn't."

"You are very good at that." I nudged him lightly.

"In preparation of our departure, Edgar and I were given new identities, as Russian chemists."

Encouraged where the conversation was leading, I interjected, "He mentioned you were assigned to a train with specific disguises. Were you scared when it passed through China on its way to Vietnam?"

"Not then, not at all. When we arrived, a North Vietnamese captain met us and took us to his base. There, they informed us of our duties. Our assignment was to identify the location of the American missiles and destroy them. It was a complicated task, but we trained for nearly a year. I had no doubt we were capable of accomplishing it."

"What happened?" My whisper came out with hesitance, this was the most he'd said, and I hoped he would continue.

He studied me carefully; we'd come quite far. Licking his lips, he took another deep breath. "There were ten of us. We left after midnight and followed the intel to the letter. We entered the American base without an eyelash batted our direction. We disabled two surface to air missiles and approached the third when they

321

spotted a comrade. A fire fight ensued, but we came prepared, since this was a possibility with how heavily the Americans armed themselves, and killed the soldiers before reinforcements arrived. Our group got back to the coverage of the jungle when we realized two of our men hadn't returned with us. Everyone chalked it up as a result of war, but it wasn't what Edgar and I believed. We weren't about to leave one man down, so I volunteered to scope out the scene. Of course, you can imagine the number of troops awakened from our visit. A rescue at that time became impossible."

Captivated with his story, I never stirred, though his grip tightened and released often.

He took a quick breath. "I made the decision to leave our comrades behind."

Years later, the effects of his choice were etched in the lines of his face.

"We arrived at our own camp with a respectable amount of success. Two of the four big launchers were completely destroyed, making the American assault less destructive. We were congratulated and shown the whereabouts of our next base, though I couldn't get the men out of my head.

"Later that night, I met with Edgar, and the two of us convinced the others we needed to go back, against the counsel of the commanding officers. We misled them with the notion we could take out the other two missile launchers, but actually, our main objective was to find and rescue our men.

"When we arrived, their night watch had quadrupled. Our men hung by ropes from a water tower nearby. Anger consumed me. Edgar stopped me from charging in and shooting anything that moved, knowing I'd be dead within seconds. He persuaded me to take vengeance through the mission. I conceded, but a fire ignited, and from then on my only purpose became destruction."

Our hands clung tight enough to keep the blood from pumping, and our fingers throbbed. I quickly let go, but placed my hand on his knee. Tears soaked my cheeks.

"Each time we arrived at another base, Ella, I came prepared to take as many Amis out as possible. Word somehow spread of the attacks, because each one got harder. At the fifth base, we were ambushed. That's when the majority of my men died. I should have too. I wanted to, but was taken prisoner instead.

"Edgar, one other soldier, and I were turned over to the Vietnamese. They took us to a prison camp. We were the only Germans, although they didn't know this because we never spoke to anyone but each other."

"What happened next?" my voice squeaked.

His cheeks turned ruddy and sweat beaded on his skin. "That's where hell began."

Silence filled the little space between us. "Stefan, I'm sorry this happened to you. Do you want to talk about the prison?"

His eyes met mine, wide and glossy. "I can't . . . I don't want to think about it anymore."

What he'd shared had come naturally and was the most thus far, but I could see how much pain it caused. "How can I help you?"

"I don't know. I wish that part of my life could disappear, simply be cut from my brain."

"Stefan," —I let go of his hands and linked one arm through his— "from this very moment, it's gone. It's over. We don't have to talk about it ever again." I squeezed him tight.

"I wish it were that easy."

"Remember when you told me about your teacher, the artist from Dresden?"

"Yes."

"You told me about his tragic life—losing everything, his whole family—and yet he maintained hope."

Stefan remained still.

"As devastating as his circumstances were, he found peace. The only difference here is that you have us. Your family surrounds you, loves you. *I love you.* Similar to your professor, I believe you can find a way to let it go and progress forward."

323

Like an ocean wave immerses the sand, a calm washed over his cheeks.

"Walk with me." Stefan pulled me to my feet and held my hand. "I know things haven't been easy for you. Your whole life has been one trial after another, and I know I've been the cause—"

"Stefan, that's the past."

"Let me finish, Love."

We reached the corner of Invaliden and Acker, only a street past Jörg's place. We stopped, and from behind, Stefan wound his arms around me. My back pressed firmly against his chest, his whispered words tickled my ear, but I refused to move. This was one of my most favorite places to be. "I'm sorry you were separated from your family." He hugged me tighter.

"It's not your fault."

My eyes caught the top of a guard tower looming far above the oak trees on the corner. From this distance I could see the end of the rifle jutting out of a window. Stefan followed my gaze.

"I was part of it." The strength in his voice decreased. "I stopped people from getting to their families."

Stefan never disclosed the details of his time commanding a tower. We both comprehended the requirements of every soldier at post. He already carried his fair share of guilt before he arrived at the wall, he didn't need another reminder.

"Stefan, the separation from Josef and Anton was devastating. Burying my father and facing such loneliness was brutal. But losing you . . . I never want to feel that way again."

His lips brushed the back of my neck, their soothing touch sweeping across as he gently turned me in place to meet him.

"I've caused you undue pain for over half of your life."

"Stefan—" I started to protest, but his fingers pressed against my lips to stop me once again.

"I want to spend the rest of our lives making it up to you."

I smiled as he stepped next to me and forced our bodies parallel. "You've had a great deal of change recently, but if you will allow me one more, I think it would make you happy."

One of his arms slid around my shoulders, the other motioned forward. "Look up," he encouraged.

I glanced upon a brick building with two wide bay windows on each side of a center door. The writing on the windows was long faded, and the dirt made them impossible to see through.

"Ella, I know the last nine months have been trying. You've handled everything thrown at you with courage—Darek, Ralf, Jurek. You are the bravest woman I've ever met." Touched by his words, I melted into him, my head resting against his shoulder. He excelled at making me feel like I was the only person in his world. "What you did for my father was the most beautiful show of selfless love I'd witnessed. And although your help around the house is invaluable, I know you miss working. I heard you mention to both Lena and Mari how much you miss serving people at the café. I want to give you something that can make you happy and busy."

"Stefan, you already ha—"

"I've leased this space. It used to be a fine café, and with your touch, it will be once again." He cut me off a third time. "It's yours."

"What?" I answered, confused. "Are . . . are you serious?" I stuttered. Nothing would've prepared me for this. I met his stare. "You got this for me?"

"Yes, I know how working in restaurants pleased you over the years. It makes sense for you to manage your own. Although it has most of the major equipment, it needs some minor repair work, but with help, you could open by May, and Mari said she would help."

My blank stare bounced between his grin and the barren building before me. I couldn't believe what was happening. *I'll have my own café?* Without warning, I threw myself into Stefan, his solid stance preventing us from falling to the steps. My lips dotted his neck and cheeks until they found their way to his lips, and then they slowed to a long and sensual union, expressing my appreciation better than words.

Later that evening, as the family joined together for our own Fasching dinner, I shared the news of Stefan's gift, and we all had more than carnival to celebrate.

"Oh, Ella, isn't it wonderful?" Mari hugged me. "I hope it's not too forward of me to offer my help."

"Of course not. I wouldn't have it any other way, but can Cade let you go from the butchery?"

Cade's arm rested casually around his princess' tiny waist. "I love having her with me, but I think she would be happier in the café." He chuckled. "When Stefan presented the idea, I knew from her reaction that's what she wanted."

Mari leaned over and kissed him on the cheek.

"I'm thinking of taking on a partner as it is. I hope to spend more time away from the business." Cade twirled his finger through one of Mari's stray curls and pulled it behind her ear.

"Really?" My brows curved. "I thought it was everything to you."

"Not everything." Cade glanced at Mari. My heart swelled for her.

Though the extravagance of Fasching's from the past was absent—the Greek statues, floral vines, and the elite class—nothing compared to what sights lay before me. The big bad wolf and his three little pigs danced around the sitting room. Snow White and her Prince toasted Glühwein in the corner and nuzzled like the lovers they were. Lena, Freddy, and their two daughters arrived in time for supper as the Shoemaker and his three elves, complete with pointy ears and bells. As Gretel in a festive skirt with my handsome Hansel in his jumper, I could not recall a more joyful time in my life, outside of my memories with Josef and Anton. Notwithstanding the wall and its scheming restrictions, today proved that happiness could blossom alongside the darkest of places.

Forty-one

PAST AND PRESENT

June 1988

"Uncle Stefan, may I have a pretzel?"

Stefan glanced towards the street vendor. "I don't know. Do you think you could eat all that? It looks twice your size."

Sofia stood on her tiptoes, trying to appear taller, and giggled. Only a week ago Katharina's precious daughter celebrated her sixth birthday. I glanced at this man who tackled the roughest of situations but crouched here, tender and gentle, with his niece. He would've made a wonderful father. At forty-four and forty-two, it was unlikely children were in our future, and imagining that broke my heart.

"Here, sweetie. Here's a mark for the pretzel." Stefan handed her a shiny coin, and her eyes lit up as she ran to the vendor and waited in line. I wound my arm through his when he stood and leaned in. My lips grazed his ear. "You're going to spoil her." I smirked. Stefan turned sharp and, without missing a beat, reached around my waist and began to tickle me. He knew my weak spots and I cringed to get him to stop.

"Look!" I giggled and pushed him away, pointing toward Sofia. Somehow the vendor kept overlooking the poor child. "Your niece needs you."

He immediately stopped, tapped my nose with his finger, and added with a devilish grin, "This isn't over." Then he rushed to her.

Chuckling, I circled in place, taking in the sights of the Pfingsten festival. Families gathered all over the city to officially recognize the seventh Sunday after Easter. Many businesses and stores closed in celebration of the holiday, and our new café was no exception. Opened only to our family this morning for breakfast, it was a rare day we could come together and leave all other obligations behind. Once the café was cleaned for regular business tomorrow, everyone prepared to leave, except Stefan and I.

"Let's take the long walk home," he suggested as he grabbed my sweater off a chair and guided it onto my shoulders.

"I would love to." I wound my arm through his.

"Me too! Me too! Uncle Stefan, Aunt Ella!." Sofia fled her mother's side the moment she heard the word *walk*. "Please?" Snuggling against Stefan's pantleg, she batted her eyelashes relentlessly until her uncle gave in.

At the park, I inhaled the sweet smell of summer. Pockets of Edelweiss bloomed randomly in this corner of the neighborhood, their white petals visible from any distance. I stooped to pick one up and held it to my nose, its strong scent curled my toes with pleasure. Pressed tightly between my fingertips, the flowers triggered happy thoughts.

Stefan never ceased to amaze me. Studying him as he engaged with his niece, I noted the reemergence of his gentleness and compassion. Although this year back together presented its share of challenges, it was one of the best years of my life. Moving to a nearby bench, my free hand brushed a pile of leaves off the seat. As I turned, a voice sailed through the air, triggering memories.

"Ella?" My eyes shot to its owner. The man stood so close I could practically hear his heart beating. Dressed in casual clothes, his hair fell longer in the back than I remembered. He sported sideburns now, and a familiar dimple in his cheek emerged when he smiled. Next to him stood a beautiful woman.

"Hans . . .h-hello," I stuttered.

"It's been a long time."

"Yes." I glanced awkwardly between him and the woman. She too shifted anxiously without an introduction.

"I saw you once," —his tone, although serious, carried a lightness to it— "a few years ago."

"Hans?" Stefan appeared at my side.

Immediately, Hans straightened his shoulders as if he needed to salute his old commander but didn't. "Sir! *Unterfeldwebel* Franke!" Surprise blanketed his voice.

"No, not anymore. Just Stefan."

His eyes swung anxiously between us until Sofia nudged her way in and cried, "It's falling!" She took random bites of her pretzel that unraveled it to the point it nearly dropped to the ground.

"Here, love, let me help you."

I didn't miss the shock creep into Hans expression. His wide eyes locked on Stefan and his mouth parted, moving wordlessly. I recalled the Stefan that Hans knew—the severe man he'd never seen exhibit mercy to anyone *except* me that night at the wall.

"Hans," I placed my hand on his arm. "Is this your wife?" She'd been ignored, her confusion evident.

"Yes," he scrambled to speak. "Yes, this is Esther." He wrapped one arm around the dark-haired beauty and leaned his head towards hers. "Esther, this was my . . ." His eyes squinted. There really wasn't a word for who we were to him. "This is my old commander and his . . . wife?"

"Oh no." I waved my hand. "We're not married." In the corner of my eye, Stefan stiffened. I quickly added, "But we are together again."

I reached out to shake Esther's hand. She met it in politeness but didn't speak. Her lips curved slowly into a forced smile.

"I . . . I'm happy for you . . . both," he stammered, and although he said the word *both*, his eyes met mine.

"Are you still in the military?" Stefan spoke.

Hans answered but never shifted Stefan's direction. "No, I left it in 1975. I'm Volkspolizien now."

I chuckled. "The police? That suits you."

"Yes. I work in Mitte mostly, along Weydinger and Rosa."

"Rosa?" my voice squeaked. "Near the Babylon."

"Yes, the Babylon." He smiled; the dimple deepened.

"I . . . I'm happy for you, Hans." I grinned Esther's direction, hoping to swing the attention off me by including her. "Do you have children?"

She nodded. "Two. A boy and a girl."

"How wonderful. What are their names?"

Her rigid stance finally softened. "Michael is eleven and Helene is eight."

"Is this your little girl?" She pointed to Sofia

"Oh no," I laughed. "Sofia is Stefan's niece." She wrinkled her nose when she heard her name mentioned. "We don't have any children." A small pang struck my chest for the second time today.

"Well, Hans," —Stefan extended his hand to shake his former comrade's— "it was great to see you. It appears life has been good to you, and I wish you the very best."

They shook. It was the first time Hans glanced anywhere but me. "Yes sir, and I wish you both the very best as well. Goodbye, Stefan." He reached for my hand. "Ella."

"Bye, Hans." I released quickly and extended my hand to his wife. "Nice to meet you, Esther." Wrapping my arm through Stefan's, we walked the opposite direction.

My thoughts dwelt momentarily on Hans and what he meant to me years ago. It was a means to an end, nothing more. Genuinely happy for him and his life, I reflected on the thrill I only felt with

Stefan. Exiting the park, our attention focused on Sofia as she licked her fingers from the butter and cinnamon glazing them. Her playful giggles became an easy distraction from the awkward silence that hovered between us.

As we boarded the tram home, Stefan held me close with one hand and the bar in the other. His lips edged through my hair and into my ear. "I'm sorry I haven't given you what you deserve," he whispered.

This caught me off guard, and I flipped his direction. "What do you mean?"

His anguished eyes followed Sofia as she bounced spiritedly in her seat. When they came back to me, he bit his bottom lip before he spoke. "I'm sorry I couldn't give you a family."

"Stefan," —my palm held his cheek tenderly— "*you* are my family. You will *always* be more than enough for my happiness. Without you, I have nothing." I kissed him softly and pulled his arm tighter around me. There was no doubt in my mind I was exactly where I wanted to be. No regrets, no sadness.

Forty-two

WINDS OF CHANGE

October 1988

The picture in the western press said it all: four prominent members of IFM holding up their passports, Wolfgang and Lotte Templin, Werner Fischer, and Barbel Boley. I recognized one of the heavily bearded men as the same man who interrupted Darek and me at the Zionskirche a year ago. In the caption below the photograph it announced their forced expatriation after a raid on the Environmental Library earlier this year. It continued on, describing the desperate act by the SED as a means to silence the outspoken. My heart rate increased with the speed of my scan through the article. Although Darek was not pictured, all the staff present had been arrested and the printing press confiscated. My gut told me he had been detained. He was always there, always working. I feared for his circumstances, but knew no matter where Darek was sent, he would continue the fight from there.

The reporter ended with this final sentence "Twenty-seven years since the wall was raised, residents of communist Berlin are tired of being silent. Their voices finally reaching the surface individually and collectively as the opposition has successfully shifted their hearts and spirits." It wasn't so much our spirits I was worried about, but the consequences that could be enforced as long as the SED was still in charge. Though East Germany was witnessing a very large movement that showed no signs of slowing down, the road ahead remained littered with too many unknowns.

"Ella, we have another party of five, and do we have any corn?" Mari entered the storage room. Ten minutes ago, I slipped into the back to retrieve a can of tomatoes and caught sight of the front page of the newspaper. For an extra mark each day, Noah, our delivery boy, slides the western circulation through our mail slot.

"Sorry, Mari, I got distracted. I'm coming." I folded the paper and grabbed the can I came for and two cans of creamed corn.

Everything alright?" She watched me carefully.

"Yes, everything's fine."

When I stepped into the kitchen, Charlie, our cook, reached for the cans.

"Excellent," he said and went back to work.

When the café opened in late May, Mari and I managed well on our own, but in the last month, business required us to hire another person. Mari met Charlie at a KvU event, but the moment we were introduced, I knew he was harmless. At twenty-one, Charlie had no family and very little prospects, a situation both Mari and I had experienced.

"Ella, taste this." He held up a spoon. Since he'd always lived on his own, he knew a thing or two about having to be creative with meals. His skill set was perfect, since the availability of ingredients varied day to day. This made way for "daily house specials".

"Oh, that's delicious. Is that Parmesan mixed in?" He was a master at blending ingredients neither of us would have ever considered, and they quickly became big hits.

333

"Yes, its baked into the corn. I made this an hour ago, and it's almost gone. I'm glad you found two more cans."

"It's our last two, unfortunately. Maybe we can find more tomorrow. This dish will definitely sell quickly!"

Charlie used his arm to brush his long bangs from his black-olive eyes that twinkled when he flashed his crooked smile. "Leon said he would be by this afternoon with fresh cauliflower, Brussel sprouts, and green beans."

"Wonderful." I squeezed his hand. "And don't forget Frau Becker's Sauerkraut order, she should be here in an hour to pick it up." Since our arrival to the neighborhood, my old neighborhood, we'd made friends easily and earned regular customers quickly.

I readjusted my apron and stepped through to the dining area. We had six tables inside covered with a thin, colorful linen, a white vase, and whatever flower we could acquire that day. The patio in front of the café offered two additional tables, and regardless of the weather, they were the most popular since we opened. Stepping down the stairs, I glanced back at the sign that rested above the front door, between the two bay windows. *Mama G's.* Every time I laid eyes on it, a warmth embraced me as if from the woman herself.

I approached the first table. "Thanks for coming. Can I get you something to drink?"

"Best concert I've ever heard." The teenagers chatted excitedly over opened menus.

My ears naturally perked up. The only concerts I'd been to were the forbidden ones a couple years ago. "What concert?"

"Michael Jackson, the American pop star."

They made no attempt to whisper, although I naturally peered around. "American popstar here . . . in the East?"

"Oh no." They both giggled as if I knew nothing, but of course, I really knew nothing when it came to teenagers anymore. "In the West, in June. Our cousins recorded it and smuggled it over last week."

Again, I glanced around at their openness. "What do you mean recorded it?"

"Here, listen. It's a cassette tape." One of the girls pulled a metal box from her lap to the table. The other placed a headband over my head. Foam pads covered my ears. Curious, I waited. A series of buttons lined the box, and once pressed, music filled my ears. My body jerked to the foreign sensation, and my jaw fell open. Although the English words were difficult to follow, the beat of the music was both light and explosive. The singer, presumably a man from the name Michael, sang at a high pitch but instantly drew me in with his compelling sound. My fingers drummed in rhythm against the table. I couldn't hear the girl's laughter, but their faces lifted with delight. My own smile confirmed it was exactly how they described.

I pulled the band off my head and handed it back. "That was fascinating, thank you. Who did you say it was? Michael who?"

"His name is Michael Jackson, an American." The girl who had invited me to listen took the player back. "It's good, isn't it?"

I agreed, yet found myself not only intrigued by the music, but equally puzzled by their forwardness. They were young, too young to understand the realism of manipulation and espionage. Could it be that the winds of change swirling in the East infiltrated the lives of the youth to where they knew no fear? For decades we watched our backs, whispered amongst friends, and every knock on our door sent terror through our hearts, wondering who was on the other side. The idea that this generation might never have to experience this made my spirit soar. With an extra hop in my step and the song by Michael Jackson the American pop star alive in my head, I smiled at the possibility.

"Hey, beautiful." Stefan's arms wrapped around me from behind. The afternoon rush had finally cleared, and only one customer remained.

"This is a nice surprise." Though my hands were full, I circled around to meet him. His arms remained in place, but now I could enjoy him in full view. With his blond locks a bit shorter and his chin clean shaven, he had found his niche. He worked most days in the mortuary with Katharina and spent his afternoons in the art room, painting. Several of his works adorned the walls in our café, the Volksbühne, Reichstag, and Brandenburg Tor.

"You're not painting today?"

He nuzzled my neck. I gripped the glasses tighter in my hands to keep the flutter in my heart from sending them crashing to the floor. "No." His mouth tickled my skin. "I couldn't wait another second to see you."

Again, my chest thumped. "Well I'm glad you remedied that." I chuckled.

"Mari?" Stefan called her name, though his eyes never budged from mine. Their brightness indicated an undisclosed reason for his bliss.

"Yes?" She stood behind the cash register calculating.

"Would you mind if I borrowed Ella for a bit?"

"Only if you return her for dinner. We've been quite busy lately, and I hold you personally responsible for that."

"Me?" Stefan questioned.

"Yes," she growled, her hands propped on her petite hips. "Don't you know we read the paper every day?"

"Hmmm." He grazed my ear with his lips. A tingle sprinted along my skin.

"Somebody put an advertisement about Mama G's café having the best food in town."

"Yes, I heard that rumor." His lips slid to my cheek. Breathless, I remained frozen, the glasses still in my hands. "I'll have to thank that person for telling the truth."

She giggled. "Uh, huh. Just go, troublemaker, but bring her back by 5." Mari stepped into the kitchen.

Stefan's half smile reached its peak. The sly and sexy one that only appeared when he was scheming.

"You little devil," I muttered.

He took the dishes from my hands and placed them on the table. Watching him reach for my waistline sent chills through my body even before his touch skimmed my blouse. The tease of his fingers as they untied my apron intensified the stir. Setting it aside, he wrapped one arm comfortably across my shoulders and guided me to the door. "Let's take a walk."

We stepped out into a bright afternoon sun, though I shivered from the crisp autumn air. Stefan held me tight as we crossed the street and meandered next to Sophien. Her walls, cracked and broken, still brought me comfort like seeing parts of my memorable past every day. Stefan knew this, and that's most assuredly why he chose to walk this way.

Across from the cemetery, one of the few remaining houses in the area had been turned into an artist's canvas. From the foundation to the windows, a garden of colorful plants and flowers had been painted on its walls. Hidden between the foliage, faces emerged and then a wall, the presentation overwhelming and powerful. Only steps down this road, the *real* wall became exposed, adjacent to where my family home and the church of reconciliation stood, now both gone. Stefan's hand slid from my shoulder and intertwined with my fingers. The sole bench that remained on an empty street of fragmented structures appeared before us. He motioned to sit.

Anklamer and Bernauer, the street sign stood alone on the nearby corner. My memories with the Kühns, some cherished, others painful, played in my mind like a moving picture. The day they brought me home, the phonograph, Mama and Papa dancing to *La Vie en Rose*, the night Anton and Josef left, Papa's final words and final breath, my eviction, the butterfly painting, hiding after my first escape attempt, the letter from Herr Brauner, the viewing platform with Josef, Anton, and Elizabeth, the demolition of the church, the wall. Numerous events played out on this very street.

"Ella," Stefan whispered. Lost in thought, I stirred, and my forehead wrinkled. I smiled at the kindness that coated his face. "I know this place is special to you, that you have loved *and lost* here."

With his free hand, he wiped perspiration from his nose. A tremble in his fingers shared more than just the love and compassion that radiated from him. I placed both hands on his jaw, his soft skin

337

warming to my touch. Tilting forward, I brought him to me. The kiss, though short, surged with desire.

Leaning back, he watched me. After several seconds he pointed around us. "Ella, this place has brought you happiness and sorrow. You have many memories here, but I want to make this very spot a memory you will *never* forget."

One brow lifted, but I remained silent. He slid to one knee on the sidewalk in front of me. Gripping both my hands and holding them to his lips, he kissed my fingers tenderly. A tingling sensation resonated under my skin. When he moved them to his chest, the thumping of his rapid heartbeat brought a smile to my face.

"Remember how we made plans?" —his voice quivered— "How we were going to spend the rest of our lives together?"

I nodded slowly.

"Much has happened since." He dropped his eyes to the ground for a brief moment. When he glanced back up, tears formed in the corners of his eyes. "We were young, and our hopes and dreams seemed so much simpler then." Small wisps of gray hair peppered his blond strands, reminding me of how much time had passed. "Many obstacles tried to derail us. Anger and sadness tried to keep us apart . . ." Completely mesmerized by his words, nothing drew me from his face. "But here we are once more, and I have never been so happy in my entire life. I don't ever want to be away from you again." One hand slipped out of our grip and retrieved a box in his pocket. *My* ring. The very same ring I wore years ago and left in the closet. "Ella, will you marry me? Really marry me this time?"

I cried and nodded, my mouth unable to form an audible word. Using both of his hands, he steadied mine long enough to put the ring on my finger. Staring at the jewel, I gasped at its brightness and beauty. It was the same ring, only this time its magnificence symbolized a greater journey.

Stefan raised me to meet him, cupping my neck gently with both hands. His thumbs brushed the tears off my cheeks, and he gazed for only a second before his lips found mine.

A simple proposal—unlike the last one, filled with toasts, exclamations and cheers. Tonight we were the only two people on the street, exactly how it should be . . . just he and I and now the best possible memory ever created on Anklamer.

Forty-three

HANDS TIED

12 February 1989

"Ella." Cade caught me in the Franke's hallway before I entered the kitchen to help Mari prepare for brunch. Every Sunday we gathered at home for one meal we could enjoy together and kept the café closed solely for the purpose of family time.

"Yes?"

He glanced behind him and then craned his neck, looking into the kitchen. "I need to ask you something," he whispered. His eyes darted past me and back again.

I hesitated to comply. This conversation obviously needed to happen in a very private place. These discussions almost always included the opposition. "Alright. Here, come in here." I directed him to the same closet I took refuge in with Lena so long ago when the soldiers came looking for me. I hadn't been in it since. I turned on the light, and Cade closed the door behind him.

"How much do you know about the mortuary?"

"This mortuary? The Franke's?"

He nodded once.

"Why?" My brows curved, skeptically.

He reached into his jacket pocket and pulled out a folded paper. "I saw a van and two Wartburgs here a week ago, when I came to get Mari for breakfast. It was early, on the 6th."

"So. They have van deliveries all the time. Bodies are brought here. That's what they do, Cade." He ignored the sharpness of my tongue, my frustration centered on the possibility he insinuated things to which he was most likely right.

"Deliveries come in a kastenwagen, not the Stasi *Barka* van."

"What are you implying?" I demanded, both hands planted on my hips. He unfolded the paper. You need to read this. It's being distributed by the Justice Working Group, IFM, Youth Convention, and Working Group on Peace."

"All of them?"

He nodded and handed it to me. "Possibly more."

Under the lamp, I read.

"An open letter to the people of the GDR:"
The Assassination of Chris Gueffroy

On 5 February 1989, 11:30 pm at night, approximately ten gunshots came from the area near the Britzer Branch Canal. Witnesses described the gruesome scene following the firings. Two men identified as 20-year-old Chris Gueffroy and his friend Christian Gaudian were found shot. Border Patrol removed both men from the scene, but only one survived the barrage of bullets. The other was lifeless upon retrieval. Friends of the men insist they were attempting to leave the East to avoid the draft into the National People's Army.

The interrogation of Karin Gueffroy, Chris' mother on 7 February resulted in her being informed her son was involved in "an attack on a military security zone" and though he was offered immediate medical care, he died from the injuries.

Clearly, this was an assassination of an unarmed man. The People's Police are not commenting and have only published the medical report from the funeral orator who described the incident in the official paperwork as a "tragic accident".

People of the GDR, we must stop the SED and their shoot-to-kill orders at the wall. We must stop those who willingly cover up the government's slaughter of innocence with lies. Enough is enough!

I glanced at Cade, my teeth clenched.

"Do you think his body was brought here?" he pushed. "That the Frankes are the ones who reported?"

My lips drew into a thin line, and my mind drifted. I knew more about the mortuary's history and association with the corrupt SED than I wanted to.

"Tragic accident?" I closed my eyes. *Please, please . . . not this mortuary.* "Cade, I have to go."

"Why?" he questioned.

"I just need to. Can I have this?"

He handed it to me as I flew out of the closet. I ran to the mortuary and yanked the doors open, ignoring the foul scent of flesh as I dashed to the office. *Their dealings are not my affair. I have no business here,* I tried to remind myself, but my legs continued forward. Without knocking, I opened the office door. Katharina sat behind the desk, Edmund leaned over her, and Stefan looked out the window.

I held the paper up. "Please tell me this isn't true."

From the distance, they could not read the writing, but their expressions confirmed their knowledge of it.

"He was murdered, Stefan!" I yelled, unable to direct my anger towards Katharina, whose head dropped into her hands.

342

"Ella." Stefan rushed forward, closing the door behind me and pulling me close, but I pushed back.

"It's wrong. How can you see a man riddled with bullet holes and lie about what happened? Lie to his family and lie to the world?"

"We didn't have a choice, Ella," Edmund spoke up, no sympathy in his tone.

"What do you mean, you didn't have a choice?" I snapped back fiercely. "You always have a choice!"

"Stop!" Stefan tugged on my arms. I yanked again, but he held tight and directed me to the couch. "Sit!" he demanded. The sharpness in his voice shocked me. He had never been so forceful with me. I sat down.

Katharina sobbed at the desk.

"You don't understand what's happening here!" Edmund hollered. "You should've stayed out. This has nothing to do with you."

"This wall has everything to do with me!"

"Not this, Ella." Stefan's tone softened. Barely. He glanced at the other two.

"No!" Edmund yelled.

"She's part of the family. She deserves to know," Stefan insisted.

"Know what?" I pressed. Studying each of their faces, it was apparent they hid something.

Stefan peered down to me. "They took Jonas."

"What?" I launched to my feet. "Who did?"

"The Stasi."

My heart raced. I pressed my fists against my forehead. Tears slipped as I recalled the ride in the back seat of the automobile and standing in front of the Stasi symbol at the door and then being placed in the remand room. Blood splattered on the walls, with chains and ropes hanging from the ceiling.

"When?"

"Yesterday."

"Why aren't you getting him back?" I cried to Edmund and then Stefan. "He's only a child. They'll kill him!" I screamed. Katharina's sobs grew louder.

"And what do you suppose we do?" Edmund yelled. "March into Stasi headquarters and demand his return?"

I glanced at Stefan, pain shrouding his eyes. We both knew the consequences of that choice, having paid a heavy price years ago. My legs weakened, and I slipped to the floor, hands covering my face. "Why did they take him?" I whispered.

"They claimed it was to prepare him for FDJ," Stefan answered.

"The Socialist Youth Organization?"

"It's a front, Ella. They're using him for leverage," Stefan added. "They know, with the opposition and protests heating up, they have to make the shooting appear an accident. They needed us to confirm their fabrication."

"So, they're holding Jonas? For how long?"

"Only until after the funeral. If we cooperate and file the paperwork the way they require, Jonas will not be forced into conscript."

My cheeks heated. The memory of Stefan forced into conscript choked me, but imagining Jonas, at fourteen, facing those same terrors paralyzed me. "When's the funeral?"

"In a week, the 23rd, at *Baumschulenweg* cemetery," Edmund answered in a much calmer tone.

"I've never heard of that one."

"It's in West Berlin. They're doing everything they can to appear accommodating, except for confessing."

I chewed on my nail as the silence thickened. Glancing between the three of them, it broke my heart. I couldn't imagine the suffering Katharina and Edmund were enduring. No wonder I didn't see her last night. "There could be repercussions to our family, possibly worse than Stasi."

"What do you mean?" Katharina lifted her head, her eyes red and puffy.

344

"This." I still clutched the notice in my hand.

Edmund came over and picked it up. "I heard about this on the radio." He read it out loud.

When he finished, I continued, "This went out everywhere. Four different opposition groups distributed it. If people find out you're the funeral orator who made that statement, there could be a riot, an attack."

"They won't know." Edmund grabbed the telephone. He dialed a number as we waited and listened.

"Herr Schneider. We need to talk."

He was silent for a moment.

"I realize I could lose my son." Katharina's face turned a sickly yellow. "But I will not lose my entire family." He spoke calmly but the handset shook in his hand. "How can you assure me that no one will know our identity as the funeral home who confirmed the death. It must be confidential!"

He went silent, and we watched, wondering what was being said on the other end.

"I don't think you understand!" he growled. "Listen to me very carefully. We have pictures of the body." Edmunds eyes flashed to his wife. Shouting on the other end of the receiver came through clearly. Edmund held the phone away from his ear briefly and then cut him off. "They are in an undisclosed location and will be distributed to every news agency in the world if you don't make sure we're protected, and additionally, if anything happens to my son—one bruise, one abrasion—your secret is over. Do you understand?" He hung up the phone. All eyes fell on him. His countenance twisted painfully, and he dropped to his knees next to Katharina. Burying his face against her chest, he cried. I had never seen him shed a tear in all the years I knew him.

Stefan's arms slid underneath mine and lifted me to my feet. At the door, I turned around. "I'm so sorry, Katharina and Edmund. I didn't know. I'm sorry."

Stefan and I stepped into the hallway. I leaned against the wall, sniffling to fight an onslaught of my own tears. Stefan held me.

"This wasn't the first time they've used threats to get what they want, is it?"

"No," he whispered, "but it's the first time they took someone."

"All those years," I mumbled. "All those years I thought it was done willingly."

"It was in the beginning, but things got harder for us when the number of victims increased."

I couldn't believe I'd been so judgmental. "Why didn't you tell me?"

"I would never drag you in. We were puppets. Though my mother had strong connections, and at times no conscience, Mielke held all the cards and used them often."

"Do you think Edmund's threats will be taken seriously? Do you really have photographs?"

"Yes, that's the one thing Katharina and I decided to do when I returned, and we started working together. We put together a detailed file of each body, including photographs. It's kept safely away from here. The three of us are the only ones who know where it is."

I exhaled loudly. "I'm glad you did that." Swiping the back of my hand across my cheeks, I wiped away my tears, but my sniffle remained. "Then Jonas will be okay." Meant to convince myself more than anyone, I had to believe that this situation was different. "The SED can't afford for this to blow up right now."

Stefan took my hand and led me down the hall.

I stopped in front of the thick doors and turned to Stefan. "We have to tell Cade."

"No, Ella. It stays with us."

"He already suspects. He's with the opposition."

Forty-four

INTRODUCTIONS

12 March 1989

One full month had passed since the event surrounding Chris Gueffroy's shooting death and the SED's extensive cover up. When Stefan and I approached Cade that same day with the truth about the open letter and the Frankes' involvement, he cried. His concern for Jonas' safe return became the upmost of his priorities, and balancing the ethics of the event held each of us captive. Though the Frankes' connection to the act was never revealed, the underground peppered the SED relentlessly with accusations.

Per the agreement, Jonas returned to the family on the 24th of February. All in all, he had been detained for close to two weeks. When they dropped him off at home, he wore the uniform of the National People's Army, the same service the two shooting victims had been drafted into. We had braced ourselves for a counter threat, but their level of psychological damage remained a mystery. Though no blemishes marked his skin, he arrived thinner and quieter. He said very little of his treatment or whereabouts. Edmund was fit to be tied, but Stefan convinced his brother-in-law of the dangers confrontation produced, knowing Jonas' condition was the government's way of sending a message of their own.

Katharina worked hard to mend Jonas and soothe Edmund's anger in her usual schmetterling way, though nobody forgot about the incriminating evidence stored against the SED. Everyone hoped a time would come when it could be released and the cowards would be held accountable. For now, the sooner we returned to normalcy, the better.

Until recently, I'd kept my relocation to the Franke house and Stefan's proposal a secret to my family in the West. I feared the years of sharing the pain and heartache of our separation might taint their opinion of him. Their initial reactions were vague during the phone call. Little was said, and I attributed the awkwardness to the fact that they'd never met him, and since the opening of the café, my communication with them had dwindled extensively. Thus, the arrangement for a face to face at the platform was planned for today.

"Josef, Heidi, Anton . . . I want you to meet Stefan," I yelled across the wall and sperrzone to the three forms standing on the platform at Bernauer Strasse. Stefan's hand fidgeted at my side. I couldn't recall a time it shook like this. I glanced at him. Sweat beaded on his forehead and down his hollowed cheeks, although the weather could not be blamed; the wind whipped briskly around us. When nobody spoke, I bit my lip.

Heidi glanced beside her and elbowed Josef in the ribs. "Hello, Ella." Her wave and subsequent smile were friendly. "Nice to meet you, Stefan."

In a completely opposite reaction, blank expressions covered the men's faces and neither one acknowledged us in the same friendly manner. I went from biting my lip to chewing the inside of my cheek.

I hoped that despite our separation, the re-entry of Stefan in my life, would be as monumental for my family as it was for me. Their sour faces, however, confirmed their unfamiliarity with Stefan and that I might have neglected to balance the good news with the bad.

Regardless, I had convinced Stefan to come meet my family today. It was critical to bring these most important people in my life together, despite the distance the wall created.

"It's good to see you all." My lips lifted halfway.

Anton straightened his shoulders and waved. "Hi, Ella. It's good to see you . . . and Stefan . . ." His pauses hung in the air. "We've heard a lot about you over the years."

"Yeah," Josef added, contempt rising quickly. "It wasn't all good."

My eyes shot at Josef. *What is he doing?* Tears began to bubble on my lower lids. "Josef?" I cried. Heidi placed her arm around him, his reddening cheeks evident, even from this distance."

"It's okay, Ella," Stefan whispered. "I deserve it."

"No, no you don't. Josef!" I yelled. "Stop acting like a child. I wanted you to meet him. This hasn't been easy for any of us!"

"Easy? You want easy? How about Herr Wagner arranging your freedom?"

"I told you!" I yelled through gritted teeth. "It's delayed."

"Don't lie to me, Ella," Joseph yelled. "I know the process. The only reason you can't come is because of him, a man who deserted you years ago—a man who shattered your heart."

"Where is this coming from?" Hot tears snaked down my cheeks.

"He's the reason you're not here!" he bellowed, loud and clear.

"What?" I flashed my sights between all three faces. Anton lowered his chin, but Josef's shot up in clear defiance.

"Ella, I made arrangements for you, and you refused to come. It's all because of him!"

"Where did you even get that idea? Stefan can go anywhere he wants."

"Then why is he keeping you there?"

Stefan patted my arm and pointed. I scanned the soldiers at the base of the wall who had stopped walking and watched as Josef continued his rant.

"You had a chance to come, and suddenly, Stefan comes back in your life, and you forget about your family."

"Josef!"

"No! I'm tired of it. You don't understand, Ella. You're not the only one that's been hurt. I miss my big sister. She was everything to me, and then she chooses dad over me. I loved dad too, but we knew he was dying, and you chose to stay . . . then on top of that, you decide to enter and exit my life over the years depending on Stefan's devotion or lack thereof. Now you're choosing him over me as well!"

My mouth dropped and a whimper escaped. The hole that started in my chest moments ago expanded.

Anton shifted to Josef's other side and placed a hand on his shoulder. Josef roughly shrugged it off.

Stefan's arm squeezed tighter around me, and he pointed once more to the soldiers who now walked our direction. Heidi motioned to the tower. One soldier leaned out and glanced between us. Anton grabbed Josef forcefully this time.

"Ella, we have to go," Stefan whispered.

"Josef!" My tears flowed freely down my cheeks. My sobs made my words unintelligible by the time I stepped off the boards.

"Ella, let's go!" Stefan lugged me away through Sophien cemetery at a brisk pace.

"Stefan."

"I know." He continued to lead me forward with lengthened strides. "Let's just get back to the café for now."

It wasn't as if the soldiers would follow us but creating a scene at the wall might bring consequences if we lingered. Our elevated conversation and even the talk of leaving most likely spurred their interest.

We zigzagged past several streets and through multiple alleys before we made it back to Mama G's. Near closing time, both Mari and Charles had cleaned up for the night. Only one patron savored a cup of coffee when we entered.

I slid onto a chair and laid my head on the table, unable to stop my cries.

"What just happened?" I whispered. I could understand Josef's anger over our separation, but he blamed me too. *I chose Papa over him!* Stefan sat next to me and held me.

"I shouldn't have gone today. I've made things worse," he said, rubbing my hair.

Mari rushed over, peered at us, and stepped away.

"It's not you, Stefan. I should have told him," I sobbed harder.

"Told him what, Ella? He's right; I kept you from your family."

"No, it wasn't you. It was me."

"What are you talking about?"

I swiped a napkin and blew my nose, but the tears flowed, nonstop. "Josef arranged for me to apply for a tourist visa. I met with a notary who comes to the East every few months . . . a coworker of his, a miracle worker. He has friends in emigration, and everything appeared hopeful. He told me I could 'visit' my family in the West and just not return."

"When was this?"

"Our first meeting was in 1984, but every time I checked in with him, problems arose. He didn't elaborate for a while. In April 1987 it was denied. Way before we reunited."

"Why was it denied?"

I glanced over to him. My lips trembled. "I have a record."

"What record? What do you mean? Like arrested?"

I nodded.

"When?"

"The Colonel."

"What colonel?" Stefan's eyes widened. "Colonel Anker?"

"Yes."

"Verdammit! That was me! Not you!" My body jerked to Stefan's yell. "Sorry, Ella. I didn't mean to scare you." He stood and paced the floor. Mari and Charles came running.

"What's going on?" she questioned.

"Nothing," I whispered.

"It's not nothing. Stefan, you need to calm down."

"I'm sorry, Mari." His crimson cheeks turned my direction. "What did he charge you with?"

"Being a spy."

"I wish that bloody bastard were here so I could kill him again!" Stefan screamed. The one patron left the café. Mari walked him out with apologies.

"I didn't tell Josef and Anton that I had been denied. I'd have to tell them why, and I couldn't." My nose stung. "I couldn't tell them about what happened to me."

Stefan appeared at my side again. His hand brushed my hair, becoming softer as it settled to my shoulders. "I'm sorry. I didn't mean to yell or scare you. I should've fought harder for you, El. I should've never let you leave the house."

"We talked about this. You know that your fate would've been worse."

"That man hurt you back then, nearly destroyed our future, and his cruelty still thrives today. There has to be a way to end this."

I rubbed my eyes. They smarted under the coarseness of my touch. "I couldn't bring myself to tell Josef why I was denied. I told the notary not to tell Josef why I couldn't come . . . only that it was delayed. I made excuses to Josef when he asked. Shortly after, you came back into my life, and they must've assumed you were the reason. I should've been honest. I should've told them the truth. Then they wouldn't be upset with you."

"It's okay. I can handle a little anger my way. He'll get over it. You don't need to say anything. It's over. It's past. I don't want you to ever dwell on it again."

I kneaded my hands together. "I can't, Stefan. You're everything to me, and if they blame you, I can't live with that." I reached for another napkin. Standing up, I kissed Stefan on the cheek. "This is one hit I won't let you take for me."

Inside the public telephone booth a street away, I closed the door and took several deep breaths before lifting the handle. My fingers trembled harder than they did that first phone call I made in 1983. When Heidi picked up, I could barely speak.

"H-Heidi? I . . . it's Ella. May I speak with Josef, please?"

"Yes, of course." The muffled sound of a covered receiver surfaced a moment before I heard a quiet call for her husband.

"Hello?" His ongoing rage emanated through the lines.

"Josef, it's me."

"I'm sorry, Ella. I didn't mean to be so rude, but I—"

"Stop! Please just listen. I need to explain something to you, and it will be very hard. Please listen."

I proceeded to tell the story from the very beginning, expecting the line to drop at any moment, but it didn't. A tender mercy from an unknown source allowed me to share the entire ordeal, as agonizing as it was.

"This is why I was denied travel, my dear brother. I'm so sorry I lied to you." The fluctuation of his breath and quiet sobbing conveyed we were still connected, though he never interrupted.

"Please don't be angry with Stefan. It's not his fault I didn't come. I wanted to."

"But what about all those other times he hurt you, deserted you?"

"I hurt others too. I hurt you and Anton, did I not?"

The line grew very quiet.

"Josef?"

"I'm sorry, Ella. I'm sorry for the pain you've been through. I had no idea, and I'm sorry I wasn't there to protect you." The guilt in his tone was unmistaken. Even out of reach and in another country, his remorse spoke loudly.

"It's not your fault, but you needed to know."

"Will Stefan forgive me?" Josef whispered.

I sniffled. "Stefan is a good man. With everything I put him through, he won't even think twice about this."

"Can we try again? Maybe give me another chance?"

"Of course, when?"

"I'm out of town tomorrow until next week, but maybe the Saturday after that?"

"Yes, let's plan for the same time, and we can talk about something much lighter," I chuckled, "like the Olympics."

Relieved this burden had been lifted from my shoulders, I said my goodbyes. "Thank you for listening, Josef. I'm sorry I didn't tell you sooner."

"I love you, Ella."

"I love you too."

Forty-five

SWORDS TO PLOUGHSHARE

7 October 1989

Sofia's tiny hands linked between Stefan and I as we walked down Karl-Liebnecht-Strasse. We held fast to our niece as we maneuvered in and out of the crowd. After a busy night in the mortuary, Katharina, Edmund, and Jonas planned to arrive late. Jonas recently took the steps to begin his training in the family business.

Finding Lena, I waved. She, Freddy, and their girls held a bench up close for nearly an hour. Once we reached them, I gave each a quick peck on the cheek and scanned the crowd.

"Was it this crowded when you came to the parade for me?" Stefan's eyes searched the crowd like me.

"Worse." I laughed and Lena nodded her head aggressively. "Since the demonstrations and what's happening at the border of Hungary and Czechoslovakia, many people have fled that direction."

"But to what?" Freddy exclaimed, "The West German Embassy can only protect so many! Have you seen the pictures?"

I nodded. That was the one thing we were consistent at—reading the press.

"What do they show?" Lena turned to her husband.

"The grounds are overflowing with refugees. People have found a way out, but those countries aren't allowing them to stay unless they're at the Embassy. It's a mess."

"Yeah, that's a security nightmare." Stefan noticed Sofia's scrunched nose from below.

"Stop talking about that. I want to see the parade!"

I chuckled. Yes, this was boring adult talk. "Sofia, sweetheart, jump up on the bench so you can see better." I helped her up.

"Hop up on my shoulders." Stefan bent so she could climb on easily. "Can you see now?" She giggled her response.

"Look, Uncle Stefan, lots and lots of soldiers." She pointed to the street. The parade had already begun. What a sight to behold, and for a child it was magical. I reflected on that very first parade I attended in the Waisenhaus. The youth celebration parade, the day Anton punched Frederick to the ground for hurting me. It was my first day with Anton: the taffy, the connection made, all a vivid memory.

I studied the crowd, surprised at the high numbers who chose to come out on this chilly October day. Of course, we were here, so why wouldn't they? My eyes fell upon the VIP section across the road and down twenty metres. A large red banner draped as the backdrop for a couple dozen dignitaries attempting to make a dignified impression. Erich Honecker stood center, on the first row, surrounded by not only military commanders but men in suitcoats braving the wind. Their long drawn-out expressions signaled professionalism, but in light of the growing dissent, might indicate tension about the unknown. They saluted the leagues as they passed.

"They don't seem to mind that people are waving the flags of a united Germany," I whispered to Cade who wrapped his arms around Mari in front of him. The banners flew everywhere, even the flags that portrayed the opposition image of the blacksmith turning the sword into the plough, the symbol on the patch Darek gave me.

"Yeah, with demonstrations every day, they've had little strength in stopping them. The size of the last protest—the one that demanded freedom of assembly and press—had to be of concern. It even rivaled this crowd." He winked back.

A mind-boggling concept, I smiled with renewed fascination. Here on the 40th anniversary of the DDR, amongst thousands of soldiers, people demonstrated their independence without being arrested for it. *What is happening?*

I wasn't the only one in our small group to notice. Lena met my eyes and shook her head and then whispered into Freddy's ear, Grace on his shoulders as they observed the crowds.

Although Stefan said nothing, I knew his mind spun long before his mouth ever moved. "You okay?" I inquired. He nodded and kissed my cheek. This had to be strange for him, witnessing it from an entirely different perspective.

"Thank you for saving us a place." Katharina's cheeks tinted a rosy hue from running. "The bus was filled to capacity. We had to stand the whole ride here." She stepped on her tiptoes to give her daughter a kiss and then systematically kissed us all.

"Why didn't you bring the car?" Stefan asked.

"Do you see this crowd?" She laughed. "Imagine the streets getting here."

Stefan smirked and messed up her hair. Katharina stood with her hands on her hips in protest until Sofia reached over and attempted the same thing, giggling wildly. Katharina tried to tickle her, but Stefan juked around the others, saving his niece. Nobody around us minded the playful badger. The entire place celebrated in their own way.

After the parade, we made our way down the walk towards an ice cream cart. The line snaked half the block but was worth the wait. The government had stocked the delicacy for this very occasion.

"Somebody's trying to make friends." Cade laughed as he handed Mari the rare, creamy dessert. I smiled his direction, acknowledging the common tie of our involvement in opposition groups. We realized the government was losing control and trying their hardest to maintain some dignity. Once everyone received an ice cream cone, we found a patch of grass at the nearest Volkspark and relaxed to stretch the day.

"Tante Ella, if you could fly, where would you go?" Sofia had practically swallowed her chocolate scoop and lay on the grass next to me.

"Flying would be a wonderful experience."

"But where would you fly to?" she repeated herself.

"Well there's this place I've dreamt about. People say its real, but I've never seen it myself."

"Where is it?" She sat up straight, completely engaged.

"There's a little village built next to a beautiful river that winds through the hills . . . and on the very top of one hill is a beautiful castle with towers and drawbridges and—"

"A princess?" she cried aloud. Everyone laughed.

"Yes, a princess lives there, but—" I glanced at Stefan. "—so does her prince."

"Oh," Sofia cooed dreamily. "I would want to go there too. What's it called?"

Still watching Stefan, I grinned. "Cochem."

Forty-six

LET'S GO

3 November 1989

"Ella!" Stefan's voice filled the café, the distinction between urgency and excitement blurred. Thankfully, his cries came between lunch and dinner when we had the least number of patrons to alarm. I quickly put down my dishes and met him in the middle of the room.

"The border between Germany and Hungary is open."

"Open?" It took me several seconds to grasp those words.

The light in his eyes illuminated with the excitement in his voice. "Less than a month since the parade and the massive protest, the borders are opening."

"What about the wall? West Germany?" I held my sides afraid I might fall.

"No, not the wall." He frowned.

"What does this mean?" My breaths came in stuttered gasps. There had been rumors among the customers that the SED was under pressure to allow travel to Czechoslovakia and Hungary.

"The thousands that fled to Czechoslovakia and camped in the West German embassies, seeking asylum, have been granted amnesty, and West Germany offered them citizenship."

"Really? And the East is okay with this?"

"Not at all. They're causing a ruckus over getting them back, but nobody wants to start a war, especially with the Brits and Amis as allies."

"I can hardly believe it."

Stefan grasped my hands tightly. "Ella, we can leave as early as it takes to get affairs in order."

"Us?" My head spun. "Together?" I found my way to a nearby stool and felt for the seat before I slid onto it, afraid I would somehow miss it.

"Yes, finally get out of the East together." Stefan came to my side; his hand cupped my neck tenderly. "We can finally get to Cochem."

Mari burst through the door.

"Ella!" she screamed. "Oh, I see Stefan beat me to it." She laughed. "Can you believe it? All those demonstrations paid off!" She glanced from Stefan to me. I hadn't fully comprehended the news.

"We can take a plane from Prague or Budapest to Paris or Frankfurt and then the train to Cochem. We could be there in a week."

"A week?" I whispered. My heart pounded outside my chest.

"Josef and Anton could meet us there."

Trying hard to wrap my head around the news, I fell silent. *Leave East Berlin . . . I can really leave East Berlin!*

"Yes." I stood to Stefan's height as Mari took a couple steps back. "Let's go. Let's do it." Stefan pulled me to his chest, his arms secure and tight. His heart beat as rapidly as mine.

We would finally be leaving and not through a tunnel or a sperrzone . . . but together.

Stefan freed one hand to pull Mari to us. He hugged her gently. "Come with us, Mari."

She shook her head. "I can't."

We both immediately released, our expressions etched in similar surprise. *Mari is family. We leave as a family.* I stuttered. "Mari I . . . I . . . can't leave you."

"Yes." Mari nodded her head sternly. "Yes, you will!" We hugged, our tears mixing on our cheeks. "You and Stefan have waited an eternity to be together far from here, and I'm not going to interfere."

"You're not an interference!" My argument came out harsh. Stefan watched curiously.

"Besides," —her mouth slid slyly upward— "I'm engaged." She held up her left hand where a simple silver band sparkled under the lights.

"What?" I cried loud enough for anyone within the block's radius to hear. "When did this happen?"

"Last night."

"And you waited until now to tell me?"

"I'm sorry, El. It wasn't intentional. My body and head are kind of disconnected right now." She giggled. "Forgive me."

I wrapped both my arms around her waist and hugged her again. Stefan joined us.

"Mari, I want you to have the café."

"No, Ella. We'll buy it from you. Although, I can't imagine running it alone."

"Mari, it will be our wedding gift to you," Stefan added and kissed her on the cheek.

Forty-seven

WHAT IF IT'S A TRAP?

9 November 1989

"Are you all packed?"

"Yes. I only need one suitcase." I wrapped my arm through Mari's as we walked to the café for the last time. Attached to the inside of my blouse, Anton's tinnie pin rubbed against my skin. Its placement, encouraged by Stefan, comforted me. He understood its importance and suggested it would be safest there.

"Just think, Ella, you could be seeing Josef and Anton real soon."

My other hand brushed against the pin, hoping the clasp held strong this time. "I'm ready!"

We peered over to the nearest checkpoint, overflowing with people. The latest news about bordering countries allowing refugees to enter initiated chaos and confusion. Though nothing led us to believe the same accommodation would be allowed at the East and

West German border, hundreds of people marched near the wall all hours of every day.

"Did you see these photos of Alexanderplatz last Saturday?" Mari held up a paper in her free hand. Between the café and the travel arrangements, I hadn't picked up a newspaper in days. I glanced over the front, astonished by what I saw.

"Look how many!" My finger grazed the pictures. "There has to be thousands of people there! And all those banners. *Freie Whalen* . . . *Glasnost* . . . Nothing remained hidden in their demands for a free election or change."

"There's a press conference tonight."

"Why?" It felt strange that Mari knew more than I about the current events.

"The article states that Günter Schabowski will report on the Communist Convention."

"Maybe the protests are working."

"I think it's good you're leaving now. It might get worse." She lodged the paper under her arm. "What time is your train tomorrow?"

"We're booked on the 10 am to Budapest."

"How long will you be in Hungary?"

"Stefan told me there's a slight chance of delay at the border. I'm not sure how long processing might take, but the plan is to leave for Frankfurt the moment we're done."

"Oh, El, can you believe it? You're really leaving!"

"I'm still trying to wrap my head around it." Reflecting on our conversation only a week ago, Stefan shared the news that Hungary and Czechoslovakia opened their borders to German refugees, and yesterday, Poland did as well. "I've barely slept since."

"I'm going to miss you!" She squeezed my arm.

"The café will keep you more than occupied." I chuckled.

"I'm happy for you and Stefan." Mari beamed and then her lips turned downward. "But the café was a gift from Stefan to you. This is such a one-sided arrangement."

"I don't feel that way at all. I only need to take the things that matter to me, with the exception of Mama G's chair, and I'm positive you'll take good care of that. I don't need much more. It's time to make new memories in a new place."

She giggled. "And new memories you *will* make!" She reached for my hand and pulled it towards her, studying the ring. "I know you said you wanted to wait to get married til everyone will be there, but I want you to know it's okay if you don't. You've waited long enough!"

I hugged her. Mari was the sister I never had, and I was leaving her; it broke my heart. Kissing her cheek, I whispered, "Thank you for being part of my life."

"Thank you for rescuing me," she cried.

By the time we reached the restaurant, a handful of customers waited outside. The sight became more common each day with the increase of patrons on the street. I unlocked the door.

"You're all welcome to come in from the cold. I can get you coffee or tea as soon as it's ready, but breakfast will take longer."

A few nods and smiles followed us inside.

"Mari, you're going to need to hire some help. This is too big for you and Charlie." I went to the kitchen and placed several full teapots on the stove.

"Cade has decided to leave the butchery and join me." She retrieved the cannisters of tea.

My mouth fell open. "He has? Isn't it his family's store?"

"Yes, but he's going to sell it to his partner. We're going to run the café together."

I beamed. Visions of Hilde and Gus came to mind, although Mari's relationship seemed a bit sweeter. The idea they could grow old here warmed my soul. "But why don't you both come with us?" I pleaded. "He'll be with Heidi again; we'll all start over away from here."

She patted my hand, and when she gazed at me, a more mature Mari came through. "We will see you, Ella. I promise. Cade and I

364

talked about it. We feel he's more useful here right now, especially with the possibility of change."

Cade's spirit was strong in the cause. I was grateful he kept Mari out of it, but equally grateful he believed in a united Germany. "Well, I'm happy for you both. I'm sure he'll love this café as much as we have."

As the day wore on, more and more people filled the tables inside and out. The energy they brought with them overflowed the café. Mothers and Fathers laughing with their children, lovers embracing over a shared slice of Bienenstich, even older couples smiling and sharing stories of what it was like before the wall. By late afternoon, it took a great deal of strength not to cry each time I served our regular customers for the last time.

"Charlie, can you check with Leon and see if he can double his delivery of vegetables over the next few days?" The supplies we used during a normal day met our needs generally, but the increasing numbers brought forth valid concern.

"Yes." Charlie placed a hand on my shoulder. "We'll be fine, Ella."

I grinned as moisture built in my eyes. I struggled to let go.

"You've taught Mari and me pretty well. Nothing will change."

I gave him a hug and walked to the dining area where darkness had descended through the windows. *This is it! The end of my last day and my life here in East Berlin.*

As the final few customers paid their bill, I removed my apron. Though my feet and back ached from the busy day, my heart stung from its own mixed sorrow. My eyes would no longer fall upon this place: its simple décor and the good people who frequented it. I scanned Stefan's paintings slowly before moving to the backroom to finish cleaning.

Sitting on a stool, I ran through the mental list of objects I packed to make sure I hadn't missed one. Papa's pipe and medal, Mama's brush and sweater, Josef's books and marbles, the records *La Vie en Rose* and Mozart, Stefan's letters, and Anton's tinnie pin.

"Ella!" Mari's cries launched me to my feet. She'd been to the Geschäft for supplies and sprinted into the back room with urgency. "Something's . . . happening!" She dropped the two bags she carried to the counter and stuttered, out of breath, "the s . . . streets are filled with p . . . people!"

"They have been all day." I took a breath, suppressed since I heard her call.

"No—" She grabbed my hands. The lines in her forehead doubled. "—They're all running."

I dashed to the front, dragging her along. My face pressed against the window as a thundering noise erupted with the flurry of bodies on the street.

I glanced at my watch—11:42 pm "What's happening? Why are so many people out this late?"

"I don't know," she said, her head next to mine.

I turned and reached for the front door. With wide eyes, Mari blocked my hand. "Wait, what if they're running *from* something?" her voice quivered.

"We need to be sure, either way." I squeezed her hand. "I won't miss that train tomorrow." I gently pried her fingers from the handle, and they latched onto my sleeve. With my one free hand I cracked the door.

Flashes of the crowd immediately drew my mind back to 1961, the morning after the wire rolled out: the chaos, fear, and unknown. Glancing at their expressions, however, they showed no signs of alarm. The noise and screams came with smiles and laughter.

"What's happening?" I cried out above the noise. Nobody responded. I waved my arms and shouted, "Where is everyone going?"

The crowd continued to move, but one man yelled back, "The border, we're going to the border!"

Confused, I reached out and grabbed the sleeve of the nearest person. "Why is everyone running?"

The woman's cheeks were streaked with tears, but her mouth curved upward. "The border is open!" She placed her shaking hand over mine.

"The border to Poland, right?"

"No," —she shook my hand— "the border to West Berlin!"

My eyes shot to Mari for confirmation on what I'd just heard. Her lower lip dropped. With both hands she grabbed the first person who crossed her. "Is it true? The border to the West is open?"

"Yes," the man shouted, "announced on television fifteen minutes ago!" He broke her grip as he ran ahead. Goose bumps covered my skin as I scrambled back into the café with Mari close behind. We darted for our radio, which had sat silent behind the main counter most of the day. I flipped the switch on and waited, the thump from my chest escalating by the second.

"The border is open! East to West Berlin is unrestricted!"

The sobs came rapidly. The words I had waited a lifetime to hear echoed in my ears. Mari held me up as I relived the moment in August 1961 when I and Herr Krzinsky's family huddled around a similar radio to hear, *"The borders between East and West Berlin are closed!"* Twenty-eight years later, everything changed in an instant.

My knees shook and then buckled. If it weren't for Mari's tight grip, I would've fallen to the floor. I stared at my watch, squeezing the moisture away to see the time. *Almost midnight.* "I need to call Stefan! I need to get to a phone!"

Mari helped me to a chair. "Are you sure you can walk?"

I nodded. Walking wasn't an option. I needed to run.

"Here, here's your jacket. I'll come with you."

The closest public phone was outside our doors and down the street a half of a block. Despite the drizzling rain, the throng expanded as word spread. I pulled my hood over my head and, moving against the crowd, pressed forward with little progress. It was impossible to get to it. Mari's face shot my direction. "Let's try the one on Brunnen."

I nodded. Although our arms linked firmly, the masses jostled us enough to separate twice. Like swimming in a fast-moving river, our attempts to break free were nearly impossible. Thirty minutes passed by the time we finally reached the corner with the public telephone. However, our effort no longer mattered. The waiting line snaked down the walkway.

The enthused crowd physically propelled us forward as they hollered, cried, and celebrated. Knocked to the side, Mari scrambled to reach me again. "Ella!" she yelled and stretched her arms my direction. I shoved forward but was hit in the jaw by a group of boys trying to run through.

"Mari, the alley," I cried and pointed to a clearing between the nearest buildings. "I'll meet you there." I thrust through the mass to reach the space with little additional bruising. As I neared the designated spot, I grabbed a light pole and used it for leverage to launch to safety. Several other people had taken refuge in the corridor, one holding his head with both hands.

"Oh," I cried. Blood trickled from a gash at the top of his forehead. "Can I help you?"

His friend removed his scarf and pressed it against the wound. "He'll be okay," he assured. "It looks worse than it is. He got hit by an umbrella."

"It's madness out there." I pointed behind me.

"Yeah, but it's the best madness to have." He smiled as he checked the bleeding.

I peered around; Mari hadn't made it over yet. I feared as petite as she was, she'd get trampled. I walked back towards the street. Within seconds, she sprinted in. Placing one hand on the building wall, she bent over, exhausted.

"Are you okay?" I rubbed her back. "I'm sorry. We should've stayed in the café."

"I'm fine. I just need to rest." She slid to the ground amongst the growing puddles, her pantlegs drenched.

"Do you think we can make it back to the shop?"

"I don't think so, El. It'd be against the crowds."

"Yeah. Who would've thought something good would be dangerous!" My eyes shifted from her to the street.

"You don't think this could be some sick joke by the SED do you?" My question was meant for Mari, but everyone heard.

The injured man spoke up. "Like to get everyone in one place for a mass destruction?"

"Yeah," I muttered. "Similar to the Jews in the showers. What if it's a trap?" My lips pulled tight, my hands shivering in the cold until I stuffed them in my pant pockets.

Another man added his opinion. "At this point, nothing is going to stop those crowds."

"They could shoot," I whispered.

"Yeah, but this time we'll shoot back." He spit on the ground next to him.

I glanced to Mari. She came to my side, and we wrapped our arms around each other. "What should I do?" Tears, mixed with raindrops, slid down my cheeks.

She squeezed. "What do you want to do?"

"I don't know." I laid my head on her shoulder. "What if the trains don't run tomorrow?"

Mari patted my back. "It's too soon to know anything. Don't panic."

Then a horrifying thought entered my mind. "What if—oh, Mari, what if they only open the border tonight and then close it again?" I broke free and inched to the corner of the building. My whole body shook as I peered into the crowds. "I need to get there, Mari." I turned, yelling back to her, "I need to see my brother!"

"Then go." She came to my side. "I'll find Stefan. He'll understand."

"What if he doesn't? What if he thinks I left him for Anton?"

"Stefan knows you love him. He also knows you've been separated from Josef for twenty-eight years. Go, Ella. Go find your family."

I kissed Mari on the forehead. "Will you be okay?"

"We'll be here." The younger man answered. "She'll be safe with us."

"Thank you. I hope your friend will be fine."

They both snickered. "Best night ever!"

I inhaled deeply, studying the crowd for an opening. The expressions that passed me ranged from extreme happiness to tears. I had never witnessed anything like this before.

I circled back once more. "Mari, here, take this." I detached the tinnie pin from my shirt. "I'm afraid it might get separated from me in this crowd. Please tell Stefan I love him, and I'll return." Even as I said it, a pang in my chest reminded me of the possibility of no return. *What if I'm separated from Stefan? He on this side and me on the other?* I hesitated. *Maybe I should wait.*

The sea of people surged as I coaxed my uncertain foot to take the first step.

"Hurry!" A woman yelled to the man behind her. "They're going to close it. I know it! Hurry!" My eyes swung from her to him and then to the others who fled down the street. *I can't take the chance of missing Josef.*

"Alright, I can do this. I love you, Mari. No matter what, you must know that."

"I know. I love you too."

I took my first tentative steps into the crowd. People continued to be jostled left and right. Some pushed, some fell, screams of delight mixed with cries of pain. *I can do this.* I charged, forcing my way in. Those that tried to keep an umbrella up to protect themselves from the rain carried a weapon. I quickly clutched onto one man's trench coat in between the sea of bodies. He didn't seem to realize I was attached, and then someone else linked to me, an assembly of strangers—one spirit and one force—all with one purpose in mind. Get past the wall.

As we neared the restricted area, the bodies came to a complete stop. My heart lurched; a cruel tease. No one was going anywhere. I tried to see ahead or behind, but it was impossible. *What's happening?* I maneuvered my way towards the side, to the dissent of a few, but I didn't care. Feeling my way forward, I met the broad side of an automobile. Peeking in the windows revealed it had been abandoned. On further inspection, a line of deserted vehicles, with nowhere to go, stretched for blocks.

A couple men scrambled over the hood of the vehicle nearest me. I quickly followed suit and crawled up the same way. Once I reached the roof, I stood carefully to my full height. Clearing both the moisture blurring my eyes and the wet strands of hair stuck to my face, I searched the surroundings for answers.

Viewing the masses of bodies pressing the partition in all directions left me breathless. Soldiers lined atop the concrete blockade side by side, hands in either their pockets or hanging on their belts, but nobody held a gun. Below them, people were climbing, scaling the blocks. One man reached the top and stood between two soldiers with both his arms raised in celebration. A deafening roar of the crowd brought a second man up, and within seconds, a dozen civilians dotted the top of the wall. I rubbed my eyes. *Am I really seeing this? Men standing next to the soldiers on the wall?* Stunned, my eyes shifted and caught the interchange of several officers communicating from the barrier to the tower. They yelled back and forth, their voices nearly drowned from the noise.

"What are they saying?" I turned to the nearest spectator who stood on the car with me. He shrugged his shoulders.

Another man near him yelled and pointed to the tower. "What are the soldiers saying?" He asked again, and on the third attempt a chant began, "What are the soldiers saying?"

The question looped through the crowd, and within minutes people shouted back. "The officer is asking what he should do? Should he give the order to shoot?" Instantly, cries rang out. With the sheer number of people present, there was no question the mob could overrun the guards. Nonetheless, this proved the stranglehold the government had on us and the fear they embedded. Nobody moved.

One man who reached the top untouched was handed a large German flag. He raised it high, gripping the pole tightly in his fists, and swung it back and forth. Shouts and screams erupted. *"Ein Deutschland!"* More people scrambled to the top, some with tools in their hands. Each time they struck the fortification, cheers exploded. Very little broke off at first, but no one stopped them.

I pinched my arm; the sting smarted. *What am I waiting for? The soldiers to seize the offenders? Throw them back into the crowd?* I waited and watched with astonishment. *Nothing. Nothing's happened!* More people started climbing and suddenly disappeared to the other side. What **am** I waiting for? I spied the access gate. It gradually rose, manually pushed upward. My eyes shot back to the soldiers. Some abandoned their posts, others appeared confused. One soldier jumped over to the West. Nobody was being stopped. It's real. *THE BORDER IS OPEN!*

Forty-eight

SWEET SCENT OF FREEDOM

10 November 1989

Each step I took felt shorter than the last. The six freckles on the man's bald spot in front of me formed a rectangle. The rain soaked his denim jacket, flattening the frayed collar, and the tear in his right shoulder opened and closed like a mouth when he moved. A woman's umbrella beside me rubbed against my leg a dozen times. Her young child whimpered nonstop. Each time I believed the checkpoint was near, it wasn't near enough. Time crawled with each glance at my watch — 2:09 am — 2:54 am — 3:18 am — 4:01 am. The red-and-white gate appeared in front of me, and my watch reached 4:42 am.

I should've been exhausted, sore, and discouraged from the wait and pressure, but the sheer shock of the moment boosted adrenaline through my veins. Ducking underneath the post, I took my first step into West Berlin and cried aloud. People all around me fell to their knees, sobbing, crying, and kissing the ground. Strangers rushed to greet the refugees with blankets, warm drinks, and an endless supply of hearty hugs. With chattering teeth I accepted a covering without reservations, sure that if it hadn't been for the body heat produced by the multitude, I would've caught a deathly cold by now.

The deeper I entered the threshold of freedom, a lifetime of memories surfaced—the separation and goodbye, Papa's burial, the letters, the tunnel, the years I plotted, wished, and dreamt for this very moment.

Horns honked, throngs of people danced in the streets. The rain slowed to a drizzle, but nobody noticed or cared. Locating a small space to breathe, I opened my mouth wide and filled my lungs with air. The sweet scent of freedom ignited every nerve, and I twirled in place until I became too dizzy to see. A warm cherry streusel materialized in my hands, the giver unseen. A group of men, arm in arm, walked by, laughing and smiling and then blew me a kiss as they passed.

Energy abounded. Reunions occurred in every corner of my sight. Envious, I frantically scanned the assembly and quickly restrained my discouragement. I had only been free for thirty minutes. I couldn't expect to see them so soon. My body rattled. *I don't know where to find them.* I wasn't sure where to look nor the direction to go. In my rush, I didn't grab their address from the café.

My steps slowed, exhaustion arrived, but I refused to stop. The sun crept upward and tried relentlessly to peek through the remaining clouds of the storm. My eyes flashed from building to building in awe at the difference. Everything appeared cleaner, stronger, and intact. Even the air smelled better. A young girl handed me a sprig of jasmine and kissed me on the cheek. Beer and liquor flowed generously as music filled the air, and strangers became friends.

I contemplated my course. *I'm standing here in West Berlin, completely lost.* I wandered in circles, witnessing more reunions and more happy people. Finding a bench, I sank to the seat, able to rest for the first time in hours. My fingers rubbed my temples encouraging my mind to calm and reflect on the night sensibly. *Where would they assume I'd go?* I made a mental list of possibilities. *The observation platform . . . maybe there.* The place I usually saw them. Maybe they would think that too.

I ran towards a group of people clearly from the West. They handed a cigar to each passing man, woman, and child, and before I could get my question out, I had one in each palm. "How do I get to Bernauer from here?"

"Bernauer and what?"

"Bernauer and Acker."

"It's two kilometres that direction. Follow this street until you reach the park and then turn right. You can't miss it. But here, have another cigar, and stay for the party!"

I smiled at their kindness. "I'm hoping to find my brother."

They grinned in return, and one patted my hand. "Off you go, dear. Find your brother."

I ran through the crowd, not as heavy as the east side, arriving at the cross streets shortly before eight o' clock. Here, at Bernauer, a large section of the concrete block collapsed to the ground, the mass of people creating a new *unofficial* border crossing. Seeing the space between the East and West free and open was more joy than my heart could handle. Viewing the partition from this side, my spirit soared. The face of the edifice had become an emotional canvas. Graffiti from top to bottom. Years and years of names, sentiments, and poems etched into its soul.

The viewing station, clearly recognizable, stood to my left. This was where my family talked to me. Tears built as I stumbled towards it. Several people climbed to the top and sobbed uncontrollably. I gripped the railing. My fingers wrapped around the same wood Josef and Anton touched. My foot lifted and connected one stair at a time until I reached the top. It was here, at this very spot, that my own brother stood and waved, spoke my name, and blew kisses. It was also here where Anton introduced me to Elizabeth.

I scanned past the wall. The cemetery remained shrouded with hordes of people. Squinting, I caught a glimpse of the brick siding of the mausoleum and then shifted to the rubble that identified as the

Church of Reconciliation. Finally, my eyes fell to the lot covered in debris that was my home. Tears saturated my cheeks. Twenty-eight years ago I reached my hand out a window and touched my brother for the last time, and now here I was, standing on his side of the world.

I remained on the stand as people climbed the barricade and poured through the hole, mesmerized by their expressions and emotions the moment they came through. I relived my own journey with each one. There were few *real* reunions, but more and more celebrated a kinship of liberty. Not one person crossed into the West without a welcome of some sort.

Turning around, I didn't recognize anyone. *How am I going to find them?* I was sure they'd be here, if anywhere. With reluctance, I stepped down to the walk and staggered to the nearest bench. My body dropped wearily to its respite. My limbs, drained of energy, rejoiced at the chance to rest. Peering at my watch again, I realized I had been awake for over twenty-four hours. Watching the continued scene develop around me, I forced my mind to stay active and alert. No doubt my time would come when I'd be hugging someone from my past, and I wanted to be ready.

Forty-nine

EIN DEUTSCHLAND!

Exhaustion overcame. Propped on the bench, one arm raised to hold my heavy head. Witnessing the vitality of the youth who danced and sang around me drew attention to my aching joints. I took the stamina and strength I held in my 20's and 30's for granted and would give anything for its return at this moment. The blanket I'd been given draped over my shoulders to ward off shivering. *Do not fall asleep, Ella!* Surely they'd guess I would be here.

My thoughts flickered back to Stefan. A momentary pang of anxiety struck, wondering if Mari reached him and explained my absence. Maybe he wandered across the border out of curiosity. Although he possessed a genuine compassion for those who were separated, I wasn't aware of any associations Stefan held in the West. *Will he believe Mari? Will he believe I didn't come for Anton?*

As the sun rose fully above my head, the limited winter rays provided an added layer of warmth. The dancing and celebrating continued and only increased above the heavy sound of construction or more appropriately, *destruction*. Tools pounded and chipped against solid concrete. In some places the cracks and fissures measured mere metres. In other areas, chunks the size of windows were hammered out. Leaving my blanket on the bench, I was drawn to the wall. Never before had I witnessed such joy in demolition.

I stepped over the ever-growing rubble. Reaching down, I picked up one of the colorful graffiti stones that had been crushed and squeezed it firmly. When I opened my hand again, I studied the rock. The significance of it resting in my palm amazed me. A handful of revelers, their arms linked together, sang *"Muss I Denn"*, a German folk song. When they passed, a man behind them caught my eye. Vaguely familiar, I pictured him standing atop a platform, raising both hands high in the air. *Josef!*

"Ella!" he cried.

I launched into a run and only slowed as his arms flung around my body, lifting me high above the ground in a full swing. My entire body shuddered. Once lowered, my head dipped against his shoulder. The scent of Josef, the man, was real. "Josef! My little brother!" Cries mixed with sputtered sobs.

"I hoped you'd be here! I hoped!" The strain in his voice increased. His cheek stuck to mine from the moisture.

"Josef!" Emotion built so thick in my throat, I questioned whether the word came out correctly. "Josef!"

"It's you, Ella. It's really you!" He squeezed my torso tightly once more and then pulled back to see me against the growing light. "When we got the news that the borders had opened, we couldn't get here fast enough." His hands gripped mine. "All roads are closed, transportation is down, and as you can see, the masses of people have halted all of Berlin."

I glanced around us; the amount of people had tripled since the night before. It was possible, although doubtful, some people actually slept through the event and awakened to a united city. "I wasn't sure you'd come."

Josef's countenance grew pale. "Wouldn't come?" One hand left mine and held my cheek, his thumb rubbing my skin. "There's no other place in the world I'd rather be." He pulled me in, his broad shoulders and round belly swallowing me in his embrace. His hands slipped from my shoulders and grasped my fingers tenderly. He turned to a woman approaching slowly. "Heidi . . . this is Ella."

"Of course it is." Her lips curved in an enormous beam. She swooped in for her own affectionate embrace. "Despite a very large wall, we have met before." She kissed both my cheeks and stepped back to introduce me to the lovely girls at her side. "Our daughter Savannah recently turned eleven and our youngest Alora is six."

With an understandable hesitance, Savannah offered a timid hug, and Alora presented flowers to me. I accepted them graciously with a kiss on her cheek. Both displayed the dainty features of elegant beauty, something they received from her mother. I chuckled.

I circled back to Josef and cradled his face in my hands. My sweet brother had grown into a man. A man at thirty-nine with a family of his own. Despite his aged countenance, his deep brown eyes remained the same—the same hope and happiness we once shared together before a wall took that away. "Oh." I let go. "Where is your son?"

Josef pointed to the portion of the barrier I had been staring at before our reunion. "He couldn't wait. He's grown up with the stories." Their oldest brandished a long pipe, striking it against the concrete barrier. It did little damage, but a few chips flew here and there. While I watched, a sudden urge to join him tunneled out of me.

"Heinrich, come!" Josef called for the teenage boy.

"No, Josef." I waved my hand to stop him. "No, it's okay." With a sly grin, I hustled over to him. "Heinrich, I'm your Aunt Ella." I reached out my hand to shake his. He placed the pipe at our feet and hugged me with the same exuberance his dad had. Nearly as tall as me, slender, with the same ruffled brown hair and eager eyes of his father, it was as if I hugged the eleven-year-old version of Josef before we parted.

"May I join you?" I pointed to his choice of instrument. He gladly picked up the pipe and placed it in my hands. I gripped it and moved closer to the manmade structure that had nearly destroyed me a dozen times over. *CRACK!* The lead smashed against the block and vibrated. *CRACK! CRACK!* My hands shook but not my spirit. I pounded repeatedly until a chunk the size of my fist finally broke loose. I hadn't realized I'd been crying with every stroke until I reached down to pick up the piece and several teardrops landed on my shoe. Josef came from behind with a pat on my shoulder and reached for the pipe. He took his turn at beating until his results brought forth additional broken chips.

Each person took a turn; even the sweet little girls had a chance. Though their strength was limited, smaller pieces began to crumble and fall to the ground. Up and down the length of the wall, the action was mirrored for miles.

My eyes lifted to the tower above. Dark and vacant, it no longer intimidated me. Yesterday, soldiers stood at their station, poised to shoot on command, and here we were, less than twenty-four hours later, demolishing the very symbol that had characterized twenty-eight years of my life.

"It's over, Ella. It's over." Josef's declaration sailed around us to approving cheers. "We'll never be separated again."

His words sunk in. The very thing I desired for decades now frightened me. Josef knew little of my Eastern life. Other than what he read in the news or saw from afar, it was abridged. The modest correspondence we shared in those years, by letter and telephone, Josef must know much had been suppressed.

At the end of our satisfying strikes, we each grasped a portion of the block in our hands, and as much as we hated what it represented, we couldn't let go. Alora slid her small hand into mine as we turned away. "Aunt Ella?"

"Yes, sweetheart." Touched by her kindness, I waited.

"Will you come home with us now?" Her long eyelashes fluttered, making me chuckle out loud. She was like Sofia, able to melt hearts for the rest of her life with a simple bat of her eyes. I considered the area, the crowds, the celebration, but I worried about Stefan—his heart and his trust. I glanced over to Josef and Heidi, nodding their heads quite vigorously in agreement.

"We wouldn't have it any other way," Heidi insisted. I smiled at each of their children. *This is my family. I'm with my family!*

"Where's Anton?" In my vision of this reunion, I never questioned Anton being here. *Maybe he's delayed or occupied.* I bit my lip, constructing a valid reason for his absence. The Anton I knew would not have missed me, not today. Despite the challenges our friendship faced in all our years apart, we shared a common hope, and that hope came to fruition overnight.

"He's away, Ella," Josef answered. "He would've been here; I know this to be true."

My sigh came louder than expected. This news brought a great deal of relief.

Josef reached for my hand. "He's in France, due to return at the end of the week."

"Do you think he knows?" I yearned for more. "Do you think he's heard about the fall?"

Josef squeezed and held tight. "I think the whole world knows." He pointed around to the various reporters set up along the wall. "The telephone lines are jammed. He might not get through if he called, but there's no doubt in my mind he's heard the news, and he would've been here if he could."

I smiled. Enveloped in tenderness, my heart swelled. *I am standing here with my brother.* The last time we touched was through a kitchen window in 1961. The idea that something as ridiculous as a **wall** could keep us separated for so long, infuriated me, but today was not about blame. Today brought love, life, and new beginnings.

"Ready?" Joseph waved his free hand forward and pointed down the street.

"Definitely."

We took our time meandering towards their neighborhood. As news of the event spread, more and more people ventured out. Though the crowds were not crazed and anxious like the East, their enthusiasm triggered countless street parties and instant celebrations.

Every step I took filled me with wonder and awe. The sidewalks weren't littered with rubbish or bordered with weeds. We weren't stepping over war rubble and scattered debris or passing hollowed shells of buildings. Store windows displayed color and excitement— toys, clothing, and confections I didn't know existed.

Before the wall, "West Berlin" was only steps from my door and part of my neighborhood. When it was cut in half and I lost access to those places, I forgot what was there. I assumed things would be different, but I had no idea how much.

Here, as I walked hand in hand with Josef and Alora, an energy radiated from this part of the city —alive and thriving. The scent of baked goods flowed, laughter emanated, and every window spread open and inviting as people cried from their perch, *"Berlin Verient! Ein Deutschland!"*

Berlin united! One Germany! Each syllable resonated deeply in my ears. I wasn't sure if I believed that was possible in my lifetime.

When we reached the corner a half block from their flat, Heidi squealed and launched into a run. A man who sat on their building steps darted to meet her. It was Cade! Cade had come! My heart pumped faster, glancing around. Surely Mari would be with him, and maybe she brought Stefan with her!

"I knew you would come," Heidi cried, flinging her arms around him. "I knew you would find us!" He probably had the foresight to bring their address with him. I ran off like a mad woman without a single item but my jacket and the clothes on my body. Their emotional embrace produced a fresh round of tears.

Once Cade released from Heidi, I timidly called his direction as we walked. "Is Mari here?" Cade's smile pulled to a frown. "No, she—"

382

"She what?" I cut him off. "What Cade?"

He sighed. "She's trying to locate Stefan."

"Stefan?" The lines above my nose deepened. "What do you mean *trying* to locate him?"

"Nobody knows where he is."

"She didn't get to him last night?"

"No. Transportation was down. She only got as far as my place. I made her stay; it was too risky and dangerous in the dark. We left the same time this morning. She headed to the mortuary and I here."

"And Katharina doesn't know where he is?"

"I'm not sure. She has no way to tell me. She mentioned your train tickets. Maybe he went to the train station as planned, thinking you would meet him there."

The pounding in my chest convoluted my thoughts. *What is Stefan thinking?* My knees quivered and fell limply. Josef grasped me securely around the waist to keep me from falling down the stairs. Heidi quickly unlocked their door and Josef helped me to their couch. My hands cradled my head between my knees. *He has to realize I'd be here. Why would he leave? Would he go to Budapest without me?* Catching a glimpse of my watch, the time indicated it was nearly three in the afternoon. Sixteen hours since the news broke. Five hours after the train was scheduled to depart— if they were running.

"Ella?" Cade came to my side. Embarrassed, I sheltered my eyes. I had turned his most wonderful reunion into a selfish tantrum. I brushed him off. "Please don't worry about me. I'm fine. Go to your sister."

He patted my hand, still entangled in my bangs. "Mari said she left him a note at the restaurant just in case she didn't find him at the mortuary. I'm sure he knows you'd come here."

I peeked his direction. "I should've waited," I whispered. "You waited. Mari knows exactly where you are, but Stefan doesn't know. What if he thinks I'm not coming back?"

Cade pulled my hand from my face and squeezed. "Ella, you forget I'm a witness to Stefan's love for you. Even if he went to the station, he wouldn't have left without you."

I couldn't stop the tears.

"Thank you, Cade." I said this to prompt his return to Heidi, but an anxiousness remained.

Josef, still sitting next to me, spoke up. "Stefan knows you'd come to us, right?" His arm draped across my shoulders.

"Yes. Yes, he knows that." My words came rushed. "I . . . I just need him to understand I wasn't coming for Anton."

"Oh." He nodded subtly. "I see."

"Oh, Josef!" I turned into his hold and leaned my head against his shoulder. "I'm sorry I didn't leave with you. I'm sorry we lived apart for this long."

He rested his own head against mine. "We missed a lot, you and me. I'm sorry I was angry with you. Papa needed you." He sighed. "But now we have a future. A chance to make up for all that lost time."

He stood to his feet and clutched both of my arms upward. I wobbled at first, and he held fast. "But first, you must rest. It has been quite a day."

I patted his cheek. "Thank you."

Josef led me. "Savannah willingly gave up her room for you." He chuckled. "She loves bunking with her sister, though they giggle most of the night."

En route to the room, I stopped a half dozen times, curiosity overtaking weakness. "Josef, your home is beautiful," I whispered. He had a separate room for a table—not in the kitchen. His living room contained one large couch, a smaller couch, and two chairs. Their television set sat atop a long wooden table with shelves underneath. His hallway was filled with pictures, decorative light fixtures, and a large vase with flowers on a niche carved into one wall. They also had a room for washing clothes. I had only seen such conveniences in the

Franke's, and although their wealth outweighed many, Josef's circumstances made me proud.

"I can't believe all this is yours." My tired eyes scanned the space. "And you said the whole building belongs to Anton?"

"Yes. Anton has done quite well in the construction business. His properties include this one as well as the one across the street. About twenty flats in all."

"I'm proud of you both. Things have gone quite well." A small twinge of jealousy broke through, my mind flashing to my small one room flat without a kitchen table. Scolding myself silently, I shoved my envy aside. I was truly happy for them.

"Anton has given us much and never asks for anything in return."

"Josef, I'll never be able to thank Anton for what he's done for you . . . for us both." I couldn't hide my regret.

Josef placed an arm around me. "What is ours is yours. You're family. We want you to live here with us. You no longer have to live in the East."

Those words floated through my head. I only dreamed that choice would come. "What do you think is going to happen to the DDR?"

"I can't imagine their government surviving this collapse. Everyone is leaving."

Everyone is leaving. His words repeated in my mind. *It's being deserted . . . like I was once.*

My jaw constricted to prevent more tears from enflaming my already itchy and swollen eyes.

As we reached the bedroom, Josef hugged me once more. "Rest, sister. We'll visit more when you awaken." He kissed me on the cheek and closed the door. Even his eleven-year-old daughter's bedroom was nicer than my entire place. Her bed, dresser, and a trunk of toys in the corner bordered pink-painted walls where the plaster didn't crack or peel nor did I find any stains. The scent of fresh flowers filled my nose over the burning smell of an overused radiator. I fell to the bed, my lids heavy, willing the darkness to come.

The next morning, I awoke to a sweet aroma. The clank and sizzle drew me upright, though I did not recognize the scent. Sitting on the edge of the bed, I stretched. Every muscle from my back, legs, and arms groaned. Rigid and sore, it took several minutes to get them to cooperate and move. When I left the East, I took nothing with me, but a small stack of Heidi's clothes rested on the dresser. I put the jeans and sweater on and entered the kitchen, finding the whole family circled around the table. The generous smiles warmed my heart as each person rose to welcome me with hugs. Though the familiarity of family gathering together brought a calm, my heart strings pinched for the family I left behind in the East

"You must be hungry, El." Josef flipped meat in a pan "Breakfast is almost ready."

"Can I get you some tea?" Heidi stood and reached for a cup.

"Yes, thank you. And what is that smell?"

"*Leberwurst, speck,* and *Brötchen!" Josef added.*

It had been a long time since I'd eaten bacon, and while Lena made delicious rolls at the house, honey was nearly impossible to come by. I picked up the honey jar in one hand and the strawberry marmalade in the other, examining them carefully and waving the open tops under my nose. I was in love. Josef placed a plate of rolls before me, their sweetness reeling me in. As I lathered them with the sugary spreads, I noticed Cade too had piled three before him. We exchanged looks and laughed. He and I were the only ones who understood the joke. Deprivation in the East would be something we always shared.

"Congratulations on your engagement, Cade. When will you and Mari marry?" I recalled her announcement to Stefan and I, with little time to talk about the details afterward. His countenance glowed, exactly how a man in love should.

"Well, with this happening, I want to marry as soon as possible."

I smiled and reached for his hand. "I'm happy for you. This is all a dream come true. Our family has come full circle."

"Yes, it has." Heidi reached from behind him and gave him another hug.

"Will you stay in the East?" Mari and I had just spoken of their intent to work the café together.

"It's hard to say. I'm not sure what we'll do. Whatever it is, nothing will keep us from Heidi and Josef now."

I nodded, knowing exactly how he felt.

After the delicious breakfast, we settled in the living room where the children wanted to show me their favorite television shows. I watched the screen with fascination. It wasn't as if I'd never seen one—I had— or that the East didn't have television—it did. It was simply a luxury few could afford, and those that could had their content controlled.

I recalled watching the speech by President Reagan, and catching a glimpse of the futbol game, as well as an occasional news show for Herr Franke when I cared for him. At times it was hard to discern the truthfulness of the statements I heard, similar to the newspaper and cinema. The DDR excelled at propaganda.

"Tante Ella, watch, watch. He's funny . . . don't you think he's funny?" Savannah snuggled up next to me on the couch. She giggled relentlessly at a young Viking boy named Vicky.

I grinned at his silly exploits, but my mind was far from the television. It wandered to Stefan, his whereabouts and thoughts. *Is he in Hungary? France? Cochem?*

Kissing Savannah's forehead, I sat forward. "Would you mind if I took a walk?" I caught Josef's attention as Alora crawled into his lap and curled up like a puppy.

"Tante Ella, you don't want to miss *Das Sandmännchen*. It will be on next." Savannah reached for my hand to keep me next to her.

I clasped her hand gently and brought it to my lips. "I'll have plenty of time to see The Sandman. I need some air, sweetheart."

"You're free to do whatever you want here, Ella." Josef smiled as he rocked his little one to sleep. It was midday and apparently her favorite place to nap. I grinned and patted his head as I walked past. "You're such a good Papa."

"You won't get lost, will you?" he said as I reached the door.

"No, I'm going to the park I saw on the way here. I don't think it was far."

"Oh, sure. Take a right at the end of our street, stay on Hochstasse, and you won't miss it. Do you want me to come?"

"No, I'm fine. I'll be back soon."

I wandered down the street slowly, as if time had no limit. The neighborhoods still overflowed with celebration, a never-ending party with food and drink offered at every corner. Music exploded from windows and cars, even balconies and rooftops where musicians played their guitars, harmonicas, and the accordion. Modern music and traditional ballads intermixed with people dancing on the sidewalk, the grass, and street. I yearned to relish in this great victory and leap for joy with them, but without Stefan, this triumph felt empty. When I reached the park, I sat down on a child's swing and rolled back and forth. The gentle sway calmed me.

I inhaled deeply, allowing the crisp air to enter my nose and circulate through my limbs. November 11th and no sign of a typical autumn freeze. I attributed the rain for the chill I experienced the night I arrived. Everything was different here—the clouds, puffy white against an endless blue, color and joy everywhere. *Does the sun always shine in the West? Do they even have a winter, or does the East possess all the darkness over Berlin?*

My legs pushed underneath me, and I gripped the chains tighter. A desire to press the cold steel into my fingers materialized—a tangible, real object, since the breeze I manufactured from the swing wasn't enough. Glancing towards the partition a half kilometre away, one entire section crumbled to the ground. A steady flow of people moved through, very few the opposite direction.

My feet slammed into the dirt and brought me to a full stop. *It's true! Darkness does hover over the East.* Gray clouds appeared, as though it was raining there, maybe storming. My eyes narrowed as they traced each building over the wall. Shadows consumed them, and what little light attempted to emanate met fierce opposition. The swing became my sanctuary. Every time I stood to leave, it drew me back. The simplicity of a child's play toy kept the unknown that terrified me at bay for several hours.

As the sun began to drift downward, I felt the beginnings of the night air chill my arms. Goosebumps covered my skin. Although I felt safe and secure in the West, I wasn't sure what the sunset brought. Humanity always consisted of a few with evil intentions, and it would be wise to return before dark.

I took one last gentle swing and jumped at the apex. Sand filled my shoes, so I walked to the grass and sat down, shaking out one shoe at a time. Hanging the last upside down, my side view caught a man approaching at a rapid speed. With little time to react, I ducked and threw up my hand as a shield.

Fifty

IT'S OVER, KLEIN MAUS

"Ella! Ella!"

Everything spun. My shoe slipped out of my hand and hit the ground with a thud. My attempts to stand failed, and I lost my balance. Anton's arms wound around me and pulled me up to him.

"Ella." His voice tickled my ear. I could hear the desperation in it. "Josef told me where to find you. I couldn't wait."

Nothing registered in my brain except that Anton held me. His hands pressed firmly against my back with no motion to release. I rested my head against his chest. It rose parallel to his rapid heartbeat. The scent of his skin tingled my nose with a musky fragrance. He leaned back and let his eyes fall upon mine. His striking green pupils fogged with tears.

"It's you." The only words I could muster cracked on their way out.

His hand brushed my cheek, nose, hair, then rested against my neck. "I can't believe I'm touching you. You're not a hallucination, are you?" He chuckled but there was an element of truth to his tone. My eyes traced his profile; the older Anton still possessed an element of coarseness about him. His tousled salt and pepper hair fell barely over his ears on the sides, and the back touched his collar. Several days scruff collected on his chin, and his light-blue jeans had a small tear in the knee, but his eyes carried the same absorbing focus and his smile . . . his ever-calming temperament.

I shook my head vigorously. "No, you're not hallucinating." His hands gripped both of mine.

"I was in Paris when the announcement came. It took me two days to get home. Everything was booked. Everyone wanted to be here."

My eyes met his, but mine were sorely blurred. "Anton, I'm sorry about Elizabeth." My sniffle masked a growing sob. "I'm sorry I wasn't there for you."

His hands left mine as he embraced me again, his breathing jagged and irregular while his chin rested atop my head. He was taller now—stronger and older than the last time we found ourselves in this very position.

"Ella, I don't fault you. You battled much without us. I can't begin to understand what you went through over there. It must've been hell."

I closed my eyes and flashes of that hell surfaced, but somewhere in between the torment, bursts of happiness broke through—flickers of smiles, laughs, and love. And each one circled back to Stefan.

"Josef told me about the Colonel and your torture." His embrace increased and released. "I should've been there to protect you." Anton reached in his pocket and pulled out a linen, the faded-blue material brought an additional round of tears even before the initials appeared. "Remember this?"

I bit my lip and grinned. Tender memories of that night flooded me: the goodbye, my father, the exchange of gifts.

"Your pin."

"The tinnie pin?"

"It got me through some really tough times. I wore it often."

"It was meant to protect you."

"Thank you. It truly did, and now it belongs with you . . . with your family." I patted my chest. The pin was gone. Momentary panic settled until I remembered I took it off in the alley and handed it to Mari for safekeeping. I feared I would lose it in the crowd. "It's with Mari, but I'll get it soon."

"I'm not worried, klein Maus. Right now, I'm holding the only thing that matters."

I reached for his hand and squeezed and then led him to a nearby bench. The moment his arm went around me, my mind flooded with memories of this man. Younger, wilder and reckless, yet when we were alone, truly alone, whether it was in the orphanage or on the street, he shared his vulnerability. That day at the Spree when an unguarded, honest Anton kissed me, our friendship deepened. Drawing me in tight, his breathing stumbled, "Ella, I wasn't sure this would ever happen, and now that you're here and real, I can barely believe it."

"I know. I missed everything." My tears fell freely. "I missed watching Josef grow up. I missed seeing you become a man, a husband, and a father. I'll never get back what they took from me, from us." I sniffled hard.

Anton handed me the blue linen, and I laughed at the sight of several holes and strings hanging loosely. Its condition suffered.

"I'm sorry. I kept it in my pocket."

"All these years?"

"Since the night we parted."

"Oh, Anton." I buried my head against his chest. "Should I have left that night? Did I make the wrong decision?"

Anton's silence worried me.

"Klein Maus. I have thought about this often. Yes, our lives would've been very different. We might have married, had our own children, but . . .''

"But what?"

"We're the people we are today because of the life we led. I don't regret my love for Elizabeth, my children. I was angry, filled with hate, but that's gone now."

I shook my head. "My hate may never leave me. I don't think I'll ever be able to forgive the people responsible for the division. They forced us to live apart all these years."

"I understand, and you have every right to be upset."

The angle of Anton's face confirmed he wasn't finished. I waited for him to find the words.

"Ella, I don't think I ever told you why I hated the Jews, back when we found the hidden room, the pouch, and the Star."

"No." My fingers rubbed over the handkerchief. "I heard rumors around the home but never thought about them. I'm sure you had your reasons."

"My father was an SS Officer."

"For Hitler?"

"Yes. He was assigned to oversee the *Wolfsschanze*. We lived in East Prussia after the war, and they were arresting those involved with the regime. We ran. We moved often for several years, all over Germany. Every time I made new friends and they weren't the right friends, or when the milkman or postman started asking questions, we relocated again. I had just turned eight, and we were living on a farm outside of Bautzen. We'd only been there two weeks when I watched, from inside the barn, trucks filled with soldiers drive up the road. They dragged my father out of the house, tied him up like a pig to slaughter. My mother tried to stop them, and she got kicked and beaten. The trucks drove away, and I never saw my father again. When I finally gathered the courage to leave the barn, I found mama on the porch. It took everything I had to bring her inside, but she never recovered. She refused to eat or allow me to find help. I watched her die."

Covering his hands with my own, I wished for some way to ease his pain. My oldest friend in the world, and here he was, sharing the darkest part of his life for the first time. I squeezed my eyes to keep tears from blurring my sight as he continued.

"I lived with her dead body in the house for days. A family in need of fresh water stopped by on the fourth day and found me. They were traveling back to Berlin, and although they wished they could take care of me, they barely had enough for themselves. When we reached Berlin, they brought me to the *Waisenhaus*. Ella, I blamed the Jews for my parents' deaths. I was filled with rage and hated anyone that reminded me of them. Your friendship saved me. It was the idea that I meant something to someone that helped me heal. When I got to the West, it was Josef and then Elizabeth."

"Family." I grinned. *They saved me too.*

"Yeah," he chuckled. "Who would've thought. This snot-nosed orphan kid with a family of his own."

"But why were we forced to be apart all these years?" My childish whine manifested.

"We have to go through tough times to become better people. All that you have experienced, all the sadness, heartache, and pain has made you who you are today. If you had never experienced those things, you wouldn't be the strong, determined woman I see today. It's easy for me to say, here from the comfort and safety of the West, while you struggled for food, peace, and your very life at times, but I believe it's true."

"But why so much heartache? Every time it seemed life was good, it never lasted."

"You have every right to feel cheated. There isn't a day goes by that I don't wish I had convinced you to leave with me, but the woman I see in front of me has grown because I was not there—fell in love and fought for that love because I was not there. You have a purpose, and that purpose was never me, as much as I hate to admit it. You belong with Stefan. He's the man who owns your heart and your soul. I believe our path was never meant to be one."

I hung onto his words. Everything Anton spoke was the truth. He was no longer the scrawny fighter or the rebellious teen. He was wise, insightful, and now a loving father.

"Thank you, Anton. I'm sorry you had to go through such a horrible event as a child. Thank you for sharing it with me. I've been blessed with good friends who loved and cared for me through my challenges, but you're my oldest and dearest friend. I will forever love you."

He pulled me in once more, and my eyes closed to his tightened embrace. The security of his arms brought comfort during most of my childhood. All those years he held me through the night to ease my terrifying nightmares had never been forgotten.

His touch should have fulfilled any yearning I had, but even in our embrace, my eyes rested on the wall. Its presence, though without breath or life, dominated. *I miss the East* and *my life.* The thought stunned me even as it crossed my mind. I shuddered in place. *I need to go home . . . my home!* Releasing me, Anton's eyes followed the lines and curves of my face before they settled on my eyes.

"Look at you," he whispered. "You're beautiful, even twenty-eight years later."

My nose stung. "Always the charmer." I met his look briefly then once again gazed behind him.

The silence that hovered created a conversation without words. Anton rubbed my arms with his calloused hands. "Ella?" He tipped his head slightly to the side. This drew my eyes back to his.

"Our whole lives we waited for this moment, this reunion, never knowing when it would come. We've missed you immensely, but—" His sigh was profound. His lips pulled into a flat line. "—but you're leaving us, aren't you?"

Tears slipped out the corners of my eyes. His thumbs slowly brushed them away.

"The East is an orphan now." I knew he would understand what that meant more than anyone. "It's where I belong." Once those words were uttered out loud, it was if a heavy weight disappeared from my chest. Breath came freely, and my spirit soared. The strange attachment I had with the very place I fought to leave had become a part of me, more than I really comprehended.

My hand cupped his jaw, and I leaned in and kissed him. It was not a friendly kiss on the cheek. His lips melted into mine, long and meaningful. My mouth drew him in, the salty taste of his lips lingering on my tongue. It was exactly how I remembered. When I released, his countenance reflected pain and awareness all in one. The kiss was goodbye, though we never said the word. When we parted, his cheeks flushed a steamy red, and my heart pounded twice as hard.

"I love you, Anton."

He nodded. "I love you too, Ella. Please come back soon and . . ." —he squeezed my hand again— "bring Stefan with you." He kissed me on the cheek, stood, and retrieved my shoe off the grass.

When he knelt to place it back on my foot, I held my hand to my heart. "Please explain it to Josef. He listens to you."

He nodded and waved goodbye. I walked cautiously to the opening that had been torn apart overnight. When I reached the space, my fingers brushed against the uneven edges, wire and rebar poking out in all directions. The structure I hated was battered and broken. Then I realized, I was the only one moving towards the East. Hundreds, possibly thousands, of people deserted what was left of the Deutsche Democratic Republic.

Once back on the east side, the darkness settled quickly, and the eternal bleakness returned. I glanced back one more time, trying to justify my actions. *I'm walking away from freedom. Am I making the right decision?* I found a nearby bench and sat to gather my thoughts. *What am I returning for? What is left for me?*

No matter what direction I turned, the face of a man with blond hair and blue eyes emerged. His half smile, perfect teeth, and inviting lips called to me, but it was his love and devotion that ensnared me. *I need to find Stefan!*

My purpose was clear. Darting into a full run, I searched for any bus traveling to Pankow.

Fifty-one

THE BUTTERFLY IS FREE

The ride to the mortuary was torturous. Two fingers and the inside of my cheek were raw by the time I arrived. If Mari hadn't found him, what made me believe I could? Before the bus came to a full stop, I launched off the step.

Charging the back door of the mortuary, I pounded until Edmund flung it open. His furrowed brow and frown initially scolded, but when he caught sight of me, it softened. He should be used to this by now. "Ella? What are you doing here?"

Out of breath, I coughed, unable to speak.

"Ella? It's Ella?" Katharina's voice soared from behind the door, nearly ripping off the hinges before her husband. "What are you doing here?" she cried. "The border is open. Go to your brother!"

I placed my hand on my chest. My heartbeat refused to slow. "I have," I cried. "I saw him! I saw Josef!"

Edmund left us.

Katharina grabbed my wrist and yanked me inside. She quickly guided me to the nearest chair and forced me to sit as Edmund appeared with a glass of water.

"Where is he?" My eyes begged, clutching her sleeve.

She glanced to her husband.

"Please. I need to find Stefan."

Katharina's hands reached for mine. She knelt before me, but her rigid jaw revealed more. My chest rose. Short sporadic breaths followed, bracing for the worst. "He's not here," she said.

"Are you sure?" My scream caused her to jump. "Sometimes you don't know, remember you said that you don't always know!" my shrieks continued. "I should go check."

"Ella, calm down." Edmund reached for one hand.

Katharina still held the other. Her lips pulled down at the corners. "I saw him leave."

"When? Where?"

"Yesterday. He didn't say where he was going. He just left." Her eyes veered to Edmund.

"He didn't come home last night?" The wrenching in my chest spread to my limbs.

"No." Edmund tried his best to comfort, but it was obvious it wasn't his forte. With shoulders raised, he shrugged. "Stefan could be anywhere."

Yeah, he could be in Budapest! A thousand pins pricked my heart as my mind conjured the possibilities.

I glanced between them. "Did he think I left him?" my voice squeaked. "Mari was trying to tell him; did she not tell him?" My hands released from theirs and pressed roughly against my forehead. *What have I done?*

"She missed him." Katharina sighed. "He left before she got here."

My hands balled to fists, and I pulled them to my lips. "Wh . . . where do you think he went?"

"I don't know." Her eyes filled with tears. "Stefan didn't always tell me things."

I wondered how much she knew of his past, the war or the prison camp. Maybe he only shared them with me.

Tapping my leg with more urgency in her touch than before, she cried, "Think, Ella. Where would he have gone?"

I contemplated her words. In many ways he was still a stranger to me. *Could he have gone through with our plans without me?* "We had train tickets to Hungary. Do you think he left the country?"

"I don't know," she whimpered. "I don't recall seeing a suitcase, but I was glued to the television. I'm sorry; I should've asked." Her body trembled in her own personal torment. Katharina's compassion for others bore a weight that wasn't entirely her own.

I clung to her. "If you see him, please tell him I'm looking for him," I whispered in her ear. "Please tell him not to leave me."

Katharina pulled back and glanced up at me with sad eyes. "If Stefan is still in the East, you'll find him. I'm sure of it. He loves you, Ella."

"He's my life." Wiping my cheeks, I stood up.

She grabbed my hand and squeezed as she walked me to the door. "Remember, you're his life too."

"I love you, Katharina, my dear sister and you, as well, Edmund." I kissed them both goodbye before I left. On the steps of the mortuary, a vision from the past surfaced. The shooting, Frau Franke dragging me down these steps and—I peered over to the bushes where Stefan emerged in his Border Patrol uniform, still stained with my blood. My sight blurred. The agony of watching him disappear that day shattered me. With a roughness in my fingers I wiped me eyes. *I need to find Stefan.*

Determined to check every square inch of the city, I caught a bus back to Mitte. Nothing could keep me from him. The rain the last couple of days had left the nights with a bitter chill, but I kept moving. I walked towards Alexanderplatz, the plaza emptier than I'd ever seen. A few teenagers stood beneath the World Clock, and a handful of families headed towards St Maria's. Besides the toll of the church bells, the city silence grew eerie, a complete contrast to the west side celebrations. I shuffled over to the Neptune fountain. My eyes darted anxiously all directions. The only sounds within range were the spurts of water spraying the underwater deity and two birds flapping in the clamshell but no sign of Stefan.

I stumbled towards Zur Letzen with its darkened windows beside the shadowy Spree. Both Dafne's and Backeri Balzer revealed an emptiness as well. Shortly after midnight, I reached the corner of Volkspark Friedrichshain, sure that if he was anywhere, it'd be our butterfly hideaway, but when I stepped through, he was nowhere to be found.

Discouraged, I sat on the grass. Despite the yellow coarseness from the seasonal change, it still felt like home. *Where are you Stefan?* He had to know, after all we'd been through, I wouldn't leave him. The butterflies were long gone, and the leaves on the trees and bushes had tinted to paler colors. Because of the late hour, mixed with the border run, the park stood completely abandoned. Back near the entrance and the fountain, I brushed my hand across the three little pigs and then patted Gretel's duck. An overwhelming urge to say goodbye to Rübezahl flooded my soul. His full-bodied statue, off to the side, had brought me comfort more times than I could count. With a simple kiss, I departed.

Conflicted, I caught a tram to the café on the northeast side. It was locked, but we always kept a spare key under a brick in the back. One by one, I lifted the bricks in the pile, nothing! *Where could it be?* My chattering lips drowned out my thoughts. *Mari!* Mari must've forgot to return it. Too far from Pankow, I recognized my urgency to get in. Glancing between the brick in my hand and the small window on our door, I justified my next action. *Crash!* Louder than planned, I paused, though the shatter stirred nothing in response. The East was a graveyard. Reaching in, I unlocked the door and hustled in.

Not much had changed since our frantic departure a couple nights ago. With the flip of a switch, I found a sweater hanging on a hook and then searched for any trace of Stefan, hoping somehow there was contact. Everything remained the same: the dirty dishes in the sink, the basket of rolls now hardened over time, even the curtains on the front windows hadn't been closed. When I passed the counter, sitting atop the register was a small scrap of paper. Lifting it, I recognized Mari's handwriting. *The note.*

Stefan,
I'm heading to the mortuary tonight, but just in case I miss you, and you find this note, Ella did not leave you. She only went to find her brother. She will be back. She loves you!
Mari.

Tears formed on my bottom lashes. *Stefan still doesn't know.*

The clock read half past 2. Grabbing a napkin, I wiped my cheeks. *How am I going to fix this?* Weary, I slipped to a stool, my head falling heavily to the counter. *I should have waited . . . at least until I . . . saw him . . , assured him. I should . . . have waited.*

Images of Josef, Heidi, their sweet children, and Anton appeared: the barricade crumbling behind them, flashes of people running, laughing . . . or screaming? Severed wire and bars protruding from cinder blocks and uniformed men guarding the way. I have to get to them . . . If I delay and they close the borders . . . wait, they're stopping people . . . shining flashlights? No, it's the spark from a gun! They're shooting people!

My body jolted. Shielding my face from the light, I shrieked, "Don't shoot!" My elbow hit the hard counter. Cursing the pain, I winced trying to focus. *Who is shining a beam at me?* I blinked then rubbed my eyes aggressively. The sun shone through the east windows. *It's not a flashlight or a gun! I fell asleep!* My heart skipped a beat.

Patting my body, I exhaled and wiped the sweat off my cheeks. *It was a dream, only a dream! What was I thinking, falling asleep?* Scrambling to untangle my legs from the stool, I tripped, catching the counter in a

402

tight hold until my feet set flat on the ground. *What time is it?* The hands on my watch stood out. *9am! How could I be foolish to let so much time pass? Time wasted from looking for Stefan.*

As I left the café, the ghostly emptiness continued, even in the daylight. If it weren't for the noise coming from the neighborhoods nearest the wall, I would've thought the entire population had disappeared. Anxious, I made a mental list of the places I'd been and the places still unchecked.

Passing the vacant telephone box that had a lengthy line two days ago, I paused and turned back, pressing the door open. I dialed Josef's house.

"Hello?" Heidi answered.

"Heidi, hello. It's me, Ella."

"Ella? Where are you? You didn't come back." Her voice stirred with more urgency now.

"I'm sorry. I didn't mean to alarm anyone."

"Are you well?"

"Yes, I just . . . um . . . by any chance did Mari come to Cade?"

"Yes, she did."

"Oh! Please, Heidi, may I speak with her?"

"Of course, just a moment."

I could hear rustling and whispering, but when Mari picked up, her weary voice cried abnormally loud. "Ella, where are you?"

"I'm in Mitte. Please tell me you found Stefan."

"No, I didn't."

My heart sunk.

"But I left him a note at the café in case he went there."

"He didn't," my voice fell flat. "I just returned from the café. Your note is still there."

"I'm so sorry," she cried. "Cade and I will come help."

"No, don't leave the family."

"Ella, Stefan hasn't left Germany. I just know he wouldn't leave without you."

"Where is he, Mari. He didn't go home. Where did he go?"

"I'm not sure. Maybe he's looking for you."

Hanging up, I rested my head on the glass. *I should have left Josef's address with Katharina. Maybe I should go back there, and he will eventually come home.* After the mental debate, I stepped out to a nippy Sunday morning. November 12th was no warmer than the last three days since the wall fell, and my life turned upside down. I pulled my sweater closer.

Convinced I'd gone everywhere important to us, I kept wandering. Discouragement followed me street after street, neighborhood after neighborhood. I went to every old memory and every new one as well. It wasn't until I stood before the Volksbühne that an idea sparked. As simple as it was, I'd overlooked the one place that intertwined both the old and the new, and it should have been my very first stop.

I sprinted towards the familiar crossroads and the bumpy path. Sophien's cemetery walls materialized on my left, and the few buildings on Anklamer appeared on the right. The wooden bench half a block away, isolated and lonely, became my lighthouse in the storm. The very place Stefan knelt to ask me to marry him—the second time.

In full view, its emptiness brought forth clashing emotion.

I slipped to the slats and inhaled as if my very breath relied on its proximity. The connection willed life and, above all, hope into me. I closed my eyes as my back rested against it. An unusual peace washed over me as I absorbed the calm it created.

I opened my eyes, skimming above the cemetery wall. The peace continued. A breeze picked up, and branches from the tallest trees swayed side to side. I watched with fascination as the unseen forces bent and curled the branches in unnatural ways, but they always bounced back . . . and never broke. I imagined Stefan and I to be much like those branches, tossed and turned in the fiercest of wind gusts only to withstand and bounce back. *I will find him!* I assured. If not today or tomorrow, it will be soon. It will happen. Our souls are forever linked—connected and unbreakable.

A family strolled swiftly down the walk, my sight drawn to their happy chatter as they headed towards the wall. I watched them pass and then followed their path to where other people gathered. I smiled, then pulled my sight back to the cemetery.

A man stood under the arched opening. Though his identity was shrouded in the shadows, his silhouette generated chills upon my skin. He took several steps forward, and when the sunlight hit him directly, he pulled back his hood.

Stefan! With a cry, I sprinted towards him and leapt, my arms and legs wrapping around him. Jagged breath warmed his cheek as my kisses landed in the hollow of his neck. Our embrace intensified. While the world spun madly around us, his arms enveloped me, pressing our beating hearts into one.

Stefan carried me back to the bench, my body still fastened around his as he slid onto it.

"Ella." Brushing my hair aside, he kissed my neck. His lips, cool against my heated skin, ignited a blaze within my chest. My head reluctantly pulled away. The blue in his eyes glowed in the sunshine. "It's over, love. It's over."

Tears surged. I regarded the wall before my head leaned next to his with a subtle nod. Twenty-eight years of heartache and sorrow woven into that concrete, yet I struggled to let it out of my sight.

Stefan's head leaned back. One hand released and reached into his pocket. When it reappeared, Anton's tinnie pin rested in his palm. "I know how much this means to you. I wanted to get it to you for Anton."

My jaw dropped. "Where did you find it?" Piecing things together in my head, the process didn't make sense. I gave it to Mari, and she never found Stefan, but here he is with the tinnie pin.

"It was with the note Mari left in the café."

"You were there?"

He nodded. "I went everywhere. The first night after I heard the news, I went to the café. It was open, but there was no sign of you or Mari, like it had been abandoned. I tried to get to the wall, thinking

405

maybe I'd see you, but once I caught sight of the masses, I knew it was impossible.

I wiped my face on my sleeve, the tears continually falling while he spoke.

"Around 1 am I went back to the mortuary and waited, although I didn't know what I waited for, and it drove me mad. I knew your priority was Josef and Anton, and that was right. I was just scared. Scared that maybe you would see what you were missing all this time and not want to return."

I cupped his jaw, kissing his cheeks tenderly.

"Ella, I searched for you even though I knew you might not be there. I went to the fountain of fairytales, butterfly garden, the Volksbühne, The World Clock, all of these places and finally at the café. With your spare key, I found the note and the pin next to it."

I stared. *We searched for each other in all the same places but at different times.*

My hand covered his, the tinnie pin pressed in the middle and pulled to my chest. "Yes, this pin means a lot to me, but nothing . . ." My heartbeat thumped against our hands. "Nothing at all means more to me than you."

His hands released from mine, and skimming my waist, he pulled my straddling legs closer. I shuddered as his lips grazed my ear, slid across my cheek, and parted with a sweetness that kindled my greatest desire. His lips reached mine in a kiss that embodied our bond, passion, separation, longing, hope, and love.

Upon release, his fingers gently traced my lips. Skimming down the curve of my neck and gliding the edge of my sweater, he arrived at my shoulder. With tenderness, his touch glided across my skin to the scar. The subtlety of his hand soothed as he leaned in and whispered, "The butterfly is finally free."

406

Epilogue

The reflection moved me. My eyes followed the contours of my face, through the curve of my neck, down my torso, to the tips of my toes. The full-length mirror revealed more than a 43-year-old woman . . . but a lifetime of experiences that brought me to this moment, as well.

"You're beautiful!" Mari's hands gripped my shoulders from behind while her chin rested next to my cheek, her flawless, white skin pale against my complexion. "Hold still." She kissed my cheek and let go, securing a champagne-colored comb into my loose bun. A single layer of beaded mesh cascaded down my back, past my waist.

"Your flowers, Ella." I circled to find Katharina holding a fresh bunch of forget-me-not blooms, their deep-blue petals in stark contrast to my dress.

By her side, Lena added with excitement, "Everyone is here."

Tears collected on my bottom lashes. "Is this real?" I whispered. Turning, visions of defining moments flashed with each embrace.

"It's real," —Mari squeezed tightly— "and your prince is waiting."

"Don't forget to touch the mermaid," Lena exclaimed. "They say if you make a wish on your wedding day, it will come true." The legendary chandelier hung above my head within an arm's reach. The silver-blue mermaid stretched out, ready for anyone who believed in the reality of dreams to touch it. I brushed my fingers across her belly. "But my wish already came true," I uttered.

Lifting my satin skirt, I stepped to the latticed-glass window overlooking the drawbridge and entryway. The winter rains nurtured the vines on the castle walls, and bright green buds emerged against the stone, extending across the trellis gardens. Brilliantly colored flags floated above the lion statues strategically placed to guard the walls. Their stately presence dwelt long in the corners of my mind. My eyes wandered past the stone columns and triumphant gate towards the river and the quaint village of Cochem below.

For many years, every stroke on Stefan's painting imprinted deeper and deeper into my dreams, generating hope this day would come, amidst my disbelief. I pinched my arm and winced at the prick. *Yes, it's real.* I laughed. All three women glanced at me with furrowed brows. I smiled back. "I just can't believe I'm here."

"The final touch." Katharina wrapped a single pearl necklace around my neck, the teardrop falling barely above the lace bodice. The dress hugged my figure and branched out past my knees like the mermaid tail above me.

One last look in the mirror brought a full breath to my lungs. "I'm getting married." My friends fell upon me again, the love conveyed in their embrace igniting my spirit. Glancing at our image, my heart swelled. Each one played a critical role in my life and made me a better person because of it.

"Don't cry," Mari giggled, "your mascara will run." She dabbed the corners of my eyes with a tissue.

Katharina opened the door, and the tears that simmered, slid down my cheeks the moment I saw them—two men, both in brown suits, each with a different colored tie.

"Ella!" Josef cried, "You're stunning!" His elbow offered, I met it, kissing him on the cheek. My lips lingered long for the brother I loved so dearly.

Next to him stood Anton. His green eyes met mine, glowing with pride. "You make a beautiful bride, klein Maus!" My blush perpetually hid in my skin tone, though my eyelashes fluttered coyly.

I lifted my hand. Anton's tinnie pin rested in the palm. Grinning, he unclasped it and attached it to his collar. My fingers grazed it lovingly with long affection for its strength and significance in my life. "For your children," I breathed softly.

He held my hand and lovingly kissed me on the cheek. "You're finally getting your happy ending." My eyes met his, and I blinked back tears for a friendship that began at the age of six and spanned decades. One could not imagine a more beautiful way for this day to begin.

My arm linked with his, the bouquet held lightly in front.

"Are you ready?" Katharina asked.

I nodded. *I've waited twenty-three years for this.*

The women went ahead. Josef, Anton, and I walked through the dining room. We passed beautiful mahogany furniture, hand painted portraits, and stunning architecture, though none of it persuaded a delay. My only focus stood at the end of our path, knowing each step taken brought me closer to Stefan.

Entering the knight's hall, I stepped to a small elevated landing overlooking the pride and honor of this noble space. Its grandeur was fleeting as my eyes followed the doors to a balcony overlooking the Mosel. Reaching the stairs, I descended slowly, blessed at having two secure men as my sides. Without them I would have surely fallen head-first from nerves alone. The elegant terrace doors, guarded by armored knights, opened to a dozen chairs, each filled with faces who sculpted our lives: Mari and Cade, Katharina and Edmund, Lena and Freddy, Edgar and Gretchen, Ralf, and Jörg. But when my eyes trailed past them and finally fell on *him*, they danced. There stood my love, my world, next to the balcony wall.

Stefan's sharp black suit and deep-blue tie were the least of his magnificent attributes. His blond locks, though touched with gray over time, were neatly trimmed just above the ears with bangs swept neatly to one side. When his eyes fell upon me, everything around us vanished. His charming smile willed strength into my lungs and limbs, reassuring each stride down the final steps. It had taken an eternity to get to this day and now an eternity to reach him. By the time we stood before Stefan, the blue in his eyes blazed a scintillating shade. My favorite color.

The two handsome men, whom I'd only seen with my adult eyes for barely three months, kissed me on the cheek before reaching to shake Stefan's hand. The clasp exuded gratitude and promise.

Stefan reached for me, the warmth transferring through our hands surged with a timeless emotion. His touch tingled my skin with the lightness of a feather but held sure.

"*Wilkommen. Dies ist ein lang erwarteter Tag.*" The pastor's welcome and acknowledgement was the last thing I heard. My mind floated into Stefan's bottomless blue eyes, swallowed by the events of our extraordinary journey. Memories of our beginning, the contempt for each other, the gradual change and understanding we experienced, leading to attraction and infatuation. Our separation, growth, and maturity, and how it evolved us and challenged us to where we were now. Years later, a love tested beyond belief yet strengthened and survived.

Stefan squeezed my hands. "I take you, Ella Kühn, to be my wife. I promise to be loyal to you in good days and bad, in health and illness, to love and respect, until death separates us."

My heart pulsated. "I take you, Stefan Franke, to be my husband. I promise to be loyal to you in good days and bad, in health and illness, to love and respect, until death separates us."

Sie sind jetzt Mann und Frau.

Man and wife! The words bound me speechless. Stefan held my hand and transferred the ring from my left finger to my right. "Man and wife." My lips repeated the words as if it required confirmation.

"Yes, we are." Stefan's half smile emerged, distinct and perfect. The man I loved and adored since I was seventeen finally stood before me as my husband. His fingers slipped from my hands to my waist and became the only device holding me upright as he pulled me to him. The familiar, rustic scent of his aftershave awakened me and unleashed my longing. When his lips parted, the warmth of his breath drew me in. The kiss, soft and tender, yet powerful enough to culminate our two souls into one, sealed our promise.

Wrapped in our own world, explosive cheers reminded us of our audience. Reluctantly we parted and faced our friends who immediately engulfed us, rejoicing in this long-awaited moment.

Celebrating through the evening, we relished in the music filling the courtyard where vibrant lanterns and glowing candles adorned the grounds. With our decision to be married as soon as the family could get to Cochem, this put us at the close of winter. Katharina spared no expense in bringing as much rich, southern flora as she could import. Evergreen vines and edelweiss wrapped the columns and lined the arches. Even the vintage well, which centered the plaza, sprung forth an abundance of greenery and lively blossoms.

Feasting on traditional wedding dishes—such as Austrian Tafelspitz and Grööner Hein and desserts, Bienenstich and Baumstrietzel—our bellies became as happy as our hearts. The pears, beans, and bacon sautéed in vegetable broth complimented the well-aged sirloin tip covered in silverskin onions and pickled gherkins. The bee sting and honey almond cakes added to the delicacies.

Deep into the night, Stefan led me away from the party. Since his childhood included summers at Cochem Castle, he guided me through the halls effortlessly. The Gothic Room, with its inlaid woodwork and stunning arches, portrayed elegance at its finest. "This was used as a *Caminata*," he whispered, "a ladies chamber." I smiled, admiring its beauty. The next room we stepped into sported animal head trophies and jagged spears. "And now we're entering the Hunters' Room." This time Stefan's eyes lit up. A massive boar's head sat opposite a beautiful window of colorful glass panes. "Each square is a different coat of arms." Stefan pointed. "They represent each of the counts who lived here." He took my hand as we passed through another set of doors. "This room is small but holds many secrets." Stefan's sly grin appeared. "It's called the Romanesque Room. Come, tap your foot against the base of this wall." I pulled my long skirt upward, and with a gentle tap of my shoe, the wall popped open.

I gasped. A well-hidden secret passage cracked open. "Where does it lead to?" I moved forward to see a staircase descending a dark course.

"Down below into the rock, and centuries ago, it led to the Monastery. This one over here—" Stefan walked to another side of the room, the walls once again completely flush. He tapped his shoe as I did, and another door cracked. "—This one leads to the upper bedrooms." He winked and smiled widely.

"But this door here—" He reached for my hand, and I followed him through the real door to the knights' hall once again. "—This one is my most favorite of all."

Glancing up to the landing I descended only a few hours ago, we stepped through the glass doors out to the balcony together.

This time there were no chairs and no guests. We were entirely alone. The transplanted edelweiss weaved gracefully through the barren vines and around the columns. Its petals filled the night air with a sweetness of the day I missed earlier in my haze. I inhaled the white bloom, no longer nervous but secure and unwavering on where I wanted to be.

Stefan's arms tenderly wrapped around me from behind, his cheek resting softly against mine. The lights of Cochem village flickered like tiny stars below and reflected against the peaceful Mosel River. Stefan's hands shifted to my waist, and with a gentle twist, he circled me to meet him.

His lips separated but hesitated, mute. Tears toyed at the edges of his eyes, and as he blinked, I marveled at the fine lines trailing from the corners. I reached up and brushed his skin with my finger and then rested my palm against his cheek.

412

"I love you," I sighed, my thumb caressing his clean-shaven jaw and tracing the lines which bordered the corner of his mouth. Despite time and age, the love I confessed for this man intensified every second.

I followed his eyes as they trailed the contours of my face and settled to my lips. He leaned in, his mouth near mine. "You are my world, Ella Franke." His whispered touch stirred my soul at the merging of our names. "I love you more than you may ever know." Bringing my body tightly against him, his lips met mine.

The tormenting years of separation, the confusion, the unknown, and the agony of grief dissolved in the blink of an eye amid the depth, spirit, and resilience of the human heart.

German Glossary

(In order of Appearance)

Öffne diese Tür- **Open this door**

Ich kann dich hören, ich weiß, dass du da drin bist- **I can hear you, I know you're in there**

Ich bin fertig mit der Gewährung von Zulagen, Sie haben eine Woche Zeit- **I'm done granting allowances, you have one week's time**

Ich komme rein- **I'm coming in**

Scheisse- **Shit**

Gorbatschow and Zaranoff- **Alcohol brands**

Wasser- **water**

Opa- **Grandpa**

Tante- **Auntie**

Hallo- **Hello**

Waisenhaus- **Orphanage**

Beamtenstippe- **A sauce usually eaten with potatoes**

Echte Kroatzbeere- **Type of German Beer**

Fleishcherei- **Butcher's shop**

Alkoholikers- **Alcoholic**

Maultasche- **Pasta dough with sausage meat**

sie ist Neger- **She is negro**

Berliner Zeitung- **Berlin newspaper**

La Vie en Rose- **Life in a Rosy Hue (French)**

Schnitzel- **Thin pieces of meat generally pork and veal**

Spätzle- **Irregular shaped pasta made with fresh eggs**

Skat- **German card game**

Arse- **Ass**

Willst du ein Bier- **Do you want a beer**

Wenn sie nicht bestellen warden, greaten Sie aus der Reihe- **If you don't order, get out of line**

Bewege es Schlampe- **Move it, bitch**

Verdammt- **Damn it**

Es tut mir leid- **I am Sorry**

Bäckerei- **Bakery**

Gute nacht- **Good night**

schwerter zu pflugscharen- **Swords to Ploughshare**

Warum- **Why**

Schweine- **Pig**

Nach hause gehen- **Go home**

Gehen Jetzt. Dieser Bereich ist geschlossen- **Go now. This area is closed.**

EINE SCHLANGE IM GRAS- **SNAKE IN THE GRASS**

Tod durch Feuer- **Death by fire**

Germnoedel- **Poppyseed pastry**

Pfannkuchen- **Pancake**

Das Boot- **The boat**

Haus des Lehrers- **House of teacher**

Obdachlos – (adjective) **Homeless**

Obdachlose- (noun) **Homeless people**

Pfingsten Festival- **Pentecost festival**

Der Bruch and *Kein Talent-* **The Break and No Talent- (Punk Rock bands in East Berlin)**

Polizei- **Police**

Diese Zeile ist nicht mehr verfügba! **This line is no longer available**

Apotheke- **Pharmacy**

Fernsehturm- **Television tower**

Kirche von Unten- **Church from Below**

Der Tages Spiegel- **The Daily Mirror Newspaper**

Grenzfall- **Borderline case**

Soldat junge- **Soldier boy**

Parokialkirche- **Parochial Church**

Fräulein- **Young lady/Miss**

Rübezahl- **German Storybook character**

An den Präsidenten Reagan- **To President Reagan**

Nach Amerika- **To America**

Nach Deutschland ein vereinigtes, **Deutschland- To Germany, A united Germany**

Apfelkuchen- **Apple cake**

Zionskirche- **Zions Church**

Wie kann ich Ihnen behilflich sein- **How can I help you**

Kartoffelpuffer- **Potato pancake**

nakt unter Wölfen- **Night under Wolves**

Beinenstich- **Bee Sting cake**

Sauerbraten- **A roast marinated in vinegar or wine, bay leaves and cloves**

Kapitales von Karl Marx- **Capitol of Karl Marx**

Fasching- **Carnival**

die Ratte- **The rat**

Glühwein- **Mulled wine**

Unterfeldwebel- **A rank in the East German National People's Army**

Wilkommen. Dies ist ein lang erwarteter Tag- **Welcome. This is a long-awaited day**

Sie sind Jetzt Mann und Frau- **You are now man and wife**

Author's Note

With a few tears in my eyes I have come to the end of a story that has changed my life. Ella Kühn, although a fictional character from start to finish, has become a part of my family and someone I have been inspired by. Without a doubt, she represents many women of war and tragedy. They are our mothers, grandmothers, sisters, daughters, friends, and even ourselves. While challenges and trials do not always end well, Ella needed her happy ending, after all she endured. I hope that as you read and share this series, it inspires you to know more about the courageous people of Germany and especially those who were personally affected by the Berlin Wall.

On 9 November 2019, we celebrate the 30th anniversary of the fall of the wall and pray that through education, tolerance, and love nothing like the Berlin Wall tragedy ever happens again.

Thank you to all those who have brought Ella, Stefan, Josef, and Anton into their lives and for your continued support and friendship. As with the previous books of the Berlin Butterfly Series, the conversations and events that occur between my characters and historical figures has been invented for the purpose of storytelling. Any events and circumstances surrounding the victims of the DDR and East Berlin, unless previously noted or referenced, is by pure coincidence.

Individuals and events such as Monika Haeger (alias Karin Lenz), her handler Detlef, the expatriated IFM officers, the shooting victims, Zionskirche, The Cellar, The Environmental Library, The Grenzfall magazine, KvU, Women for Peace, Protests and demonstrations, The open letter to the people of the GDR*, Punk music's influence on the fall of the wall, and the skinhead attack are all factual and can be further researched at the Berlin Wall Memorial: Bernauer Straße 111, Berlin Germany.

*While the letter about Chris Gueffroy's assassination itself is factual, the contents of the letter in this story were recreated for storytelling purposes. As we recognize all of the victims of the Berlin

Wall shootings, Chris Gueffroy's death represents the last known kill recorded. After the wall fell, Karin Gueffroy, Chris' mother, pursued justice for her son's death and "filed a lawsuit against the unknown" responsible. The four border guards involved faced varying degrees of punishment. Three offenders received probation, and the gunman who took the fatal shot was sentenced to three years and six month imprisonment. In 1994, however, this was overturned, claiming the shooter acted on orders from his superiors.

"At least 140 people were killed between 1961 and 1989 at the Berlin Wall or were killed in connection with the GDR border regime. In addition, at least 251 travelers died during or after checks at Berlin border crossings. Countless are the people who died out of grief and despair over the effects of building the wall on their lives."

Often times, either in research or online, the number of deaths vary. These numbers are provided by the Berlin Wall Memorial. Please take some time to read the biographies of the victims at:

https://www.berliner-mauer-gedenkstaette.de/de/todesopfer-240.html

About the Author

Leah Moyes happily lives in the sunny state of Arizona . . . year-round. She is the biological mother of four but claims many more. After a career in the airlines and teaching high school sciences, she has pursued her life-long dream to become an Archaeologist and currently works under the guidance and direction of amazing Archaeologists at Arizona State University. Between writing and archaeological digs, the world has become her playground.

Berlin Butterfly is her first Historical Fiction Series.

Made in the USA
Middletown, DE
29 June 2020